SUSAN DAITCH was born in New Haven, Connecticut, in 1954. She attended high school in New York then went on to Barnard College, interrupting her studies for a time to take part in the Whitney Museum of Modern Art's Independent Study Program. She graduated in 1977, and for the last ten years has lived in New York, working in a variety of jobs whose 'only common denominator', she says, is that each has allowed her time to write. In 1984 she received a Graduate Fellowship at Columbia University's Writing Program, and her short story, 'Storyland, U.S.A.' appeared in *lo Spazio Umano*. A novella, *The Colorist*, was published in 1985. She is currently working on a second novel, set in New York in 1930.

L.C., her first full-length novel, is a remarkable evocation of the life of a young Frenchwoman, Lucienne Crozier, whose diary records her progress from onlooker to activist in the tumultuous months before and after the French Revolution of 1848. After the uprising she flees with her lover to Algiers, then disappears without trace, her name and diary forgotten. When discovered some 120 years later, the task of translating her extraordinary memoir falls first to a reclusive American with a predetermined view of the revolutionaries, then to a younger woman, a veteran of the riots at Berkeley in 1968. Three women of different ages, motivations, perspectives: each finds in the diary her own truth. Marvellously original and inventive, L.C. is a novel about the recording of history itself.

L. C.

SUSAN DAITCH

To my mother

and in memory of my father

Published by Virago Press Limited 1986
41 William IV Street, London WC2N 4DB

British Library Cataloguing in Publication Data
Daitch, Susan
L.C.
I. Title
813′.54[F]   PS3554.A3/

ISBN 0-86068-758-9
ISBN 0-86068-763-5 Pbk

Lyrics from Love Potion #9
by Jerry Lieber and Mike Stoler:
© Copyright 1966 by Chappell Music Co. Ltd.
Used by permission of Carlin Music Corporation
of 14 New Burlington Street, London W1X 2LR.

Typeset by Goodfellow & Egan of Cambridge,
and printed in Great Britain by
Anchor Brendon Ltd. at Tiptree, Essex

INTRODUCTION

Provided all relations, friends and so on are long dead, even the most precise portrait of a citizen is, without a corresponding name, difficult to identify. A portrait in print is no different. Certain fundamental facts about the life of Lucienne Crozier will always be a mystery, but if we can believe what diarists write about themselves to be true, then we have access to the private thoughts of a woman who witnessed a revolution and vanished several years later, an indirect casualty of its aftermath.

What is unusual about the life described in her journal is the degree of latitude available to Lucienne Crozier in mid-nineteenth-century Europe. Whether this degree of latitude was freely available to her is questionable, but free or not, she took it. She may have shocked some of her contemporaries, but it's not clear if she suffered for it. Henry James's Mrs Walker told Daisy Miller she was old enough to be reasonable and old enough to be talked about, but what the Mrs Walkers of Paris in the late 1840s thought of Lucienne Crozier she barely tells us, and for all appearances doesn't really care. Readers should remember it was a time of revolution, and the hierarchical structures of social order were shifting, grinding against one another, flipping over. It was as if the physical laws of gravity, in select circumstances, weren't being followed according to the customary fashion. It is just this February 1848 Revolution which is central to the diary.

Take any point in history and you find contradictions, or a profound turning-about-face of a segment of the popula-tion. 1848, which saw the publication of both *Wuthering Heights* and the *Communist Manifesto*, was a time when many who had felt passionately about revolution quickly turned their backs on it. Frustration and disillusionment aside, when faced with torn up streets, crossed by great walls of chairs, tables, paving stones, carriages and people's minor possessions thrown out of windows; when faced with random open firing by both sides, there is an impulse to stay indoors.

If Lucienne Crozier initially led a sheltered life, her ideas were shaped by the same sources as those of many other women of her class and education: romantic novels, popular newspaper serials, *feuilletons* written by Eugène Sue and Alexander Dumas *père*. Marxism and fluff may seem like strange bedfellows but from stories of proletarian adventure Lucienne drew conclusions antipathetic to romance. Everyday events aren't simply the easily forgotten commonplace but have a slot in a societal index, a chain of causes and effects. Beggar girls don't become heiresses overnight. Workers don't own the means of production. They will never become millionaires. The stories which illuminated the lives of Paris's working class had, when it came to happy endings, little basis in truth.

Lucienne had heard of the utopian socialists Saint-Simon and Fourier. At meetings of the revolutionary cell, *14 Juillet*, she became familiar with theories of how capitalism functions and survives. She read Pierre Joseph Proudhon, some Marx, perhaps Bakunin, learned of François Babeuf, who founded secret societies during the French Revolution, Louis August Blanqui, one of history's first professional revolutionaries whose Central Republican Society was active during the February Days. The notebook's last owner, had he read her diary, might have said Lucienne Crozier's political beliefs were more emotional than theoretical, but I think she had enough information to argue convincingly, and her convictions are admirable.

The bourgeois regime of Louis-Philippe, dull, oppressively pedestrian in its values, was particularly repressive in its attitude towards women. Women's work was poorly paid and, in consequence, many were forced into prostitution. Education beyond the secondary school level was forbidden.

2

Marriages were often arranged by families for economic reasons. The respective man and woman might have met only once or twice before the wedding, and divorce was nearly impossible. Women were considered part of their husbands' accumulated property; they were denied citizenship, had the same legal rights as lunatics and the mentally deficient.

On 12 April 1849, Daumier published a cartoon in *Le Charivari* which depicted three women placing their hands on a top hat. Is the laying on of hands part of a witches' spell? Are they going to toss the contaminated hat over their shoulders? The caption reads, 'The insurrection against husbands is proclaimed the most sacred of duties.' The women are ugly. Nineteenth-century cartoons, as a rule, represented suffragettes, socialist women and blue stockings as harpies and harridans. The satiric attitude towards these groups wasn't an original product of Daumier's comic vision; his series on women's movements reflected the popular sentiment of his time. Much of the French press and theatre portrayed feminists in exactly the same absurd light. These are women who divorce themselves from domesticity and conventional sexuality, threatening to skew society's established lines of gender straight to hell. This aberrant gang has the power to run masculine/feminine classifications upside down and inside out. Many radicals, such as Proudhon, were outspoken anti-feminists. The movement was seen as something ominous, outside any political sphere, a threat to the social order of the family if you were an anarchist, to the family and the state if you weren't. Unlike Proudhon and his scientific socialists, the utopians such as Comte de Saint-Simon, ironically of aristocratic lineage, were much more supportive of women's rights. (In Fourier's case, this support was manifested in spiritual form. His followers sought the female messiah in the East.) There were exceptions among the socialist and right-wing factions, but generally women's rights was a question all sides agreed on negatively. Daumier was reinforced by Babeuf, Balzac, Napoleon, Talleyrand, Gavarni, Guizot and King Louis-

Philippe. Women, as Delacroix himself painted them, were involved in the fighting of each revolution from 1789 to the Commune and after, but, unfortunately, the patriarchal system and its biases were as pervasive on the left as on the right. In spite of isolated support, 1848 marked a moment of activity before women's groups were banned in August of that year. Opened and closed within a few months were the *Club de l'Emancipation* founded by Jeanne Derouin, *Club des Femmes*, founded by Eugénie Niboyet, and *Tristan*, named for Flora Tristan, a feminist labour organizer who died in 1844. There were also many journals, such as *La Politique des Femmes* and *La Voix des Femmes*. So by 1849 Daumier was beating a horse which was already quite assaulted, but not dead.

As a footnote to this discussion on women I would like to add that we have no idea what Lucienne Crozier looked like. Delacroix's portrait of her, even if it were to be absolutely verified, is a vague pencil sketch whose quick, general features resemble those of many European or even American faces. Nowhere in her diary does she describe herself. For every reader there will be a different mental picture of Lucienne Crozier. It is unusual in a text written by and often about women that there are so few physical descriptions. The subject of women's appearance is nearly entirely ignored. This absence almost precludes our thinking of these women in sexual terms at all. For such a personal work never meant to be read by anyone other than the writer, she felt it necessary to describe only what struck her as unusual, rather than that with which she was familiar. The decisions behind conscious omissions on the part of the author are a continuous yet invisible chapter.

(In a year of revolution, the sight of women in trousers aroused a kind of social provocation which had nothing to do with suspicion of androgyny or disgust with the idea of fashion.)

It is a testament to the nature of books, even hand-written ones, that Lucienne's diary survived at all, travelling as it did through Paris during a revolution, across France,

4

across the Mediterranean, landing in North Africa, then tracing its steps alone back to Paris. Diaries (especially translated ones) should be read with an element of mistrust. Diarists are under no obligation to write the truth about themselves. Sometimes it isn't even a matter of playing with truths and actualities. As Virginia Woolf noted in her diary, one tends to write more often when one is in certain frames of mind than others. The final picture, in spite of the best intentions, in spite of private oaths of objectivity, tends to be distorted. The balance shifts and the reader is left with an exaggerated profile of depression and dissatisfaction. A diary, however, comments on a life in a way consciously edited memoirs and biographies can't. When one writes for oneself, one is allowed to be unselfconscious, invulnerable to threats of being tripped up by the outside world. Allowed or not, there is such a thing as tripping over what one perceives as one's mistakes, and keepers of diaries are susceptible to retrospective embarrassments. Solitude eggs the diarist on. At various points in the text, Lucienne looks back, notes that all the time she was thinking X, Y was really going on. The reader, having time on her side, knows these shifts weren't so explicit but underfoot all along. The very nature of remembering and recording establishes a counterpoint pattern. When Lucienne's memories, observations and expectations were jumbled, confounding any logical narrative sequence, I have made every attempt to regularize passages within a given dated entry. No surrealist booby traps here.

Unfortunately, it's not possible to reproduce the physical quality of the original journal: the newspaper clippings glued in at intervals, pasted letters, changes in handwriting when she was writing under pressure, drawings in the margins. A diary of many uses, occasionally Lucienne wrote letters out in her diary first, later copying over this first draft and sending the revised version.

The inclusion of letters in the diary provided a clue which led to the only supporting evidence for the existence of a Lucienne Crozier outside the proof represented by her

5

diary itself. Her friend Fabienne Ruban, who became Madame Ruban-Xavier, died in 1896, leaving her estate to her two children whose heirs (Fabienne's grandchildren) were very generous in allowing me to examine the family archives. The letters to Fabienne first copied in Lucienne's diary were also found in Madame Ruban-Xavier's papers. Identifying documents kept by the Xavier estate was an interesting task. There was a box of partially burned letters which Fabienne's son, when old and senile, had attempted to destroy – stopped, according to family legend, by a niece. These letters revealed a number of incidents. Late in 1859, the Croziers learned of Delacroix's portrait of Lucienne in Madame Ruban-Xavier's possession; they tried to force Fabienne to return it to them. Since Lucienne and Charles Crozier had never been legally divorced, under French law all her possessions should have passed to him. Lucienne, in fact, never possessed the portrait. Delacroix gave it to Fabienne, as her last letter will prove. I've included only one of Fabienne's letters at the end of the book to attest to some of the circumstances surrounding Lucienne's death.

It is ironic, given Lucienne's relationship to her husband, that the name Crozier is the only name history has left her. When she and her husband finally separated, the Crozier family of Roubaix had her name struck from family and church records. A deeply Catholic family from an insular part of France, the thought of husbands and wives living separate lives was profoundly threatening, neither discussed nor tolerated. When her name does appear there is no maiden name, so her place and date of birth remain unknown. The 1792 law which allowed divorce was rescinded in 1826. The Code Napoléon which followed reduced the rights and general state of women considerably, and one has only to examine the life of George Sand to determine the difficulties facing a woman who found living with the man she married an impossibility and the process of obtaining a legal separation almost as tortuous. Charles's family responded to Lucienne's unfaithfulness with vehemence, although they were late in surmising the extent of her

6

infidelities and supported her almost up until the moment of her departure. The thoroughness of their erasures notwithstanding, many records in the Nord and other parts of France were destroyed in the course of two world wars. Research in France turned up scanty evidence, thin hopes for any references to Madame Lucienne Crozier outside of the aforementioned sources, and many dead ends. Of others mentioned in the diary, corroborating evidence was found in more obscure locations. One source was police reports such as were kept for political prisoners and criminals at large. Jean de la Tour, for example, was wanted by the police for involvement with *Quarante-Huitards* who, the authorities believed, had planned the February insurrection and the murder of Maxime Aubuisson (also known as M. Arbuite, Robert Arbust, and César Robert). According to the report, Jean de la Tour was clever at eluding the police in Paris. His quick-witted alertness, well known to the Préfecture, was a side of his character much less apparent to Lucienne, of whom there are no police records. According to his file, the *garde municipale* believed reports which indicated that when he departed from France he fled alone to Italy. Lucienne's diary contradicts this information so secret and so valuable to the Préfecture at that hour.

Eugène Delacroix doesn't mention young Madame Crozier in his journals or in *Le Corréspondance*. The journal of 1847 was lost during that year, but were it to be found, the absence of her name wouldn't be unusual. By his fifties he rarely described his lovers in his papers with the exception of his cousin, Josephine de Forget. Any letters Lucienne wrote to him either were not kept at the time or were lost after the painter's death. *The Portrait of a Woman in Moroccan Costume*, believed to be Lucienne Crozier, is housed in a private collection. Its companion, the portrait she drew of him, was never seen after the February Revolution. Lack of substantiation may give critics cause to wonder if Madame Crozier was, in fact, ever involved with Eugène Delacroix; was their affair a daydream made real in notebook pages, a way of dramatizing her own life? Others may point to the slightly disjointed narration, shifts in tone indicating the writer's mental instability, but I think all of this is beside the point. Whether her affair with Delacroix actually occurred or not, it indirectly served to fuel her social consciousness. At the time Lucienne wrote, Delacroix's opinions and his art were extremely apolitical. Her arguments with him were a necessary step towards her radicalization. She beat her head against the wall of 'how a painting means', like many literal-minded twentieth century viewers of abstract art; she just couldn't get it. The routes between life's events and their representation through painting were, to her, murky and unreliable. The Delacroix debates map her rejection of romanticism and her inclination to embrace the kind of realism practised by some of his critics of a younger generation. Practitioners of realism from Courbet to Dickens and Balzac (both admired by Marx) used art and literature for purposes of social criticism. The information Lucienne gathered even from the sloppy realism of Rémy Gommereux made the ideological step to socialism an easy one.

Translating a work never intended for publication, written by an unknown woman, the translator is compelled to make decisions which, naturally, never entered the writer's mind. The voice of the translator, therefore, is destined to appear in the literal and metaphorical margins of the text.

The original French-language diary had a faintly bitter smell, the mustiness of old paper turned sour mixed with attar, evidence of the scented drawer. The book was hidden from the family for decades, left to solipsistic fermentation, the vinegar battling the sugary, until I blew the dust from the journal's cover. Since I live alone but haven't always, I can imagine Lucienne's need for secrecy. The back of the drawer acted like a precipice which separates hostile tribes. The simple box was a piece of geography which kept the need to record her thoughts from the eyes of servants and husband. It might be a friend or visitor whom she knew went through the papers on her desk when her back was turned. There is always that other person in the house.

Before World War II, at a time when some of the original pages from Delacroix's journals were turning up in Paris book shops, it might have been possible to find a book like this one: worn brown leather covers, streaks of gold still clinging around the edges, initials engraved in the centre. In the case of this document, the letters read: L.C. As one turns its pages, a breeze threatens to blow the whole thing apart, but it is treated carefully, wrapped in paper, secured with twine, carried off and forgotten about for a few more years.

I would like to acknowledge the help of Monsieur and Madame Odilon Xavier, without whose generous assistance this translation would not have been possible; also Mademoiselle Eugènie Redon of the Bibliothèque Nationale, and Monsieur G. A. Braque of the Préfecture of Police in Paris. Finally, I wish to thank my good friend Luc Ferrier who gave me no time to change my mind.

Dr Willa Rehnfield
New York City
May 1968

It is because it is 1968 that I've undertaken a formal translation of these pages. In the newspapers this year, a bomb goes off and suddenly one is confronted with the personal background (in print, film or video tape) of this member of the SDS or that member of the Weather underground. The interviewers, the reporters, say they are nearly always children of the middle class. One learns to make pipe bombs while events pass by her indifferent sister, as if violent protest, as if terrorism happened only within the shallow dimensions of a television screen.

Going backwards.

He didn't so much put the Lucienne Crozier diary in my hands as lead me to it. Luc Ferrier had more or less stolen it and I wasn't meant to keep the book long. He had just flown in from France, had had many drinks on the plane and Customs, usually a breeze, had given him a hard time. His clothes were rumpled. Mr Ferrier was agitated, as if he knew this scheme might not make it, might backfire, and his affairs were so tangled even a battery of lawyers would get nowhere trying to sort them all out. I gave the diary back to him. That was the last time I saw him alive.

Someone had recommended me to him three years earlier. He got my address through the university and wrote me a letter. Would I appraise some paintings? I knew from his note he had corporate stationery and a secretary who did his typing, but when I did meet him he approached me like a fence. He might have been a genteel blackmailer, an art consultant to corporations or kingpins of drug empires. I could see him in a dark crammed office at night, headlights of passing cars catching the silver rim of a fan or an art deco teapot. Here was a man whose fortune was a combination of education, chance and vice, I thought. I looked at some glabrous paintings he claimed were by Juan Gris and told him they were fakes. Mr Ferrier laughed.

None of my friends knew much about him. One story, not really reliable, said he'd been tapped on the shoulder by the Intelligence Service while still in college. I can imagine him at twenty-four being drawn to the agency because the combination of power and good manners can be compelling to those who instinctively know they have neither. Perhaps he had a passport whose stamped dates and places mapped an index of covert American foreign policy. A man who lay awake nights playing with a calculator and practising dialogue for dinners with Argentine secret police or Greek military attachés. I don't know why I had those suspicions. (Because he carried a calculator? Not many people did and it seemed an affectation.) At some point the difference between his licit and illicit enterprises became blurred; his sponsored trips, and those he ran for himself, completely overlapped. I could write he ran a forgery scam but all this conjecture is a way of mentally filling in a lacuna and probably erring in doing so.

Luc had a soporific voice and a licentious manner. I didn't ask him what he hoped to do with the phoney Juan Gris. He touched my arm when he wanted to point out something about the fakes.

He was in a hurry when he took back Lucienne's diary and I never saw either one of them again. My remorse over the loss of Madame Crozier is much more concrete. Luc just appeared with the book and disappeared again. That had been his habit since he first presented me with what he thought were early Cubist paintings. Lucienne I lived with quite solidly, for a few days at least.

Dr Willa Rehnfield
September 1968

11

4 JANUARY 1847

Near the convent school in Boissey Saint-Leger lived a solitary woman in a funny house. She was very old and didn't like children. In spite of her apparent condescension she often traversed the yard when we were playing in it, deliberately crossing our paths when she might just as easily, in fact with more directness, have taken the straight route into town. Mademoiselle Pitou or Pistou, I'm sure she wasn't as spooky or as perverse as her actions led small girls to believe. Her favourite story was the tale of the three shepherdesses. It was more of a fable than a true story yet she claimed it was a true story and if we weren't careful we'd grow up to become one of the three shepherdesses in perpetual mourning. One longed for the past, one for the future, and a third for the present. It was a question to think about while standing in line – past, present or future; if you had to pick one to be, which would you pick? At home I asked my grandmother about the three shepherdesses but she'd never heard of them, some tale from the Haute-Marne, she thought, there were no lost shepherdesses in this district.

You grow up, the family needs money, they send you to Paris to marry into a rich family, you return to visit your mother and an old woman enters your train compartment, settles herself in a corner, and wants to tell you a story. She boarded the train in Paris as I did but must have spent some time looking for a suitable compartment. The train had already pulled out of the Gare d'Orléans before she opened the door to mine. She travelled alone, carried her own

13

small valise and a book, its place marked by her ticket folded into a triangular wedge. Silence for a half hour perhaps, then, when the train passed over a bridge, she shut her eyes and crossed herself. Was she afraid the bridge would cave in, train, passengers and baggage tumble into the water like a line of peas sprung from a pod?

'Spirits live under this bridge,' she said. Here was the Mademoiselle Pitou of my twenty-fourth year; spirits in a ruin, spirits in a useless well under the piers of a bridge.

'It was during the Terror, some people were shot under this bridge, no one knows who they were, where they came from, who killed them or why. The bodies were found face down, nobody claimed them, two women, one man. One of the women was shot in the face. Horrible, it makes you think the guillotine is an instrument of mercy. A fellow from Paris came down, made some inquiries. One of the women was believed to have been the daughter of a wealthy family from the Nord; she'd been missing for over a year at the time of the murders. There had been talk of a kidnapping, talk of her running away from an arranged marriage thirteen months before. An innkeeper's wife thought she saw the trio in La Varenne the day before the bodies turned up, and a lone rider said he saw them on the road two weeks *after* their corpses were found. Special police were sent down from Paris, perhaps spies as well, but nothing turned up. Little portraits of missing persons were shown around, to the innkeeper's wife and so on, but the mystery was never solved. The bodies lie in a common grave in what is now the Joinville churchyard. The curé who, of course, was not a curé then, [*] told me he used to see odd souls visit the unmarked grave until about 1810. Thinnish, with turned-up collars, these visitors never said anything to him, and the curé is dead now himself. He believed someone didn't want the murderer or murderers found. You no longer hear anything about the

[*] During the Terror, the Catholic church was banned, priests were beheaded, graveyards destroyed and churches turned into *Clubs des Jacobins*. Willa Rehnfield

14

bridge murders, but the silence makes you wonder how people can live their lives, then be completely erased from the face of the earth as if they were no more than a smudge on a page.'

One is born into the world, is given a name, a class identity; one acquires a more complex identity as one ages. Murder comes cloaked in mystery (according to Mademoiselle Pitou), perhaps muddled by a deliberately inept constabulary (according to the curé), completely dissolving the accretions of memory, so there one is in an unmarked grave, a life gone without record. If anyone had knowledge of any of the three, he didn't claim them. My new Mademoiselle Pitou crossed herself again and with the second crossing her efforts at conversation ceased. She stared out of the window in silence as if she herself had been one of the elected and had said too much. One of those elected to see corporeal representations of the three eighteenth-century revolutionaries, thieves, aristocrats, wayward petty bourgeoisie or whatever they were: a woman in a white and blue dress lay face down in the dirt and blood, a section of her skirt looked like the French flag. My travelling companion was young then and threw up in the grass. The Mademoiselle Pitous of the world, tale couriers, gentlewomen who've lost the extra bit of money they thought they'd always have. They ride trains, push schoolgirls with their sticks and become a little cracked maybe, but it's they who carry on the private history of each department of France. Over the generations the history turns into tales. The bridge murders become travelling spirits, and before too many years they are the three desperate shepherdesses.

I would mourn for the present.

It wasn't my mother's fault. Fortunes and debts accumulate, marriages and births establish and tip balances: amassed capital on one side, serious deficit on the other. Our family took the gradual descent. My father was lost at sea. His loss is considered a fact now, but a fact initially received with reluctance and presented to the world under a heavy coating of story and fib. The man disappeared. My little brother was told disappearance didn't mean death, father was still alive shipwrecked on an uncharted island the nineteenth century had yet to discover. He was a king, an emperor ruling a spot in the middle of the South China Sea. Little Etienne examined maps with a magnifying glass for the tiniest overlooked island, comforted by the empty blue spaces which might contain land configurations still unknown in 1842. He could have been on one of those. Father might not have been a Micronesian king at all, but upon swimming ashore he might have become assimilated as just another member of the tribe whose job was to make harpoons or string instruments, abandoning any desire to return. Probably he was drowned in 1842 and gradually this truth was acknowledged. No mysterious fortune of coffee, spices or Arabian stallions arrived in Marseilles to credit the family income as my father had promised upon parting. 1843, 1844, fortune reversed itself. Bit by bit, parcels of our land were sold until almost nothing but the house and immediate garden remained. There were no dresses from Paris, no trips for pleasure, all extra money went for my brother's education. Naturally he was to redirect our family to a course of prosperity. Lucky fellow born too late, we couldn't wait for him to grow up and save the house, so the role of champion fell to me. To give the impression that all my mother's (should I write our?) aspirations in life were pinned to an income and a man lost at sea is not altogether accurate. She was willing to submit to all kinds of substitutions and cuts in her style of living. The years of gradual cutting back and selling off – as I write of our fallen position, it doesn't seem as though it was so painful. My mother used to tell us to grow long noses because air is free, but I know she felt acute hopelessness in her inability to remedy our situation on her own. She had no experience in the world of production, in the spheres of making money, investing it, gaining more. Sewing was boring and painfully slow work, running a shop demanded some knowledge of book keeping and capital to start with. The expression is to earn one's living.* My good-natured mother was hopeless at it, and the responsibility became mine.

I was sent to Paris to become acquainted with and eventually marry into a wealthy family, good friends of both my cousins in Paris and my closest friend who lives there too. It was this friend, Fabienne Ruban, who gave me this blank journal.

How is a book like a life? A riddle whose solution escapes me, a riddle I thought I ought to answer before I sat down to write. I could begin 4 January 1847; today I packed a bag, was driven to the Gare d'Orléans and boarded a train travelling south, but I feel some explanation or introduction is necessary. If only for the Lucienne C. who'll read these pages twenty years from now and won't have the remotest clue as to what memories these recordings sprang from. It's a question of doubting continuity. I expect my life to take a course more like my father's than my mother's (in spite of Monsieur Crozier). My mother spent all her life in the same town, my father travelled all over the world (and is certainly a king of longstanding in Oceania, having forgotten even the words to the *Marseillaise*). As far as diary writing and inconsistent memory goes, it's not enough to list a day's actions: packing, boarding, driving, travelling. A life doesn't begin on page 1. This train ride began when we received news of my father's drowning and only my mother and I breathed the truth to each other. History, background information, pattern of cause and effect leading up to the very present moment, a cold afternoon, four days after New Year's. Why do I write all this down? To put a present to use? I began with the intention of strictest privacy, thinking I would die of embarrassment if anyone besides myself opened this book, but the act of committing my life to paper belies a secret wish for someone other than myself to crack the binding, for there to be other witnesses, someone to be sympathetic, to take my side. But privacy

* Literally translated, 'to earn one's life', the connotation is that you get the situation in life you earn or deserve. W. Rehnfield

17

is endangered when publicity is flirted with. Even if the flirtation isn't acted upon.

I am on a train travelling south, the illusion is that I'm being projected forward, an old woman entered my compartment, said 'Let me tell you a story', and I'm taken backwards. The train pulls out of Boissey Saint-Leger, my brother meets me at the station and takes me home.

8 JANUARY 1847

The first year I lived in Paris I stayed with Fabienne and her father. Barely a week had gone by when I received an invitation to dinner at my cousins' of whom little needs to be written except that it was in their company I met Charles Crozier. The intention of this dinner and the ones which followed was obvious – meet the fellow and marry him as soon as possible. My end of the bargain was slight. By marrying me the Croziers acquired an odd strip of grazing land. It had never been worth much, but of late there have been rumours of a rail to be built through it, in which case the land might, indeed, become worth something. I used to dress slowly and carelessly for the dinners, even eating beforehand, so the occasions themselves were reduced to the social formality they truly were. When presented with Charles's passive features and simple inquiries I believed I faced an evening of complete boredom and I was absolutely right. The early evenings were totally boring events. Then the cousins, freethinking women that they were, got the idea we were old enough to be left alone. Should tap on shoulder turn into a grasp, should mild advances grow aggressive, they believed I, though not a sensible girl, would know what to do. The rules of Paris are not those of provincial society. My cousins excused themselves after dessert and went into another room. It was Charles Crozier's air of conspirator during these moments that endeared him to me or at least made him appear interesting, as if we could only truly behave naturally and honestly when other people

18

were out of the room. Our behaviour was innocent but we engaged in a code of secrecy as if that weren't the case at all. This act was particularly convincing when I was invited to the Crozier house on Rue Saint Gilles. Charles's mother was unconquerable. From the moment I met her and the sisters, their conversations were all of Deauville, Cornwall, and as a rule went around me. So rarely was I addressed directly I was like an inanimate document – something one has a legal obligation to keep around but can ignore at the same time. Against their oblique manners Charles was a hero of tact and good conduct, a picture of charm. Surrounded by his female relations his patriarchal instincts knew no threats, no serious threats. I also think he chose me to be contrary, to fly in the face of their obvious though impotent wishes. They were convinced I was after Charles's money, which was true, but it wasn't my idea originally and I needed constant encouragement to carry on. Charles's fondness for me co-existed along with knowledge of my mercenary ambitions. Finally fondness excised knowledge, obliterated it. He has never accused me of marrying for francs instead of for Charles, himself.

Although my marriage hasn't been entirely insufferable I write as if the wandering pen will provide some connections, because my engagement appears to have been a mystery, a curious lack of appraisal. Return to the dinners. What did we talk about? Charles had many ideas of what places he ought to occupy in French society but none of these niches turned out to be the right one. Upon taking a place at the Bourse, he severed the ties of a brief early life, mainly remembered as a lot of spare time. Nights at the opera, gambling at the Frescati were finished, and his appreciation of the wits who frequented these places dulled considerably. As a social misfit he's miscast. It's the air of impatience marking his opinions that would lead a woman to think this man is misunderstood and apart from the crowd in his judgements when, in truth, he's as snug as a well-fitted dovetail joint in the scheme of things. His colleagues are his father's age, and when presented with a companion

19

from an impoverished, if perhaps remotely noble family, I was his way out. But during the Crozier dinners his mother never left the room. Charles had a way of making me certain that all he shared with his punctilious relations was an accident of biology. We were the initiated. We let her cling to her suspicions. At some point in time my attraction towards him became more genuine than trumped up, but exactly when and how the balance shifted I have no recollection. Madame Crozier, supported by her daughters, opposed the marriage. I had nothing to offer the family that they could put in a bank vault; there were many young French women who did. Charles never met any of these women. He had met me but Madame C. said no, absolutely. Madame C. collapsed from a heart ailment and tumbled down a flight of stairs in the Rue Saint Gilles, pince nez on a gold thread wrapped around her neck. We were married in the autumn. Indifference, aloofness, mild repulsion, in actuality, not so mild when I spent the afternoon thinking about it; and then such extreme embarrassment. Charles – things aren't settled – this niche, too, has warped walls, corners which are far from plumb and I want to give all this up. Give up a marriage? Suddenly doubts are forced into retreat and I'm told respectability gets the majority vote. How can someone elicit such conflicting sentiments? When Charles admires me I feel I'm duping him and only take my last clothes off when the candles have been blown out.

My brother assured me that if he were going to medical school in Paris instead of Rouen there would be unpleasant scenes between himself and Charles in which he would assert 'French great fortunes are a crime against humanity and Charles, keeper of the keys, would have no defence against me. He would become an acquiescent mass.' You might say Etienne doesn't respond with my mother's grace towards Monsieur Crozier's generosity, or, more directly, Etienne resents being in a position where he's forced to accept handouts from what he considers a tainted source. Where did the C. money come from? Coal seams, fields of sugar beets, linen and wool works from land in the Nord –

Roubaix, to be specific. Most of the family still live there. It isn't lumps of coal, beets or shreds of wool that produce the income; it's miners, peasants and underpaid labourers who live under execrable conditions. The profit margin is expanded by low wages and sixteen-hour days, my brother points out, to say nothing of the Caribbean plantations managed by another branch of the family. My mother turns her back on him. If there's a corroded spot in the edifice of her plans, he'll scrape away the cosmetic camouflage and expose the fault. It had seemed so perfect to her until he knocked down the house of cards. Etienne grows self-indulgent, whipping himself up like a schoolboy without thinking of the object he taunts. Mother says even if everything he says is true, when we're about to be thrown from our house what does this history have to do with us? How were we to know what manner of criminals the Croziers were, and are they really and truly criminals, darling earnest Etienne? Criminals are vulgar, unlettered people who take your money or your life at knifepoint. The Croziers work hard – Charles does, no question about it. Etienne describes how miners and their children are worked to death, and how weavers' families, scores of them, huddle in tiny rooms with a loom, working continually. His scenes of squalor and destitution aren't lost on our mother. Isn't this a kind of violence? Isn't this the knifepoint in the Parisian street? She responds with an infuriating maxim about not judging people. What could be more boring? Etienne claims he's just being analytical. Not me though. My powers of perception are fuelled by calumny and mean-ness, the way Charles eats lemons down to the rind, the way his sisters count their change. But my mother isn't a complete naif. Who knows what our father, republican that he was, or any of us given the chance, when placed in a position of power might have done? Mightn't we commit similar sins of exploitation? Charles is a nice gentleman, he can't abandon what he's inherited. ('Why not?' says Etienne.) She reasons with him: if you want to be a saint, give up eating bread because the wheat was certainly grown for a landowner

21

more evil than the Croziers, and the jocular baker we've known all our lives may beat his wife behind closed doors. My brother says we must be able to make choices; in our secluded lives we get very few chances to act responsibly. The evening ends in an argument, my mother leaving the room.

9 JANUARY 1847

She spoke of the household, its upkeep, and of my brother. She spoke of remorse and guilt without naming the word. Responsibility is a popular notion with both my mother and brother, although the specifics of their respective prejudices conflict. Like my father who had a terrible fear of ships and their fallibility in high seas, I just stepped on board because money was needed and all ways of getting it in a pinch are probably equally unpleasant. My responsibility has, I think, been fulfilled with only a slight personal kind of deficit. Etienne's arguments are too late but seductive; more than that, they're an accurate articulation of my ambivalence regarding my marriage. To Etienne, Charles's avaricious profession can only reflect his lack of generosity on a smaller, personal scale. My distrust of Charles as a person is a translation of Etienne's broken code. What Etienne sees as larger moral transgressions, I interpret as a wariness I have of the man, the person I live with. Although my brother has lately adopted an oratory tone of address which I also mistrust, Charles's remoteness is tangible, something I desire and resent simultaneously. It isn't just a man, it's a life which must be accounted for, he's the sum of his experiences. Madame C. was right: there are many French women who would give the family valuable assets and who would do so quite willingly. She and I both knew romantic love is an unspoken and often absent element in marriage arrangements, and I can write this statement without feeling unduly mercenary.

Etienne makes her more of a target than he intends. He's too young to edit his speeches, directs them at everybody indiscriminately and just can't keep his mouth shut.

16 JANUARY 1847

While drinking coffee with Fabienne at Café Tortoni today a clinquant animal accompanied by a dark musician strolled past. Straight black hair, almond eyes, almost Oriental, we were told the flute player was South American, and his woolly beast, draped with gold tinsel, covered by a red blanket, was what's called a llama. They were a cynosural presence on the street, and later, as we wound our way home in the twilight, we heard the sound of the Incan flute, saw the glint of his animal turning off a street as we entered it. Fabienne and I parted at the corner of the Rue des Archives and the Rue Pastourelle. She hurried home to dinner with her father, disappointed with the prospect of a quiet evening at home. Perhaps obliquely directed by the vision of the Incan, she will try to read *Lettres d'une Peruvienne** but it won't hold her attention because café society is excluded from the account. But for me, someone else's narrative I can enter completely to the exclusion of Paris upsets no delicate balance, presents no intrusion on my domestic circumstances. Temporary absence is justified and I have no sense of the city going on without me. I caught up with the Indian musician on the east end of my street near the statue of Saint Gilles, touched the llama's neck and dropped a franc in his hat. The llama resembles the camel, I think, about the eyes and face. A strip of gold paper clung to my dress. My husband asked me where I'd been.

23 JANUARY 1847

Fabienne's boredom is a great chronic pit. She consumes diversions as readily as I dream them up: operas, comedies, jugglers from Tuscany. Today we went to look at paintings.

'He painted the Maréchal to look as if he's just returned from the Indo-China peninsula or the Sahara, still remembering the swamps, the desert.'

---

* A satiric romance in letters by Madame de Graffigny. Willa Rehnfield

23

'Yes, but brave, not too sentimental, he doesn't miss the campaign.'

There must be a point in artists' lives when inspiration fails and the production of paintings is just like the repetitive fabrication of any other object. One day in the studio follows another and painting becomes a job like any other, a series of mechanical steps, some intellectual justification supporting the less automatic decisions. Fabienne accused me of thinking like a horsedriver. My disinterest might border on the heretical but I'm not impressed by mirrors of nature, still less by artificial drama: landscape after seascape, bowls of plums after plates of pears, nude after nude. Until we came to a section whose subject was the Orient and North Africa, the view out the window was more interesting than the reflection of bits of French life presented in the rest of the gallery. Scant clues to life in the East I have found in Paris so far: the image of an eccentric acquaintance of Fabienne's smoking a hookah, wearing a fez and slippers with turned-up toes; Japanese screens and fans in a tea-shop window, herons flying over the pleats. I had seen nothing as detailed as the reality presented by these pictures. Here were views down narrow streets, not grey and loaded with European history as in France, yellow Moorish arches; bits of calligraphy, a different lexicon of shapes and signs; men praying in a mosque, women still wearing auriferous garments, looking outward at us, the Parisian voyeurs. One painting held my attention longer than the others: a Turk about to spear a leopard. I think he was a Turk. He wore a turban but a true adventurer or explorer who knew better might tell me there are no leopards in Turkey. Some artist in Belleville daydreamed him into painted life. The picture reminded me of another image: St George slaying the dragon, a parallel man and beast snarled around each other in mortal combat. The difference lies in the question of which antagonist wins. St George is the historic victor, but with regard to the little Turk it's not clear. He looks beaten. Blood runs down his naked shoulder, his pantaloons are in shreds. The leopard is all posed muscle, frozen in the middle of a flawless arch.

24

The memory of St George's story is in conflict with this picture of animal cunning clearly on the mark, and my expectations are tripped up. In the suspended attack, I want the man to win, but the painted narrative has no sequel. My expectations in Charles have been tripped up also, another suspended attack this, with nightly sequels which add nothing further to the narrative. He could be cat or Infidel, it doesn't matter. I don't know if he'll win. He appears alone like the solitary Turk in his forest, a painted illusion. Charles's forest is teeming with creatures, and he is well acquainted with each bit of life in the Bourse. He moves with increasing smoothness and skill but it really is a battle for him. At home, over dinner, he drops the stiff decorum, the manners and language of business transactions and speaks of the wounds, claws, broken spears of finance. My brother would be appalled, but for Charles dinner with me is the one occasion when all his defences tumble. He confides he isn't St George, and the skills of manipulation and exploitation may not always come to hand with conciousless facility. He is in the precarious position of the painted Turk. When his mother was alive she took a somewhat active part in managing the family investments. I qualify her active part by 'somewhat' because female involvement in business has grown marginal during the reign of Louis-Philippe; any participation beyond the marginal appears unseemly. Old Madame C., ever sensitive to appearances, gave way to her son's management, but ensuing empty days sharpened the edge of her bitterness. Her ambitions would not be curtailed. She would look after the family fortunes in her own way, and stopping our marriage while alive was about the only power left to her, for all the good it did. So I wish Charles would not feel free to speak to me about the finances as he did to her. I don't want to know about his plans for investing in railroads, buying land cheap from the desperate: illiterate peasants, impoverished landowners. He pays the asking price to counts and minor princes who know land's true worth and desire railroad shares. In all cases, the spear could easily snap and Charles

Crozier could fall prey, soft victim caught off guard, unable to fight back. I don't know which image to believe, the sharpy from the Nord or the floundering, isolated young man who, but for the servants, confides there's nothing he'd like more than to unbutton his shirt and eat dinner partially unclothed. The average time it takes to look at a picture is an unknown unit of measurement. Fabienne was twenty paintings ahead of me.

1 FEBRUARY 1847

It isn't that Charles is losing the battle, but he'd rather have orders executed from behind the lines in Flanders than command in Paris, the front. Brussels or Ghent are both closer cousins to Roubaix. They are also in wool. He spent happy childhood summers in Roubaix and it is appropriate that this corner of the country is his destination in retreat. Arguments for and descriptions of the lovely countryside are weighted towards the future: the city is unpleasant and unhealthy for children. Like someone who is trying to persuade another of a venture suspected unpleasant, he stared into the distance above my head. There was a painting of a ship behind me, mast, sails and tiny sailors to his rescue. He will go first, establish offices in Brussels, find a house in the country to the south. I will follow eventually. If I tell him how reluctant I am to leave Paris he insists this is just a trial, he's not coercing me into anything permanent; but my trust in him is stretching thin. I wished for a disease, anything to prevent the imminent trip. If I could invent an illness which would prevent me from being moved, I certainly would. I did begin to grow ill the very next day, but for all the wrong reasons. Mathilde, one of the old servants, interprets all the symptoms as pointing to one conclusion. Her inquiries, her maternal concern, don't appear to me as altogether altruistic. The real objects of her concern are Monsieur C. and his heir. I'm almost reduced to a human conduit; in the way, necessary but secondary. The streets of the third arrondisse-

26

ment have turned into a geography of entrapment. I run to Fabienne's, refusing to stay in bed as if by prolonging a girlhood friendship the condition of girl might be maintained and that of mother seem a contradiction, out of context, impossible. I had thought there was a system of preventing this. There will be no more pretending my marriage is some kind of abstract, financial arrangement. We will move to Roubaix or someplace just across the border and after the children have grown up I'll be allowed to stop lacemaking and work for Catholic charities.

No red rewards, not the slightest pain, nothing at all. The finitude of being sent away to school was like this; thinking I would never return, a station in life had been reached and I would never be a child again. I thought I was being taken to a convent full of the most severe palatines, but for the duration of the trip I also felt independent. To the contrary, it's 1847, and Charles's trip north has nothing to do with even the most illusory or temporary sense of independence.

To Fabienne my marriage is a serialized drama; several times a week she hears another *feuilleton*. Fabienne imagines herself stuck managing her father's household for decades. Nothing will happen. Arguing with the housekeeper over the price of coal one week, firing the new maid, fifteen years old, just come from Saint Ybars, the next. If she's sympathetic for voyeuristic reasons, I'm unhappy enough to exploit the moments of potential exhibitionism when they occur during our meetings. I tell her everything. We do these things by choice, not chance. I'm destined to disappear to an estate behind a woollen mill, our arrangement in a state of collapse.

There has been a terrible storm and everything is white. The streets are impassable. Nobody is in them. Thick snow covers roofs, balustrades, balconies, friezes of carved men, angels, animals. Afternoon looks like early evening and has a somnambulant effect. With the day so dark I fell asleep. Upon waking, Mathilde told me that when a woman is overcome by sleep it is another sign.

27

I had been late. I kept my coat on and watched him drink cabbage soup and cream, eat pork liver sausage with sage. I try to think of my marital enterprise as a job, the repetitive fabrication of images for a salary and I'm the tardy clerk. Then Charles elicits such pity as he eagerly describes each portico, each cupboard of the northern house. Birds migrate; I don't share the ornithic instinct. The second dinner subject was partings. At each possible turn I have regrets. Perhaps we will go and then we won't. Mathilde cleared the table although that's not her job. Somewhere in the social hierarchy among the servants it was understood that among them only she could be witness to this private scene. Privy is the wrong idea. She puts objects on the tray as if deaf and dumb. I sat at the table with my coat on and watched her, knowing she is far from deaf and dumb, and possessed of all her faculties.

Charles gets up early so I don't see him. Women aren't allowed in the Galerie de la Bourse, the fear being that *cocottes* will distract men, bribe them to buy or sell this stock or that, or worse, solicit them for purposes blatantly sexual.

Fabienne and I wandered through Les Halles today. It smelled completely bad from the poultry which is slaughtered there. The vendors shouted at us. ('My birds are fed on pure grains and champagne, my birds are aphrodisiacal.') Rolled jacket sleeves, aprons spattered with blood in patterns of arched spurts, layer upon layer, brown to bright red, red grins, raw-looking hands and forearms. Stalls are set up on the street, geese, chickens, ducks lined up in wicker cages or hung in rows by oozing neck stumps. Sticky with coagulated blood, feathers drift over mounds of hard dirty snow. Some buy live birds, others not and scoop up into sacks the headless birds which have taken a few steps over icy pavements. Ladies such as F. and myself were clearly out of place in a corner of the market mainly patronized by cooks. One *vendeuse* shouted with particularly derisive glee: we should feel her fat birds, stick our fingers into their guts. It's a puke world, overtly visceral, a closed door in polite society. We arrived here by accident. This closed door bars a room I desperately wanted to see, a room where bodies can be turned inside out as easily as dresses, guts and seams on the outside, clearly visible, and each individual is reduced to a physical presence. We heard two women talking about a friend who died from a Caesarian. The baby lived but the mother died slowly from fever and infection. These things are rarely discussed, even among women. It was a conversation tossed in our path in the middle of one of the noisiest streets in Paris. Fabienne was affected more deeply than I because no one had ever told her about fevers spreading outward from your middle.

It's not just fear of pain and babies, there is the fear of running away. My abrogated marriage would mean work; work for which I won't be paid enough to live on, meagre employment which won't pay for medical school or my mother's house. The women on Rue des Halles can, in the context of Rue des Halles, snicker at us, but for a simple sacrament I could be reduced to setting up shop next to them.

I caught Mathilde knitting little white caps and, again, couldn't become angry with her. Caught implies a crime. I should write *found*. The inhabitants of this house and their innocent pleasures seem to me a game of conspiracy and counter-conspiracy. The innocence questionable, the pleasure perverse.

15 FEBRUARY 1847

At Fabienne's this afternoon I became very ill and the rumour of a new heir or heiress was brought to an end. We drank *lait de poule** (with rum) and read *feuilletons* in bed as if husbands existed only in dreams and we could go on reading in bed like children.

One of Charles's sisters has been staying with us, and in flawless convent French learned in Lille she insists she will stay with me when Charles is away, a woman alone is 'not quite the thing'. She would be afraid to live in the city by herself. Her main occupation is changing her dresses to suit the fashions, altering sleeves, adding ribbon, cutting off lace, an infinite metamorphosis of costumes. If she stays the household will be paved by bits of cloth. No lewd edge, no suggestive surface will be left bare.

My protests against the move north are feeble, exhausted. My ill health, Charles is certain, will be temporary. I feel like a cowardly child caught red handed with a stolen toy.

At dinner he made two announcements, giving equal weight to each: 1, he will leave for Brussels at the end of next week and 2, his gold cigarette case is missing, stolen, he believes, by a pickpocket. As soon as he discovered the theft, he reported it to the Poste de Police. It will be easy to identify; the case is engraved with his initials. As he waited in the Préfecture he began a conversation with the butler of an acquaintance, the Vicomte de Roussey. The butler was with a woman he didn't know, introduced as a servant of the same family. The man, not the most discreet of servants, revealed that a Rembrandt had been stolen from the Vicomte. Detectives had come around in the morning but the chief inspector wanted the servants, the only witnesses, to give another detailed physical description of the two felons at his offices. Two men had arrived after the Vicomte and the Vicomtesse had left for the day leaving only a few minor servants in the house. The men claimed to be picture restorers hired by the Vicomte to touch up the Rembrandt. Since there was no one in the house who might have known otherwise, the scullery maid led them to

---

* A heated mixture of milk and a raw egg, often given to young women as a means of restoring health. W. Rehnfield

the salon. She stayed long enough to see them open flat leather cases full of brushes, tools and rolls of paper. When she checked the room an hour later the two men and the Rembrandt were gone. At that moment, on the street, the Vicomte's personal butler saw two men loading what appeared to be a large wrapped painting into a cart. One short, one tall, wearing workmen's smocks, one blue and spotted, one white and more so (though both garments looked soft from many washings), patched woollen jackets, polished boots – an attempt to pass as workmen out to make a good impression. The butler, after a lifetime of letting people into doors, out again, and turning them away, gave a sharper description than the scullery maid who became even more flustered when one detective suggested someone in the house tipped off the thieves as to the exact moment when the house would be so nearly empty. What was even more odd was the note the butler brought with him to show the chief inspector. It had arrived in the afternoon. The robbers didn't want ransom money and had no intention of selling the painting. Their demand was the release of four anarchists held in Saint Lazare.

Charles waited for the two to finish their interview with the inspector. It was a so much more interesting case of theft than his own, and it would be amusing, knowing the truth, to see how the Vicomte would disclose the affair in public. His patience was rewarded, and this is what he learned. The inspector checked the records and found that two of the anarchist prisoners were guilty of organizing strikes at mills belonging to the family of the Vicomtesse. The third had run a satirical journal highly critical of the king. It had been shut down in a wave of repression: these waves, ever growing in frequency and duration, are the result of the king and his state feeling particularly assaulted. In the middle of the night, presses and typefaces were smashed, papers burned, ink spilt and smeared in such quantities that black pools spread on to the street causing black footprints coming and going in all directions and for quite a distance. Children laughed but the ink remained sticky, taking an unusual length of time to evaporate. The fourth prisoner had tried to assassinate a general or perhaps the king himself during a parade. According to the note, if the thieves' demands aren't met in forty-eight hours, they will send the Vicomte a 4 × 4 centimetre square bit of the painting every two days until the men are freed.

Charles says he guessed from the start the thieves were either half-witted Bonapartists, loyalists or anarchists. No one could hope to sell such an obviously stolen painting. Who would buy it? An ignorant American industrialist? A shifty Prussian baron? The agents of an isolated Russian count? They couldn't smuggle the painting out of the country, not a chance. And he doesn't think the scullery maid had anything to do with the theft, she seemed a daft girl. He remembered her name, Pascale. He regrets his trip will prevent him from following up on the affair. De Roussey may have enough power to have the prisoners released and the Rembrandt is an enormous investment to lose, but he bets de Roussey would rather receive his Rembrandt in little square bits through the French mail. The Vicomte is enough of a military figure to reject bargaining with the enemy, and he'll reject that option with no regrets or second thoughts. His friendship with the armed Vicomte had intimate beginnings at school but was later abandoned. Charles did not know the exact title or subject of the painting. He doesn't expect he'll see his cigarette case again, and we don't discuss the eventuality of my joining him in Belgium.

27 FEBRUARY 1847

An idea of personal liberty at the mercy of a temporal anomaly; very early in the morning – an accidental privacy. I gave most of the servants time away, a holiday. Mathilde will not go. She has no place to travel to. Vacations, for her, are undertaken awkwardly and reluctantly. No family to visit, no friends to take along; the house of Rue Saint Gilles is everything to her, but I find no flattery in her fidelity. Devotion isn't directed at me. Perhaps there was a butcher in Paris or a butler in Lille who fancied her years ago but as far as I can tell there was no romance so compelling that she would find pleasure in reunion.

'*La Vrai République*, Madame?' Mathilde picked up my newspaper as if it were a dirty object the dog brought in by mistake. I pointed out an article about a meeting of silk workers in Lille. The police had broken up the meeting brutally.

'Didn't Charles have a relation in that trade in Lille?' She told me it had been an uncle and took away the paper as she removed a bunch of dying lilacs from a vase.

Caginess wasted, disguised as maternal concern, all spent on a single, insignificant family. Charles could be in New Caledonia and she would look after his domestic interests like a game warden. Her current superstition passed on to me by Hortense: I will myself not to have children. An idea that came with her from the country and has resisted years of living in Paris, as if will had anything to do with babies. The population would be halved if that were so. Can't she send those little white hats to her nieces? I told her to return my paper, I was not yet finished with it.

Entries read like studies in frustrated vindictiveness. To engage in self-portraiture is to court foolishness. I didn't mean to write this way. I'm fulfilling Mademoiselle Pitou's prediction, becoming a woman who mourns for the present. It's a temptation because this journal is a bound, mute book which nods in collusion and doesn't argue, but some passages present an unattractive reflection. They join with Mathilde and talk back to me.

My mother's letter contains only domestic information: formulas for removing candle wax from linen and brass polish for convoluted door knobs and key holes, especially useful because it never hardens in the jar. Even if she knew, my mother would turn a deaf ear to the scenes on the other side of the brass key plate, polishing it until it shone, regardless of time spent at the task. My brother's letter, in the same envelope, described his Carnival tricks. Disguised,

33

I hope beyond recognition, he and his friends carried on their shoulders a life-size effigy of a light cavalry officer of the *garde municipale*. The man who was the model is, in reality, one of *les notables** of our district. My brother is under the impression I don't know anything and can be duped into believing his pranks are innocent and childish. By torchlight, their route went past the fellow's estate, through the town and up to a bridge, where they decapitated the figure then threw it in the river, all the while singing obscene lyrics. Why rude songs instead of the old ones from the Revolution? The idea was to insult, not to antagonize, although I'm sure they succeeded at both. Etienne wrote he had expected Monsieur le Maréchal to chase the band through the town wearing a smoking jacket and waving a billiard cue and cigar. During the next days inquiries were made but the identities of Etienne and his Carnival comrades have remained a secret. My brother is lucky.

5 MARCH 1847

The Rembrandt/de Roussey case has finally appeared in the newspapers. They claim the Vicomte has received only two tiny pieces of the painting and the police are in possession of new secret clues which they expect will lead to the phoney picture restorers. I don't believe any of it. Not wanting to admit defeat publicly, I calculate the Vicomte has by now received about a dozen slices of his Rembrandt through the French mail. The newspapers obscure the case by failing to mention the imprisoned strike organizers or journalist. The press reports that the price of ransom is only a lunatic held in an asylum in Brittany, a confirmed menace in the last stages of an unmentionable disease. Just before incarceration he had attempted a murder, not uncommon, the papers said, for souls so afflicted. It's not an equal exchange. The ransom of the Rembrandt will be ticklish; the gesture could fail if the Vicomte resists. Reasons

* *Les notables* refers to a member of the franchized class. W. Rehnfield

34

don't penetrate what he imagines is his great wrath, and the peer of the realm, a man whose accumulated history of title and privilege goes back to the Carolingians, isn't converted to the cause of the revolution. To him, it's an episode about the preservation of power under duress.

The stations in a woman's life are marked by public ceremony, with guests invited, christenings, weddings, funerals an unalterable chronological sequence. Having participated in my own marriage, I'm supposed to know certain unspoken things and therefore be possessed of the self-confidence of a young married woman, not a girl, and sometimes not even what they call a young lady. But it doesn't work that way, it turns out you can go backwards. Sometimes I feel more adolescent than anything else, because with Charles's absence the rules grow flexible, subject to interpretation. The married woman isn't something continuous and automatic. Those two images, stations supposedly consecutive, are in conflict and the battleground is most marked during outings with Fabienne. The language of flirtation is not among my sluggish talents. Fabienne uses clever chatter like an actress being interviewed, and repeats aphorisms I never hear her use when we're alone. When I enter a room, people say, 'There goes a serious girl.' I could retire into the role of Madame C., the neuraesthenic who never goes out, except Monsieur Ruban insists his daughter be accompanied by another woman. His idea of some kind of guard for Fabienne's chastity is the presence of a married woman.

15 MARCH 1847

'I want to escape my chaperone, go to one of those tiny boulevard theatres full of out-of-work printers and journalists who write for the kind of papers that have disappeared or been outlawed by the following day,' said Fabienne.

'Do you think the unemployed will behave quietly and elegantly while you never take your eyes off the stage?'

'You'd complain of the smell.'

'I'm not the one who wants to go. You were so offended by Noun's suicide in *Indiana*, you wouldn't read any more George Sand. "Servants don't kill themselves for love," you said. "She'd have had the child and disappeared into Belleville." Belleville is where you're going to have to go if you want to see those plays.'

21 MARCH 1847

A shade of green that's so black it's hardly green anymore. The north pools of the Jardin du Roi, meeting place for *lycée* students, sanguine nursemaids, coachmen out of livery, old men clutching walking sticks.

Through the winter the carp hide at the bottom of the pool, far below the collar of ice. Old fish, the really ancient ones, are covered with many veils of mould, living down there in the muck. They are supposed to be over two hundred years old, thrown in by a handmaiden of Catherine de Medici. Every spring they reappear, the same fish, hungrier and more obscured. As often as I meet Fabienne and as often as I walk through the Jardin, the ugly fish are a sign of spring I greet with ambivalence. Persephone emerges from the underworld. It's not that I would send her back, inverting spring to autumn, but I look on the new season with some trepidation. The clues of change are portents viewed with dread. I've just lost comprehension of the alphabet for reading these particular symbols. I want time to slow. That's really what this journal is about as much as it is about preservation, as if writing can attenuate and magnify memory.

Fabienne arrived a little late, red in the face and out of breath. We broke off chunks of bread and threw bits to the fish. Fabienne, realist, insists that fish live in water and omens are another thing. They don't augur love or bad luck. Spring is spring, late or early, the signs are of significance only to farmers. She concerns herself with hard facts, what she sees as simple truths: Charles is absent, off arranging deals in Belgium, and on Thursday at Saint-

Hilaire's[*] I met a painter whose name begins with D. Hard facts have nothing to do with a bunch of old fish who have acted on the same biological instincts for over one hundred years. Ice melts, they swim towards the sun and food. Feminine orange mouths appear at the surface of the water and they snatch like famished carnivores, predatory and vulnerable at the same time.

Charles is the sort of creature people know as an acquaintance from the Bourse. They might call him 'the most affable of men' but for all this splendid fellow business, each day his image grows more vague, his memory reduced to a smile and an overly used phrase. Even the duration of a short absence is enough to erode particular details, the shadow where jawbone meets neck, the inside of the arm where muscle meets elbow. I try to picture my husband engaged in one of the most mundane actions – shaving, for example. He is in front of the glass, slowly fiddling with brush and soap. I do miss him but in the way one misses a dull elementary school teacher whose routine has become habit. Now that he's gone, as well as the routine, I remember what I took to be foreignness when we first began living together. And as I remember that strangeness, that sense of foreignness which comes when you live with someone you don't know at all well, I suppose Fabienne is right. I'm looking for a substitute. Someone who is as Charles was at first.

Forget about charming interpretations, forget about bending an attentive expression into something lewd and fixed. At Saint-Hilaire's Fabienne left her fingerprints on the front paws of a life-size bronze tiger, unable to talk about genus, varieties of rodent species in Central Africa, the development of genetic hybrids. Zoologists, chemists, biologists, she accused them all of malapropism in lieu of her own misunderstanding. She looked away from the stuffed python, the gorilla skull. I was in a book-lined

[*] Augustin François César Prouvençal de Saint-Hilaire was a botanist, director of the Jardin des Plantes. Willa Rehnfield

37

alcove with two men, tall obsequious Phébus, the animal sculptor who moved to grasp my arm when he wanted to emphasize a conversational point, and a small man who held himself stiffly away from those points but closer to me. She could see half his body, black elbow, hands in pockets, studied boredom.

As she scraped the mud from her shoe with my umbrella, she told me the man on my right was looking at me like one who waits on the stair for someone to pass, wondering if this time they will say hello. I don't think Monsieur Delacroix is a hopeful man, or one who spends a lot of time waiting for his chances, especially in affairs with women. Fabienne could see only half of his body. She didn't witness the humiliation of Phébus who had to bend his shoulders under the curved alcove ceiling. I can tell her he was very restrained and that reluctance can be misinterpreted as malevolence.

Fabienne adores rumours. 'Eugène Delacroix is a dandy in the less familiar English sense, but it's only a social pose. A misanthrope devoted only to his paintings, his flirtations are parodies of manners. He might be the illegitimate son of Charles Maurice de Talleyrand, and he keeps a Moroccan monkey and a pair of parrots in his studio on Rue Notre Dame de Lorette.'

Another rumour is about his mistress, his cousin Josephine de Forget, who lives near his studio. She is a baroness who, along with her mother, smuggled her father out of La Conciergerie* in 1815. They dressed her father in her mother's clothes and hurried past the guards *en travesti*. The trick worked but her mother stayed behind and went mad in prison. Fabienne admitted she had always loved that story of switched genders, and often when she couldn't sleep she fancied herself a Madame de Forget rescuing an imagined lover.

* La Conciergerie was a prison in Paris at the time of the Revolution. W. Rehnfield

The invitation from Monsieur Delacroix wasn't for a secluded dinner, didn't indicate the kind of privacy I anticipated and Fabienne expected. Instead of *chambres privées* in the restaurants of the Palais Royale with silent waiters and thick walls, we went to a large party at the house of one of his friends.

Frédéric and Pauline Villot live in a tall house behind two courtyards on Rue de Nevers and from a northern oriel you can see the Cour Carré of the Louvre. The double courtyards perform the function of delaying or obscuring the accessibility of the house to a mob, in case of revolution or invasion. As we passed through the courtyards he remarked on the face of Paris architecture, so different from London. He attributed the difference, in part, to the delay devices, these courtyards added to courtyards. 'Rebellions, revolutions, workers, students, each group takes its quarrel, its theme of oppression into the streets. Street violence leads to life behind a series of empty boxes that don't trick anyone.'

His contempt surprised me. He has always been imitated by republican engravers. * While we were still in the courtyard, he said Villot needed greater protection from his critics at the Louvre than from radicals or street gangs (the same thing in his opinion). Frédéric's restoration of some paintings has been considered excessive to the point of monstrosity.

We were shown into a salon lined with prints and small paintings, and Villot hurried to greet Eugène with the anxiousness of someone who suspects he's not well liked and wishes it were otherwise. He spoke rapidly, enthusiastically, of a marvellous red, the elusive red of Tintoretto, of Veronese. It was wonderful, he told us, he would try it on some damaged paintings at the museum as soon as

* Lucienne Crozier is referring to the many imitations and variations on *Liberty Guiding the People* that appeared in French periodicals during the 1840s. See Courbet in *Le Salut Public*. W. Rehnfield

possible. We left the salon to see the marvellous red in Villot's workroom. Pauline left her guests and followed us with a tray of absinthes. There were awkward moments at the doorways to certain rooms and at stairs until a servant relieved her of the tray and the five of us finally descended into the cellar of the house.

The room where he ground paints, binders and blended oils looked like a scientist's laboratory and smelled slightly offensive, like rotten eggs. Rows of shelves contained many sizes of shallow glass and porcelain dishes, gradations of mortar and pestle sets, glass tubes and coiled rubber hoses. Sections of wall not supporting shelves were covered by colour charts and swatches of canvas and paper daubed with paint. Every colour imaginable was somewhere in the cluttered little room. After all this, the famous red looked like a rather ordinary red to me. Eugène said the red in the dish looked fine to him and it looked fine on the sample bit of canvas but it might look different on the actual painting because it has, after all, a different chemistry from the original, and will dry and age differently. To be anything less than cautionary would result in travesties. He went on; each painting will age differently, the amount and density of each area of paint old and new will vary. Who knows the true composition of Rubens's red, of Piero della Francesca's blue? They were entitled to their secrets. One ought to take only so many liberties. Painted women are no more amaranthine than the living and breathing ones. 'Living and breathing,' he said. As if I were a homunculus, a shell of rubber skin whose motor reflexes were controlled from within by a gang of fairies. I turned to Pauline who was absently coiling a small hose. We discussed the Victor Hugo affair. She whispered he had not been very cautious, should not have let himself be caught. Pauline drew me into conversation when the two men disagreed, as if to set up a sound barrier, so as not to hear.

After dinner we walked down the Boulevard St Michel then took a cab to the Café Tortoni. Eugène seemed to be still thinking about his disagreement with Frédéric Villot or the dishes of ground pigment, or perhaps it was Pauline who really occupied his thoughts. He began to talk about an artist's peculiar social needs which isolate him from other people, having an occupation which utterly seduced him to the exclusion of other people. When I was unsympathetic to his studied self-concern he said women see only the literal side of human needs. The metaphorical is lost on them. It seems to me there are genuine tragedies in the world and this turmoil of his own manufacture isn't one of them. He looked straight ahead. There was nothing in his expression that might remind me of the short man who stood by me so quietly while Hippolyte Phébus talked about marble fauns and brass Caligulas. Any relation between the two diminished and he grew as sour as Malfrère at the Tivoli Circus. I decided to return home alone. A profuse flatterer couldn't have triggered more antipathy. Then I became less sure. Sincerity is an elusive quality at best. I half changed my mind as we parted at Place Vendôme, but didn't in the end.

14 APRIL 1847

A letter arrived from Charles today. He hasn't found a house yet. He writes of the churches with their intricate altar pieces: triptychs with wide unfolding wings, the Annunciation, the Adoration of the Shepherds, Nativity, Madonna Enthroned. Angels wear brocaded robes and every detail is a religious symbol, a cipher. Doors carved in patterns of cinque-foil and trefoil, portals and tympanum house figures of everyman, prophets, demons of luxury and avarice, the Angel of Death, the Mystic Mill: Moses and Saint Paul grinding corn, Grammar, Pythagoras, Music. He steps back and tilts his head to see the clerestory and that's the end of his letter.

A letter from Eugène arrived but he is too late. Sorry, no thank you, my regrets, regards to your paintings, I'm leaving tomorrow for Boissey Saint-Leger to visit my mother for Easter.

41

Fabienne called before I left. She had just received a rare note from the nuns in Normandy with whom her mother had been staying for twelve years. She lost her mind in 1835 when Fabienne was eleven years old and was subsequently sent to a convent where they take in the mildly deranged. Fabienne now lives alone with her father who works in the office of the *sous-préfet* in the ninth arrondissement. She has two older sisters married to men with military careers. Unfortunately much of the family income went into their dowries. Fabienne with a few thousand francs has dim prospects at a time when many suitors assess quick fortunes more eagerly than pretty faces. Men look at Fabienne, who likes to spend money but has little of her own, as an invitation to debtors' prison. Unfairly, her father thinks most of her companions are frequenters of low haunts but he remains essentially oblivious to affairs of his family and she can often do as she pleases. Conversations with Monsieur Ruban are all about the value of the franc and 'Louis-Philippe is doubtless one of the most underrated kings in the history of France.'

Madame Ruban's afflictions began shortly after she started attending the salon of Alberthe de Rubempré, a self-proclaimed sorceress of far-ranging faculties. Although the workings of her illness must have been in place long before, once exposed to the theories of Alberthe de Rubempré (also known as Madame Azur), all the fevers that had been dormant for years started to dominate her behaviour. Slowly the tables in the Ruban house began to turn and talk, expound, in fact, through the medium of Fabienne's mother. Dead grandfathers, aunts and cousins gave all kinds of advice. Monsieur Ruban ignored his wife's spiritual dialogues until she, in turn, began ignoring him. Suspecting Satanism or undue Bohemian influences, he sent her to the nuns. This also avoided embarrassing the elder sisters' suitors and skirted further scandal. At eleven I remember Madame Ruban dressed in black and red velvet with a turban round her head, greeting me saying, 'Don't touch! Don't touch!' I don't know if she meant the tables or herself. If Fabienne's sisters were embarrassed by their mother's conversations with people who weren't there, Fabienne thought of her performances as a kind of game with costumes and resented her sisters' conventionality.

When I was taken to Paris to visit I wanted to be independent of my mother, to walk in the park with friends as if I were an orphan, self-reliant, able to take care of myself. My mother never looked strange or talked to herself but she embarrassed me by insisting on looking after me when I thought I was old enough to be left alone.

22 APRIL 1847

During the journey home no old woman entered my train compartment with a story, an axe to grind or complaints about her grandchildren and the state of the Republic. Travelling to my mother's home is a gesture which puts Paris affairs in a drawer, slammed, locked shut. She opens long green shutters and steps out on to the terrace, the garden: new purple irises, banks of old lilac bushes, apple trees planted in a crescent. My brother is home and we visit the cemetery although my father's not buried there. In the evening there are callers. They drink cider and beer, play *bouillotte*.

It's not so much that the quality of masculinity differs from person to person but that my perceptions of how traits of gender manifest themselves vary so much. I don't notice it in most men, but if I were in love with one then smell, stance, voice, all those differences would become interesting – if I were really in love, to the point of obsession. As I retrace my steps from the Café Tortoni, I can't attenuate one of Eugène's short mannered kisses into a seduction scene. My thoughts run out of control but it just can't be stretched. It was as if I heard Madame Pitou euphemistically telling girls what it meant to stare too long at a boy, as if you could be poisoned by any nitwit. But lately in the isolation and provinciality of Boissey Saint-Leger the kiss in the mind has turned into something else entirely. Eugène's deficit

43

characteristics are filled in by my imagination. That's what causes the addiction and I know one or two things about him. I regret having gone home alone.

My mother rarely asks direct questions, as though certain answers ought not to be named. She has developed a new fear based on hints and suggestions and her shrewdness collides head on, not with what I would call prudery, but with the wish not to be accused of prurience. She says only that she doesn't understand why I continue to live alone and that rumours which circulate in a city must be more vindictive, more prone to exaggeration. The thought makes her ill, headaches, it's her liver. Since I was eighteen, no, since my father was lost at sea, she has never considered me quite safe and she has always been concerned more for my welfare than for my brother's. Although I married to send him to school, his basic survival was always assured as the quick handsome son. If I were to have remained unmarried, my mother is certain I would have become a destitute old woman.

28 APRIL 1847

Fabienne and I spent another Thursday afternoon at Saint-Hilaire's and heard a lecture on the enormous lizard skeletons some farmers unearthed near Avignon.* E.D. never appeared.

3 MAY 1847

There were pictures finished and unfinished, hung on every available centimetre of wall space or leaning against the wall. Most of the paintings were his; others, obviously painted by another hand. He smelled of the thinning agent, a kind of alcohol used to soften hard paint. Props, costumes, model stands were stored on shelves or half displayed on tables. The evidence of the search for subjects was cast around the room like scattered clues to the end of a play staged in the storage house for the Comédie Française.

* Probably les dinosaurians d'Avignon. W. Rehnfield

44

Looking up from a table littered with drawings like a valley of paper strata, he dismissed his servants, Andrieu and Lambert. Fifty serpentine human figures with helical spines rivalled pythons. They drew claws, unfolded shadowy wings, displayed pulsating, hermaphroditic chests, Eugène's *fantasiste* inventions. Wingless Apollos, Virgils, Homers and Dantes bearing spears, staffs, charcoal swords, they never sweat or shiver, little paper men and voluptuous women. An arm is hidden by a creased edge; a rider is about to tumble from an Arabian stallion, but the violence is only smeared water colour, Mars black and veridian. A hand is extended, the hand is withheld. The jaw is about to bite, the spear is about to pierce. Little angels, cherubs of Greece and Rome scattered over the sheets. Each fragment is a contribution to the final narrative. Each finished painting is the moment before; about to kill or to be killed, about to accept or to reject, always and forever just on the edge. As my eyes narrow the multitude into a morass of graphic sludge, an Apollonian face peers through. My eyes focus the shifting population: figures, animals, torn curtains and armour.

Drawings as recordings, documents of human and animal motion, a way of producing and fixing graphic memory. The pencil as a precursor of Daguerre's invention. Odalisques stretched out on divans: these are Eugène's mental daguerreotypes. Erotica, chapters of. He confessed the existence of a private notebook filled with such drawings as would help him pass the hours of loneliness. These drawings, from refined imitations to explicit lewdity, betray naive dreams mixed with brothel worldliness. Hands clasped behind the neck, the soft curved lines where stocking end and thighs begin, the two lines meet as legs cross. The tension creates a shape like a long ' ⌒ '. Baudelaire suggested these drawings be preserved in a special archive named The Museum of Love. Eugène's odalisques would surely have a hall to themselves – hard to find, a left turn easily missed. This gallery would be open only on alternate Tuesdays.

Unfortunately the confession of the notebook put our relations on a different ground, paralysing flirtation. Up until this moment I could have been any woman touring his studio, an admiring patroness who made neutral platitudes of approval and was received the same way. As far as appearances were concerned the incidental hand on my elbow was a steering mechanism and yet it was not. His acknowledgement of the private notebook acted like a cord pulling down specific painted flats. Self-consciousness descended upon both of us, though I remarked on the pretty odalisques as if they were sexually neutral like paintings of birds or ships at sea. He let go of my arm, said painting was nothing more than sticking brushes in goo, yet a dictatorial mistress all the same. The impulse to be critical of his paintings out of jealousy was a useless and misguided one.

Changing the subject, Eugène explained his friendship with Villot. One had to behave a certain way with him. It was terrifying to think what Frédéric V. might do to his paintings if he were dead. He has had nightmares of mutilated, severely truncated paintings: Hamlet's black cloak touched up with sanguine, *The Prisoner of Chillon*'s chains lopped off because the restoration, in the end, was far too garish.

He led me to a steamer trunk, opened the lid and began to take out dark velvet trousers (Turkish), shirts of raw silk, scarves hung with gold ornaments. These were part of the collection he brought back from Morocco. He began to unbutton my dress and then untie my laces. I stood as mutely and as passively as a painting, thinking about the red marks the laces made against my back but, half naked, afraid to turn around. Eugène pulled Arabian clothing from the trunk. The objects were little more than very white lengths of cloth with a few seams. *Chechia, haik, kufiyeh* which is tied around the head: he named them as he tossed them in my direction. E. undressed without looking at me. Over my shoulder I stared at his spine, the line of bones nestling white against each other as he bent over, and at that moment I did not want him to touch me. He put on an Arabian costume. I was going to be a drawing. That was what he wanted. I finished taking off my dress as if the room were empty, put on a green velvet jacket and a small hat with veils tied under my chin. Gold disks sewn on the clothes clinked as I moved. Eugène sat back in a chair, picked up a drawing board with paper tacked to it and began to draw me. The effect of being drawn and examined so closely was difficult to bear. It's very much like being touched, as if the eye were a hand. The pencil outlines your ear, your cheeks, the top of your forehead, and the sound of curved strokes against paper is the same gesture against skin. It's as if you're being touched on the ear, neck, shoulders. I found a smaller sheet, bent over a table and started to draw Eugène but I didn't imagine my pencil touched him in the same way. He seemed immune to suggestion, entirely absorbed in his drawing. E. finished first while I was still trying to follow the lines of drapery around his head. He walked to my side of the table, bent over close to me and looked critically at his portrait. He moved my hand still holding the pencil to add some lines and correct others. It was a patronizing touch but standing as close as he did his suggestions made little sense. His arm was against my arm, through the thin costumes I could feel his chest against my back. I suddenly imagined Fabienne's high inquisitive voice:

'Where will you go when he starts moving his hand up that flimsy Arab thing you're wearing? Will you just lie there on the cold floor?'

Not to the model's room, a little chamber with a narrow couch, odd bits of curtains lying across it. We spent most of the afternoon on the rug, Arabian clothing scattered in heaps, tinkling as the charms hit the floor.

5 MAY 1847

A letter from Charles lay unopened next to a crescent of crumbs pushed to the edge of my plate. The letter

47

will contain descriptions of a house. Charles thought, short of death, he would have only one wife. Monsieur Crozier, for whom marriage was a solid edifice, not to be chipped away at by chance flirtation or deliberate seduction.

I went to see his paintings: *Shipwrecked Men in a Boat*, *The Entombment* and *Jewish Musicians of Mogador*. A sense of suspended violence; its potential threatens me personally in each picture. I can't reconcile the language of colour and light with these pictures of covert brutality. Painting of pain isn't the experience of pain but an interpretation, a fictional reproduction. I find the combination of beautiful painting and doomed content frightening and I wonder if these contradictions aren't a clue to the nature of the man, the painter himself. Which of these women might have been painted after Josephine de Forget? Which one has her eyes, her mouth? Women in paintings, in letters, late nights ending in early mornings. He claims to be a painter of morals, a moral painter.

I met Fabienne at Baratte's between Notre Dame and Les Halles. She slid into the booth as if she'd just fled the Conciergerie. Her father wants to marry her to a clerk, a marriage probably arranged in a place like Baratte's, aristocratic food served in haphazard surroundings. I'm afraid my consolations rang false. I know there can't be any for a ceremony which will link her to a tedious little clerk and she's sure that's exactly what the person is. While she spoke she kept pouring vinegar and pepper sauce on her Ostend oysters until her plate brimmed over. I stacked the empty shells on the table's edge to signal the waiter. Fabienne made a useless dam of shallot fragments.

What does Eugène know about physical brutality? What does he know about mental brutality, monsters lying chock-a-block in the recesses of an uncontrollable imagination? Having led a middle-class life of comfort in the shadow of aristocratic cousins, perhaps nothing.

Mathilde brings me Charles's letter, still unopened.

We arrived early and she opened the door for us herself, speaking greetings and endearments in a whisper which I found phoney and annoying. Princess Belgiojoso's rooms were dimly lit, and, dressed entirely in black, her body seemed to disappear as she stretched out in a black chair. Loops of garnets sparkled around her neck when she turned, and if she hadn't turned her head a few times, she would certainly have projected the illusion that her opaque white face was a flat card pinned to the wall, framed by garnets. (She looked so chalky, Fabienne later said, she must have been beautiful when she was alive.) The walls were hung with all kinds of astrological charts, metal, clay and wooden figures. A bookcase near my head held tall glass jars filled with dried herbs which bore unfamiliar labels: *Girande mandarine*,* for example. The Princess spoke of the mysterious rites of Ceylon and Java, the rituals of the primitive which have a more immediate link with the spiritual. We would all do well here in Paris, the Princess said, to be a little more primitive, and therefore closer to the spiritual.

When more guests arrived we sat at a round table and the Princess performed the ritual of table turning, the same performance which had so inspired Fabienne's mother twelve years ago. The room was entirely dark except for a few candles in niches. Passing her hand over her face the way one shuts the eyes of a corpse, she suddenly choked and gagged violently. The spots of recessed light flickered as if a door somewhere had opened and an unseasonable draught blew through.

'Stay calm, *Messieurs et Mesdames*,' said a man, apparently a regular visitor. 'Who are you?' This inquiry was directed at Belgiojoso.

---

* *Girande mandarine*, literally translated, means mandarine's fireworks. The herb is said to figure in some French folklore originating in Italy. W. Rehnfield

In a voice at first very deep, then very high, the Princess said, 'MADAME PEY-TEL'.*

Collective shuddering followed.

'Who murdered you?'

'How does it feel to be dead?'

'Who is that rude person? Be quiet, let her write!'

The Princess's long hand like a pianist's moved slowly across a sheet placed in front of her. A few words, false starts and halting pauses, nib stuck into paper. Her head fell on her chest. Across from my seat a cluster of silver skulls from Mexico seemed to glow more brightly on the wall exactly above Fabienne's head. The Princess whispered incantations in a mixture of old French, Latin and unidentifiable languages, perhaps some kind of Gaelic or Celtic. When she opened her eyes fully, she began to speak in a normal voice again.

'No one in the government listens to me. My premonitions, my warnings, fall on deaf ears. Cynics render my skills mute. You all know of Dr Koreff who has successfully infected Paris society for fifteen years: a doctor, a mesmerist, an occultist, a quasi-encyclopaedist. Herr Doktor Koreff from Munich is also a spy in the service of the Prussians. How many times has this thin-lipped man with his blinking eyes and his wig of dog grass and hemp come to me in a dream and the message is always the same. In his salon he has a cage filled with books of every language like a modern Faust and he can change his human form at will. Those who take his venal medical prescriptions might as well sleep with a viper.'

After her advice, meant to terrify, the group left the table and broke up into small clusters. The line written by Belgiojoso/Peytel was barely legible. It seemed to read:

'The source can be found in Lyon.'

* A famous murder case of 1839. Monsieur Peytel was accused of murdering his wife and servant. He was guillotined, though many, Balzac and Thackeray among them, believed him innocent. W.R.

People conjectured as to the meaning of the sentence. There had been some question in the case as to the ownership of the murder weapon. It may have originally come from the shop of a curiosity merchant in Lyon. Was the murdered servant from Lyon? Did the servant, as Monsieur Peytel claimed, attempt to kill him in order to steal 7,500 francs? I was too young in 1839 to remember the details of the horrible Peytel murders. I'm sure they were kept from me. Regular guests to the salon remarked how different the handwriting is each week. I listened to the Princess tell the story of Mary Shelley who came to her a few years ago asking if she could contact her dead husband, but Princess Belgiojoso declined. She had read Mrs Shelley's book and found something lacking in the fictional monster of Dr Frankenstein, insulting to those committed to the serious psychic sciences. The monster was child's play compared to the very real and terrifying powers of the supernatural and the occult. She admitted feeling some regret at turning down the Englishwoman's request but suspected such a writer would never be truly satisfied with the Princess's talents. There would be too much mutual suspicion to make the seance worth the risk. She said with doubtful sincerity she didn't like turning anyone away but one gets so many requests from so many, the great and the small. (Fabienne later told me the Princess lost a brother at Waterloo and just doesn't like the English one bit.) Changing the subject, someone mentioned the American writer, Edgar Allen Poe. She admires Poe much more.

'The Americans at least make an effort towards accuracy.'

As we were leaving, one of the guests, nearly in tears, pressed Belgiojoso to attempt contact with her son, missing, believed dead in Tangiers. The Princess agreed and shut the door on the departing guests, leaving herself alone with the woman.

Fabienne and I walked part way down Rue Bleue, turning up Riboutte and therefore avoiding the address of the rival occultist, Madame Azur, who had been such a favourite of

51

Fabienne's mother. We got in a cab close to Rue Notre Dame de Lorette. I didn't want to walk too near and risk meeting Eugène. We both smelled of incense.

23 MAY 1847

A note from Eugène finally came two days ago containing his apologies. He'd been with a sick friend. Fabienne believed the note would refer to Chopin. Eugène takes his friends' affairs very seriously and, trusting to appearances, he derives a certain amount of pleasure from the role of middle man, especially insofar as the Chopin-Sand liaison is concerned. He is rather secret but his discretion isn't inflexible. Letters full of confessions and confidences, as many sent out, I suppose, as received. Chopin was gravely ill but has since recovered; Eugène is more inclined to take his side and is less sympathetic to Madame Sand. Good intentions aside, when he showed me their letters, noting dates and recriminations, I felt like an innocent witness who'd stepped into a basket of live crabs.

Mathilde's suspicions are urbane in character and source, while Jenny Le Guillou's are of a relentless and rural Breton nature. In spite of their differences, both would entertain each other tirelessly. Jenny disappeared after serving dinner. In a domestic setting Eugène takes on some of her character, except he is the master. If I didn't know about the studio, didn't know his reputation, I'd find his dinners as bad as those of the Croziers. Stubborn, opinionated, mistrusting, twenty cranks just like him could be found in the café down the street.

In another room full of dark wooden cabinets made up of long, flat drawers, the kind used for storing drawers and prints, he pulled open a drawer and asked me to look at its contents. Under a pane of glass lay a yellowed drawing of shipwrecked men on a raft. Little figures dying and falling overboard, a genuinely frightening and depressing picture. Then, as if he regretted an indiscretion, he quickly shut the drawer and we went upstairs.

In the morning it was raining lightly and being cold for May we dressed quickly. Jenny brought us bowls of coffee. In the silence between swallows, I tried to think of something to say to him. Indifference: I was already far from Rue Notre Dame de Lorette and he was already arranging his models. In what perverse arrangement is a man's indifference found compelling? Is this what Fabienne calls a fatal attraction?

'I saw your *Shipwrecked Men* at the salon. Like the drawing you showed me last night, they are very frightening pictures.' I tried to explain the difference between my terror at the idea of drowning, with nothing under your feet but fathoms of water, and the documentation of the horrible. A painting of people dying of cholera, for example, that would be horrible.

'These aren't simple Robinson Crusoe adventure drawings.'

I know all about the *Ancien Régime* and its scandals and I might have said so but didn't. He was already offended by what he incorrectly saw as my squeamishness in the face of fictional documentation. He spoke of allegory and as he spoke the paintings became transformed into representatives of Doom and History. Rather than seeing more clearly, I remember my mother telling my brother and me fables while my father, poor unhappy republican, sat around complaining about the monarchy. Politics and La Fontaine side by side. Art, chafed by the juxtaposition, seemed trivialized by graver accounts. Then, after listening alternately to each parent, my mother's stories appeared to comment on the morality of the government scandal my father reviewed, but that wasn't what Eugène was talking about.

'My friend Géricault did the drawing in preparation for his painting, *The Raft of the Medusa*.' He asked me if I knew the story of the ship. I shook my head no, although I knew the name. His lecture wasn't fair, but although I was dressed I didn't think I could just walk out.

'Before you were born Louis XVII appointed an incompetent emigré, a faithful monarchist, as captain of a huge ship, *The Medusa*. The ship was sunk under his misguidance

53

and over one hundred sailors were drowned, an unnecessary loss of life owing entirely to the appointment of the royalist. Croneyism, political favours; taken for granted by the cynical, disappointing to idealists. Shock is short lived, nepotism is an easily forgotten arrangement. Géricault intended this painting to arrest the evaporation of collective memory. The *Raft* is a historical reminder which will remain emblematic of Bourbon behaviour even when people no longer remember this particular line of kings. I'm sure you must find it unusual that a painter would find a source for subject matter in a newspaper story. You might also find it nasty that he went to hospitals to watch men die so he could draw their dying psychologically as well as anatomically correct. As for the horror, people your age can always turn their heads and say it didn't really happen, it's only a painting, just the product of an artist's imagination, vision impaired by hashish. You can do that, you can stubbornly defeat the intention of the painter. You may be right to feel trepidatious but for all the wrong reasons.'

I told him he wasn't really answering my question.

'Perhaps you are too young and haven't the capacity for memories which contradict the evidence that life is just fine and getting better. I have always had notions of what progress ought to mean and my constructs conflict with what I see around me. You don't remember a time when there were no factory smokestacks on the horizon.'

A sense of the cyclical nature of things relinquished to an idea of progress built up in steady positive increments; a replacement represented by telegraph poles and factories. He hated all of it and said there would be no narrative in the modern age.

'Science,' he said, 'may be useful for explaining the physical world but test tubes, models of the planets and so on have no place in the studio.'

He went into the hall and returned with his coat and a package. He put the package in my hands and said that, of course, he was very fond of me, then went out, leaving me with Jenny standing in the doorway. I got my things together and, as she watched, opened the package. The string slipped off easily and thin paper crackled like onion skin, nearly blowing away. Bit by bit, the image appeared. It was the portrait I had drawn of him in Moroccan costume. On the back he had written:

> To Lucienne from Eugène. I've kept the portrait of you, hanging it in the studio, between a drawing of Marphisa, from Orlando Furioso, and Marguerite.

I took a Dame Blanche omnibus to Rue Drouot for no reason except it was the first to come along, a truly random gesture with no narrative connection to anything else.

A letter arrived today from Eugène. Last night we slept in the little spare room alongside the studio. Like the first night, the paintings are a silent, dominating presence, like one's brother or sister asleep in the next bed or shamming sleep, more real to Eugène than political issues, than women, than actual day-to-day life around him. Within the perimeters of this room heartbeats, the expansion and compression of lungs, swallowing, are all grounds for suspicion. I'm an intruder in a library of portraits. When I'm indifferent, he pretends to plead with me, as if I were as virtuous and as multiplied as all the Margarets reproduced in his Faust illustrations. It's a trick; he pretends my mercy will change his life for at least thirty minutes. As I lie on my back with one hand under my head and the other braced on the window sill, I'm as mute and as passive as my picture and he might just as well have that bit of paper in bed with him as my corporeal self. I'm beginning to feel cynical in the face of Eugène's obsessive narration.

Once in the Louvre he profusely admired a cluster of marble statues, magnificent women without human floridness. He claims to be a submissive student of the feminine. Women's posture, he claims, naturally spirals, we twist rather than turn, have voices which arch over and under expressions of desire of any sort, have long fingers on small hands. He wants the distraction of women present, yet in the flesh their demands or even simple presence can send him off into a fit of bad humour. He's afraid of impotence yet seems inadvertently to wish he were so afflicted. I'm surprised at my susceptibility to marked flattery and his obvious kind of seduction. Last night he spoke of the waiting, listening for my footsteps on the stairs, the sound of the doorknob turning, but in the next sentence he wants to be free of torment and that is a word I distrust. Not about Jacob wrestling with the angel, not the suicides performing for Sardanapalus's daydreams but a word which has kinship, in the context of this Paris bedroom, to melodrama. At other times, most of the time, I feel totally powerless. I could be anyone at all in this particular body, my portrait on the wall.

Last night when he thought I was asleep, Eugène got up and went into the studio. Through the door I could see him, candle in hand, sit down at his desk and begin to write. It was one of those rare minutes when dreams recede, thoughts gradually acquire logic, and you lie there, eyes open. The bed is a waiting room. One leaves it. Empty or near empty, one leaves or is chased out. The transgressions against sleep are invasive, night after night. Acts of sedition committed against the pacific state. Insomnia, a preventative measure, keeping at bay the state of forgetting.

3 JUNE 1847

Dear Fabienne,

You always think men will behave a certain way and then what you thought turns out to be completely wrong. At Saint-Hilaire's you thought the way E.D. humiliated Hippolyte Phébus he would take on anyone, but I can't imagine him on the barricades. These are some of the snares the mind is capable of creating and sustaining through unchecked perversity.

He reads newspapers and forgets everything he reads, making no distinction between the left and the right. They are all guilty, they will all make his life miserable. At twenty-six, he wanted to paint his century, but at forty-eight he has yet to do so. Once Eugène said to me, 'I'm simply a kind of grocer; a grocer who deals in pictures.' But these are not day-old pictures, reduced. His bins are full of antiquity and nature, sticky with preservatives. As his choices become increasingly private and contracted, this perspective is translated literally and metaphorically into the pictures. Pictures limited to flowers and animals, inoffensive subjects, difficult to critique.

His sense of privacy extends to the point of refusing to show me his paintings and sometimes I'm inclined to go home in the middle of the night. It isn't that I need to know what he's doing or thinking, the disturbing part is what his refusal represents: my place is in another room. I am a human reference point, a footnote positioned in relation to the population of women occupying the studio around the corner and if I feel threatened by his exacting privacy there is nothing I can do about it. I have my place in the index under F. The world of women and the world of ideas are antipodean and it's by this rule one conducts one's liaisons. There are his living women and his paintings of women and between the two ranges his solitary masculine intelligence like a male dromedary who traverses a desert looking for water holes. Even knowing that in his darkest humour, painting and its illusions are his reality, I feel the act of kissing is an automatic gesture, not a desired decision but the instinctive reponse to animal, not sensual, impulses. I start to put my clothes on. My sympathies are worn out. George Sand says man is never satisfied with the present but embellishes the past and imagines the future. Her axiom is E.D.'s as well. He shuns realism for the concept of the heroic enterprise as revealed through myth and allegory.

Whether one is discussing Louis-Philippe or his critics, for him all political debate is a source of revulsion and boredom. Insofar as he is successful, his paintings are visual parables whose characters are well disguised. No dandies or grisettes, no workers or bourgeoisie. These are

57

ancient Romans, Greeks, Bible heroes, but I wonder if all these don't represent, or aren't some kind of metaphor for 1847, despite Eugène's ranting to the contrary.

The collections of costumes and props stored in the studio are often used theoretically, if not actually, in the corridors and rooms beyond. He isn't a dishonest person but I think his affinity for disguise enters into his dealings with men and women. Practising the power of obliqueness, he speaks around the object of his desire. So the other side of this coin is his abhorrence of the realists. The hint, the suggestion, the indirect approach is his way.

4 JUNE 1847

Fabienne and I drank many *café filtres* at Café Momus. Drinking many coffees made me feel tough and nervous like a certain class of prostitute who wouldn't want to appear drunk in public so treats strong coffee as a substitute. A silly illusion, like the games children play to shorten a long trip.

6 JUNE 1847

Charles has returned to Paris for a few days. The reunion was not pleasant since I couldn't pretend I was happy to see him. I was very tired and tried to talk about food, what would he like for dinner? The house became a nightmare of animated objects, spilt pitchers, overturned bottles, dropped glasses. If Charles had a terror of deception, he didn't take on the role of interrogator. Perhaps he didn't care if I betrayed him, perhaps he wished for it. He said he had not encouraged me to join him because he expected he might have to go to New Orleans, something about cotton mills. Or was it sugar cane and Martinique or Haiti?

17 JUNE 1847

It still seems much too early in the night, although the clock has just rung twelve. A woman's shadow crosses a room on the far side of the courtyard. Her silhouette traverses many small panes of glass turning an otherwise smooth shadow into a dark, fractured grid. Her shadow appears to be tracing her lips with her fingers. She opens the window but doesn't see me. I'm by myself again. The portrait of Eugène is propped between the inkwell and the mirror. I haven't hung it on the wall.

19 JUNE 1847

Eugène invited me to the home of a Comédie actress, Mademoiselle Mars.* Dressed entirely in white, rows of pearls and a Japanese fan, her smile stretched across her face to the breaking point, then retracted abruptly as if she suddenly realized she was reinforcing its lines. She spoke of the inequality of the sexual exchange. She told me she didn't imagine I had piles of drawings of naked men in my house yet male artists drew naked women and used these when live ones wouldn't oblige them. I didn't know what she was talking about. Spontaneous vulgarities were forgotten with the same alacrity they were off-handedly uttered. I suddenly thought of Charles sitting at dinner sectioning off the parts of the day as if it were an orange.

A young man introduced himself to me as Jean de la Tour. The top half of his face looked serious, the bottom comical; a vision of two sliced Carnival masks glued into one. With an air of ennui that seemed made up he told me none of these artists interested him and offered to take me to the Club des Haschichins. I questioned his invitation. If women were admitted to this notoriously latescent club, Fabienne would have visited it long ago. He spoke of the

---

* It was Mademoiselle Mars who suggested Delacroix accompany the Count de Mornay on his trip to Morocco in 1833. W. Rehnfield

ritual of drinking tea made from coca leaves as practised by South American Indians. Jean claimed to be a former companion of Baudelaire's, but he has shrugged him off. He, Jean, belongs to a secret group in Montmartre, followers of a German, Marx. I asked him who that was but his answer was evasive and then he left the house. He has large round eyes. I can easily imagine them inflamed by coca leaves.

20 JUNE 1847

Dinner with Eugène at Divan Lepelletier on the Boulevard du Gand. He said, now I'll tell you a story which explains the link between the history of food and the history of the French government. Look at the life of Germain Chevet. He began as a horticulturalist but sold roses, potatoes or pâté according to the political whims of the king or emperor. He sent elegant flowers to Marie-Antoinette, hiding love letters in the buds. When these were considered too bourgeois, he switched to the populist spud. He survived prison and the famine of 1794 to found one of the most famous restaurants and cooking schools in Paris.

27 JUNE 1847

Eugène's letters from his house in Champrosay describe Margaret of Navarre's patronage of da Vinci, Cellini and Andrea del Sarto, Charlemagne's court. His romantic language doesn't describe serfs or men but souls, the spiritual posing as an anodyne for everyday misery and triviality. There is no Black Death, no mad priests, no paper currency.

28 JUNE 1847

Saw a Haitian woman blind in one eye near Montmartre. She was muttering in a pure French of the last century. I remembered what Princess Belgiojoso said about their voodoo rites and made the appearance of the half-blind woman into some kind of omen.

Roads lined by fields of blossoming grass and clover became willows then dark woods again. No smokestacks; women poked sheep near the horizon. Champrosay, island-like, although not altogether rural, not a peasant town.

'When I first came to Paris I was obsessed with becoming a painter and thought of little else. I thought of little else seriously. A friend and I made a few francs by painting illustrations of machines. We had a system. He drew the machines in ink and I filled in the colours. I pity the mechanics who had to make reconstructions from our drawings.'

Some illusions die long protracted deaths; others, cut back early, are never given the chance even to grow convulsive. When Urbain le Verrier determined the location of Neptune, French science seemed like a heroic pursuit but one which didn't involve a sea voyage, a desert crossing or physical danger. When I first came to Paris, just before I met Charles, I thought I might study optics and astronomy. Quietly, in a room with windows on four sides, I could set up a telescope, read about Newton, Galileo, achromatic lenses. One of the first presents Charles gave me was a series of prints showing how draughtsmen analyse landscapes.

6 JULY 1847

Thin white paper, black ink, the writing made an illegible pattern, loose knitting across the folded page. I held the note up in my hand and listened. The house was completely quiet. Usually Jenny follows me as if I were a thief. I was very bored.

Dear Eugène,
    I hope you are having a pleasant holiday at
Champrosay. You write of the workmen in the house
who are much too slow, of the garden and the forest.
I'm sure the workmen distract you. Is it one or are there
several?

All the familiar objects, the pervasive smell of paint: none of these foolish things have the meanings I'd originally engendered. Endearments turned sour, the room has all the sentimentality of a cabin on a sinking ship. I heard a door open and close and knew it was one of two people who arrived several minutes too late to prevent or even discover my crime. However altered, I had to pretend the centre of gravity hadn't slipped from the place it was ten minutes ago. When Mademoiselle Pitou told me of the shepherdess who mourned for the past, she didn't tell me that the past could dissolve into something frail, silly, romantic, and far from true.

Just as Eugène imagines himself fighting some Hellenic battle and transforms thoughts into paintings, I turn a letter into a displacement of the validity of my own desires. My anguish can hardly be transformed into anything concrete like a painting. Pictures lend tangibility to his imagined, unspoken passions, but my only product is thought, rehearsing a single scene over and over again.

7 JULY 1847

He was so involved in his *Dictionnaire des Beaux Arts*, it was easy for me to leave on the coat tails of a half-plausible excuse. For a while all I can think about is the J. who signed that letter. J.'s character is composed of all that I lack. I can see her looking into shop windows on the Rue Vivienne, talking easily to Dumas *fils* at Place d'Orléans, a woman as gracefully oblivious to the migrant workers in Paris as to the gossip of the salons.

10 JULY 1847
Boissey Saint-Leger

Husbands have French law firmly on their side. According to my mother, I have tried to introduce choices into a situation in which there are none. My brother considers Charles a domestic translation of King Louis-Philippe:

dull, boring. Etienne reads about the 1789 and 1830 revolutions and dreams of another, believing the Orleanist dynasty has nearly run its course and will be finished by an insurrection like the one which initiated it. This time the revolution must not be stolen from the people as it was in 1830. He compares the reign of the petty bourgeois values to a coach pulled uphill by an old horse. 'Passengers become anxious, agitated, desperate to go faster. Finally, natural incline makes speed possible. Timing of revolution is the same natural phenomenon as the downward side of a slope, it's always there, inevitable.' As the moment approaches Etienne is afraid he'll be studying in Rouen and miss everything, but he has plans to get to Montmartre somehow. We stayed up late talking while my mother slept soundlessly but unhappily over our heads.

17 JULY 1847

It's not a secret system. Only citizens who own property can register to vote: bankers, industrialists, speculators at the Bourse, barons, successful artists, too, can elect to keep the government functioning. When I democratically included artists with traders and vicomtes, Eugène grew indignant but it wasn't clear to me why. It was as if I had hit a nerve, and I wonder if that hadn't been my intention all along. Once you pass the point of ineligibility, in the restricted domain of voters, all are equal; it's not even very interesting to talk about. No, not just the influences of recent discussions with my brother – there was more to my argumentativeness than late-night conversations with Etienne in Boissey Saint-Leger. Behind the slightly blunted attempt to insult, I was illustrating an idea which had nothing to do with artists servicing a conservative government. I was trying to separate myself from his ideas. I have always been so acquiescent. Sometimes I do hate the pictures. I hate the expressions on their faces, the way their clothing is so often windswept, never to know still or stagnant air. Sometimes

63

I admire the paintings, sometimes I engage in a pretence of admiration. This afternoon I began to recognize the pretence and tried to dissemble it.

Dear Lucienne,

I hope you are well and enjoying the city as best you can manage. Many of my associates and their wives take a dim view of Paris society. They are well-mannered, intelligent people but ignorant of ways of life which vary even the slightest from what they're accustomed to. They tend to be suspicious of anything or anyone perceived as foreign. Everyone asks about you and inquires when you're coming. 'Is your wife short or tall? Blue eyed or brown?' To be left alone is a sad thing, you see, and the married ladies sympathize with me.

I can't deceive you, life here is not interesting. I'm afraid you will find it very dull.

This was part of an old letter from Charles. He hasn't written since his visit. Whether the silence is due to inertia or another married woman left alone I don't know, and spend little time conjecturing.

20 JULY 1847

He told me about the group who met on the eve of the 1830 Revolution, Victor Hugo, Alexander Dumas *père*, St Beuve, de Musset. Now he watches the July Monarchy grow as mouldy as his own timorous desires gone stale, half-hearted and consummated only fitfully. After a dinner, the dinner, any dinner, they joke about the bluestockings and the women of letters whom they find so intolerable. Eugène says to Pierret, 'Young women are interchangeable except for the aberrants, the androgens.' An entire sex made up of all sorts of victims ranging from the toadying and submissively ignorant to the militant. (Jean de la Tour had said all men and women are victims of the ruling class. He clearly never had to sit through a dinner like this one.) I stared at Madame Fortune's loops of hair, playing as dumb

64

as Eugène when Madame Sand's name was said with derision. Unsure of my ground and my arguments in the face of all this camaraderie, I felt I needed allies and so, to my embarrassment, said nothing. I thought of those lovely, boring Egyptian artefacts, tiny things in glass case afer case at the Louvre. I felt stupid, one of many nearly identical scarabs or Greek coins in a glass house. A hundred subtly different beetles of turquoise, onyx, carnelian or gold but identical in shape and intent. Initially I felt a personal degradation then, secondly, the sting of the collective insult. In the safety of the late hour and the solitude of writing in a notebook, I can pretend to be outraged and preserve a kind of self-respect.

Eugène was involved, at least emotionally, in the 1830 Revolution but he is quite different now. 'People respond to images, symbols of events, not true moral issues.'

I'm not sure anything can stay on its own plane, oblivious, spinning its own tale, each minding its own house.

Why have I written nothing about affection? Affection isn't interesting to write about. Writing at least lends split, unchannelled emotions dignity; sometimes entries appear all the more insipid for having been turned into language.

25 JULY 1847

'Painting,' he began, 'isn't just another commodity whose security, well-being and profit-making capacities are guaranteed under the Citizen King.'

It disturbed him that I reduced his ideas about high culture to an unwitting but accurate reflection of the bourgeois frame of mind, historical or mythological narratives which compliment, not comment. Was Sardanapalus supposed to be Louis-Philippe?

He is aware the system of patronage sometimes dictates what will be put on a wall and that that in itself lays a form of censorship upon the lives of painters and their choices of subject, just as the Academy's selective policy perpetuates pedestrian standards. Eugène clings to the belief that the progress of his work is somehow immaculate, unpolluted, untouched by the strategies of Academy theoreticians, opportunists, the power of flattery and jealous colleagues.

He is critical of them, the lovers of fashionable art, the idiot *savants* of the cafés, ladies the whole of whose thinking goes into their dresses and the unreliable servant class. A moment in front of *Milton Dictating 'Paradise Lost' to His Daughters* might enact great changes in lives as disparate as my brother's, Monsieur Ruban's or my mother's, despite Eugène's likely aversion to all three and what they represent.

At a party, at dinner, in an opera box, in bed, we drop remarks in public that fuel our private confrontations. Confrontation isn't always the right word. I do a lot of listening. The kind of listening that's like being handed thirty kilos of wet laundry. I am intrigued by the idea of 'taking a stand against' while Eugène is all about retreat and condescension. His withdrawal is the well-thought-out position of a man nearing fifty and it's in kicking against this confirmed position that I begin to form my own ideas. Suffocating miners, permanently bent weavers, children worked to death, hoards of destitute unemployed, oppression by the dominant class, the owners of the means of production – he would cover his ears if he were to meet Etienne. He is so aloof with his Moroccan buccaneers, medieval knights, Faust, Orlando Furioso.

Paintings could be a delicate bridge between the painter and the present tense but they only root him more solidly with his back to the window, his back towards Rue Transnonain.* The Rue Transnonains uncap his tubes and dry out the paint. Beyond habit, in acute depression, it seems pointless to keep turning out drawings and canvases, so the Rue T. is erased from the map. Deliberately dreaming, he turns to flowers and odalisques. Odalisques, the historic anodynes. (Not me, I'm too thin and not nearly so

* Site of the brutal police murder of several innocent families suspected of leftist activities in 1834. See Daumier lithograph done in the same year. W. Rehnfield

66

lascivious-looking.) From Champrosay he wrote how wrong it is to think peasants or workers could have a harmonious relationship with their masters, didn't I know peasants were as devious as the spiritless middle class? They are all an expanded version of the art world flunkies employed by the Institute. Analysing society's structures is futile, results in laziness, nothing gets done. Why do I persist? Am I so naive about human nature? He's lethargic and in the agony of inertia; the caked useless brushes, the half-finished drawings threaten him more fearfully than the havoc to the external world that class struggles threaten to provoke. He is in despair, he writes to me as if giving lessons. People are animals, it's all about greed, appetite, barbarity, and the willingness of the human soul to be corrupted.

One hundred and twenty years from now no one will remember Louis Blanc but everyone will still be familiar with Macbeth, Hamlet, the Greek and Roman heroes. There are times he feels deluged by the events of the present, the recent past, and amnesia would be a blessing. He sees himself as an old man huddled in a warm corner muttering about the light going out. A romantic, the *light* is a symbol for you know what. Mutter, mutter, nature and fate are constant under any monarchy, any republic. Governments change with the snap of your fingers; it can take months to paint a small picture. The spectacle of revolution is horrible, it takes no time to tear things down. He links the masses with this kind of destruction. Masses = revulsion.

Eugène thinks of himself as an individualist. You have only to look at his paintings next to those which didn't provoke the ill favour of the Academy. It's not just a case of bad luck. When I say the *réformistes* should be taken seriously, he accuses me of sounding like an echo.

'You repeat what people tell you,' he says. 'You don't see the demons in the pit, this seething horror,' and he describes it as if I'm too young to claim unpleasant memories of my own. I accuse him of being jaded. He agreed with me, he probably was.

67

1 AUGUST 1847

My mother received money from Charles. There was no letter inside but it had come from Port-au-Prince. At twilight as I walk home I wonder about the lives behind newly lit windows in other people's rooms. If he were here he might be rushing home from a meeting with gentlemen financiers, speaking in a new language about investments and capital, mutual interests expanded and protected, but he is not here and I'm on my way home from Fabienne's alone.

Eugène has gone to Valmont, the Normandy estate belonging to his cousins. There is a ruined Gothic abbey adjoining the house. With his cousin Léon he used to make castings from chunks of carvings: heads of Saint Paul, Saint Mary of Egypt, or Roland ambushed by Basques. A stone hand grasping a sword hilt, a granite ear and half a jaw were found under a pile of leaves among the wreckage. Fragments of glass, three banana-shaped shards from a shattered window, bits of Mary's robe or the sky above Eve's head.

23 AUGUST 1847

It was the kind of day when the egrets and peacocks kept their tails stubbornly folded. There were new birds from the Emperor of Shanghai but he wanted to talk about his murals. How to organize the myths, the lessons and allegories which will hang over the heads of an untold number of future ministers and librarians for hundreds of years, barring fire or flood. This is where, according to Eugène, Auguste Comte* is useful.

Human ideas, he says, fall into three divisions: the Theological, the Metaphysical and the Positive. In the paintings Civilization is represented by great men from

---

* Social philosopher, 1798–1857. He was a positivist and an early disciple of Saint-Simon. A believer in social reform, he endorsed scientific method and systems of ordering experience but had the idealism of many social reformers. The idealistic side of Comte probably held no interest for Delacroix. W. Rehnfield

Adam to Seneca. No modern-era patricians or plebeians, no women, no Greek orphans, no barricades. Order on one side, Chaos on the other – cleanly divided spheres of influence. Each Great Man bequeaths Reason upon the Chaotic. As Orpheus calmed animals and Sirens with his lute, so the faculty of Reason may perform the same function. I refrain from questioning the role of Orpheus's music in Paris in 1847 where citizens are in a state of uneasiness and discontent. We don't discuss the historical fact that not just fire and flood but people could deface his murals. As we stand in front of the ibex house, he remarked that no amount of scientific invention or social philosophy can predetermine relationships between human beings, especially in affairs of the heart.

An alarm was sounded because an ape from the Ivory Coast had escaped, the kind with a blue nose. I saw Phébus in the crowd. He had said he often spent mornings drawing at the zoo. He was wearing a long blue scarf in spite of the heat and startlingly white shoes.

'Hello, Delacroix. Hello, Lucienne. The monkey is probably sitting in a café in Montparnasse eating an orange.'

Eugène told him the African kind can be dangerous, they snap at people. Phébus disagreed. If they would only let another one, a female, out as bait, and follow her until the two apes find each other. While the animal sculptor dropped names like snow in Nivose, I felt sorry for him, but not too much. He talks smoothly like a solicitor with a malicious edge. I would find his eyes disturbing were it not for a slight affliction which causes him to look a little to the left or the right of one's face. I feel hollow after he's left, as if nodding and blinking at a vacuous pantomime which has sucked you up in a moment of inattentive boredom. You play along, your eyes follow his animated face and it is only at the moment he walks away you feel cheated by his vapidity. At the north end of the ibex house I saw Jean de la Tour walking in the opposite direction. It appeared he had decided not to approach us and was swiftly leaving the zoo by way of Rue Cuvier.

Since Charles has been away I have found cause to re-examine my relationship to the servants, or rather his servants, the ones I inherited when I married him. These thoughts were precipitated by the desire to censure Eugène's servant who is protective to the point of obsession. The sharp words are withheld, the dismissal notice is never executed. Mathilde, too, often expresses reproach bordering on the hostile. They represent an undercurrent or underlife which I often wish would go away and live its own life away from me. We cling to each other in symbiotic co-existence. The little tiny mutual dependencies are legion. Mathilde and Jenny represent the old school; Hortense, my cook, is much younger. She doesn't say so but I can tell she has no intention of remaining a cook in my employ for the rest of her life. We are the same age and a little sympathy springs from sharing in a particular generation. She has trouble with Mathilde, doesn't like being told what to do in the kitchen. Mathilde, talking to herself, says the house of Crozier is witnessing a grave decline, coming apart at the seams. Our household is sustained by a shaky kind of security. No one, whatever her misdemeanours or transgressions or complaints, believes she will be let go. Jobs are relatively secure and I am allowed to go on thinking nobody knows of my affairs. I really have no way of knowing what these women know, what they've guessed from beds unslept in or from conversations overheard when Fabienne is in the house.

We had dinner at the Villots last night, a Russian style dinner which means you serve yourself from a large table then go back to the dining room to eat. Eugène thought the whole arrangement was ridiculous, designed to disrupt conversation, and the French ought not to be so keen to eat like Muscovites. ('People were meant to sit down and be served.') The Villots would have done well to consider the attitudes of their guests before issuing invitations because opponents found themselves standing next to each other in the absence of a seating plan. Sides were quickly drawn for or against King Louis-Philippe, or so it appeared. Even if the more vocal participants were in the minority, the sheer pitch of their arguments would indicate otherwise, and the antagonism was played against an uncomfortable backdrop of balanced plates. One lawyer sprayed peas all around him while explaining that the king was the least aristocratic of all French rulers. Little green points fell into the rose-patterned rug, some squashed in as the lawyer stepped forward or back. A long wine stain down the side of her dress, Liberty Guiding the People said she was only afraid of two things, but I never heard what those two things were. For many of the guests, political debate is heavily laced with gossip, transformed to reactionary opinion and 'Did you hear this?' It is, for them, like discussing a play. They're removed from the action. The theatre closes at a certain hour and it is far from their homes anyway. There isn't any analysis, it's either thumbs up or thumbs down. Opinions are bantered back and forth on the private lives of the protagonists. Arguments are reduced, the real scandal lies backstage with the actress herself.

Pâté à la financière, chicken à la Saint-Cloud, crème d'Argenteuil, he spoke as he chewed and he hated George Sand. She gave thousands of francs to radical causes, why did she not give that money to him? He didn't approve of women behaving like philanthropically inclined gentlemen. By attempting to combine two identities that won't mix, they stretch the limits of gender far beyond what is acceptable. Who knows what combination of organs they really have under their trousers? Once they have discovered the freedom of masculinity, there's no putting the genii back in the bottle. They will all espouse radical causes like G. Sand. A drunken partner who'd given up holding his plate in favour of the more readily negotiable glass agreed. They concluded that the emancipation of women will lead to the dangerous dwindling of the population and with fewer than

71

fifty individuals in towns, maybe one hundred or so in major cities, the downfall of the Republic will quickly follow. Women belong in two places. The drunk held two fingers up before my nose. 1, the convent and 2, he didn't say; I think he winked. It wasn't late but Eugène was impatient to leave. Boors, dandied-up men, chatterboxes, he thought he was performing with delayed chivalry by taking me away from them and I ought to have been grateful. He detests verbal skirmishes regarding affairs of the state and grew vituperative as we walked along the Quai Malaquais. The 'Russian' dinner was completely silly. He will never knowingly accept such an invitation again. We went for a proper dinner at Les Frères provençaux. They are known to indulge their patrons with chairs.

The sound of short conversation, questions and instruction, came from the entrance hall. Eugène was sending his assistants on their way for the evening. Heavy drawings were spread before me, something to read while waiting, drawings still wet from saturation with watercolours. Others bore a clinging aura of pastel dust. Women are everywhere, more prevalent than any creature in his imagination. Women as property and as victim, postures of spiralling supplication or solitary flirtation before the mirror. Desdemona before her father, Sardanapalus's murdered seraglio (women destroyed along with the treasure), Rebecca carried off half-conscious, slung over a horse, her vertebrae as flexible as a sack of chick peas. I like the sketch after Rubens. Water nymphs, a creature of lower cast sprung from a bestiary; with curling tails, half animal, half human; a literal version of all partially humanized women. Crushed sanguine and paint; vermilion, crimson, scarlet, cadmium red stuck to my hands. Art in league with seduction, two halves in constant dialogue.

He left early to attend to the ceiling murals at the Bourbon library and I slept very late. Everything in the room looked wrinkled by two bodies that were physically at odds with each other all night and my dress had become a

72

twisted mass in the corner. I put it on slowly, too much of the day had already passed and my clothing bore hapless evidence of other people's dinners from the night before.

11 SEPTEMBER 1847

Fabienne believes the violence will begin over a trifle and rage unchecked: buildings will implode, gutted walls will be instantly marked by shells. Even in the salons, she said, you hear people talk about subjects like the workers' strikes, the ruling middle class and Utopianism. I asked her what Utopianism is but she didn't know. Some kind of theory of government, she wasn't sure.

As I was waiting for Fabienne in Café Anglais, I heard the proprietress talking to a neighbour about the protests that are beginning to grow in frequency and intensity. You see a knot of people as you pass Place des Vosges, or close by Les Halles you hear shouting and you know it's not been an ordinary case of theft that drew the crowd. Journals of dissent, a few pages long, appear, vanish and are reconstituted under other names. Rumours of cells, of clubs whose names no one really knows, are overheard in the backs of omnibuses. The woman complained that the north part of the quarter has become overcrowded with provincials. They leave their farms to find work in the city and it's a mistake because misery is only compounded here. Everyone is out of work, the glaziers, joiners, printers' apprentices, and the exiled field labourers are added ballast in a sinking ship.

'Paris is filled up to the brim with them. They live in single rooms, like pigs trundled into dirty pens. Have you ever seen the kinds of rooms in which buckets catch the rain from leaky roofs and rags are stuffed into broken windows? They live in buildings that should have been razed in 1830.' She sounded half sympathetic, half disgusted.

'This is the way it is after every potato blight,' said the woman from the bakery next door. 'Tenants are tossed off bits of land, thrown out of work, and there are no jobs for them here. There aren't even any places for them to live.'

'Overnight drops in fortune, shabby gentlemen farmers reduced to cellar and attic dwellers. I don't understand why they crowd into Paris. This is no paradise. Louis-Philippe should pass laws. They should be made to stay in Burgundy or the Auvergne. They should be made to stay where they were born.'

'Factories instead of farms, we have them here and somebody's got to work in them. I prefer the hands behind the pumps to be French rather than Spanish or Prussian.'

The proprietress looked at a spot out of the window, across the street. 'After dark the Marais grows entirely unpredictable. I don't dare go into it alone. From doorways you hear bits of conversation spoken in dialects, a pattern of wild gestures. You don't know if they're begging, trying to snatch your purse, preparing to drag you into an alley or inquiring the way to Rue Monsieur le Prince.'

'What am I going to do? Lock up my daughters? You spent too much time with the nuns. If there are no lines at the butcher and you can sell chocolate to ladies in your café, the storm will jump from Montmartre over you to the Tuileries. Nobody cares about our sins. There's no grand day of accounting and retribution for us. I don't believe there is. In a revolution, it's the extremes who go for each other's throats. Anonymous citizens are allowed to sit still while the haves and the have-nots slug it out.'

'What if the storm doesn't make it to the Tuileries and lands on our heads? The pressure builds, as it did in 1839. What if I were to lose my business? How would you or I recover from something like that? The resilience you think you can lean on is a myth. Revolution is not about relieving people of their horses and jewels while they're on their way to the opera.'

'I'm reluctant to confess a dream I have – sometimes once a month, sometimes every three months.' The proprietress looked back to the street. 'All my fears of the city, all its potential to overpower me, is realized in concrete ways in this dream. For example, in part of the dream my daughters and I are sucked into slums which have covered Paris and the two girls are forced into prostitution rings.'

74

'Even if Jews took over, your dream has no basis in any reality I can imagine. Changes don't come as quickly as students, idle young men and cells of revolutionaries would have it.' The woman from the bakery held up her hand and counted on her fingers. 'Your mother and your grandmother ran this place.' Then she, too, looked out into the street. 'The king walks around here with his umbrella in case it rains. I've seen him with it like a grocer, and attempts have been made on his life. If someone tried to kill me, you wouldn't find me strolling down the Boulevard du Gand swinging my umbrella. Charles X was another story, the *ancien régime*, I was glad to see him go.'

'It's not so much the king as the Assembly, old roués and thieves. Draped in enough gold braid to strangle everyone who comes in here in a day, their hands are never where they ought to be.'

'Gentlemen and their honour. What does honour mean? For women it has something to do with fidelity. Something dreamed up during a waltz. Something dreamed up after a duel. The scandals keep people preoccupied. During the summer the Duchesse de Praslin was murdered, brutally bludgeoned by her husband, Monsieur le Duc himself, encouraged by the children's governess with whom he'd been carrying on an affair for six months. The Duchess was the only daughter of Maréchal Sebastiani. The mob rushed to the Duc's mansion and overturned the guards. They wanted to block the Duc's escape should he try to make it out of the city. It wasn't so much to see justice done as to see an aristocratic head roll and that's as far as the revolutionary impulse will go. The Duc took arsenic. He missed the guillotine, and avoided giving the people any satisfaction.'

'A posthumous trial is being held for her murder. Hanging a dead man will only stir up the Blanquists.'

'Scandals are what people remember, not history, not politics. That's for boys in gymnasiums. Two minutes after graduation, and they too have forgotten everything. I like stories about lost sanity. When Count Mortier tried to kill his children in a remote château, or when Prince d'Eckmuhl stabbed his mistress with a medieval blade, a family halberd – those are truly black affairs.'

'But you treat them as if they're of no more importance than yesterday's *feuilletons*. The deputies behave as if they were just released from Charenton, have returned to their palaces and can still act according to lunatic rules and perverse instinct. The Cubière episode* made us look like a nation of suckers. Some day the Prussians will come marching through here, as if the Boulevard du Gand was their own and had been all along.'

15 SEPTEMBER 1847

I asked Eugène what Utopianism is, but he said it had something to do with a cult of artichoke eaters† and not to bother him with politics.

Monsieur Ruban had to dinner the clerk he's arranged as Fabienne's suitor. The scheme, dormant for some time, has undergone rejuvenation treatment by way of the young man's unexpected legacy of several thousand francs, an inheritance which caused no end of pleasure in the mind of Ruban *père*. The suitor seemed generous in spirit but gluttonous in appearance, enormously fat. What would one do with a husband like that? Impossible, horrible to imagine a mountain of flesh, no evidence of bones or muscles, even when stripped of jacket, shirt and trousers. As each article of clothing fell away, so would another shred of dignity for each of them. The impossibility of hiding embarrassment would discourage any romance. My grandmother used to say there's a lid for every pot and somewhere there's a lid for this fellow, but it isn't Fabienne. The suitor is such a gross caricature,

* General Cubière was brought to trial in May 1847 for accepting a 94,000 franc bribe for granting a salt mine concession to an interested party. He had been a Minister of War. W. Rehnfield
† This statement is unclear in the original text. He was probably making some kind of pun based on the French word for Jerusalem artichoke, *un topinambour*. Willa Rehnfield

it's unfortunate he isn't on the Bourse but only a clerk in the office of the *sous-préfet*.

17 SEPTEMBER 1847

Alone at night I took out his portrait. His face betrays the man in my head, only faintly related to Monsieur Delacroix of Rue Notre Dame de Lorette. The man of the drawing creeps under my door in a vaporous form, rustles the crinolines to make me aware of his presence. I turn around, surprised by that old trick, and he takes off his costumes: Virgil's laurels, a Greek orphan's smock, Faust's collar, Milton's trousers, a sultan's turban, Lord Byron's jacket, Hamlet's stockings, Macbeth's kilt, a pasha's scimitar, Liberty's flag, a caid's umbrella, a harem girl's slippers, a visigoth's armour, an Ojibway's feathers and an ordinary Frenchman's shirt. Underneath the shaman's robes there's just an ordinary naked man who will fall into my bed on Rue Saint Gilles and leave me the morning for myself.

21 SEPTEMBER 1847

Fabienne took me to see a vampire play at the Odéon. She says we absolutely must see one of these, they're not the fairy tales I thought them to be. She means this sincerely, believing people must be of their time, of their season at the very least, and the vampire plays are very popular this fall. Fabienne isn't a woman so acutely aware of fashion as to exclude everything else, but she has an awful fear of the boat sailing without her. Devotion to popular imagery is a faculty in constant need of updating. This week it's vampires. Next week it may be Orientalists: dancers from Alexandria, snake charmers from the Indus valley; the following week we may return to the salons of fossil hunters, botanists and astronomers.

Works with slight political interpretations are fashionable. They must be political enough to cause something of a stir but not result in censure. It's an issue of falsification or translation. The vampires equal the blood-sucking bourgeois monarchy, the widening gap between rich and poor, I think. No, the syllogism fails. For if human bats and shadowy hypnotists represent the dominant class, who do the palest, most naive girls in Paris represent? Are these actresses symbolic of the labouring classes, the pickpockets and prostitutes? Somnambulant narcophiles draped in layers of white lace and diaphanous veils, there is no rebellion in them, no starch. They must be rescued by a third party who knows what combination of silver bullets, crucifixions and garlic will arrest supernatural tyranny.

Fabienne, no languid doll victim, started up a conversation with two young men who were sitting near our box. Afterwards, at the Café de Paris, they spoke of their recent losses at the Bourse. I went home alone.

25 SEPTEMBER 1847

Mathilde has spoken to me about the dangers and uncertainty of crossing the Atlantic: snapped masts, mutiny, piracy and diseases known only to Port-au-Prince. She may have loved Charles dearly but her concern is a way of not talking about food shortages, fighting in the streets, random shots, another revolution. This is what Hortense tells me and Hortense hears every conversation of everyone in the house who talks to herself.

Supported by faint cracks in the plaster, the image of the portrait coalesces on the ceiling, best seen from bed. It's possible to find a dozen faces in an hour. I strain my memory but can't actually visualize his picture of me. His painted and drawn women with whom I'm so familiar crowd out the memory of my portrait. Dead, dying, martyred women, women who've been to hell and back, the ones who've nearly used up their time, consistently so.

30 SEPTEMBER 1847

The moment before the barricades of 1830, Jean de la Tour had said the close of 1847 would parallel those days exactly. In 1830 Eugène had not yet withdrawn into his studio repeating the names of old lovers and dead friends as if sentimentality had the power to mend rifts and turn back clocks. In 1847 he really does believe in sentimentality and nostalgia. He calls barricaded streets fatal stage sets and argues he is not a stage manager. He wants no responsibility. To exploit this parallel moment and paint the symbols of the revolution as he did in 1830 is to walk into a trap, to walk in circles, to be a flunky, brush in hand, for the left or the right. It doesn't matter. I can talk to him of the plight of the peasants, the urban proletariat, but he will have none of it and less of me. He condemns rumoured communists. Calls them termites. Baudelaire is their living patron saint. Something about the overly sweet smell of perfumed decay and bleeding purple blood. 'Men who are all rhetoric are the first to inform. They will stay indoors when the battle begins and in code tell the *garde municipale* where to fire the first shots. Talk to Baudelaire about the relationship of the urban proletariat to the scarcity of his books in the shops.' But finding Baudelaire wasn't my idea.

2 OCTOBER 1847
Le Boulevard de la Révolution
Le Boulevard des Marionettes

Fabienne and I stopped to watch a marionette show near the Place des Vosges. High on stage, the jointed figures looked bigger and taller than us although they are really quite small. One portly marionette was obviously a caric-ature of Louis-Philippe.* The audience hissed when he

* Louis-Philippe was King of the French (as opposed to King of France, the former title) from 1830–1848. His reign was known as the July Monarchy and he was called, satirically, *Le Poire*, because of his pear-shaped head. Caricatures of the king often portrayed him this way. The name is a pun because *le poire* means both pear and fool. Monsieur le Poireaume is also a pun (pronounced Poirhomme – Pearman). *Poireaume* means leek, pear, and man. W. Rehnfield came on stage and he sat heavily in a little gilt chair. It wasn't clear whether his weariness was due to his wife's harassment or the jeers of the audience. The queen was tall and icy. She addressed her husband as Monsieur le Poireaume. When Fabienne and I got close enough to hear, Monsieur le Poireaume was in the middle of reciting some kind of list of his possessions and property.

> My printworks: horses, machinery, paper, desks, chairs, closets. My buildings in Paris: the house on Quai Voltaire, the shop in the Palais Royale Arcade, carriages, horses, suits of clothing, gold watches, silk hose, boots, linen, plate . . .

Madame le Poireaume soon heard enough and boxed Monsieur's wooden ears. Their comic harangue was interrupted by a third marionette who burst in through a paper window. His short frock coat signified one person to the French in the crowd: Napoleon. Monsieur le Poireaume screamed, 'A thief!' and gathered objects in his arms as if he were about to begin a long exodus. I felt a little sorry for him and his precious toy possessions, but had to remember he was a tyrant, reduced. Children standing near the front scooped up the falling props. Monsieur le Poireaume was less concerned with Madame. The Napoleonic marionette distributed the wealth of the bourgeois family among the tattered puppets representing the working class. It was an easy story to guess. Everywhere you turn lately Napoleon is pointed to as a symbol of an heroic French past, a true ruler with hair in his ears, no waffler from the Bourse.

The puppet shows have grown hard to find, plays are often cut off in the middle if a lookout spies a policeman. They've been shut down because tourists, the English and the Americans, can hear mockery and satire directed at the king in his own streets. Hinting instability to foreigners is frowned on and so the Chamber declared the large stationary crowds which surround the shows a breeding ground for pickpockets. Immobile crowds are Christmas to the sticky-fingered. The marionettes are banned in the interest of the public good.

'He's out.'

'But his light is on in the studio.'

'I'm cleaning.'

'I saw his silhouette in the window as I walked up the street.'

'He's working. He doesn't wish to be disturbed. He's out.'

'It's very urgent. I must see him tonight.'

'That is unfortunate.'

'I'll wait in the café across the street. If he wants to see me, if he wants to stop working just for a few minutes, he can meet me there.'

'You can wait but I can tell you now, he's working very hard and he won't see anyone.'

'Will you give him my message?'

'It won't do any good.'

Jenny shut the door.

10 OCTOBER 1847
The Hôtel Frescati

'Ladies and Gentlemen, play your game.'

The last, the only time I'd been to the Frescati, I'd thought gambling was for the desperate, a man's sport. The women present are perhaps widows or heiresses who have control over their incomes, can afford to play and like the suggestion that they can go out in the world all by themselves. It was Fabienne's idea to go, she'd never been, but I indulged in the illusion I was a woman alone.

Men dressed in livery were stationed in the front of the ante-chamber. You could tell they were predominantly men from southern France who had come north for work. The rooms that followed were large and well lit. Many men and a few ladies played *rouge et noir* at the green-covered table. The green cloth was checkered, marked into coloured squares, and rouleaux of gold coins were piled in sections of the table. The room was very quiet, even the mechanical sounds of the games were muted by soft-covered tables. The silence was broken by the men who ran the games at each table. They called the cards.

Black wins
Red wins
Black wins
Red wins

The gold coins on the losing squares were transferred by means of a long rake to the great pile, the 'bank', the 'capital' of the man who keeps the table and stakes against the company.

Fabienne deserted me for the silver room. She wanted to play but I was seduced by the people betting high at the gold tables. Fixed to my spot, a hopeless voyeur who couldn't begin to pretend otherwise, I watched three people in particular. A man with dyed black hair, perhaps an Italian; a younger Frenchman, and a woman with an I-dare-you-to expression aimed more at the wheel than in flirtation. Each player held a pasteboard card marked with red and black ledger lines which were punched out with little steel pins as red or black was called out. In this manner, players can keep track of the chances and hazard another play.

Black wins
Red wins
Black wins
Black wins
Red wins
Black wins

She tossed money out, little came back. In the span of a moment she looked at the man with dyed hair two, three, four times. He never so much as glanced back at her. She touched her upper lip quickly, as if she wanted to deny the act of sweating, Mannered, wax figures, everyone was spellbound by the wheel and the squares, one and then the other. I wished someone would open a window. Summer had gone on too long, artificially attenuated in that hot room.

500 francs on 27
2000 francs on 19
1300 francs on 38
8000 francs oh, on 72

The man with dyed black hair was betting high. I heard his name again. Monsieur Guillaume Baptiste. Baptiste was said with a slight Italian accent. A gambler's intent calm. He had an air of indifference but a hurried manner of movement and average betting luck. Once in a while he would turn pink. A waiter circled the table with glasses of cognac, Malvoisie and vermouth. The younger man did not seem to be doing at all well. I soon lost sight of him in the crowd and his place was taken by a German with a square monocle and a gold-topped cane. The rouged woman was winning fairly steadily. She seemed so obsessed by each full minute of the game that when her luck began to reverse she couldn't stand up and leave. (There is always the hope the plummeting action will reverse itself.) I was addicted on her coat tails – just five minutes and then another five: the green table was an insidious magnet, a drug whose side effects included acute forgetfulness. A trickle of sweat ran from the woman's ear under her jaw. Monsieur Guillaume Baptiste left but I hoped he would return. The game had a finite set of players. The inclusion of new personalities changed one's expectations.

A hand touched my elbow. It was the young man with bad luck. He offered me a drink and told me his name in a barely audible voice. The rooms in the Frescati are so quiet, the inclination is to whisper all conversation. I left him to look for Fabienne but couldn't find her in either the silver room or the gold. The sets of players had barely moved, frozen in their positions, but she had disappeared. Rémy Gommereux made a feeble effort to help me find the woman in the blue dress. Clearly she had gone and we ended up on a group of chairs in an alcove near the silver room. He offered me another drink. He is a painter. Gambling and painting have a lot in common, much the same human activity, he says. I had a vision of a sea of coins and franc notes and men and women drowning in this sea: images of Géricault and Charles, chance, capitalism and canvas. I went home with this Gommereux fellow to a room above a tailor's on Rue du Bac. Recklessness can become a strict code of behaviour when you've lost your way home and survival instincts are utterly confused. Deliberately throwing caution to the wind, falsifying a devil-may-care attitude, the uninhibited gesture is well rehearsed. He had large, nervous features in spite of his pretensions and I guess I was drawn to these, at least for one evening. If not a bit desperate, it seemed all right.

11 OCTOBER 1847

Fabienne appeared this morning. She had her reasons for leaving me stranded, without explanation or good-bye. She had met a man who said he was a poet and they went to play the *guinguettes*.* She said the poet dropped puns across Paris; a poet in the comic tradition, not a tragic romantic, not like a ceiling painter who spends most of his time on his back.

Each evening her father proposes this engagement or that marriage, Fabienne responds by going out and falling in love with the second poet she trips over in the Café Anglais. She has a keen sense of what other people call decorum, stretches her activities to those limits, hoping people will still say she is an obedient daughter even if they are not quite sure. It isn't the language of flirtation but its absence. Fabienne doesn't need slightly cut dresses or late arrivals, she doesn't look the other way and wait to be asked. The tough artists and fragile

* *Guinguettes* are small taverns. In the first half of the nineteenth century, there were clusters of these around Montmartre surrounded by carnival games such as 'nine pins' and 'Russian mountain', an early form of the rollercoaster. It is these games surrounding the taverns which Lucienne refers to when she writes, 'to play the *guinguettes*'. Willa Rehnfield

poets will never cross the threshold of her father's house, which is why I think she's chosen them as a kind of anti-anguish drug. She will never elope with one of them. Garrets and meals in outdoor restaurants aren't her idea of a good time. Instant remedies have their second chapters. My friend must know this. Although she packs her trunk, she never does leave.

18 OCTOBER 1847

Mathilde left the mail on the table in Charles's old library. A note from Rémy Gommereux but nothing from Eugène. I slipped the Gommereux note in a book and searched all my coat pockets to make sure I hadn't forgotten to mail my own letter; it might have fallen out somewhere. Mathilde asked me if she could help me look for whatever it was I might have lost.

Rémy's birthday last night was marked by a dinner at Les Frères provençaux in the Galerie de Beaujolais. A friend had had a good night at the Frescati and reserved a large table. Fabienne skipped an evening with one of her Ledger King future husbands in order to attend, but I was afraid E. might appear with one of his friends. My chair faced the gardens of the Palais Royale but I twisted my head every once in a while and looked around the room. Women seen in public parties, he would say, risk compromising their reputations. He would be critical of loud company who inflicted their celebration on surrounding diners. Les Provençaux was full of strangers. 'Vin de LaFitte 1802': a prolix drunk leaned over my shoulder, asked me why I twisted around to see the room. It was Phébus. 'Had I seen Eugène?' he asked, and in the same breath quoted Brillat-Savarin.

'"The truffle is the diamond of the kitchen." Isn't it fortunate that in the modern state a member of any class can eat game. The hunt is no longer restricted to those who own forests.' He swallowed more partridge à la Périgord and hoped no one would refuse the asparagus

Ferdinand because it was named after *Le Poire*'s eldest son. He called the champagne *coco épileptique* or *coco aristocratique.*[*]

Sitting on my left was Mademoiselle Desormeau who wishes to study painting but has been denied admission to each *atelier* she's applied to. She paints by herself in a small room in her mother's house. Madame Desormeau doesn't take her daughter's painting very seriously but hasn't discouraged her either. She has tried making copies in the Louvre but men stop and talk to her. She gets nothing accomplished, so when her mother will give her the money she hires models, makes up scenes and paints them in her room, or she paints from the Seine which she can see from her window.

21 OCTOBER 1847

I expected Rémy's drawings to be familiar reproductions of the masters, subjects from Greece, Rome, Byron, Shakespeare or Scott. On the contrary, Rémy is a new realist. He bragged a little less in rooms smelling of sweat, wine and turpentine.

He draws obsessively, documenting everything. Rémy claims his practice is 'like the unedited surface of a lake', but he's wrong. His realism isn't simply an all-inclusive mirror. There are schemes of elimination, the encyclopaedic impulse is often only a glib repetition of ideas that are in the Parisian air. Here are the Café Momus, the puppet show and the pickpockets, a woman soliciting a customer, perhaps not. In another stack a laundress with curly red hair and happy, round cheeks looks up from her drudgery; a laughing concierge, clothes full of holes, leans out of her window. The title is *The Gossip*. Rémy's sentimentality is that of a relatively young man, brush in hand, who sees these women as something they're not. Paintings that shut their eyes tight as Rémy declares, 'I'm truly thinking about

---

[*] He is alluding to cocaine, not chocolate. W. Rehnfield

what is.' They show what might be but probably isn't. If these relations of Delacroix's Rebecca, Ophelia and Desdemona were to meet, Rémy's women might envy the heroines their heroes but would be pleased to be painted as true as daguerreotypes, vividly coloured in. They bore none of Eugène's hazy emotion, no buffering plumes of cloud and veil. They looked like any woman you might see in certain streets except their occupations don't bear out their optimism. Rémy spoke a great deal about realism but until the vinegar of day-to-day actuality overwhelms the sugary aftertaste of his opinions, social realism is just going to be something he talks about and his paintings will be as popular with the Ledger Kings as they would be with Charles in a moment of questionable taste.

Fabienne is worried about her mother. Monsieur Ruban is oblivious beyond sending money to the nuns. Her sister Chantal would go to Normandy but her husband is about to be stationed in Paris.

28 OCTOBER 1847

Monsieur Gommereux frequently dresses entirely in black down to tapering trousers and shining shoes. It's not so much a sign of mourning as an affectation of seriousness. The antithesis of Monsieur Phébus. He knots a white silk scarf around his neck, ties it tightly like an expensive bandage: the wounded earnest young man.

We meet in public places. I never allow him in the house on Rue Saint Gilles, not because of Mathilde but because I don't want Rémy to examine the evidence of Charles's existence; don't want to hear myself forbid him to rifle through my husband's clothing, his papers, saying, 'Please leave those things alone.' For Rémy he is a curiosity. It's not his lack of jealousy that disturbs me but the way he acts so sure of my reasons (a dull, absent husband) for desiring him.

So we met today at the Brasserie Andler, a favourite of Fabienne's poet. The poet spoke with familiarity of the

Andler, a café which reflects the contradictory notions and trappings of its patrons. Intellectual radicals play billiards there while they drink whisky and discuss aesthetic realism or Hegelian dialectic. Rémy is intrigued by Bohemia and tried to imitate its manners. He might announce his commitment to atheism, then start going to church. Religion isn't the point. It's all in the service of shock or nonconformity.

Did I wonder why he came to this place, he asked? No, I didn't. He told me the story of his life. When he first came to Paris from the country, he took a job at the Préfecture of Police, a smart decision for a painter. Why? During the street fighting and riots – an annual event at least – the Préfecture is closed. The *garde nationale* is called out. On these occasions Rémy would go to the Louvre to study. He distrusts paintings of the Orient and mythology. French is his language, especially its slang expressions, and he seems to indulge in a fashionable affection for the gutter. Nothing was said about his family. Was Gommereux *père* a post-master in Rouen? A tax collector in Ornans? A magistrate in Dijon? I never found out.

Then he told me that after he'd worked at the Préfecture of Police he decided he needed some contact with painters and so worked as a studio assistant for Eugène Delacroix. Employees rarely tell you their bosses are nice people and I was afraid Rémy would repeat rumours and the obvious kinds of malignities. He's unreasonable, transparently cranky and inflicts his perfectionism on his assistants. They are salaried and easy prey. I could hear him say, 'Would you like to hear about the time I had to walk his dogs, buy soap for the models, leave while his cousin Josephine de Forget was in tears?' But I was wrong, he didn't talk about any of that.

Practitioners of romanticism represent the ideas of another generation, one which rebelled in 1830. They lost and subsequently their rebellion became absorbed, incorporated into Louis-Philippe's schemes of bourgeois culture. The passionate young men aged into peers of the artistic realm, notions of romanticism no longer the sword but cloaks to wrap oneself in, narratives one could sink into or hide behind. Rémy considered Delacroix, particularly, guilty of escapism, although he often took an adversarial position in relation to the Academy. Rémy, as an aspiring painter, could see advantages in becoming a sort of apprentice. In such a situation he would learn how figures were plotted out, limbs mapped on to artificial landscapes, how the restraints of commissions became hindrances, or not, how letters were answered. He was intrigued by the persona of a man who engaged in the dominant culture and at the same time disputed it. He produced hundreds of paintings and drawings but the man's convictions about the whole enterprise didn't quite seem to stick – at least it seemed that way to Rémy. Transvestite paintings, androgynous paintings; half one thing, half its opposite; half the image of the instant of conflict, the moment of epiphany; half parable, moral, newspaper story, which stays lodged in the brain long after the picture itself is forgotten. The planning and forethought which went on before the paintings were sent to an exhibition was lengthy and taught Rémy that making art is just a job like any other. He acquiesced, gave up any thought of asserting his character in the studio, allowed himself to become part of the support structure of Rue Notre Dame de Lorette. He would even choose to eat exactly what Eugène Delacroix ate on any given day. Eugène was never interested in Rémy's work or the stories the assistants told of their evenings, days off, their childhoods. 'So then I moved my chair closer and said to her . . .' gave way to silence when the old man entered the room. There had been rumours about the execution of the murals in the Bourbon library, how much had been done by Delacroix's own hand, how much had been done by his assistants. It wasn't a public scandal but the stories cast doubts. If authorship was misplaced, trust in Delacroix wavered. Rémy claimed to have painted the *Hésiode et la Muse* panel. Sleeping Hésiode, the Muse drops ideas into his somnambulant imagination. She hovers over him but the only thing between his legs is his crook. Was Rémy hinting at a kind of pictorial plagiarism?

89

Many of the people who visited the studio left some kind of impression on Rémy. Mademoiselle Mars, mistress of the Count de Mornay, wore a scarlet dress with sleeves like balloons, and ochre morocco boots. Baudelaire would burst in talking of Proudhon, of Daumier. Madame Sand was not pretty, argued like a man and maintained opinions on everything. Chopin was frail and came wrapped in her shawls. Josephine de Forget was beautiful and quoted Madame de Staël. He knew little of the painter's life beyond the perimeters of the studio. The assistants often conjectured but they didn't really know. At the same time Rémy insinuated that he had been an insider, an intimate, he had known things while I waited in the hall.

A man recognized Rémy from across the room and made his way to our table. The friend, a tall man with an aquiline nose, told lewd stories. I laughed but felt embarrassed for having laughed. Not out of prudery, but because in company whose rule is the desire to contradict, laughing at dirty jokes might be wrong. Eugène's polite society wasn't any easier. In each the truth lies somewhere between the conventions of mannered behaviour and the necessity to break every manner, code and all the bits of unspoken etiquette. When the friend returned to the bar, Rémy said the fellow wrote pantomime plays. A few of them had been successfully received at the Funambules.

'Champfleury is really still the best,' he said in a low voice, as if his friend were still at the table. He jerked his head vaguely in the direction of the bar. Had I seen *Pierrot Marquis*? Pierrot is a miller's assistant and he is always white, covered with flour, still the traditional white clown. When Pierrot takes a wife, he is so disturbed by the colour of her skin he covers her with flour. She is then *en paillasse*. Rémy liked the idea of painting a woman's entire body like that.

Walking quickly down the Rue des Prêtres Saint Germain l'Auxerrois, thinking Rémy's connection with Eugène made me uneasy and the reasons were partly about snobbery, a man walked sharply in front of me to enter the Café Momus. It was Jean de la Tour. I hadn't seen him since the day at the zoo, and didn't know what to say.

'I had credit here,' he pointed at the Momus. 'I can no longer afford even bad food at the Café de Foy. You come here when you're broke. The waiters are rude and expect no charity.'

He told me he had written a piece on the Committee for the Defence of National Work, a secret group made up of influential men with large investments in sugar, iron and steel who want to obliterate unions and reverse the social reforms that have affected their particular marketplace. * It was easy to locate the members, more difficult to prove their activities. Jean linked his arms through the back of his chair so his chest stuck out and spoke of the private social codes – I think he meant manners – of an aristocratic class. Even new members seem to know these codes. Once, to gain entrance to a meeting, he told a footman he was Baron de la Tour. In borrowed clothes, they never caught on to him. Guizot was about to shut down *La Réforme*. *La Vrai République* would probably be closed soon. There were no newspapers left for Jean to write articles for.

Paris is full of secret clubs, cells, meetings in cafés, attics, back rooms, ministerial chambers. When they are mentioned, I think of men scurrying like beetles in dark alleys, giving signals. The edges of Jean's lapels were shiny like his idealism, which seems rather more borrowed than naive, an idealism antithetical to Rémy's sheltered cynicism and Eugène's paralysis.

'All of Paris is bored, bored with Guizot, bored with Louis-Philippe and his ministers. We are so dull-witted that the memory, the cult of Napoleon, ferments in the imagin-

* A conservative think tank? Nineteenth-century trilateralists? Jane Amme, 1982

ations of everyone from failed journalists to doctors of philosophy at the Sorbonne to unemployed printers.' Jean explained this as if it were a new idea. There is a vast amount of discontent casting around for a target and so, according to Jean, you end up with self-negating contradictions like the resurrection of N. Bonaparte, no champion of the working class.

' "The July Monarchy is nothing other than a joint stock company for the exploitation of French national wealth, the dividends of which are divided among the ministers, Chambres, the 240,000 French eligible to vote. Louis-Philippe is director of the company – Robert Macaire* is on the throne." Karl Marx,' he quoted.

He offered to take me to one of his *14 Juillet* meetings. A few women are allowed to join, and the group is not, he assured me, involved in Utopian† ideas. As if to demonstrate his seriousness, he declined to kiss me good-bye but shook my hand instead. Jean wears tight clothes but I don't think he does so intentionally. His contempt for the Utops. is chilling.

7 NOVEMBER 1847

The red-haired woman, not unlike one of Rémy's women except for the expression on her face, sat on a gilt chair, crocheting. It, like other proprietors' chairs in Paris shops, is on a slight platform. She makes out bills and the customers pay her when they leave. Another proprietress came in from the *tabac* across the street. The red-haired woman adjusted her pencil behind her ear, put her crocheting in her lap. The second woman pantomimed a story, gesturing with her thumb and forefinger as if she had a gun in each hand. They both laughed and returned to their respective businesses.

* French prankster popularized by actor Frédéric Lemaître in the 1830s. W. Rehnfield

† Some Utopian groups whose original philosophy involved theories of the collective and communal enterprise evolved to the point where 'free love' was almost their exclusive doctrine, reflecting the tastes of group leaders. W.R. 1968

Nobody writes to these women telling them to close up shop and grab the next carriage to Belgium. I ordered another cup of coffee and wrote another letter to Eugène, crumpling the first and stuffing it in my bag.

10 NOVEMBER 1847

At dinner I said too much about the wrong things and felt transparently childish. I wanted him to talk about himself so that I wouldn't, but of course the reverse happened. A catching-up kind of conversation, like the exchange of notes between business partners: one in Lyon, one in Rouen.

In the cab going home I felt as if I'd slipped out of my place in the network of lives that make up Paris. Partly because I'm going to leave soon, I feel I've been more like a visitor during these last weeks. If having my portrait drawn by Eugène Delacroix gave me some sense of definition, that's an erroneous definition; but to be robbed of a false identity – that provokes no less a sense of loss. Without a word being said, it was clear that I would be put in a cab after dinner and returned to Rue Saint Gilles. And then I feel it's all very small and trivial, not worth any sense of loss at all. From the very first portrait, this affair was sparked by flints of inauthenticity. Fabienne says it's not that I give the streets of Place d'Orléans emotional tones of memory, but for me the Paris geography is infused with a hysterical colouring. I wasn't really in love with him, didn't like his big square jaw like an American's, thought his sky-blue cravats embroidered with E.D.s fussy. He put me in a cab as if I were one of his silly nieces from le Midi whose sense of direction grows scrambled at every corner and must be carefully sent on her way. However, as the fourth arrondissement came into view I was glad to be on my way home and didn't really care.

93

In a chocolate shop window in the Palais Royale arcade a steam engine plated with small mirrors crushes lumps of cocoa in its circular path. Canopies of small mirrors faceted into columns and tunnels all simultaneously reflect the afternoon sun. I suppose the concentration of light softens the chocolate, makes it easier to crush. It's somebody's job to clean these things every evening, and then chocolate is just like dirt. The train runs on a mirror track in an infinite chocolate landscape. The tea shop next door has a similar arrangement. Three china mandarins with bobbing heads are infinitely multiplied, a population of Oriental princes. In cafés and brasseries whose walls are covered by looking glasses, you can see what your neighbour is eating.

I watched barges float down the Seine carrying piles of wood and charcoal. The newspapers have said there may not be enough fuel to last the winter. Washerwomen sit in scows moored along the edges of the quays. I walked against the direction of the river to Rue de la Bienfaisance.

Fabienne was still in bed. She was not ill but could not get out. She was thinking of things, she said, and moved over to make room for me. I finished her bowl of coffee and told her if she could think about bathing it might be a start towards putting her feet on the floor. She could think lying down in the bath, turning into a prune. She was already sitting up, tying and buttoning clothes around her. Fabienne did spend a long time bathing. A young man in a tall hat and white silk trousers entered the bedroom. Not a hidden lover, not a pushy suitor, but Fabienne herself. Few women have openly followed George Sand's example. Few can count on reserves of daring or nerves of steel to outweigh the frailness and vulnerability which make up our movements. Without these reserves, the escapade would be doomed. Fabienne has yet to wear her suit in the street. She has yet to get past her father in men's clothing. She suggested she might change into the trousers at my house, then meet her poet at the theatre. He doesn't know if she is only going around in

94

trousers as some kind of sport or if she would really like to be a man, and in the end he told her unconventional clothing is just another bourgeois flap. Referring to George Sand again, Fabienne said they had begun smoking *poetic cigars*. The poet obtains them from a friend in Marseilles who gets them from someone in Morocco who cannot be named. Poetic cigars are smuggled over borders at night, overland, and transferred by small boats to end up discreetly passed around at the Café Tabourey, l'Hôtel Merciol, or the poet's attic where he writes verse on the wall and Fabienne draws around them anthropomorphic fish, birds, pictures of saints and maenads.

In the Luxembourg Gardens the poet saw Gérard de Nerval walking a lobster on a pale blue leash.

12 NOVEMBER 1847

When Charles first left, his departure created a disruption more serious than the simple break in routine. In his departure there was a moment I thought I might love him because he no longer lived with me, but the habit abruptly ceased. There was no being put in a cab, no scenes of hysteria or rage. Even then, I didn't want to admit the marriage was completely finished. My celibacy left Fabienne incredulous, his absence a gift thrown away, but I have made use of that 'gift' since. I have an inordinate fear of regret and consider the possibility of returning to my marriage, malingering over it. For a brief moment of his absence Charles could be perfect. Perfect in the way an actor at the Comédie or Opéra is perfect to a young girl. Perfection is part of the baggage of infatuation, but I was never infatuated with my husband. Whatever the feeling was, it's turned archaic. What all this is really about is money and what I will do when there is none left. The envelopes addressed from New Orleans or Martinique have stopped unless there's been some kind of accident or series of transatlantic typhoons. There were no letters in them, just money. Even the ones addressed to Mathilde no longer arrive.

The cook is happy to remain in Paris (Mathilde is not) but this week she has been complaining that the city is not what it was. It's becoming difficult to obtain meat and coal and the newspapers are becoming scarcer and limited in length. Several stands have to be tried and hardly the same one is open twice. The conversations in cafés infuse shape into the confusing anatomy of the creature French politics has become. The skeleton and musculature is given a name: the Opposition.

The Opposition, they say, refers to anyone who is critical of Louis-Philippe, his cabinet, the National Assembly. The Opposition is forbidden to hold public meetings, but to circumvent this edict the group has been holding banquets. These are masks behind which the meetings can convene. Everyone knows the banquets have little to do with eating and they, too, have come to be banned.

On the Opposition

The woman who runs the brasserie:
She thinks the banqueters are after their friends' jobs. There are only so many places in the Ministry, there are only so many holes for all those pegs. She no longer pays any attention to what this guild or that party say their politics are. Her husband felt passionately about such things when he was alive and she ignored both sides then. Beyond the perimeters of her business, she doesn't care much. The price of a glass of wine is not negotiable. It's not graded according to the salary of the drinker. That's her theory of economics. If she could vote she probably wouldn't use the privilege.

Mademoiselle Desormeau, a painter:
'One is robbed in the streets by gangs of barbarian twelve-year-olds, then robbed by the oligarchy, and that's quite legal. They have all sorts of lawyers to defend their interests. I'm told in some parts of England the propertied classes

build high walls around their homes and some hire little private armies in case of a mass revolt in the mills and factories. I don't know about universal suffrage. It would be a novelty to vote. They'd never give the vote to women in France.'

There are so many perfect little worlds plotted out in men's minds. She remembers Fourier* and his simple kitchen gardens, as if all your needs could be satisfied on communal bits of land with no one having formal husbands or wives. (That's the main, unspoken aim of the post-Fourier reformers: science and sex for everyone. But I don't think everyone will benefit. Some will be excluded.) She isn't sure progress should be that rapid. There's a danger in trading one trap, a real one, for another trap, disguised as some kind of freedom a man dreamed up sitting in a chair at the Bourbon library. The anarchists are half way on the right track, but only by half.

Baudelaire:
He would fight with the rebels.

Woman sometimes seen in the company of Hippolyte Phébus:
There are two kinds, the professionals and those who do it part time. The ranks subdivide from there along varying degrees of luxury and penury; the classes of prostitutes are a microcosm of the class system at large. Professionals can do very well – as well as wives, sometimes better. The man sets you up in a place, something discreet but not pokey, perhaps on the Rue Lafitte. He provides necessities and indulgences: glazed salmon, morrells, red Chinese silk dressing gowns (from money often denied his wife). Restraint and commitment are self-determined. Several

---

* Charles Fourier, a social philosopher, developed a kind of Utopian socialism. Eliminating what he considered restraining social structures such as marriage, he and his followers believed in the emancipation of women and complete sexual freedom for both men and women. Fourier designed 'phalansteries', an economic unit of 1,620 people, basically agricultural communities, systematically arranged. W. Rehnfield

lovers may be admitted to the theoretical rooms on Rue Lafitte as long as everyone pays his bills and doesn't get intimate with the maid. Part timers try to have a foot in each world and nobody has long enough legs to do that. Girls who do it part time are seamstresses, laundresses and domestic servants, usually those who don't live in. Revolution or not, business on the Rue de Langlade* will continue as before. Certainly if there is no revolution, the ranks of their fellow tradeswomen will continue to grow; especially increased in numbers will be those on the downward end of the scale. Women's work: sewing, scrubbing, peeling potatoes, legitimate work sanctioned by religion, pays just enough to starve slowly and gives you enough time to think about how unfair life is while you're in the process of attenuated dying. Shrewd women on the Rue de Langlade aren't immune to bitterness. For appearances, proper citizens stick to the Rue St Honoré, bundles of alarm and outrage at the suggestion of what goes on in narrow streets behind its lovely broad boulevards. Many take the long route back after dark to pay in marks, pounds, dollars or francs, and to sell.

Monsieur Ruban:
A family man, he also believes in each person accepting his or her lot. It follows that he does not believe in the use of violence but he has a voyeur's curiosity about such acts. He believes people should help themselves and not depend on the government; therefore, he sees reforms as a sign of laxity and laziness in the French. A follower of Guizot's maxim, 'Enrichissez-vous'.

Fabienne's poet:
'You make a mistake about revolution. No one starts a revolution. Not the southerners, not the Prussians, not the Jews. There are no conspirators. Just mobs, and the emotions of a mob aren't premeditated; they're ignited. Conspirators,

* Area of prostitution, see Balzac, Les Splendeurs et Misères des Courtisanes. W. Rehnfield

98

if there were to be any, must act spontaneously. They must take advantage of the general malaise the way an explorer at sea uses the prevailing wind. De Tocqueville said something like that. (De Tocqueville? Are you sure?) So much is the result of chance or a series of fortuitous chances. It's more a question of sensing the wind, the gales within a crowd.

'If you want to blame something on foreigners, the cholera plague is more suitable, less messy in the end, since people, not buildings, are affected.' Fabienne tells him some day these *bons mots* are going to get him into trouble.

Jean de la Tour:
It's like Carême-Carnaval. Marx says, 'The financial aristocracy, in its mode of acquisition as well as in its pleasures, is nothing but the resurrection of the lumpenproletariat at the top of bourgeois society.' It's like Carême-Carnaval where fools rule for a day but the day has gone on for far too long. Marx writes of the debauchery of the ruling class where 'gold, dirt, and blood' flow together, but you don't have to read Marx to witness exploitation by the bourgeoisie. The irony is that the current artifice was built on the revolution of 1830 which bankers stole from the workers. You can't have 1830 back but you can correct the mistakes of the last eighteen years by giving labour back the revolution it fought for in the first place. A change brought about by revolutionary blood, not a ballot box, the passage* of time or the bargaining table.

Eugène Delacroix:
Given the chance of walking into an eggbeater or not, he prefers to stay at home. When the events surrounding his studio nag and threaten his privacy, he nags and threatens in return. He agrees the government is a house of cards stacked by conniving half-wits, but *The Death of Sardanapalus* isn't a metaphor for *Le Poire*'s treatment of workers. 'I don't

---

* Lucienne, in describing Jean's words, may mean the *evolution* of time, but the word evolution was not in common use until after 1850. W. Rehnfield

wish to install myself in some made-up self-endowed office of social criticism. Rue Notre Dame de Lorette, business hours 10–6, Tuesday through Saturday. Those young social critics who prod and prick, whose pens are busy twenty-four hours a day and who would rush for their guns if the knock on the door was right, they have indulged in greater sins of romanticism than I could ever be accused of.'

Hippolyte Phébus:
'Louis-Philippe isn't all bad. You must realize he's done some good. More men have the vote now than twenty years ago. It's possible to improve your station if you know about finance and can learn about the new technology. Machines can do the work of twenty men and cost a fraction of what twenty men will cost; also, a machine can break down but it won't strike or join a mob. My friend Snarlet near Lyon has transformed, mechanized his silk works completely. The worms never see real sunlight. Snarlet has enough capital to qualify as a voter, he's nearly a peer of the realm. Snarlet's ancestors never knew a moment like this one. They were stone breakers or grave diggers. Money flows around us in all directions, it's only human to put your hand out and try to retain some for yourself, invest it, obtain more. From the time you are born, the clock starts ticking; you have to eat, you have to pay someone, you have to find a way for the river of currency to flow past your door.'

20 NOVEMBER 1847

My vocabulary for describing scenes of seduction is limited to the extent that my experience of being seduced is limited, and the way in which I have been persuaded by men has been very indirect. Eugène wanted to play dress up. Rémy became slightly drunk and very serious. Jean just announced one night that he would like to stay and so he did. He was conscious of each motion, each part of his body and each article of clothing: buttons slipped into and out of holes, ribbon and strings untied, hooks slipped out of eyes. His manner didn't quite match his offhand speech. No Lovelace, no Raymond de Ramière, no Lucien Chardon, he doesn't believe in gifts, epistles, preludes, footnotes or postscripts. His presence at Rue Saint Gilles made me nervous, as if Charles or Mathilde leading the ghost of Madame Crozier might open the door any minute.

25 NOVEMBER 1847

The language of subversion, of potential revolution, appears at every turn; even in the most mundane café conversation, some clause is tacked on the service. Most people know someone or know of a citizen who has been jailed by Guizot. As Jean's poverty and his failures increased, so did his radicalization. I suspect this is true of many members of *14 Juillet*, but I don't mean to imply their commitment springs entirely from lack. Jean is quick to take the didactic approach. A secret pedant, he explained that the process of criticism involves taking a thing apart, and so his theories are a combination of the interesting, the constructive, and the long-winded. At first Jean frequented the marginal Tabourey, the Andler, the Café de la Rotonde. At these places he had listened to Baudelaire and Courbet but they only made him depressed. Artists like them, however controversial, had some kind of forum or stage for their works – or so it seemed to him. The acceptances of his writings were limited, not so much because the pieces were bad – I don't believe they were – but because the Ministry had been closing papers and journals all over town. Jean knew this and knows it still, but he spent too many hours swallowing watered-down drinks while the artists at the next table were not. He was certain. His political ideas are based on the experience of extreme deprivation, not the detached knowledge of destitution to which, he says, I'm privileged. We could get into endless arguments about who's the genuine article. I could say his convictions grew out of personal need, mine from a series of rational, objective decisions. But this isn't exactly the truth. There have been good reasons and bad, or you might call it a combination of sincerity and sheer imitation. The questionable source of my opinions lies in my curiosity about Jean. I wanted to be sure of the reasons he felt so passionately that the Louvre and the Sorbonne should be burned as well as the palace. Jean has no knowledge of these motives. My sincere reasons Jean considers just as questionable. He condemns my social conscience as a soggy kind of humanitarianism. No, it's not a *kind* of humanitarianism, to him all 'good will' is soggy and blandly liberal at heart. It's like mending a thoroughly warped table: pointless. At La Galerie de la Bourse fraudulent companies, stocks and bonds mingle with the genuine. Jean believes there's little difference between them anyway. Both the self-made industrialists and the aristocrats simply switch horses whether there's a monarchy or republic, always retaining their controlling interests.

The 14 *Juillet* wants to minimize the role of management and eliminate the ownership of the means of production by a non-labouring class. A few have gone into factories in order to help organize unions. They say if people are employed, children will no longer be abandoned. Claiming to take a synoptic view, the *Juilletists* rarely examine a specific problem. The 14 *Juillet* isn't interested in distribution of bread to orphans.

Fabienne repeated some of these statements to her father. 'Like Marx,' he told her, 'your friend will be thrown out of France.' Monsieur Ruban, Charles, the Ledger Kings, for them the world is too full of gnats and mosquitoes. The throne and all it stands for is bolted down as it should be, infallible and taken for granted as such.

Sometimes the club meetings are about numbers. I've read some of the statistics before, often wondering how the counts are taken. In 1846 only 250,000 men had the vote. In 1840, 85,000 are on the dole, and so on. In the slums, eight or nine people are crowded into a single room in the lodging houses, men and women together. One of our members, César, has a special fondness for reciting these figures. In his head, there must be an endless loop of numbers. Some day he'll separate them all into two opposing columns and begin a process of addition which should occupy him for years.

30 NOVEMBER 1847

Jean was suddenly impatient with Mathilde and she responded like a defenceless house cat, defiant but cowering, unable really to assess the source of the attack. They almost don't speak the same French. Their use of language, their actual vocabularies, are so different. He began by asking her about her childhood, her family's connection to that of their masters, the Croziers. The relationship goes back two generations at least. Flattered by his attention, she told him about her grandmother who had been as strong as a man and believed martyred animals could be saints if they had led noble lives. Most bewildering to Mathilde, Jean asked her why her family stayed with the Croziers, why they didn't follow one hundred other possibilities open to enterprising citizens in the modern era? Why, in the middle of the nineteenth century, persevere in the feudal way with its oppressive modes of labour practice? I'm not sure why Jean persisted. She's not about to go into business for herself, putting her savings into a shop on Rue des Tours des Dames, for example, or become a pioneer in America. Mathilde isn't going anywhere. She's too old and she probably has no savings. What would he have her do? Organize the country's maids? She doesn't think her life in the service of the Croziers has been a mistake and is very unlikely to change without sacrificing her lucidity, without going mad. I would like to believe Jean was being sincere and naive but the real source of his antagonism was misdirected anger.

The only way I can divorce Charles, according to the law, is to find him in bed with another woman and to do this I'd have to go to Martinique. It would be messy,

103

unpleasant, take years, and once I reached the island Charles could have me locked up as a mad woman. Husbands can do this. They have the legal right. He could declare me insane and have me locked up with Fabienne's mother, if not on an island thousands of miles away from here. I'm not sure Charles would really do this but Jean, in his passion, certainly might, which is a curious contradiction.

2 DECEMBER 1847

Restlessness is an endemic second language now. Every day Mathilde tells me of something she couldn't find in the market or had to wait in a long line for, including bread. Unspoken at the *14 Juillet* meetings is the question of the actual mechanics of the revolt they are so sure of beginning soon. Although living, animated people, they remind me of Eugène's painted people, always about to do something, always on the edge, about to kill or be killed, about to accept or reject, always and forever just on the edge. The difference is that the *Juilletists* might very well do anything. They just haven't, yet.

10 DECEMBER 1847

Under French law a woman who commits adultery is a felon, but when the July Monarchy ends we shall all take new names and no one will be responsible for a dimly remembered authority's idea of crime. My marriage for money embarrasses Jean, it's a kind of hopeless taint, a contagion I can't be quite rid of. It's easy for him to pretend I had other choices, and I don't want to be dependent on him in turn. (That would be useless.) I still have time to sell a few things, jewellery, silver, a sentimental little Fragonard. Jean would like to buy a small printing press.

14 DECEMBER 1847

Drawing the curtains, I lie in a cold bed until the sound of his scribbling puts me to sleep. Every ten or fifteen minutes, the pen stops. A few minutes of silence, then he says out loud:

'With the termination of the National Workshops, the July Monarchy ceases to uphold the pretence which was only a pretence to begin . . .'

or:

'In the Angers factory a fire of suspicious nature spread up the stairwell. Twenty women were working in the upper storey and they were trapped, the stairways being full of flame.'

17 DECEMBER 1847

Often something about the *14 Juillet* meetings troubles me when I descend the four or five flights of stairs to Place des Italiens or Rue de Bouloy. I must admit, although not to Jean, it is the vagueness of the language, pure sloganism at times. Certain men manoeuvre the discourse until it's reduced to a general consensus of agreement on simple ideas. When these members are absent we engage in more pointed debates. Sides are taken, rifts become serious schisms and I fear the group will split up into a series of trios and quartets. Most of the *Juilletists* are men; one woman is very vocal, the rest, I'm afraid, are followers, like myself. Grey haired Pascale is often shouted down, unable to finish sentences or ideas. We are told she is divisive. The entire structure of society is rotten, we are told. When women demand attention it diverts the drive of the movement, saps its vital strength. César leers: women are supported by men, taken care of, their problems reside in the domain of the household, the family, not the political or theoretical arena. Bourgeois women don't work and would vote in the same way as their husbands and fathers. Their slot in society is a position of determined parroting. Our position is like that of the dirtied mirrors in chocolate shop windows. Working-class women have a measure of economic equality, therefore a feminist approach is superfluous, unnecessary, a distraction really. Pascale remarked that women in mills are paid about thirty-five centimes a day, a quarter of what men are paid. César addressed her without looking at her – would Pascale please be sure everyone had enough paper and wine? Such calculated dismissal, such unceremonious condescension, makes me suspect the two categories: the oppression of women and the struggle of the proletariat represent entirely different sets of circumstances and have little relation to one another. Although I cannot think of women as different as the Mademoiselles Crozier and Pascale belonging to a single oppressed group, insofar as they'd be treated the same by César or Guizot perhaps Pascale's vision of women as a single class is just, at least in part. As the meeting broke up she told me she would have nothing more to do with the *Juilletists*. There was *Les Femmes de la Révolution*, there were other groups. She had given the post-Fourier Marxists a few months and now she was finished with them. The nature of the members' domination assured her elimination. I am bewildered, feel I should leave too, but am not sure how. My submissiveness is underlined, made traitorous by comparison. But who am I a traitor to?

The street full of slick, undefined shapes because of the rain, I paid no attention to the unfamiliar direction we were taking. I let Jean and César walk ahead of me. I didn't want to hear their conversation, wanted to pretend I was alone or at least partly alone. Twin hunchback beggars huddled under an arch. Tonight was not even an early bout of winter misery for them. The season starts earlier for those who live on the streets than for people who live in houses. I know something about clamminess and the impeded vision of clouded, diseased eyes, in metaphor if not in fact. I tossed them a franc. Jean and César turned at the sound of the coin hitting the pavement. Perhaps I don't know how they felt. It was late. Street performers wearing saturated costumes were looking for shelter. I think I even saw the llama, no longer bright, but shivering and whining, led off, disappearing around a corner.

Jean dominates in the way pain, when acute, becomes the only perception capable of ruling the body. Pascale is gone, the orbits of power re-align and sigh in relief. I don't have the force of lung or articulation to adapt Pascale's voice. I'm unable to find a separate mode of action for myself. Whole sub-cities are about to erupt and shatter the everyday Paris, the complacent city. As the fissures appear, it's too late to jump from one side of the fault line to the other.

21 DECEMBER 1847

My portrait has remained wrapped in white paper in an empty drawer. That funny period of time seems to me now like five minutes' airing on a balcony during an all-night party, a respite from weariness but not an altogether re-freshing one. Somewhere in Paris, lying in another drawer, is another picture, two deceptive records of those five minutes on the balcony. Deceptive because these portraits seen side by side can so easily be misunderstood. The sitting was not about comedy or theatrical enterprise. What I think about now, as I look at the old paintings in the Crozier house, is what I can sell and how many francs I'll get for each picture.

Fabienne appeared at Rue Saint Gilles today with a parcel under her arm: the white silk trousers. She changed in my bedroom but her courage slipped at the outer court-yard door. We trudged back upstairs, Fabienne crying on my shoulder. Life is rotten, she has no freedom, the poet's attention drifts, he's not worth being in love with, she has no money of her own, and the final blow is always her mother who will never return and her father's good-humoured indifference. As I looked down, the curve of Mathilde's jowl seemed caught on the illusion of a cusp of the banister.

I can't turn Mathilde out and I think she knows this. Superannuated, she could hardly find work in another household, and there is little room for charity in Paris at the moment. At night the cook can follow Mathilde's every word of conversation with the lately deceased Madame George François Pierre de Crozier, and the pleasure Hortense takes in repeating Mathilde's monologues comes from love of gossip and fear that Madame's spirit might be watching her peel potatoes. Hortense turns to confiding in me as a protection against being dismissed. I can no longer pay her. I have sold a few things but I'm not sure how much longer I can keep her.

' "She's been looking at pictures and things in the house, writing down little notes and amounts of francs, what these things might be worth and so on, as if she means to sell them and without Monsieur Charles's permission. She spends her time with all kinds of men, sometimes she's away for days, spending Charles's money on them. One's a painter, maybe more are painters, I can't tell really, it's the way the clothing comes to smell, Madame. One of the men is a Marksist but he knows as much about Saint Mark as a hottentot." ' Hortense quotes Mathilde.

So Mathilde scowled at Fabienne and me. Was she rehearsing tonight's one-sided conversation? ' ". . . and then they both went into her bedroom, leaning on each other in such a manner as to leave no misjudgement regarding their intentions . . ." ' she will say to the dead Madame, the cook and, through the cook, to me.

Fabienne said angrily I was no comfort to her and that some day I would discover the *Juilletists* feel passionately about one thing and one thing only: the idea of revolution, just as her father and his friends feel passionately about one thing: francs. Neither the act of opposing nor attempts at making francs have done anything but affect her life adversely. Fabienne reminds me of Eugène as I think he might have been at twenty. Voluble and reclusive, an endorser of extremes; all men are deceivers, all women are victims, all women are flighty, all men are self-involved, or the other way around in each case. In another twenty years Fabienne will retreat into her marriage or whatever her life becomes, just as Eugène retreated into his studio, rejecting everything and everyone who bewilders him to the point of irritation or boredom.

28 DECEMBER 1847

After Christmas a deceptive mildness replaced Jean's feverish, agitated writing. I write deceptive because I don't know what he's actually thinking. He agreed to spend a few nights at Rue Saint Gilles. Mathilde left for Roubaix one morning, scarcely saying good-bye to anyone, and the cook's gone to her family in Lyon. We're alone in the big house and for days we spoke to no one but each other. Jean went about the house from scullery to attic like a child in a museum who must see everything.

'So this is how you live.' As if he were standing in front of an imperial Crozier coat of arms and suits of ancestral armour rather than the entrance to the house of a very successful merchant family. The ancestors of its owners never came near wearing armour.

'Where did the Croziers come from? Where are their lands? How did they get their money?'

I know very little about their history; his inquisitiveness takes me by surprise. Trying to turn the questions round to him proves unsuccessful; he doesn't like to talk about himself, won't ever mention his family and avoids all references to ever having had one. He sprang fully formed, slouching in a chair at the Café de Paris, glass and cigarette in hand. He imagines he will leave my life and the lives of other friends as he entered, without a past or a future. Snap, snap, a bolt of lightning imperfectly fixed in one's memory: that's Jean de la Tour. It's a sort of pretension. He's not so much a man of the streets as he'd like us to believe. He's not that tough. He's not that reckless. He's no buc-caneer. He's too careful. He doesn't drink to excess, even when the *sous* are jingling in his pocket. So I asked him a question I might have asked him a long time ago. An obvious question, as if I were writing for *La Réforme* myself. And through his answers it became very clear that the one thing Jean would really like is to be interviewed, to be taken seriously as an authority, to be called upon to expound in print – legitimate print with lots of like-minded readers. Only through print, he believes, will he be taken seriously. Through print his ideas could take on the solidity they lack in their present form – flyaway notebook pages and fluid café conversation. The running metaphor for social theory is architectural: building blocks, bridges, foundations, pinnacles, minarets. Not so Jean. In de la Tour's garden of social discourse, Jean is the gardener, carefully tending each cabbage, each rose, explaining the source, the precedent, the history, the growing cycle and future of each. With my chin on my knee, I take the aural tour. I am not a printing press but Jean is very self-conscious before his singular, if ephemeral, audience. He quoted Proudhon:

. . . if the air and water were not of a fugitive nature, they would have been appropriated. Let me observe in passing that this is more than a hypothesis; it is reality. Men have appropriated the air and water, I will not say as often as they could but as often as they've been allowed.

5 JANUARY 1848

Jean claims to have worked in glass factories when he was between school terms. His descriptions of the drudgery and dangers are dramatic but they might be the stories of a man who spent a lot of time looking in factory windows or talking to glass workers in bars. Some members of the *14 Juillet* are craftsmen and shopkeepers. Not all are intellectuals, not all are like Jean. They talk of demanding the formation of workshops, *ateliers sociaux*, workers' production associations, although the organization of these often leads to fights.

110

'Collective ownership must replace private ownership.'
'Class conflict is inevitable.'
'Property is theft.'
These quotes might have been titles and subtitles for the speech Joseph Pierre Proudhon gave to the club. He considers rent, interest and other such profit-making schemes unjust. Workers, he told us, must begin to assert their right to profit from their labour. The class system based on profit is so entrenched that there can be no hope for role reversal between owner and worker. The whole order must be changed so there are no bosses jimmying the racket to ensure the last drop is squeezed. Proudhon's loose smock, costume of a son of a cooper, and his narrow spectacles of an intellectual, are symbolic of what he tries to do: contradict. More antagonistic than Rémy's benign Bohemian attempts to shock, Proudhon's whole presence I found jarring and far from heroic, but I'm in the minority by endorsing the latter opinion. He was hostile to the whole idea of being asked to address the group. Even this gesture smacked of 'leadership' and 'authority' and he chafed under the position we'd assigned him. His irritation soon melted into the subject at hand, but not for long. Without warning, like an abrupt jump in a book which has lost a page, he asked the few women who were present to sit at the back. Proudhon is known for his disdain of women, but some say it isn't so much women (or any singular woman) he staunchly disregards as any party which might clutter up his clear and precious schemes. The question is, what kind of threat is cluttering, exactly? In his schemata, if you've been placed between a pair of brackets, that's where you must stay. The authoritarian order from one who only a few minutes earlier had spoken of the tyranny of proprietor and legislator was a contradiction. The six of us meekly stepped to the back and tried to sit down as quietly as possible. He paused to allow us to become settled and took up a new subject. All art of any kind should be burned. (Delacroix's and Rémy's women going up in flames together like witches at the stake.) No painting or sculpture would

111

be made for fifty years. I don't know if this is a good idea or bad, but I thought this self-proclaimed Everyman whose costume party worker's shirt made him look twice his natural size was completely intolerable. I stood up and left. I hope my departure wasn't taken as a vote of sympathy for artists, because as far as that issue goes I'm not particularly concerned. Four of the women followed so I don't think there could be any mistaking our displeasure. César made a cynical apology for our departure. I couldn't quite hear him. We went to my house and talked all evening, considering the possibility of resigning from *14 Juillet*. The question of how to leave – should we make some kind of statement or leave in silence? Each option became eroded, deemed somehow ineffectual, paralysed by my own sense of futility. One argument defeated the next. *14 Juillet* itself wasn't at fault, the object of criticism was Proudhon. But the group did endorse his opinions. An optimist among us believed at some future point in history, everyone, not just women, would leave the room in the face of Proudhon and the sycophants who parrot him. The men, those who stayed, were as guilty as their speaker. None of them had defended us. Two women did decide to withdraw from *14 Juillet* and will never go back to another meeting. I remain ambivalent.

Jean was shocked at our rudeness. Leaving in the middle of the lecture was an unpardonable affront to Proudhon, will only convince him that women do not belong in the clubs, and he's certain to repeat the story of the incident wherever he goes.

14 JANUARY 1848

We stayed alone in the house for nearly a week. Jean wrote all during these days, working on an essay in response to Louis-Philippe's 'Speech from the Throne'. His thin body seemed to float in space, jabbing the air above the angry pen to which it is attached.

He talks to himself. In half-comic speeches he challenges

the velvet and gilt objects that belonged to old Madame Crozier, things that still remain in her empty bedroom. Crime paid for this. Larceny paid for that. We are presently living off the 'vile and dirty' Crozier fortune and the golden spigot may shortly be turned off. Two months pass, but still the expected words from Charles remain unwritten, perhaps even unspoken; a mystery in Martinique. The silence could materialize into a confrontation at any minute and I wait for it as if that's what I want. The catastrophic part has already occurred. It's the impending *articulated* catastrophe that latches on to every moment. I pretend I'm rallying all kinds of courage by waiting for mail that doesn't arrive. The truth may be that I accept this disturbing state because the alternative will be fairly grim and will arrive soon enough. So I wait, partly forgetting about the virtues of caution and avoiding a scene.

Sequestered away from the streets and cafés, Jean may not know what I found out today when I went out for the first time. There isn't very much food or firewood to be had in Paris unless you had thought to store things up a few months ago. Crozier money or not, there are long queues and not much to buy. The cook had the foresight to save some flour before she left. I went out today thinking it would be good-bye forever to Rue Saint Gilles so tonight we'll have smoked trout, champagne and fresh raspberries. My values don't always match my idea of a good time. These extravagances were meant to be props. As I left tracks in the snow I daydreamed about this last dinner at which Jean might pretend he's Baron de la Tour. He can keep up the pretence until tomorrow when we trudge back to his solitary rooms. Today I went out to buy trout and returned with dried apples and stale bread. Not having seen another face save Jean's for so long, faces looked foreign, as if everyone would be expected to wear his face to maintain a peculiar continuity for my sake. Jean the baker. Jean the fishmonger. Jean the butcher and the dairymaid. It took me so long to find nothing that I had no time for Fabienne. There is so little food that to recall a time when my

113

husband would play with his is more reckless than nostalgic. He would mash his pâté into a lump, a series of lumps, as if giving a geography lesson: 'Say this is Senegal, you bring slaves through the interior, ship them out of Dakar then across the Atlantic.'

28 JANUARY 1848

'Fraternity is a form of solidarity.'

The *14 Juillet* has disbanded. César, the ferrety man with the figures and statistics, turned informer and the group was forced to scatter in order to avoid imprisonment. With the unexpected abruptness of a knock on the door in the middle of the night, we received news that the Club of Convictions I chose to abandon was compelled to disperse owing to rottenness at the heart. One who was trusted by most turned out to be committed only to saving his skin: César, the first one across the picket line.* But this is no *feuilleton*, no serialized caper with perilous episodes and nice rewards. We have to go underground. I know this expression isn't meant to be interpreted literally but I can't help but think of Hippolyte Phébus's friend with the silkworms which never saw sunlight. To some giant Snarlet we are the errant silkworms forced to eat mulberry leaves in a sub-terranean cell, artificial and bleak. Careful not to draw attention to ourselves, careful not to break any of the superficial rules, painfully conscious of appearances, we'll spin our cocoons or whatever it is they do, and pretend the old passions are just that, old and vestigial.

Jean sat at the edge of the bed, explained the situation but did nothing until morning. The following day, Jean found rooms in a remote quarter of Paris where no one is likely to look for us. We packed a few bags and boxes; one cab ride and we were here. How different from Charles's move to Belgium which required so much packing, arrange-

---

* I don't believe that the word or concept of the picket line existed in 1847. Jane Amme

114

ment, movement of goods and services, buying a new barouche.

This is a very final move. There will be no going full circle, no returning to a point in time when I wondered about the private aspirations of my cook or hid letters from a painter like Eugène Delacroix in a roll of stockings. I don't measure my station in life by the fact that I can carry all my possessions in a few bags and cartons, a rather literal and superficial form of measurement, but it does indicate a certain change. Looking at the bare flat and the small pile of boxes at the door, a kind of freedom is signified, a freedom allied with the gift of speed and lack of remorse. I like to think my poverty means my life finally matches what I think my principles are, but the root cause of our present state has to do with institutions completely outside my control or Jean's. We didn't choose to live in hiding or choose to take vows of poverty and silence, like monks. Our fate grabbed us by the collar, shook us by the lapels and bounced us down the stairs into the street, escaping from an undivorcable husband, the Censorship Committee, the Préfecture of Police, invisible forces whose arms are rumour, closed doors and shut-down printing presses. In a mythical society they might have handed us a road map and train tickets as well as letters of recrimination, and politely but comfortably sent us on our way. On the contrary, realistically, it is 1848 and there are no accommodating police marshals or gaolers. Our movements are dictated by letters and knocks on the door in the middle of the night.

4 FEBRUARY 1848

In this quarter far from Montmartre we are viewed with suspicion; strangers, almost foreigners, in the eyes of the inhabitants. The old cafés are a long walk and an omnibus ride away, and the end of the *14 Juillet* meetings leaves Jean feeling particularly powerless. For police inquiries, the club must never have existed and the *Juilletists* must seem to have disappeared off the face of the earth. Rumours reach us; one fellow is in Ornans, another in Chartres, another in Spain. César has been stabbed to death. The *garde municipale* is in a hurry to solve the murder, acting under pressure from superiors who want informers to feel assured of protection. While in hiding we are more likely to believe that seven out of ten crazy rumours are true, although the odds may very well be the other way around. There is no way to gauge. César may not even be dead but I do believe he ratted, and if he is dead, his murderer could easily be a felon of the criminal class, not a fugitive *Juilletist* at all. While most citizens partake of concrete information systems – newspapers, café conversation, and so on – we participate in a system of guesswork, an information lottery. What we need to know is unprinted, not discussed; those who might know are unreachable. Once I thought I saw César turn down a narrow street near the old Café Tabourey. I hurried to catch up with the little phantom but he was gone by the time I reached the corner.

6 FEBRUARY 1848

Jean has begun to go to the banquets organized to circumvent Louis-Philippe's edict banning political meetings. The banquets are exactly that, meetings of dissenters thinly disguised as dinner parties. It costs you ten francs, and if you don't pay you can't eat but you can listen to speeches condemning the July Monarchy.

I walked past Rue Saint Gilles today. The house was partially boarded up and I haven't a clue as to who ordered this, the police or Charles. My key let me in a back entrance. The furniture was covered with sheets. Dust lay on surfaces bearing fingerprints and footsteps but I didn't know how to interpret them. A stack of mail; someone had arranged the envelopes neatly on a table but none of them was slit. I walked through each room, taking only two bottles of wine, an ordinary blue dress and a book I began two years ago but never finished, thinking, now I'll have time to read it, but I haven't opened it yet.

116

When I ran into Eugène near the Andler it was like seeing an old classmate who still wears the same uniform although she's outgrown it. I might have been wearing the same old suit, too, or at least was perceived that way. We had the same conversation we always have.

Eugène

The tenor of life in Paris is at odds with the tranquillity needed to make art and understand art.

Lucienne

You would have it Guizot's way. 'Peace at any price' in order to do your work.

Eugène

I would rather have peaceful servitude than danger and constant threat. You say it's in the name of your revolution but it's just another form of oppression.

Lucienne

George Sand writes that art must not only be beautiful but socially useful. This idea is exclusive of art about art, art about flowers, art about half-naked women and half-eaten meals.

Eugène

The barricades and what they represent will flip around and evaporate overnight, sides cease to be meaningful, a moment may seem like forever but is really only a moment long. What reads to you as vividly coloured and fade-proof is only a boring chapter in a future book on social sciences. To make art of modern history is to make art which can't possibly endure. You will grow into a tiresome and boring old lady waving tracts in the faces of *flâneurs* on the Boulevard des Capucines.

Lucienne

The average French worker earns less than two francs a day.

Eugène
The average French worker is not a noble creature.

Lucienne
The rich invest money all over the country, all over the world; railway shares, banana plantations, the colonies, speculation here and there. You say 'So what?' You never think of what exploitation means.

Eugène
You don't remember the barricades of 1830. You don't know what terror is, what violence looks like. It will make you old rapidly.

Lucienne
Nearly half of Paris sustains itself on charity. When charity fails to provide, theft fills in the gap and this practice will continue as long as workers have no control over the means of production and receive no profit from their labour other than an inadequate salary. The system is so iniquitous and all you do is paint fruit and tigers and tell women they'll age prematurely, their vanity will suffer, if they think too much.

Eugène
Once I nearly ruined my eyes reading the newspapers. I read several every day. I had to know exactly what was happening in France, in western Europe, in the factories, on the Prussian front. It was a kind of bug-eyed addiction and ended in complete withdrawal to the studio. I do not need to know. I do not need to co-operate. Nobody is going to consult me anyway.

Lucienne
Gangs of boys terrorize small businesses, prey on people in the street. The women who mend your shirts, take in your washing, most of them must become prostitutes as well in order to eat.

He said something about warm beds and the last bottle and hoping for something better. He took my arm but I pulled it away. We had been practising our monologues, thoroughly concentrating on delivery, reception or perception of the other's be damned. He thought the little room joining his studio on Rue Notre Dame de Lorette would cure all difference, but to me that gesture, that desire, only made our differences more clear.

22 FEBRUARY 1848

I am writing from Fabienne's. Walking home last night, the streets were filled with people and soldiers. It was impossible to sense the tenor of the crowd and dangerous to trust to appearances. Was a certain knot of people joking among themselves or taunting a silent group of soldiers? Who were the soldiers loyal to? It was easier to identify the others: shopkeepers, clerks, workers, gentlemen and ladies lined the curbs and stood in clusters on the boulevards. Spaces grew tight, clogged with people and churned-up paving stones. Ordinary objects took on the characteristics of weapons. A walking stick became a potential club. An oyster knife could be transformed into as damning an implement as a bayonet. Real weapons appeared from hidden arsenals, pistols in sacks of onions and boot tops, larger guns in carts of potatoes. Conversations, no longer harmless, turned into threats and realizable ones. Vengeance could be wreaked. No more what if's and how might we's. I didn't see any of the soldiers' faces, afraid if I looked squarely at one of them he'd fire in return. Tension, random death imminent, lives perhaps about to end in bullet fire as predictable as roulette. I felt such apprehension during that marginal period of time just before an event, an unannounced occurrence, is about to happen. I remember one day at school, just before the Christmas holidays, there was a fire in the convent adjoining the classrooms. The nuns rushed us out while the smell of smoke was just faint in the air and we had no idea what was happening. That short period of time between the initial nervous agitation and the definition of the cause – fire – I remember those minutes more vividly than the subsequent collapse of the convent into flames. It is the moment of marginality, before the *cause* is given a name, and only its symptoms have a reign of the imagination. There appeared to be no sides. The antagonists may have been invisible in the palace but the results of their antagonism were plain. Some of the people in the streets, however, were visibly armed. It would take hours to get home so I turned off the avenue and walked the ten blocks to Fabienne's.

Her father came in shortly after I arrived. Monsieur Ruban had tried to get to a dinner party but gave up after a few blocks and returned home. Probably few guests arrived anyway, he explained, taking off his opera cloak, and it would have upset his liver to have people knocking through windows with rifle butts while he was trying to slice his meat or swallow an asparagus spear. He heard the riots began not far from Rue de la Bienfaisance, at Durand's, * where a huge banquet was planned. Monsieur Ruban curses the secret societies and freemasonry; they are the root of France's troubles. Just outside the Ruban door he heard that the *garde nationale* had gone over to the people while the *garde municipale* remained loyal to the king. People would be killed, people were probably lying dead in the streets already. It was such a waste, he said. Their cook won't go out to the shops tomorrow for surely massacred people will be cluttered everywhere. 'It's 1830 all over again.'

Unknown to any of the Ruban household, Jean was at that banquet at the Place de la Madeleine. I didn't tell them because the family wants no link, however associative or circumstantial, with someone they think of as a renegade. Monsieur Ruban, sprinkling benevolent indifference on all women from the lunatic he married to his daughters and servants, still wants to think of me as a good girl, a suitable companion for Fabienne. He knows nothing of my life since Charles left and still thinks of me as Madame Crozier, with all that title would imply to a conventional mind. I

---

* A restaurant in the Place de la Madeleine, popular with radicals. Willa Rehnfield

feel trapped here but control my anxiousness, or at least let them think it's due to the general state of things.

24 FEBRUARY 1848

Yesterday, the morning of the twenty-third, Jean came to fetch me at the Rubans'. He had been in the middle of the crowd and knew a great deal more than Monsieur Ruban, whose main cause of displeasure was the cancelled dinner party. Monsieur Ruban thought Jean was just a nice man who intended to conduct me safely back to the Crozier house. Fabienne, knowing his real identity, begged me not to leave, all the while her father telling her not to be childish and that I should go back to my house on Rue Saint Gilles, where there were lots of servants to take care of me.

Jean knew the route I was to have taken home the night of the twenty-second. He had discovered it to be impassable and hoped I'd gone to Fabienne's. Finding his way to the Rue de la Bienfaisance was difficult even late at night, and he didn't arrive until morning, the twenty-third. He had to hear shots before they were fired, see soldiers before they judged a crowd likely to turn antagonistic. Men were shot a few feet away from him. In some quarters the *garde municipale* hadn't yet advanced and in these the streets were being torn up to form barricades. Back streets, rooftops, cellars; a forty-five-minute walk took four hours. He was going back out into the streets and would take me along, not back to Rue Saint Gilles, as the Rubans expected. Jean was intoxicated by the prospect of the barricades, no longer satisfied with reading the correct journals and spending his evenings at leftist clubs sitting in an armchair.

A few blocks from Rue de la Bienfaisance the crowds I'd observed the day before remained in place. The tension maintaining the mob at such a pitch was beyond human scale. It peaked, receded but never quite dissolved, then peaked again. As for what happened, even now I don't accuse myself of naiveté. All the socialist ideology, all

121

conceptions of moral behaviour which I was, and still am, quite sure about, none of these offered mental constructs to prepare me for what I was to witness. Eventually ideas will re-align and enforce experience again, but when confronted all I could do was be a witness, initially.

The government prohibited the Opposition's banquet of the twenty-second and a crowd grew at the Place de la Madeleine in protest against its cancellation. The banquet had been planned to discuss extending the vote.* A shot was fired into the crowd. Some say an unemployed baker walked up to a gendarme and blew his brains out; some reports say it was a lieutenant who was shot. A group of students from the Left Bank arrived, a section of the original crowd broke off and joined them in a march to the Chamber of Deputies. Monsieur Ruban was right, the disaffected garde nationale sided with the people; in the poor arrondissements they are quite radical. The garde municipale, known for its brutality, continued to stand by the Crown.

As Jean and I hurried toward the Boulevard des Capucines the shops were all closed, there were no street vendors or carriages about, frightened groups of neighbours met in doorways, exchanging news and rumours. Like the Rubans' cook, they say the government is trying to massacre people; it's repeated on each corner. As we advanced the groups spilled into the streets and ceased existing as units. The streets were filled. A hospital was shelled, its corridors streaked with blood; houses and schools were torched and shelled. Silently, quickly, the trees, lamp posts and sentry boxes that line the streets were cut down and stacked to form barricades.

The rain was hard and relentless at first but as we reached the Boulevard des Capucines it lessened as the crowd grew in density and aggressiveness.

* Under Louis-Philippe, only property owners who paid a certain amount in taxes could vote. This ensured an electorate and an assembly whose values tended to be in sympathy with those of the king. The Opposition forces wanted to extend the vote to those who, although not landed property owners, had some position. W. Rehnfield

A bas les grands voleurs!
A bas les assassins!
Mourir pour la patrie!
Vengeance.

We heard gunshots, and all the latent combativeness of the months, years, totally animated the crowd, no longer an incipient menace but a genuine threat. We were assaulted and we might have expected more than moderate confrontation. No one appeared to be thinking more than twenty minutes ahead. The riot expanded, out of control. Troops opened fire somewhere ahead of us. I felt Jean fall against me, the pressure of the crowd pushed us forward off our feet. Finally we made our way to the edge and up a barricade at the corner of Rue le Peletier. I was aware of the sound of breaking glass but I don't know if the looting began at that moment. Dead and wounded tumbled from the barricades and became incorporated into the wall. Someone near me said something about 'thinning the ranks', and I had a horrifyingly silly image of hair being cut unevenly or small grains slipping through a sieve while the larger remained – all in the interest of finding some kind of metaphor for the separation of living and dead that was going on around me. In a moment that demanded acute attention my mind took odd, undisciplined turns. I was afraid to join the singing. My sense of purpose slipped and I felt hopelessly like an observer, at best an opinionated yet penless journalist. This wasn't my fight, I was a fraud who sought shelter at the wrong moment. Perhaps I wanted to be shot, perhaps I thought to be a true revolutionary I would have to be martyred. It was as if my convictions were theoretical and I didn't know how to behave when really pressed.

A woman fell against me, bleeding down my back, and I caught her in my arms. She had been shot near the throat, tried desperately to speak and then, finally, just to breathe. It might have been a stray bullet but I think it was a soldier whose accurate aim was the result of constant practice, who knew his mark when he went for it, even if the mark was a woman's tiny neck. She had been holding a pen knife which I picked up from a chink where it just nicked a wooden sentry box. I held her hand until she died a few minutes later and someone carried her away. The soldiers retreated or went to the Tuileries, I'm not sure which. I sat dumbly next to Jean on the barricades, perhaps for twenty minutes, perhaps for hours, blood drying my dress to my skin. Then we saw a hideous cortège, an open cart led by four men carrying torches. Piled in the cart were the half-dressed bodies of the dead. Some still bled, others had already gone stiff, lifeless, utterly without breath, picked up just at the moment of death. The knowledge of death is the last fact of a person's life before they're just another hunk of inorganic crap* and that's all there is to them. The moment of death is the last chance to speak of them in the present tense, the very last. Lines formed behind the cart and the Boulevard was quiet, then two men started banging tocsins and the cries began:

Vengeance
Vengeance

They moved so slowly after the convulsions of the mob, I breathed deeply, perched on a felled lamp post several feet above the crowd. As the cart approached I could see details of the dead: a bare foot, the curve of a cheek, a long braid, and this is where I made out what was left of Rémy Gommereux lying near the very top. Half of his face was blown away and the horror with which I write still rivets me: impossible to turn from it, to hold the revulsion at arm's length, I could count his teeth, so white and red and

* According to Eleanor Marx's 1886 translation, towards the end of *Madame Bovary*, Monsieur Homais began 'talking in slang to dazzle the bourgeoisie, saying *bender, crummy, cut my stick*, and *"I'll hook it"* for *"I'm going".*' Although *Madame Bovary* was written eight years after Lucienne wrote in her journal, the slang words were probably the same, or, one could assume that Monsieur Homais, residing in Tostes, took several years to assimilate what had been current usage in Paris a few years previously. Eleanor Marx, the youngest daughter of Karl, committed suicide in the same manner as Emma Bovary, twelve years after she completed the translation. W. Rehnfield.

so close. What nascent republicanism had drawn him out on a rainy February afternoon? Why didn't he stay at home with a pipe, home where such men belong? Caught by chance because he did not believe in riots and even looting would seem desperate, admitting poor origins. Perhaps Rémy Gommereux wasn't Rémy Gommereux at all but someone else entirely, another underground radical from a group in Montmartre or Ile Saint Louis, a desperate extremist group, a cell known for renegade attacks on the offices of the right-wing press. Rémy hardly seemed the ex-tough guy, representative of a group who didn't hesitate to use violence, but when it's a matter of saving your life you go underground and switch identities in order to survive. Is that why he liked Champfleury's Funambule pantomimes so much? Since he wasn't what he appeared, Pierrot's flour disguises and those of his wife may have been close to Rémy's heart. The fighter* played the artist. Rémy was exactly what he professed to be, but I hesitate to believe in the accidental and try to formulate explanations out of bits of memory. The fragments resist solvency. But for a span of a few feet, it could have been him up here on the barricades and me lying dead on the cart. Dead, mangled Rémy brought to mind stories my grandmother told me of the Terror, of the travelling guillotine, of how the blade became a symbol of arbitrary fate, going by the name of (1) justice, or (2) politics. It was all a code, a fake. Random and rigged like the wheels of the Frescati, as Rémy learned. But for a few feet it could have been me. My grandmother when very old would say to my brother, 'Fetch me some cider and be a good fellow or the guillotine will come for you when maman's back is turned, then no one can save you.' My mother scolded her, my father, too, but she stuck to her tales and the image of the blade until a few months before her death.

* By fighter I think Lucienne means what we would now call a guerrilla or terrorist. Jane Amme, 1982

The crowd chanted, moving towards the Tuileries. We made our way back home slowly, told to avoid one street, and then another, saw bloodied bodies, still groaning, a bit of life saving them from the cortege. Through the night we heard the sound of trees being chopped and paving stones prised up. By morning hundreds of barricades banded streets throughout Paris. The insurrection had spread rapidly from the Boulevard des Capucines. Errant gangs of malefactors of no political persuasion broke into houses and shops in the revolution's wake. 'Faubourg de Montmartre lies in ruins,' a woman told me, as she threw the boards from her windows on to a barricade. On the street a pile of small white calling cards fanned out at my feet. I picked one up.

HIPPOLYTE PHÉBUS
SCULPTOR

RUE MONSIEUR LE PRINCE

A pathetic remnant of another man who should, I would have thought, stayed home by his fire. What was the fate of Phébus? Were his yards of gold chain (after Disraeli) snatched from his shot-silk waistcoat? Were his tight checkered trousers (fit for the races) caked with mud and his olive kid gloves bloodied? The rain soaked his poor cards to a soft pulp. The things we leave behind us, the clues. I felt like crying for the feebleness of his cards, his vital makeshift dignity. I remembered accepting one at Saint-Hilaire's nearly a year ago and kept it lying around at the bottom of a bowl of odd latch keys and buttons, unable to toss it out altogether. He had pressed it upon me so earnestly, his important little card.

The citizens who survived broke into the Chamber of Deputies looking like the front lines of Napoleon's Grand Army without uniforms, covered by blood and gunpowder. Statesmen who had planned to read about the skirmishes in tomorrow's papers were confronted with the news in living form. They submitted and became former authorities. The deputies in their expensive coats with wide padded lapels never produced a more convincing illusion of power than at that moment before they knew defeat. That moment was very brief. Wools and silks next to harsh material, grimy cheek a few inches from one carefully powdered this morning, guns leaning against the Speaker's podium. An entire world was flipped around, just as Jean predicted, but far from Carnival time: this switching of power roles is very serious. It was a moment of victory, a short span of time in a relatively small bit of legislative space. Language and speeches deferred to force. Deputies like Comte de Lavallois tried to gather what remnant of power they imagined they could still exercise and warned us to remove ourselves from the premises or be levelled on the spot by the *garde nationale*. As more people poured through the door, it was evident the *garde nationale* was not on the same side as the Comte. The whole scene was like a great tiered bowl full of Daumier's caricatures of politicians. Many fat or pinched-looking elder statesmen, peers of the realm, businessmen, some from the Bourse, scores of Poireaumes. Supporters and look-alikes, cartoon people, bereft of power. A child next to me held a long chunk of gilt picture frame, a baroque club. The indomitable appeared vulnerable, a conversion which may be temporary; and for those short of memory, it is a transformation which may be rendered meaningless. The faces of those startled Members of Parliament signified a kind of victory, even if it turns out to be a very singular moment. I could call it power in transition or power dispersed. Even if the moment is never repeated, those men must know now and for the rest of their lives that dirty, angry people can come crashing through their chambers and unseat them, no matter how solidly they believe themselves ordained.

Is it worse to die at sea, drowning, completely conscious of the act of dying, or to die instantly, unaware, bullet through the brain or heart? A crash, an explosion, a revolution has its own timing and never happens at one's convenience. There's no time to pull on your shoes, brush your hair, compose your thoughts. Even if one was initially motivated by principles and politics worked out months or years before, one's actions become only reactions, and one is reduced to animal instincts. Or maybe it's just being in the wrong place at the wrong time and whole people are turned into cripples rattling tin cups. To be blinded, to lose your arms and legs, you become a veteran, a bit of you has died and the rest waits. Random violence separates the witnesses from those who stayed indoors on untouched streets, the voyeurs, like Monsieur Ruban, ever curious yet they stay safely behind, furniture piled up against bolted doors. The lives of the survivors are changed, a corner is turned and even the memory of the street you left behind is altered. The statue on the corner, the fountain which never ran, all become precious or ravaged, depending on your recovery.

I wasn't there when the Tuileries was ransacked just at the moment the king and queen fled by a back way. Their clothes, jewels and personal possessions were taken and left in broken heaps throughout the palace as if all of Paris had rifled through their closets and desks. They say paupers sat on the golden throne before it was tossed out of a window and burned. Men and women drowned in the flood of wine from broken kegs. One hundred years from now in some back room of a shop, an old woman will give her daughter a gold chain or a snuff box, saying this is what your grandmother stole from the Tuileries in February 1848. A great wealth of stolen heirlooms becomes legitimate property by virtue of new ownership.

The barricades are now abandoned, the felled trees and

128

sentry boxes are slippery and bright in the rain. Not indelible, the trail of blood will wash away by tomorrow. Some future history book can map the sites of street fighting in a more permanent ink.

A provisional government has been set up with Dupont de l'Eure, old grandfather of a revolutionary, as a figurehead Monsieur le Président. Lamartine, Minister of Foreign Affairs, is in charge. Others: Arago, Garnier-Page, Cremieux, Ledru-Rollin.

Louis-Philippe fled to England under the name Mr Smith.

Eugène saw political activity as a vast pit thronging with confused, hideous monsters. Fools think they can intervene and alter situations. He'd say interference is a trick and you'll only be converted into another pit dweller. If I were to knock on the studio door, he would condemn my description of the February Days as a love of the gutter. Would a row of marching paintings, proceeding towards the Tuileries, have, like Orpheus's music, calmed people, have silenced the chants? Would everyone be sedated into giving up the revolution, turned around and sent home?

1 MARCH 1848

Jean covered the table with his papers, writing endless detailed descriptions of each of the February Days. Everything he saw or heard is documented and the doubts I express aloud as I look at maps or out of the window are of no interest to him.

Jean accompanied me on a walk back to 4 Rue Saint Gilles. I nearly wrote *home* out of habit, although in actuality it had become more like a temporary warehouse. I looked upon the familiar houses still standing as symbols of security and happy childhoods. To call this familiar walk a trail of innocence is an artifice that doesn't really fool me. There never was such a time. We could see that the devastation in some parts of Paris was enormous. Rooms lay wrecked behind smashed windows, forced doors and shutters;

littered courtyards could be seen behind twisted gates. Through one such entrance I saw an outstretched arm, from elbow to fingers, lying on the court flagstones. The rest of the body was hidden from view and I tried in a weak way to reason with myself; the person might be asleep, fainted on the stones, that's all. Of course it was one of the dead. A sight is repeated over and over and it becomes incorporated into the commonplace, the everyday. These new dead were victims of looters, regular street crime gone a little more berserk in the wake of the insurrection. Houses now could be seen into. People moved inside; new tenants, or the originals, could be seen continuing to eat, sleep or argue with each other among the wrecked chairs, scattered books and vandalized paintings in old rooms.

When we reached Rue Saint Gilles I felt some relief. The house was still standing, but bit by bit details of the building became visible. Windows had been smashed, doors forced in. I tossed my keys into a window box. We walked directly in. Dirt and boot prints indicated a mysterious trail that led through hall and rooms. Furniture was broken, pictures ripped up, mirrors shattered, wardrobes and jewellery boxes prised open. Teacups, stuffed into holes, ripped into chairs, clothing left on the stair as if the person descending were invisible: a surrealistic* scene. Almost everything of any value had been stolen. It's unfortunate I hadn't sold more of Charles's family's things before because I couldn't be held accountable for their loss now. Mathilde is in Roubaix, Hortense in Lyon, but if any other servants returned to the house for any reason I was not aware of it.

In the kitchen, blood, dried and hard to distinguish from splattered encrustations of wine and dirt. The marble pastry slab lay in chunks on the floor; among the slivers was a lock of blond hair. Jean stood in the kitchen doorway and as I opened the pantry door it is a measure of how much we have witnessed that I didn't scream or grab Jean. A man sat on the pantry floor, his pants bunched up around his

* This must be Willa's word, not Lucienne's. Jane Amme, 1982

ankles, his legs stretched out in front of him, the top half of his body leaning against the wainscoting, one of our carving knives in his back. His worker's smock might have signified reprieve for Jean or Proudhon, but the half-undressed body aroused no sympathy from me. Here was a rapist, calescent, flushing crimson with rolled-down trousers. What would be worth stealing from a kitchen other than the women who might be hiding there? Food, it's true, but this character looked rather well fed. Just when he was about to present himself, a second woman struck him. His legs gave way but he managed to lean against a wall of formerly sweet-smelling cupboards. Perhaps that sweet smell was his last sensation. Judith was a heroine for slaying Holofernes. The anonymous maids ran away.

Jean took my arm and said we should return, there was nothing we could do in the house. We couldn't sleep there. The police, more vandals or more Croziers might reclaim the house at any time. Perversely, I responded to the dead man in the kitchen as just another hunk of meat that the cook might have salted away. If I was so offhand and unconcerned about a murder in my house, one can only guess at the prevailing attitudes of the majority. It's easy to believe he got what he deserved. We left things as we found them, I took nothing with me. We had started to walk through the courtyard when I remembered and ran back into the house, upstairs to my bedroom. My desk had been hacked to firewood cords, letters strewn on the floor, inkwells spilt. The thieves had been looking for a secret compartment. My writing desk doesn't have one, as they must have discovered. Jean waited in patient ignorance while I searched through the mess but Eugène's portrait was gone.

2 MARCH 1848

Early March, it's suddenly warm, then it rains, fog blunts the edges of broken faubourgs. Tops of women's bodies wrapped in tight shawls mimic buds, portents of spring.

Time for adding up losses and gains on each side. The fog and smoke have yet to clear so I should say these days might be a time for assessment but aren't quite yet. Through the past week I've felt compelled to write about loss. Death of a man I hardly knew (I didn't particularly like him but felt remorse, nonetheless), loss of life, loss of order (whose order and what gains balance the losses?), losses of material goods. What's true loss? The disappearance of a portrait of Eugène Delacroix dressed like an Arab? I don't want Jean to guess my defection; not a true defection like César's but an indulgence, rooted in the value of lingering sentiment, fear of slipped memory and the fatal attraction of contradictions. I'm no longer interested in him as an artist or as a lover I'd like to see again. It's because I'm afraid of starting at point zero, and after the revolution Jean believes there will be a tremendous erasure of history, public and private, Proudhon's wish come true.

We're running out of money. Jean writes under a different name but I don't know if it will have any more success than de la Tour. He is hungry, he doesn't want to think about subtraction and addition. X sous for butter, Y sous for bread, and 1 franc 15 sous for *vin de Bourgogne ordinaire*; it's left up to me.

If the next week were a chapter in a *feuilleton*, I would go to the Frescati every Friday night and play against the Bourse, against the house, and always win, nobody knowing my identity or what I did with my money. Attempts to follow me home after a night of gambling would end in tragedy. I would wear scarves pinned to my shoulder by a little gold nine of hearts. There is buying and selling on the black market. '*Il y a un dessou des cartes*',* Phébus once said about the black market in Montmartre. I walked through Montmartre and there were no more *guinguettes*. Shutters, even nail-studded ones, were torn off their hinges, whole sides of houses looked broken off, black rimmed from fire,

* 'There is more than meets the eye' (in Montmartre) or, the man meant underhand games (*cartes* = cards) are played in Montmartre. W. Rehnfield

walls which weren't levelled by cannon bore the marks of hundreds of musket balls. The *garde municipale* had thought the root of the insurrection lay in this quarter and yet were arbitrary in their thoroughness. I saw no evidence of a black market. It would be dangerous for a woman alone to try to insinuate herself into the racket, and with only bits of things to trade or sell I'm afraid I would appear pathetic, or even mad. Phébus would be attuned to the disbursement of small properties and valuable objects across the city after the looting, and he would know how to profit from it. Those selling don't often know the actual worth of material goods once so dear to sheltered homes. Phébus would buy silver cheaply claiming it was only plated and make an exorbitant profit based on a looter/bricklayer's ignorance. I'm too undemonstrative to drive a hard bargain, I do know that much.

If anyone read this journal I would consider the transgression part of the fraternity of acts of vandalism. I suspect Jean has looked through it when I've gone out because it wasn't in exactly the same place I left it yesterday. His intervention in the life of a memoir was a joy ride on the wings of mutual confidence.

Eugène had lost his 1847 journal, left it in a cab as if he wanted to lose the whole year altogether. Cerulean blue meets scarlet lake and all he really wants is to be left alone. The turpentine spills, layers of drawings dissolve and grow brittle and warped as they dry. His ideology is an embrace of unwelcomeness, a constant revision of what and whom to exclude, to avoid. All he wanted to do was paint Homer, Dante, bowls of flowers, compliant women, images to coat gaunt screechy ideologues until they disappear.

4 MARCH 1848

Today was the official funeral for those who died in the street fighting. As we marched up the Boulevard des Capucines I thought I saw Eugène on a balcony but the reduced figure waved at the crowd. I don't think he would have waved.

I tried to determine how the bits of what I knew about Rémy Gommereux added up to his participation in the February Days. The Frescati, the Andler, part-time policeman: it doesn't add up neatly. Was he hiding clues to his true identity from me when I climbed the stairs at Rue du Bac? Like Jean now, many are wanted by the police for subversive acts, for belonging to an illegal club, for murder. Playing the dandy at the Frescati with a voice as smooth as *crème fraîche* in a silver bowl, the injured artist at the Andler and the Bourbon library, these are clever identities for a fugitive to assume. He might have been as much of a fop when he played the socialist as when he played the artist, yet went out that rainy afternoon to shed his costume. The artist suit, in fact, was less clever, since some artists, like Courbet and Daumier, aren't content to fight studio Saracens. I don't know how he faked all those paintings and drawings. It's hard to believe he was at the Place de la Madeleine spurred only by a detached curiosity or purely by accident. He was too canny about the tenor of the streets to feel it was the afternoon for a stroll.

The march was slow. I didn't know what to think about. Whatever had been sparked off last week, it's over now and everyone knows it. The moment of the revolution appears to be just that – a singular moment – and the days of the *14 Juillet* appear to be really finished this time. I have accused myself of weeping over symbols of innocence, of an innocent time frozen in the representation of a street or a portrait, but the symbols are fake, the innocence is riddled by knowledge. Our minds range around the vacuum 1848 seems to have become. After so much promise, the disillusionment which I scorned in E.D. is a confession of failure I'm not prepared to sign. The February Days were a membraneous divide, my sympathies slip back and forth between areas which I used to be sure were either good or bad, and my sentiments are no longer directed by my politics or even by my intellect.

The city behaves like a human body, unable to rid itself of disease. The convulsions made it look like one possessed; the blood-letting relieved a touch of the fever. The idealist believes the worst is over and the body can repair itself, but some, lachrymose, feel the slow pulse and express reservations about the healing process. Mauled streets and broken glass, debris from the barricades, was pushed to one side; it doesn't disappear, so it's pushed back the other way.

Mutinous instincts increase as Jean does little but write on both sides of each leaf of paper and within every margin. His production is formidable, not of this world, an enslaving process. There is no discussion of his assembling the sheets for an editor. Editors, by their very nature, he has come to believe, exercise censorship and imperfect understanding. In a few days I'll be forced to buy *harlequin* in secret from the *houilleurs*** on the Rue de la Mortellerie. Each of my thoughts dwells on the relationship of currency to food and how the disparity might be remedied. Short of theft, the gap between price, bread and amount of money at hand must be bridged. I don't want to end up at the *Hôtel Dieu*† living on fifty centilitres of cheap wine and broth so vile that any meat or vegetables were long ago corroded in it. Jean lapses pathetic, driven only by his pen.

---

* Translated literally, *houilleur* means coal miner. These were scavengers who rooted through garbage for half-eaten food which they sold to the poor. They were also known to buy morsels of refuse from restaurants and households who in turn may have been using leftovers from some more upper-class kitchen or dining room. (This custom was called *serdeau* or king's dessert.) The *houilleur*'s mash of scraps bore the name *harlequin* because of its multi-coloured appearance. *Houilleurs* were harassed by police inspectors, but indeed, little food in Paris was actually gotten rid of until someone, somewhere down through the strata of classes, swallowed it. Willa Rehnfield
† The poor house. W. Rehnfield

Fabienne sat on a rug reading her father the most recent episode of *Prosper Bernard* from a newspaper *feuilleton*. He ran down a crumbling Montmartre stairway, not realizing the men dressed in the uniforms of the *garde municipale* were really friends, or at least acquaintances. Except for the bits about stealing vegetables and sleeping under the Pont des Arts, the real Prosper and his friends couldn't read or write properly and they wouldn't know one end of a church nave from the other. Their language is the language of the streets, and the syntax of polite behaviour is alien to them. Hyacinthe, at fourteen, would have had a baby by now and left it to die in a doorway or church yard. She wouldn't be a maid or work in a shop. Children like them, even adults of their class, are considered a cut below animals, completely outside the structure of social order. Parasites who steal and scavenge, tumours that live off their hosts and grow alarmingly; that's how the bourgeoisie view this mass of children. The irony of the names, Prosper and Hyacinthe: their real nomenclature would hardly sound so nice or so well-off. They would have no interest in plotting revolution. In the event of street fighting and riots, the looting which occurred in the aftermath would be a language of possibility they would understand. Apprenticed as children, masters as adults, their craft is criminality. Even the *Juilletists* called them barbarians but in the *feuilletons* they are heroic waifs. The way I look back on my life before my marriage can be fairly sentimental, just as the innocently libellous journalist who profits from Prosper sees cunning and writes of cuteness. On another raining Tuesday I might have sat still and listened. Monsieur Ruban complained of hypostasis and shut his eyes.

He was appalled by the tremendous destruction which had taken place in the Tuileries Galleries, the whirligig of calamity seemed, to him, to be spinning out of control. All kinds of people are turning up at the Louvre to return what they claim is stolen art. They insist on their innocence and they want rewards. Most of the objects aren't worth much, some are fakes or paintings stolen from private collections. The populace engages in an attempt to trade in, to profit from a redistribution which has nothing to do with an equalizing of wealth. It's all about trying to negotiate the gap between currency, price and commodity when you've barely had anything to eat for weeks.

For Eugène, the February Revolution was a meal destined to be thrown up in sickness all over oneself, disgusting. Something, however, is accomplished if only that Louis-Philippe, Guizot and the lords of the Chamber must know they can be replaced or at least seriously threatened now, by other than natural causes.

21 MARCH 1848

Every brick, chair or bottle thrown from a window in February has missed its mark. Everything which, months ago, seemed illegal or subversive now appears as useless, a thing too much fretted over which failed anyway. Control of the government has reverted to a ring of moderates preoccupied with proper parliamentary procedure. Elections have been postponed and the problem isn't just that all systems are in a state of chaos but that the confusion is being used to advantage by the right. Yesterday, thousands marched on the Hôtel de Ville. The workers, artisans mostly, were met and escorted in hostile silence by the *garde nationale*. Jean says it was a moment about to break but held in check, only to grow all the more violent in the next round. Extreme Jacobin clubs are springing up again, meeting in back rooms and corners. Jean doesn't trust anyone. In even the most committed cell, in even the band most on the fringe, a César may be found. Underground means hiding, hiding means solitude. He's impatient and accuses me of not understanding simple cause and effect relationships. Blanqui continues to appear as a revolutionary conspirator, advocating violence as a means of overthrowing the government. As if in response to general hopelessness, the mechanisms of everyday life in Paris do not run well. Lines form in front of all kinds of shops, especially for food. People blame the left for the failure of the trains, the conservatives for the empty shops and lines trailing from the bakeries. Casting around for blame, these are easy targets, facilely contrived absolutes. Was it really Rémy Gommereux on the cart? Has Hippolyte Phébus simply gone on a long trip? Collective memory is an unstable element, and to rely on it is to rely on something whose longevity is questionable. I could be accused of writing fiction. It will be said she wrote what she claimed was true but the history books fail to provide corroboration.

Dressmakers are busy each spring regardless of what may have transpired in February. New bolts of lace and linen are brought into the city for vicomtesses and wives of perfume merchants. Some omnibuses have ceased to function, there's no money for parts or repairmen. It's ironic: some of the parts would have to be imported from England where the king has fled, but I don't think the *Poire* is having a merry time. He seems more a figure of confusion than malice. Loyalty to him perseveres in some corners. Louis-Philippe's bankers have rescinded all support of the provisional government although it's nearly as conservative as his. Long boring speeches put everyone to sleep. Alexander Ledru-Rollin* hops from branch to ideological branch. Louis Blanc's National Workshops have no money to pay workers. Predictions on the outcome of the February Days run the gamut of all possible disasters. A flood: the Seine could rise over the rooftops. A cataclysmic earthquake: Paris could be swallowed in a westward gulp by the Plaine de Brie. I can barely read newspapers. *La Voix des Femmes* is difficult to find. I don't really know what is happening in the rest of the country. Were other streets dug up, were other barricades built from paving stones? Did citizens in port cities and towns in le Midi divide and sub-divide into

* Alexander August Ledru-Rollin, opponent of Louis-Philippe and a minister in the provisional government of Lamartine. W. Rehnfield

138

all kinds of factions with Jacobin, Orleanist or Royalist tendencies too intertwined and complicated to sort out? Jean says, no, the rest of France is remote. Paris is a small, rarefied geography with tightly defined perimeters. A topography, he says, which doesn't exist anywhere else. In practice, revolutions have occurred all over Europe but I still think of these events as central to the capital of France. Sometimes I'm so tired of the city and its failures I would go anywhere, but then I reconsider the provinces. I had reasons for leaving: the parochial citizens, *les notables* who always vote the same way, the subjects of Etienne's effigies. There were the careful doctors prejudicial towards superstitious remedy, the kind of people who would never question the story that the Rembrandt was stolen for ransom money. The ones I wanted to get away from, I would find them again if I returned.

25 MARCH 1848

This afternoon I put another veil on Jean's hat. During the funeral march on the fourth of this month, he stood near me disguised as a blue stocking from the Left Bank. Since it's dangerous for him to be seen in Paris, we construct disguises: a chimney sweep, face covered with flour; a fireman. Jean is thin and not terribly tall. He shaved his moustache long ago and I painted black around his eyes, red lips. There was something frightening about a feminized Jean who couldn't quite change his walk without looking exaggerated and silly; dissimulation took on ridiculous proportions. It was impossible. I cut seams from a black dress, put in bits of blue silk to make it larger, but the silk was old and tore. I found a wig and an old hat on the street, and added veils of black lace. This one would be for me, so my face too would be obscured and I looked like I was in mourning. I gave up the idea of a deep bonnet like those worn by women in the Nord. This kind of hat is difficult to see into but it is unlikely such a woman would participate in a demonstration and suspicion would be aroused. It was important for Jean to be part of that funeral march and very dangerous. He wanted to be seen by some and go unnoticed by others. I don't know how well he passed but we seem to have gotten by.

28 MARCH 1848

Midnight tonight like midnight last night, Jean is not at home. Tonight he's dressed as a fireman. His sorry quests must be seen in the inconstant and sickly light of post-revolutionary chaos. I counted the dishes from rinse water to drying rack: four, five, six glasses; one and two. At the fourth spoon I decided I'd turn around and ask him where he goes. One spoon, two spoons, three spoons, four. I didn't ask, uncertain of my right to inquire. Across the airshaft I could see a lamp in a window and a woman combing a child's hair. She can see the window below mine. In a line of vision zig-zagging down the airshaft, each learns about the lives of strangers.

A nasty, defeated edge turns up everywhere: in the press which still exists, in the lines at the bakery with no papers to read and in apartment stairways, especially as you approach the top floors. I have given up the idea of asking Jean where he's been. He sits at his desk, sometimes the pages form stacks like towers under construction; they mount up in inches and become a way of measuring the passage of time. Papertime is a variation on the hourglass or the Chinese water clock but far less reliable, for sometimes the flow of paper stops for a few days.

Jean leans against the airshaft window and says the same gang will get elected. Shrouded in their exclusivity, they are men for whom the world is a marketplace where the lives of the populace exist for their own personal use. In Paris the working class itself is divided. Suspicion is endemic. People are afraid of losing the miserable jobs they do have, they act without hope, without unity of action or purpose. There will be worse Februaries. People have nothing left to lose.

The 14 *Juillet* might have been a surrogate for action. Jean is no conquistadore, no musketeer; the club meetings were his arsenal, the speeches his firearms. He sees himself as a little man with no voice and no recognition unless it arrives so belatedly he'll end up an elderly symbol of a forgotten revolution like Dupont de l'Eure.

César's interference has prevented Jean from becoming a public figure of any kind. César, who dogmatically recited his figures, meeting after meeting. His disguise was numerical. Was he truly an Orleanist, a fanatic recruit of the *garde municipale*? Or was he just a man who needed money and wasn't sure where his sympathies lay, who didn't even think about differences in class or sides in a battle? Maybe he did think remotely about the fighting part, knowing a moment would come when sides would be drawn and everyone would know of his betrayal, but I'll never know why he chose to do what he did. Explicitly the message of César and his numbers: this is the way the world is, we use numbers to represent reality. César's code brooked no projections of Utopia. César believed in hard facts like cold cash, yet César himself was not as he appeared. An operator, a two-penny actor, a saltimbanque who had us all fooled: most saltimbanques in France are radicals and are persecuted for it, hounded from town to town. He was not even an acquaintance but profoundly influenced our lives in his ratty way. Dead as he is, he's our gaoler. It wasn't so much what the man did, there have always been stoolies, but why was the 14 *Juillet* a target? Up until February, Jean and I didn't believe in grey. Sides were clear: good against evil, left against right, and so on. Since February, even with César's defection, our lives have become muddied by the provisional tumult around us. People fend for themselves. Everybody has their reasons. Barriers between justness and treachery are permeable, subject to the memory of the person doing the describing. I mean barriers that ought to be some kind of ordinary moral fabric are shot to hell.

As the cortège passed the barricades, I was repelled from the spectacle and temporarily turned with half-hearted romanticism towards the part of the city that suffers no burns: the only way out. I was thinking of a means of survival. My favourite impression of Jean: fleet of foot, sprinting between threats of starvation and mortal enemies. Something has slipped. Lately, I've become the one with the canny sense and he's the dreamy one, retreating to his teetering desk as if all answers could be found in the pressure of pen against paper – his way of facing the parade of the dead. If they changed the names of the months, we would stand by the decision with supportive glee but shiver in cold rooms, having lost all sense of time, weakly measuring it by the towers of paper, scaffolds constructed by Jean's chronicles, his unpublished writings.

Clear-cut, easily defined sides are like the memory of an infallible innocence, a thing of the past. The innocence turns out to be fallible and shoddy, the sharply defined sides are blurred and turn out to be fake. I used to know how I thought the world should be and now I couldn't tell you anything.

1 APRIL 1848

Why do some people become completely immersed in the events of their time while their closest friends, the very people on the other side of the wall, are passed by? The latter continue to live their lives as if, barring the seasons, each day were undiscernably just like the last.

I saw Fabienne in the street and felt compelled to cross before she saw me. At her house two weeks ago she kept demanding to know my new address, the disclosure of which Jean has forbidden. He barely has confidence even in me. How many times can I say, 'I can't tell you'! Intrigues, she thinks, are the stuff of newspaper *feuilletons*. She interprets my secrecy as unfairly aloof. With unusual timing, an omnibus stopped in front of her and she got in it. Seeing me from a window she waved quickly and mouthed the words of a message I couldn't understand.

142

An emergency tax of 45 centimes has been levied to keep the government functioning. The lines grow longer. In them you might learn where to find cheaper bread or butter not so close to growing rancid. You might hear a man condemning an Orleanist scheme or fingering a Marxist plot. Sometimes a student, sometimes a shopkeeper or a gendarme will propose mass executions. This is the social critique you hear in bread lines.

The police are still looking for César's murderer. Although an arrest was made, the man was held only for a few days. The criminal, real or not, will be exhibited like a medal when he's found, as if to say, 'This is what we do to protect ours'. Jean is despondent. To go deeper into hiding, give up even his nightly trips and lie in a virtual closet where speech is limited to a whisper is impossible. He has begun to talk about leaving Paris. We have enough money between us to travel to Marseilles where we can board a boat and travel to Algiers. Jean addressed me, the window, shelves, desk, his reflection, as if he were spinning on a plate. Does he really believe in exile or is he just making a dramatic scene out of an impulse? Jean buttoned his coat up all the way, sat on the bed and spoke of a network of favours which eluded and excluded him, spoke in metaphors of grabbing and calcification. I didn't entirely understand him and I'm not sure where exactly this money we have in common will come from in order to get us to Africa. I find it difficult to trust the image of placid exile. How can he think Algiers is a clean slate, a new toy, starting out from the first day as if no others had preceded it? He might think self-effacing sultans and reticent women in diaphanous clothing will welcome him and all he thinks he stands for.

I suggested Switzerland. There, at least, French is spoken. Jean says no. People speak French in Algeria too. The Swiss are not very accommodating to foreigners with debts; fugitives are banned entry entirely. There are many French emigrés in Algiers, a large colony of *Quarante Huitards*, he's heard, and a friend of his has an uncle there who's all but promised him a job at his journal. Who is this friend? This person, this friend, emerged at exactly the wrong time. I wish I could manufacture such a friend in Geneva, Trieste, Venice. I wouldn't choose for the liaison to be in Africa, Brazil or New York. I don't believe in the virgin New World and question what I think will be a miserable life in Algiers. Jean, however, is intoxicated. How different our trip will be from Eugène's chaperoned excursion to Morocco. Phébus, too, had been there. He didn't stay long. ('The heat! The food! The Arabs don't trust the French. Why should they? Beggars and holy men done up in sheets. The women, too, unapproachable.') Both he and Eugène never stopped being European while in Africa. We will take a lot of the baggage of received ideas with us. It's a kind of colonialism unless Jean is willing to become African in a way I'm sure most European travellers are not.

4 APRIL 1848

We received word that the police are looking for the four women members of the *14 Juillet*, as well as the men. I don't know why we thought women would be treated in a discretionary manner. As far as rounding up suspects for the murder, suspicions don't stop at gender. I am no more safe going abroad in daylight than Jean, but I continue to go out sometimes. One of us must. The room Jean occupies grows too oppressive, rancid, the walls close in. Freedom in the streets is worth the risk. There are moments I believe someone is following me. I try to glimpse him in window reflections, trying not to turn around. So far all my shadows have been *flâneurs* or messenger boys.

Jean's speeches, which continue to sound idealistic to me, are also naive – even I can tell they are, and I'm to depend on him. It is his *idée fixe* that exile will be free from the edifices of institutions of culture and government and he wishes to leave behind the ruling classes of Europe which suffocate with their web of controlling interests. He's convinced social change will only take place in Europe after earthquakes, cataclysms and revolutions enough to erase all of it.

There is an empty place in the imagination of my contemporaries, a place of barrenness constantly in need of some kind of performance. The artists who were young in the 1830s had their romanticism born on the eve of one revolution, only to sputter out on the coattails of another. Jean believes this trip to be a consuming passion. Passion may turn into drudgery in North Africa. He makes up lists, makes boxes out of fragments of cardboard for his papers. I neglect cleaning, leave dishes and clothing scattered. I have a sickening fear of remaining alone in Paris; that the February Days may be repeated and the luck of a few feet and a few minutes may not be on my side this time and there may be no Jean de la Tour who thinks he knows all the answers and likes a narrow bed for two. We are to leave for Orleans in three days.

16 APRIL 1848

Two days ago over 10,000 workers assembled on the Champ de Mars. It was said to elect union officials but actually they planned to stage a march on the Hôtel de Ville. A panicky Lamartine called out the *garde municipale* to 'escort' the workers to the Town Hall, which they did in columns. Lamartine has a nervous man's sense of timing. He runs no chances, takes ill will for granted, and expects the worst at each hint of a problem. The incendiary element was in the air but the second revolution of the year was caught in a container of guards, always one step ahead. Jean says this last act by the provisionals has completely alienated the true *Quarante Huitards*.

Another voice in the lines, a man: 'The crazy journeymen bastards didn't know when they were well off. France should return to the Bourbon plutocracy and a genuine system of justice. People who don't respect the value of property ought to be made to pay for the damage they've done.'

145

February 1848: a date made into a symbol by both sides. As I become convinced of my own personal disappointment and collective disillusionment, the symbol casts events I thought quite complicated into simpler and simpler categories. Perhaps my ability to think critically is no longer up to the job. Symbols are a mental convenience.

28 APRIL 1848

We haven't enough money yet to leave Paris. The trip may not succeed at all. Jean no longer talks of Algiers very much but he has bought several maps and is still organizing his papers in cardboard boxes.

For each young man like Etienne or Jean who says the elections are meaningless, nothing's changed, there is a bitter person who says they knew it would be so. It's as if the paving stones formed barricades out of their own volition. The same group slips out of power and in again with a few names slightly changed. Some, like de Tocqueville, fall back into place as if nothing more than a gentle breeze had lifted them up and set them down again. *Les notables* remain in trust of the provinces.

16 MAY 1848

There have been revolutions all over Europe: Austria, Italy, Ireland and Poland. One hears speeches suggesting a great common alliance of the people against the kings and bankers. Yesterday Polish sympathizers congregated at the Place de la Bastille to march on the National Assembly. Many were arrested: Blanqui, Raspail, Thoré. Lunatics of every stripe were mixed with the genuine on each side. The offices of *La Vrai République*, Thoré's paper, were raided and ransacked. Everyone has their own private set of suspicions. If someone looks at you slyly you can report them for subversion, or they can have the finger pointed at you in return.

Eugène would say revolutions prove that the labouring

146

classes are just as greedy and devious as the bourgeoisie given half the chance. They are only less circumspect about it. I might tell him he's the one with the romantic vision; the bourgeoisie are ignoble, truly avaricious consumers, investors, ruthless exploiters – but he and I have been through this before. Who were all those people throwing bricks into windows and running out of shops with plates, top hats and hams under their arms? Didn't some of them have fashionable addresses, weren't they people who wanted to get something for nothing? What does it prove even if I'm wrong? If he were here Charles would tell me the disagreeableness was marginal, minor, happened on the periphery. He had a way of ensuring comfort beyond the material.

28 MAY 1848

Everyone suspects everyone else of something. While arranging his oranges, a greengrocer turns red, has a coughing fit and suddenly the whole block sees him shaking hands with *le père* Communism. All the imported oranges must be trashed. Expunging is the job of the police. The police compare themselves to surgeons rooting out diseased parts. Jean has stopped writing. All the neighbours wear César's face, anyone will expose friend or acquaintance. It clears grime off their own names a bit and makes them look good, or at least better than the next guy. Jean and I finish packing in a few hours and silently board a train at the Gare de Lyon for Dijon.

12 JUNE 1848

It isn't just the buildings that receded as the train pulled out but the spirit of Paris itself faded with an alacrity that hints at mental vacuity. Hours into the provinces I found a postcard in the train aisle of a vaudeville scene, a girl in a striped dress and a d'Artagnan figure. The city already seemed like a foreign place visited for a long time but a long time ago. The *Quarante Huitards* and all they represent are behind us and there is nothing but fields on either side, above or below. This is the Midi.

This is a story which isn't about storytelling, has no characters, no unfolding over time. Time is a context, a date scribbled on a page so as to endow the discourse on social theory a specific point in time and, therefore, a specific point of view. The date says, 'This is when I'm writing', not necessarily 'This is when it happened.' I envy the Madame de Staël of 1848, whoever and wherever she is: analytical, with an eye towards a world view, the institutions and literature that shape meaning and events. A woman who can forecast cause and effect from a hot air balloon that seems to rise through time, not space, and who from a height above Paris speaks most lucidly on revolution. History and human nature follow patterns: Roman against Visigoth, *Sans Culotte* against the king, capitalist against communist. It's not about La Fontaine or the Count of Monte Cristo. Let's have the facts straight out, not through some drama in three acts or many chapters, not through parable. (I know who I'd assign the roles of fox and hare but the exact mechanics of the rabbit's trick remain to be discovered.)

Other version:
The personal memoir: this is my life in a city that anticipates, then has revolution. Meetings about hoarding smuggled firearms and rhetorical speeches about class struggle, and then I'll tell you about how I bought oysters, very rare and unusual but fresh from a woman carrying them off a barge. It had just moored and the women came from a place where no news had yet been received about the February Days. I won't linger long on the personal because what everyone will want to read about are skirmishes in the street. At this juncture in the memoir, truth will yield to the more forceful stuff of embellishment and recast history. I will explain my changes in this way. Not everyone had procured a weapon,

certainly women were not armed. When guns were smuggled into cellars and garrets, women were instrumental in this process but nobody thought to get guns for girls. Because of my associations I was able to get a pistol, and although I'd never practised marksmanship by any means I became a perfect shot overnight. Be certain we're not just speaking of perfection, qualities of precision or other personal attributes. I'm a heroine in this memoir and the man or men I shoot are absolutely evil. I could afford to dine at Les Frères Provençaux each night but eat only bread and water like my compatriots.

The motion of the train projected us forward. The train consumed track the way my eye followed words on a page, one right after another in sequence without skipping. Railroad ties as they passed under us and sentences as I read them were perceived as units of time, the hours of travelling. My seat faced backwards while Jean faced ahead. I wanted to change places with him but he had fallen asleep.

We stopped in Dijon and engaged two seats to Lyon by carriage.

16 June 1848

Avignon

After a few days in Lyon we got places on a carriage bound for Avignon. Our fellow travellers were representatives for the textile trade. Their conversation became another way of measuring time while travelling: the going over of accounts, the discussion of each deal, each business transaction, concrete blocks, tailored facts, a game they're accustomed to, a game forged over generations occupied by the same family business. The reason, the structure supporting every decision, from firing an employee to selecting the right shirt, has precedent, history based on unvarying tradition. A game played with neat, square cards: shipping bills, franc notes and wool plaids. In their occupation there is an element of chance – the sheep could come down with a plague and lose their wool, silkworms could suffer from blight, or the workers might organize a strike, but there's really very little chance in this business and a great deal of security. Jean started to argue with them and I could no longer listen, but there was no train aisle, no hall or stairs, no way to find a few minutes of quiet.

Could I have continued to live in Paris alone? The further south we travel the more my sense of deracination increases, knowing the true desert is ahead, not behind. I could go back. I could take my passage money and return to Paris without Jean. Before we left I considered remaining alone, and it was at that moment I realized I was more dependent on Jean than I had ever been on Charles or anyone else. My situation in Paris has become dangerous to the extent that we've been forced to remain intertwined fugitives. I'd like to believe I'm capable of living alone in spite of the exigencies of the law. At the time she left *14 Juillet*, Pascale believed women should work out their own destinies apart from those of men. Men print newspapers, are elected to office, become educated as doctors, build houses. Women push brooms behind them, limited to truncated, insignificant kinds of performances. Once in a while someone casts a backward glance at the brooms and by virtue of that attention you have the exception who has eluded anonymity. Without the right to vote, own property or be educated, wives, mothers, mistresses, daughters play the role of sweeps to history, as much a part of an anonymous support system to men of the left as to men of the right. Pascale was not interested in maintaining the position of table legs while the dinner went on above and around her. She was extremely disillusioned with the men who called themselves revolutionaries, who sheltered themselves in secret camaraderies but were, in her mind, replicating the same patriarchal scheme they believed themselves fighting against. Their language recommended different economic remedies but these theories alone were no victory banner as far as she was concerned. She once told me they were all

150

chasing their tails, screwing themselves into the ground. If one were set on packing all the demons into one vast villain, Pascale believes its nomenclature ought to reflect the true enemy: tyranny of gender.

Fabienne, dim and distant, like the memory of 4 rue Saint Gilles before it was burnt, and she couldn't get past the door in white trousers. There were moments, days, when Fabienne was the animating spirit in my somnambulant brain, giving purpose to my irrationality. The last time I saw her it seemed her strength and impatience had only been rechannelled into an unhappiness over her own life. She was shocked that I'd acquaintances who knew how to make bombs and had no doubts as to the importance of using that knowledge, of passing it on to others and implementing those rudimentary explosives. I shouldn't have betrayed that particular secret because her shock disappointed me so much. To return to Paris now, I would have to change my name, find some means of employment, find new friends who wouldn't know I had been a *Juilletist*, wanted by the police. The secret police: the police of secrets, the men who root out secrets, the police who are secret because nobody knows their identity. One of them could appear to be snoring into his drink next to you while absorbing every word you whisper to your companion. So I would have to be scrupulously careful to avoid anyone who sat too close. I would change my name, change the colour of my hair, avoid certain parts of the city. Paris is invested with too much personal history. There are too many citizens who would recognize me from across the street and shout my name out loud with nothing but the best of intentions. Living constantly imperilled on familiar streets may shorten my life but I have no way of ascertaining how much more hopeless it may be in Algeria. The success of either project is not a venture I would stake bets on. What might I pursue?

I've the qualifications to earn my living as a governess to small children of wealthy families. There would be all kinds of contradictions inherent in that new life, giving private lessons to tiny barons and baronesses. Gradually, in spite of fear, I'd seek out sympathetic spirits, perhaps try to find Pascale, whom I'd like to see again, or even Fabienne's poet. Ultimately my identity as a subversive still living somewhere in France might endanger my mother and brother, or so Jean says, and I assume he's right. Soldiers have been known to torture families until they reveal the whereabouts of fugitive sons, daughters, and so on.

23 JUNE 1848

Dear Fabienne,

I am writing quickly in a little compartment in the train which runs from Avignon to Marseilles. When I was nine years old, my father took me on a trip to Avignon to visit one of his uncles, and fifteen years later sites, images I thought I'd never seen before have hints of familiarity. Avignon is circled by a great wall built as part of a fortress for fourteenth-century popes. The streets are close and narrow, almost passageways, the sense of enclosure, thereby, is continuous and I find it comforting, rather like the way you feel when you huddle under lots of blankets. A ruin of the palace built for the popes, a fragment of a medieval bridge which spans the Rhone; my father pointed to a bit of crenelated parapet and told me stories of great exotic feasts (food brought in from the east, spices never before tasted in France) and intrigues: dukes and bishops manoeuvring their authority within the rich papal see. Stories of children whose fathers could not be named, poisonous letters and infamous churchmen, tales uncomfortably transplanted from a stormy north to a sunny, warm south. I believed every one of them. When I returned to Boissey Saint-Leger, my brother had been born. His imminent birth had been the reason behind our trip all along, to get me out of the house. Young children don't witness these things, as you would know if you had any younger siblings. I don't suppose there'll be any surprises at the end of this journey. People are more open and talkative than in the north. Jean's lips are pinched together, guarded against the slightest slips. He resists any friendly bit of chatter because if information has a price, anyone, he says, can be bought. The cost of a dinner, even here, is too high for us to be idealistic about the other man's nice scruples. Surviving has a lot to do with flexibility, and nobody, Jean says, knows this better than the southerners, descendants of bishops. Jean, for each shopkeeper, becomes a symbol of the silent northerner. They know that rather than speak to each other, Parisians tear up their own streets. Jean and I went to the markets in Avignon which smell from piles of roasting hazelnuts, mussels and bowls of yellow *aioli*. The vendors yell across the squares to each other aggressively, as if their conversations required a much higher degree of animation in order to communicate simple exchanges. We were, indeed, starving in Paris. In the spice market we bought small bottles of marjoram, coriander and cumin which, although capped, still leave their smells in the upholstery of our second-class compartment. If you could persuade your father to leave the office of the *sous-préfet* and come here for a short holiday, he might find inspiration to change his notion of the comfortable.

On either side of the train tracks are very small *mas*, the Provençal word for farmhouse. These houses are one-storey buildings with flat roofs made up pink tiles. Sometimes the train passes small towns built on top of hills, centred around a church. Miles of vineyards become cherry and apple trees bearing green fruit, then return to vineyards again, and I often wish I could get off the train in the middle of a grove and migrate from farm to farm, doing what exactly, I don't know. Labourers look as patched and as ragged as the lowest dregs of Paris. You often see shepherds and shepherdesses in the middle of a few hundred sheep waiting for the train to pass so

153

they can move on. They probably speak a mixture of French and Provençal which we wouldn't understand.

Since I left Paris I keep asking myself how I got here, how I came to be on this train, fleeing to a location I can't name. Last year, as soon as Charles's phaeton turned into the Boulevard Beaumarchais, you leaned on my shoulder as if you were a bent old woman who'd had a completely impossible life but was full of advice due to her own bad luck. You stage whispered how fortunate I was to be rid of my husband, how as Madame Crozier I was out of my parents' house, had an independent income from the absent Monsieur C., to a certain extent could do as I pleased, and, for the outside world, appeared beyond reproach. At first, the pretence of virtue was slow to die, it was enough just to live alone and not plan my days around someone's presence or absence. *

30 JUNE 1848
Marseilles

Marseilles has a justified reputation as a southern city of free thinkers and so the news of the June Days in Paris arrived quickly and was greeted with interest. I have mixed feelings about these events, a desire to have participated and relief over the distance between me, the fighting and its aftermath. Regardless of the intensity of the convulsions, the final outcome makes all suffering appear an exercise in futility. It was just another temporary fit; now we're all obeying the laws of grammar, respecting syntax and speaking properly. The government disbanded the National Workshops, precipitating riots which made past demonstrations look like rides on the gay *guinguettes*. Barricades popped up again, 5,000 dead, many of them from the *garde mobile*, young men not yet twenty. Before we left, many foretold a final devastating confrontation

---

* In no form does this letter appear in the Ruban-Xavier archives. Apparently, it was neither finished nor sent. Willa Rehnfield

between the reigning gentlemen and the proletariat. These predictions were commonplace but the dissolution of the National Workshops finally set it off. Paris has become very dangerous, there are mass arrests daily – arrests based on the flimsiest complaint, or suspicion, before crime is even considered. The Préfecture of Police speaks of the 'possible attempt' at crime against the state. In order to deter it, to nip it in the bud, fill the jails. These are the June Days. From a distance the effect is like having the third act of a play described to you second hand after having seen the first parts for yourself. Jean is a jealous soldier and is impatient to leave France altogether.

2 JULY 1848

After three days in Marseilles, Jean has made a contact which will bring us some money. We have none left. A friend of a dead *Juilletist* met us at the Gare de Marseilles when we got off the train. It is a mystery how he recognized us, a mystery Jean prefers to ignore. The further away from Paris we travelled, the more control and command of the situation he exhibited. Jean de la Tour is not one to be hoodwinked by any provincial and he seems not to recognize his own fallibility. He knows all the lame horses, all the faults in the engine car, all the variables before they arise. Away from the criticality of his Parisian colleagues, he cuts the figure of a musketeer, or tries to; now we go to Orléans, and then on to Morocco. His canny sense, however, often puts him right on the mark, the horse does go lame and the train engine grinds to a halt half a league before some little town. But this train station contact, the man who smoked Turkish cigarettes, aroused my suspicions. The deal is we smuggle certain documents from Marseilles to Algiers in exchange for our passage and 7,000 francs upon safe delivery. Our means of passage is not exactly the vessel which brought Marie de Medici to Paris but a trading ship ultimately bound for the Ivory Coast.

There are several major prostitute districts in Marseilles: one near the opera (expensive), another near the harbour for sailors, and one close to the garlic market. It is *Foire aux Aulx** in the market near the centre of the city. Wreaths, garlands, long braided tails; from pale green, yellow and golden to withered brown cloves. A member of the lily family, a cure for colds, a remedy for arthritic conditions, a tireless cleanser of clogged arteries, stiff hearts, a restorer of virility and fertility. Tossed aside, they squelch dryly underfoot. I wandered into the prostitute quarter with a cluster of garlic dangling from a string round my neck, small white garlic skins clinging to my dress. The older ones are here at the edges of the market. A woman with glitter on her eyelids and at the corners of her eyes, I saw her first. Eyes enflamed and twitching from disease, early blindness decorated with glittery artificial crocodile tears. She sang to another who mimicked a Moroccan dancer, a wad of wrinkled veiling around her head. She twirled like an awkward little girl who had just discovered the momentum of spinning, turning on one leg and then another. The long yellow veil swirled around her, a Daumier satire of sensuality, an aged escapee from Rue Notre Dame de Lorette – but Daumier's satire is misdirected and offending. There is no image of their customers. No drunken sailors, magistrates or ship owners staggering from the *Foire aux Aulx* to their arms. The crocodile tears are for herself, since the disease originated with him.

I wandered into the fish market where *poissonières* yelled into the square about their fish. They seemed to direct their screams at specific individuals. I couldn't really understand their dialect, bits about fish smells and 'the head is the best part to eat'. Their gestures were vulgar and disturbing to me because they were so loud, pointed and incomprehensible, and I have never been so lost. I stopped in a café, bought

* Garlic Fair. It is still practised in southern France. W.R.

the cheapest food they had – *aigo buido*, a herb and garlic broth. In an old dress with garlic around my neck I thought I looked like the other women, and as long as I refrained from speaking to anyone my accent wouldn't give me away. An old woman sat down next to me with a bowl of *bourride*, fish and garlic soup. She asked me where I was from and didn't believe me when I said Aix. I told her my name was Marie-Laure. She said her name was Chantal. Her destiny had been Corsica, where she has two cousins, but when she got this far south, she heard that the French military in Corsica had become very strict, arresting anyone, especially those who are recent arrivals. Her cousins aren't well known on the island and could easily be considered 'free thinkers' by the local citizens. Chantal decided to go back north, perhaps to the Netherlands by a round-about route. She travels alone, carries a pistol, and often dresses like a man. Men have passed her by on the road when they might not have done so otherwise. She was afraid of getting conscripted into the Army by mistake. There was a story of a woman who'd had such a misfortune in Germany, ending up in jail, and Chantal would have to avoid the Prussian Army on one side and Alsace and Lorraine on the other. I didn't tell her I thought she was too old, although she explained she sometimes dressed as an old woman carrying a basket of hens or leading a dog on a string. Once she pretended to be blind which is easy to mimic. A woman like this presents no physical or monetary treasure. Concealed, anonymous, rogues of all classes have dismissed her as dross. Sitting beside a companion and occupied with eating, you need never actually see her face. Someone off near a cauldron screamed. Hot soup spilt and I jumped, and at that moment I turned around and saw the woman's face closely. She bore a few long scars on her left cheek. When I faced her she looked less old than I'd originally guessed. She was a woman who had called herself Chantal but certainly was the same woman I had known in Paris as Pascale.

I could imagine Jean saying, you trusted a woman in a café, you told her our plans. She had your confidence because she went to a few *14 Juillet* meetings. I could hear his detailed objections but I spoke to her as if I'd no responsibility to Jean, and confessed nearly everything. Our destination is North Africa. Pascale warned of the African myth. Like Corsica, Algiers is occupied by the French Army; be careful of the Zouaves, there's a different law there, it's not Paris. Jean knows this and he says in Algiers it's possible to undermine from within; in Paris all you can do is throw haphazard shots from the outside through a damaged and curtailed press. At best you could blow up a wing of the Louvre. Pascale/Chantal asks why should an Arab trust a Frenchman? In France you can be sure others will join your cause and be faithful to it. She dipped a chunk of bread in my soup without asking if I'd mind, a gesture which made me nervous after my confession. Pascale left Paris for reasons which are obscure, she didn't want to elaborate. The story of César didn't surprise her, he stank like a rat from the first and the secret police planted squealers in both unusual and obvious places. After leaving the *14 Juillet* she joined another Montmartre group which excluded men. There were vague spots in her narrative but I trusted her. Let Jean figure the double-spy logic to her story. Then sometimes I think, are Jean de la Tour and Lucienne Crozier really such significant fugitives? Aren't there worse murderers? Worse felons liable to create or smash empires at the slightest provocation are allowed to roam about as they please. Pascale reminded me there are many loose crimes casting about for scapegoats and nobody in the chaotic mess Paris has become is being too fussy about proof beyond the circumstantial. Pascale plans to leave Marseilles soon, perhaps in two days. She suggested I return to the same place tomorrow because she comes often. She wasn't interested in going to our rooming house with me. She asked me why Jean didn't change his name from the aristocratic de la Tour to Delatour. One part of Pascale's story impressed an additional fear of Paris upon me. There was a time when the word police suggested simple nouns and verbs related to concepts of law and justice which went relatively unquestioned. Even when questioned, when challenged, even when I knew the simple divisions of hero and villain were structures of childhood, I wasn't prepared for the meaning 'secret' attached to the word police. A branch of a department which enforces laws can be bent towards political ends. No, an inaccuracy, it's beyond mere bending. This is a state of extreme twists, of deformity. Their existence had been hinted at when someone disappeared but then there was always the possibility the missing person might just have gone off somewhere. It wasn't discussed openly, at least not in front of me. Once at a *14 Juillet* meeting a fellow seemed to have disappeared. People often came and went but this instance was considered odd because the man in question was a responsible fellow and due to address the club that night. His wife came to subsequent meetings hysterical; she'd found one of his shoes in the street. César gave a highly emotional speech about common criminals but I think he was acting cagey, presenting us suckers with a diversion. Yes, of course, Honoré was knocked on the head by a gang of illiterate boys, that's it. Many nodded, agreeing, and then one day there was nothing. No Honoré, no wife.

Pascale's twenty-two-year-old stepsister, too, had disappeared on her way home from work. She had taught at a school in Montmartre. Pascale could not go to the police because they were looking for her, so the friends from the school reported her disappearance. Her step sister arrived home a week later, ragged and delirious. The parts of her speech which made sense were horrible to the extent that these passages too, Pascale hoped, made no sense. Her speech didn't seem to describe the behaviour of humans, and so at first the stepsister's sanity was in question. Three men, she said, had grabbed her and taken her to a cell in what appeared to be part of a prison or police station. It wasn't dirty, she saw no other prisoners, so perhaps the place was neither of these; it had an anonymous character. She didn't know where she was or the identity of her captors, the perpetrators of what turned out to be a modern *auto-da-fé*. During the next days she was raped, beaten and asked where her sister was, but she genuinely didn't know because Pascale was in hiding. Finally they put a hood over her head and led her away in a carriage. She believed she was being taken away to be executed. When the hood was removed she was lying in her doorway. She died a few days later. Pascale now wishes she had given her secret to her stepsister if she would have suffered less. Even if it meant betrayal, they might not have tortured her. One of the sister's friends went to the police. She said she would go to the newspapers and the mayor if she had to, although why she made these naive threats Pascale didn't know. The friend, too, disappeared. A disfigured body floating down the Seine; mad rapist, the papers said, women should stay indoors after dark. Two more women died and the substance of their obituaries was altered to suit a crime wave. And nobody had a clue as to the identities of the real murderers. Pascale was bitter, no longer interested in claptrap about social reforms, she wanted to part with Paris entirely.

They say you get used to the smell of fish, that after a while the smell becomes an integral part of the air you breathe, but by the time the day of oblivion comes for me I'll be in the desert, far from flounder, mackerel and *poissons de roche*. On the waterfront, people creep around piers, boats, rooming houses such as ours. They lurk around waterfront bars by day and take boats out by night. These are dealers in Fabienne's poetic cigars, not the sort to traffic in legitimate plaids like the men with whom we rode into Avignon. Her poet had detailed the story of the leaves' provenance, savouring the element of danger, emphasizing the risks. From North Africa by boat, over the Pyrenées, borders crossed in the dead of night, contraband sewn into borders of dresses, hems of trousers, coats, and hidden in secret compartments of portmanteaus.

8 JULY 1848

Jean regretted not seeing Pascale, and the intensity of his

regret suggested the extent to which he misses Paris. He never expresses remorse about anything. Sensing doubts, I propose we reverse our steps and travel to the Netherlands, but for Jean the water closed over our tracks a long time ago. We have no choice but to continue south. 'Amsterdam, why Amsterdam?' No reason. Respecting Pascale's confidences, I didn't lay my head in Jean's lap and reveal everything. There's little chance we'll ever see her again. Jean sticks to making the concrete arrangements for the journey. We no longer talk abstractly about North Africa and I've given up asking him questions. We discuss the practical as if we were preparing to do something very simple. The ominous threat, lurking and emanating from Paris, has begun to recede a little. I'm not to know the documents we're smuggling out of France.

I spent half the night preparing a letter to my mother and brother, to be mailed just before we board ship for Algiers tomorrow. My brother may be mildly excited: his sister is a revolutionary, she lives in exile in an exotic place, and so he'll feel a cut above his dull classmates at the university. My mother will be disconsolate. Even if she attributes my departure to an inheritance of my father's republican spirit (he was a hearthside revolutionary), even if she believes it began with the bad business of the Crozier marriage, she'll derive no reassurances from the justification.

Dear Christophe,

There are two items in this package, both are for you. The first you are familiar with, the second, no one but myself has ever seen before. The drawing of the woman in Moroccan costume you know as just an old drawing that hung above my writing desk since you can remember. I have chosen this moment, your twentieth birthday, to tell you this drawing is a portrait of my friend Lucienne Crozier who died in Algiers before you were born. Before she died she sent me her journal, begun in 1847. She didn't want to destroy the diaries, nor did she want them read by the people around her after her death.

In her last letter she asked me to write to Eugène Delacroix and request the portraits. I did what she asked and he sent me the Moroccan costume portrait and a drawing he did from memory perhaps prompted by my request for two pictures. Lucienne could not have known about the latter as it is dated after her death. I suspect that in her delirium she may have been referring to the lost portrait. In any case I am sending you the Moroccan portrait, signed by Delacroix, and her journal. The other portrait will go to your sister. You are old enough to know what these things mean. I have always regretted not travelling to Algeria to be with Lucienne at the end, as I believe she was quite alone. Write to me when you receive this package so I may be assured of its safe arrival.

Love,
Your mother

Fabienne Ruban-Xavier
Neuilly-sur-Seine
France

EPILOGUE

In her introduction Dr Rehnfield neglects to tell the reader how she acquired the original French-language diary begun in 1847 by an otherwise undocumented Frenchwoman. There's not a single reference to who gave her the text to translate and under what circumstances the job was assumed. Of well-known diarists the provenance of their journals as objects is literary history. After their deaths Anne Frank, Alice James and Virginia Woolf had father, brother and husband respectively as caretakers of their private writings. Delacroix's journal was copied over by a man named Robaut and the original subsequently disappeared. It was found again in 1924, but had this not been so the Robaut version would have had to be trusted. Compared with the original, they say the Robaut copy contained many discrepancies and misreadings. Before the time of the camera never lies, before the days of xerox, the clerk's language could supplant or even contradict that of the original, opening up all kinds of possibilities for scholarly back-tracking and confusion. Dr Rehnfield pressed her passages over the lines; a blurry palimpsest, she was the Robaut of Lucienne Crozier's diary. Her language has become L. Crozier's, her framing intrudes into the picture, her involvement with the papers has become part of what the diary is. Like *The Aspern Papers*, this is a story of deceit and subterfuge, but unlike Henry James's narrator, no calamity befell Willa Rehnfield. She got the papers; perhaps they were a footnote to her real goal, but she did acquire them, and without having to pretend she was interested in old Venetian gardens, court the suspicious or feign love for the reclusive. The draft of the introduction found with the translation has a personal manner, as if Willa were having a friendly little chat with herself on paper. I began to consider what the translator skipped, blanched at and erased, or forgot to include altogether, as if by accident. It's a lacuna the eye ignored because the overall pattern was taken for granted – suddenly the gap stood out and became the whole text, the whole story.

To find the missing configuration, we can start with a name mentioned in the acknowledgements, Luc Ferrier, or perhaps we should start with me. I'm the one who packed up Willa Rehnfield's papers after she died in 1982, packing them off, according to her last wishes, to be donated to her college library where they'll be sealed in storage until a future student of literature or art history expresses a desire to see the Rehnfield papers. A librarian, one month, may think they'll make an interesting display in one of those glass cases near the card catalogue and, with single-edge razor blades or scissors in hand, she'll slit the bands of tape. There is nothing more inert than barely legible papers on subjects which, though once of grave importance to someone, death renders nearly meaningless. Meaningless, at least, to the person into whose hands they fall. Not all heirs are or were devoted. I was neither heiress nor fanatic but an employee. Anonymously, unknown to future students and librarians, I executed Willa's request honestly and to the letter, armed with cardboard cartons, reinforced paper tape and catalogue checklist. Every book, every bound manuscript and folder was packed away and picked up by a man from United Parcel Service, except for this translation which I took from a file drawer and kept. Stolen, as certainly as the original was, I took its copy, carrying on a tradition. I excised *The Lucienne Crozier Diary* from the catalogue (under the category *Unpublished Works*) so nothing will appear to be missing when the dozen or so cartons reach Amherst, Massachusetts. This was my first task after Dr Rehnfield entered the hospital and the last thing I ever did for her. She gave me the keys with misgivings, I could tell. For an apartment which held so many valuable things,

Willa believed the fewer keys the better. Her dominant sense of a work ethic was at odds with her suspicions. She relinquished authority to me as late as possible.

Everything in Dr Rehnfield's life was documented some-where, from plots of novels never written to observations on city dogs in the rain, but as she grew ill and forgetful, these became more extensive. C for Castro, M for Manet; as I went through her files after her death, I discovered notes on the backs of income tax forms, receipts, envelopes, margins of magazines. Willa was inescapable, but the bits written in the last months of her life reflected the break-down between her ability to make concrete decisions in the present and her memories which inserted themselves as the present at odd and unpredictable moments. In the path of her drive to label and annotate lay the fear of discovery. Knowledge of her lapses and dwindling state elicited pity, which she didn't like, but worse, she thought someone might exploit her moments of flighty judgement and she'd end up on the street, wandering lost in Central Park. She also expressed a fear that the barrier between certain thoughts and speech would cease to hold. It was as if her mental slips might preclude all kinds of admissions of guilt. Anxious as a guilt-ridden murderess whose crime had remained undetected, she grew nervous. If disease eroded enough of her guard, all kinds of con-fessions might slip out. She was afraid of being mentally burglarized. Her hair receded, making her head appear fragile, vulnerable; the skin around her eyes approached an ashen purple and then grew altogether grey, as if she had been weeping a corrosive chemical. Mirrors became in-explicably cracked, were removed but never replaced. Her vanity, up until now, had survived the incursions of ageing fairly well but couldn't adjust to so many rapid transform-ations, most of them brought on as much, she thought, by the medicine as by the illness itself. Before she entered the hospital she had grown so cadaverous, the moment of death had already been attenuated into several weeks. The notes, the process of thinking in sentences and writing in words, were, for Willa, as much evidence to the contrary as she could summon. She refused a wheelchair but often had to lie down. Lying down, eyes shut for a few minutes, the minutes grew into an hour, two hours. I opened her mail, answered letters as if she were there but she wasn't there. She slept. With little to do I'd go to the kitchen, have coffee with the cook and the new nurse. The cook wondered whether she should start looking for a new job or stick it out and apply for unemployment later. The nurse laid out beautiful sets of pale blue, green and speckled pills, disposable syringes. She would always work. Mornings usually maintained a business-like plan but by afternoon the difference between her waking speech and her speech as she emerged from sleep grew indistinct. Not a fragile or submissive woman, disease had to win a large percentage of her body and mind before she would allow me to have any major responsibilities as far as her work was concerned. At that late point, when she entered the hospital for the last time, I needed to have access to all her papers if I were to organize them. She warned me not to keep the keys together with my address book in my bag. She was afraid that if it were snatched somehow the keys would be linked to the Rehnfield address and tried in the door which, of course, they fit. Willa asked me not to scratch any initials on the keys for the same reason. It wasn't the kid with the nylon stocking, the do-rag tied around the top of his head like a *haik*, the one who happened to take the #3 downtown or the F train in from Brooklyn. There are other kinds of thieves with a more sophisticated network of fences than Flatbush Avenue dealers. The ones who know who owns what and when owners take vacations. Smart crooks in suits, Willa feared these white-gloved men, but how would they ever recognize her keys out of millions? During her last month the aberrations caused by Dr Rehnfield's fears exerted themselves as if she lived (and had always lived) in a remote, isolated small town where everyone knew everything about her. I found an ancient bottle of Raven Red nail polish in one of her drawers and painted her keys to distinguish them from my own. No one would connect her address with a pair of red keys.

The doorman, she had thought, was too friendly and too naive. To obscure gender, her mailbox read only Dr W.E. Rehnfield, and occasionally an elderly resident of 12 East 84th Street would ask her for medical advice. To the residents of #12, the term of my employment represented no time at all, and now it's just about over. The doorman's uniform, the dark veneer of the wood, the faithfulness of employees and the gratitude of grandchildren are intended to last, to endure. I would have liked to sit in the dark foyer, watch a man named Frenchie and the doorman run numbers in their spare time. Like a good boarding school in financial straits, the lack of capital, or perhaps just lack of interest, was beginning to show. The opulence was restrained, the evidence pointed to rich people. It didn't matter that chair cushions were wearing thin, baseboards and the tops of frames remained dusty. The ground floor was irregularly shaped; oddly placed alcoves sheltered heavy chairs, tables and mirrors; the group near the stairs held a Chinese vase filled with parrot tulips. A few purple-black petals lay on the table. This is a signal: the cleaning woman who sings Christmas carols to herself all year had Thursday off. Two weeks have passed since Dr Rehnfield's death. The condolences no longer arrive. Frenchie sticks his head in the hall, says to the doorman, '171 Maurice', and disappears down the street. Maurice pulls at the cuffs of his jacket and looks out of the door to 84th Street. For perhaps another week, maybe two, Dr Rehnfield's assistant can pretend she's in Paris riding the glass elevator to the fourth floor.

Had she not been born into a fortune, had she been forced to have some kind of job, I used to think she would have done well as some kind of lab assistant, constantly feeding rats, putting them through their mazes and recording data. Not bound by the restraints of having to make judgements, she would have been happy interpreting symbols into numbers and back into language, codifying systems of meaning. This was one of several initial misconceptions I

167

entertained about Willa. She was much more than an anonymous hinge. Her bailiwick extended so much further than that of an objective observer, based unobtrusively on the margins of the text, innocent, beyond reproach, stripped of the responsibility of drawing conclusions. Her prejudices were invasive of her translations and she felt both weighted and compelled by them. There was an element of the missionary in the translator.

If it's true the role of translator requires at least a pretence of neutral, objective behaviour, the pretence held only sporadic interest for Dr Rehnfield. Choices of words are bound to be influenced by bias, predilection and whim, and Willa often indulged in her ability to affect style, if not meaning. She was offended by suggestions of restraint or arbitration. A word, she might explain, is not simply transformed with equal weight into another. One hour doesn't translate into sixty minutes; an ice cube isn't the same as melted water in the bottom of a glass. As the value of pounds to dollars to francs shifts in the process of conversion, so does the power of suggestiveness between languages, and the currency of influence is inflated or devalued accordingly. If, as a translator, she was supposed to be a faithful conduit, her neutrality was malleable, riddled by hard and fast opinions.

There was a pattern to the kinds of subjects which held Willa's fascination. Over and over she underlined passages about women who might describe barricades, picket lines or cellar meetings of the partisan gun runners. She searched for precedents among the documentation. The fixed core of her everyday life was an unalterable code of inactivity. Self-imposed invalidism, with or without actual illness, undermined her perceptions of her favourite subjects or perhaps made her interpretations more resolute, less mincing. Without the original, the point of view of the initial narrator might be as difficult to pin down as the ace of diamonds in three-card monty. She wondered why some women, all of whom were born in 1824 and read *The Three Musketeers*, cocked a snook at authority while others stayed home. What turned some nineteen-year-old women into bomb throwers while others just covered their noses with wet handkerchiefs (against the tear gas) and took the long route to class. She felt affection towards those who went to class no matter what. I never told Willa that firebombs and Molotov cocktails were the only bombs which were actually *thrown* and they were used infrequently. Most bombs were planted by deliberate design. Lucienne would not have approved of her. Whether I did or not no longer matters. I needed to be paid off the books. Dr Rehnfield assumed I didn't want to pay taxes. She didn't ask for references.

Willa jumped when a glass was overturned, screamed if she accidentally touched a hot object, though she rarely did her own ironing or approached a hot stove. Split seconds of panic, chaotic overlords reigned, reason eliminated, booted out – not for good, but what if the fit didn't pass? She interpreted these bits as micro versions of the experience of large-scale violence. So they held no fascination for her, contemporaneous rebellions or terrorism. If a United Nations mission was blockaded she walked a distance out of her way to avoid it. In the shards of broken glass lying on her floor she saw gutted buildings. In the second her electrocardiogram expressed terror she saw no hope of that terror subsiding. She predicted weeks of panic.

For years Lucienne was the subject Willa searched for in the mustiest, least-travelled parts of private libraries, in collections of papers the heirs didn't know what to do with. As each file was opened, each portfolio untied, the dust blown away, there must have been some disappointment. The brief, crabbed diary of the uncle who liked to sail off the New England coast, or the letters of a cousin in the Peace Corps in Malaysia, none of this was interesting to her. Documents which constituted a grave disappointment to her, she sat cross-legged on the floor, spine leaning against the bookcase, until the Lucienne Crozier diary was presented to her almost by a combination of chance and Odilon's lack of curiosity.

Che Guevara said, 'There is nothing which educates an

169

honourable man more than living in a revolution.' Willa, had she lived in Paris in 1848, would have resisted education, as she did 120 years later. Her resistance was the resistance of a passionate voyeur, and the notebook labelled *L.C.* was an open window with all the lights blazing. During the execution of the translation there was no editor, no publisher, no heiress holding Willa to accuracy.

Rémy Gommereux wasn't the only one who romanticized simple working women, fixing them on to lambent fictional scenes of interesting, satisfying labour. For Willa these romantic notions were rooted in what she saw as the mercurial nature of her family's fortunes. She was always doubtful of its perpetuity and as a student she feared its sudden collapse, an open abyss which would leave her on the other side. She would have been obligated to give up school, return to New York City and take a job. She would become a worker, an adult who punched in and out of a job, who received a paycheque calibrated according to the accumulated sweeps of the time-clock hands. Reading *The Maltese Falcon* or *Mildred Pierce* between the eight and ten o'clock shows in the ticket booth of a Broadway movie house, she would be a figure in an Edward Hopper painting which was never painted. It didn't occur to her that the softly lit scene of a woman in a three-sided glass booth might represent, among other things, a dull job. Willa never did learn this. Her fortune was good for another generation, at least. Willa never had to apply for any sort of employment. The financial cataclysm didn't happen during her lifetime. In early 1968 Willa was waiting in the lobby of a cinema watching Mademoiselle X collect francs and pass tickets back under the glass. The telephone may have rung. '*Le film commence à vingt et vingt-deux heures, Madame.*' Willa watched coloured tickets for different shows spew out. After 10.30 Mademoiselle X would have locked the cash box, handed it to the Indian manager and taken the Metro home, or perhaps met a friend at Café Voltaire. Willa instantly conceived of a whole French history in volumes, going back in time, starting with 1968, a history from the point of view of the ticket taker's family. Lucienne Crozier was her great grandmother. A fictional epic conceived by chance on a rainy Saturday night on the Boulevard Beaumarchais.

She read, *'Tu parles comme une charretière'* and wrote, 'You talk like a horsedriver.' It was 1968 and she watched the Chicago riots on television, travelled, translated and made out a will. She mourned Luc Ferrier's death, and briefly puzzled over it. I was at Berkeley. Later on I would arrive in New York under the name Jane Amme. Amme is Emma spelled backwards, for my grandmother, for Goldman and for Bovary. *L'âme* is the French word for soul and there's a pun on aim. After 1970, when I arrived in New York from Berkeley, I might have seemed to have anything but definite aims.

The file room was a kind of paper purgatory. Her system for cataloguing worked like an accordion, always expanding to accommodate future additions, treating the ephemeral as if it were anything but mass-produced. Once I read a table which rated countries according to the pounds of paper consumed per year per citizen. The table included all kinds of paper: books, hamburger wrappers, social security cards. The United States, Japan and western Europe came first, and from there the poundage dwindled to something like two pounds for Somalia and Bangladesh. Fragility: paper garbage blows down streets like Willa's, as well as mine. There is so much surplus to go around. Doormen and supers sweep, windows are shut but the surplus continues to pile up. It always returns. Fire was a big threat to the file room. Years ago Willa had a layer of asbestos installed, deciding that if the insularity of her life and perishability of her work necessitated a carcinogenic aggregate, she'd take her chances. Locked in the file room, a kind of giant diary sealed in steel, the audience she sustained was primarily my own solitary investigations.

The main purpose of the files was to account for her translations and notes. Translation is a filter, there is always some refraction. Willa was no novelist, poet, screen-writer, playwright or journalist. She may have wanted to be but never was. Given a text, it's a ready-made, like Duchamp's bottle rack, but she goes further than Duchamp. She would begin by taking the work apart. Later it would be reassembled. First the most important sections, chapters and passages would be translated, then she would work backwards. The last step, with paper-clipped bundles of pages lying around her, was to reassemble them back to their original order. For other translations she would extract one character, follow him or her through the entire text, then go back and fill in the rest of the narrative. This technique contributed to the maintenance of a very personal relationship with the characters. There have been a few characters for whom she felt qualified to write biographies, biographies entirely independent of the books from which the characters themselves sprang.

Surrounding the file room was a U-shaped room. They fit, one nestled inside the other, like a larger-than-life dovetail joint. Willa turned the room into a gallery, another room which required not only lock and key but also burglar-alarm systems. A glass door opening on to a balcony one storey above the street caused the burglar-alarm and insurance people furrowed brows, but curling iron grilles were installed and everyone's fears, including Willa's, receded with the click of the lock. Instead of white walls and track lighting, Willa moved oak panelling from another room into the gallery and had little brass lights fastened over each picture. Apart from the use of electricity, it was a nineteenth-century manner of displaying paintings. The gallery was not unlike the file room it invisibly sheltered, a combination sanctuary and warehouse.

Art handlers have come from the Metropolitan for the Turkish manuscript illuminations, the Napier photograph of a French suffragette, and the tiny Cézanne, but I couldn't find the portrait of Lucienne Crozier in the gallery or in storage. Delacroix dressed her as if she were the five-jointed Barbie doll of his late Romantic dreams. Lucienne

172

treated him in the same manner but she was powerless. Her cavalier attitude didn't get her anywhere. They engaged in a drawn conversation. The woman smiled and looked west. It had been 1847. She and Delacroix pulled clothes off and on each other as if it weren't 1847 and the July Monarchy would go on forever, and neither gave much thought to the Cult of the Rev. That moment was all about pleasure, accuracy and disguise. The Rue de Faubourg Saint Honoré was not yet fashionable. Napoleon's body was brought back to Paris for a hero's reburial. The portrait probably told little. Except for a date or a signature, it would have eluded a context, as if the face might have belonged to any number of women, at any moment, one hundred years before World War II. Willa might have told the owner, Luc Ferrier, it was an anonymous picture, inconsequential. There had been no trunkful of Arabian clothes, no ransacked house on Rue Saint Gilles, no search through post-revolutionary debris. She told him that in 1883 Pissaro drew Gauguin, handed him the paper, then Gauguin drew Pissaro. Twin portraits, the seer and the seen and back, the portrayed and the portrayer, then reversed.

4 January 1847

Near the school house in
woman in a funny house
herself and often
moiselle Pit
girls

A corner of Willa's handwriting. I saw the edge sticking up out of a trunk, a brown spiral notebook, plain and ordinary, covers bent back. Willa often wrote in them. What school? What funny house? I pulled it out, rolled like a calyx, and unfurled the pages. Dr Rehnfield's Introduction was clipped to the back cover. Here was a code which would help me decipher Willa's filing, a sign pointing to a scheme of organization. I knew I was looking for a particular hand, a

173

bundle of documents written in French, not Willa's English. There were clues to the end of Lucienne's story hidden in the towers of paper Dr Rehnfield accumulated and produced during her lifetime.

Her files were arranged alphabetically, from A to Z, but the contents of drawer M, for example, might not contain folders whose contents uniformly began with that letter. Willa had her own system, from Abstract Expressionism to Zeus. Under C, for Childhood, was the record of her first European tour: a notebook with postcards and candy wrappers glued in. In London in 1945 Willa's aunt suggested she keep a notebook to record her impressions of her first trip to Europe. In London and in Paris she saw the lone walls of burned and bombed-out buildings like sharks' fins sticking out of waves in a sea of brick, twisted pipe and splintered wood. She wasn't deliberately taken to these neighbourhoods, the car drove past on the way to other places. The aunt felt responsible for her little niece's tour but did not indulge in the maternal instinct for editing. Aunt Megan bought her a notebook, blunt scissors and glue. Following her descriptions of the Elizabethan portraits at The National Portrait Gallery and the white dresses of the Royal Ballet, Willa wrote how at the theatre her Aunt Megan rubbed a spot on her blouse over and over, absentmindedly, as if she thought no one was watching. A few days later, fearing Aunt Megan would read the page, she tore it out and tossed it in the can near the bed. Her aunt had been gone quite a long time but was expected soon to take her to dinner. Willa lay on her stomach, wrote, watched the clock and waited. As she waited she retrieved the wad of discarded paper and smoothed it out again. Listening for the sound of her aunt in the hall, she glued the sniping note back in the book. At some point in the future, she reasoned, she might want to remember that lovely Aunt Megan could suffer embarrassment just the same as everyone else. She returned late that night and took Willa out for cakes shaped like hats with cherry brims.

From this savings bank of notes, a tentative self-portrait could be constructed. There were sections, periods of years which eluded documentation or remembrance. In the weeks following her death, this shadow of language became an almost identical twin of the real, the late Willa Rehnfield. A helter-skelter paper sibling expressed a kind of solidarity for her. When Dr R. pulled a chair up to the PSY-RAT drawer, she felt sure her life was constructed along clear narrative lines. What happened to her, how she arrived at her position, hadn't been the result of a series of random meetings on trains or in waiting rooms. Because there were days when she felt like a little animal swatted across the room by a big dog, because she felt herself a marked victim for random violence (collapsing tunnels, international terrorists, Hurricane Alice), surrounded by her works there was purpose and linear structure, cause and effect.

As her assistant, my job after her death was a sort of final chapter and index combined. I moved all the file cabinets into a circle under the sloped roof of the library, uneven teeth in an architectural yawn. After a week of sorting, reading and packing, my Dewey decimal system of organizing the papers was working, the masses shifted and I had a beginning to the story of Lucienne Crozier's diary. It began in 1968.

She was in an airplane over England when the plane began to shake. Engine trouble, turbulence, whatever it was, Willa didn't pay attention to the explanation. She flew often but had a tremendous fear of flying. It wasn't the idea of crashing on impact or being trapped in a huge cigar wrapped in flames, but what really frightened her was the duration of the instant you realize you have sixty seconds left to live, still able to see the burning engine and flames slicing up the body of the plane. They were over the Channel, perhaps over Lille, almost to Paris, then the plane arrived at Orly. There were no warm greetings for Willa when she descended from the plane. No one was there to meet her save the silent chauffeur of Monsieur Xavier who drove her to the Xavier house on Boulevard Beaumarchais. No, Madame, Monsieur Bob, the chauffeur, hadn't heard any of the reports of airplane trouble. Monsieur Bob's silence made her feel as nervous as Jonathan Harker being driven to Count Dracula's castle but far more neglected. She noticed a racing form on the front seat next to Monsieur Bob. On the plane she wrote a letter to a man, two sentences, not a letter really, thinking it would be her last, hoping that as the Air France lost altitude somehow this sliver of paper could survive although her corporeal self might become charred beyond recognition. In the back of the car, driving into Paris, the sensation of solid ground seemed like the most wonderful gift. She felt as if she'd slipped out of an elevator just before a blackout, survived the electric chair, escaped over the Berlin Wall. She was at the narrow end of the wedge, the acute corner, luck was on her side and she rolled her last letter into a wad, opened the latches on her suitcase and shoved it inside. (A few days ago I found it smoothed out and stuck in the FA-KYR file drawer.)

Odilon Xavier, the great-grandson of Fabienne, lived with his wife in a large house when they were in Paris – about half the year. Since she arrived in the middle of the night, the Xaviers were asleep and the maid showed her to her room. Dr Rehnfield had been referred to the Xaviers by a mutual American friend, Luc Ferrier. The Xaviers were in possession of a number of works of art they wished to sell; paintings by Bonnard and Vuillard, some drawings, a Delacroix among them, a few letters written by Baudelaire, Saint Beuve, Julian Halévy, Proust and others. Madame Xavier had collected these but was too old and infirm to take much pleasure from them. The Xaviers had no children and Monsieur X. wanted to dispose of these objects and invest the money in a business venture with Ferrier which required capital. Willa was to examine the documents, translate them and courier them back to America. It was and still is illegal to sell and transport works of national importance out of France. Monsieur X. wanted cash. A means of smuggling the works out of the country had been arranged but Willa wanted to be ignorant of it. Airport

176

contacts, private boats travelling at night, closely watched ports, strange men on trains – she believed if she were ever engaged in a confrontation she would be a lousy actress and all manner of names and secrets would bubble out of her in a long unedited list. Luc waved her doubts aside, as a man who held down his tie with sprays of diamonds might, but he respected Willa's wish not to know. It may have been a problematical yet undiscussed point between them, a sticky matter which involved accusations of flexible morals and cowardice on each side. She was afraid he resented her flashes of puritanism, flashes like the one she felt when she saw the racing form lying on the seat next to the chauffeur. He was ignorant of that impulse, but had he known he would have asked her why Monsieur Bob shouldn't read about the horses? Why should he care whether an unknown American woman dies in a plane crash over the United Kingdom? Why shouldn't Ferrier take paintings out of France?

She had told Luc a story she knew to be true. A seemingly impoverished aristocratic family, which lived somewhere in Champagne, wished to sell a portrait which was, in fact, a work of national importance in France. Not a *Madame Récamier*, but a valuable painting by most standards. A German dealer was contacted as a potential buyer. He visited the family and all seemed genuine. He wished to buy the painting but all parties involved knew it was illegal for the painting to cross the French border. The French dealer, middleman between the family and the German, suggested that a landscape could easily be painted over the original portrait and the landscape layer simply removed once the portrait was in Germany. This was done, the painting paid for, and the work shipped to Munich. When the German dealer removed the new layer of paint, however, the image underneath was not the portrait he paid for but a worthless still life. Oranges. Bananas. He'd been tricked. And impotent, too, since he'd been part of an attempted ruse to begin with. Apparently this French team of family and bogus Parisian dealer staged this scene many times. They were making quite a lot of money.

177

Beside the notes on this story was an article clipped from a newspaper, probably the *New York Times*. The reporter had spoken to a detective from the New York Police Department, a representative of a new division whose purpose was to investigate art theft. In large letters in the middle of a column: 'Great paintings are being sold on street corners.' Organized crime was getting involved, stockpiling stolen art. When the squad recovers art from a heist, he had said, they rarely retrieve every object. Many things just disappear. 'Any painting or sculpture over 100 years old has changed hands illegally somewhere along the line.' Willa had underlined this hypothesis. It could have begun with Napoleon, Magellan, Roman conquerors. There had been Goering and Goebbels. There were whole Incan temples transported half-way around the world.

When Willa woke around noon, Monsieur X. had long since left for his day at the Bourse. In the middle of spreading butter on a brioche and swallowing strong coffee, the maid brought her a package wrapped in thin-striped paper, the stuff paper-doll business suits might be cut from, and a note.

Dear Mademoiselle Rehnfield,

    I hope your journey was safe and you will be well rested by the time you read this note. It is unlikely that we will actually meet until the end of the week since I leave very early in the morning to attend my business and, unfortunately, engagements each evening prevent me from returning to Rue Beaumarchais at a sociable hour. I regret, also, my wife is not in Paris at this time. She convalesces in Aix. I leave you this bundle of letters and other documents which I will sell to our friend Luc Ferrier and look forward to your opinion as a scholar. Luc's Cuba-Spectrum scheme is very intriguing, do you not think so? I look forward to meeting you. Luc has spoken so highly of Mlle Rehnfield. Again, accept my apologies for not being able to perform as a visibly gracious host.

    Odilon Xavier

I found one letter in Willa's file about Cuba-Spectrum, the venture that required the art sale. It was a letter written on Cuba-Spectrum stationery. The letterhead bore a logo which combined the letters 'C' and 'S' and looked suspiciously like a cigar. His company was to act as a liaison between American corporations with business interests in Cuba and the Cubans. Things were still a bit tentative, the letter suggested, but if the Cuban door were opened just a crack, there were lots of anxious clients in the waiting room. Willa wrote an unmailed reply on the back of his letter.

The Cuba door sounds very much like the Chinese door and the Brazilian door, to say nothing of the oil door, and 'door' as far as Luc Ferrier's schemes are concerned, is a ridiculously diminutive metaphor. He is as at ease talking sugar industry to the Mr Coca Colas as he is talking to the Senor Martinezes, formerly of Havana, now of Miami Beach. The ideology of any government is as immaterial to Luc as a half-chewed cigar, as long as that government makes things easy for investors, as long as the half-chewed cigar doesn't fall in your soup. What interests L.F. is profit margins. When we first met, his conversation had been threaded with theoretical 'if you could separate A and B, or merge X and Y' but he had long since actually been handling A, B, X and Y, as well as many other letters. There is overt business and there is covert and to most of the world they are separate systems which mix only in spy stories or novels written by former State Department aides or journalists. Luc mixes the two to his advantage but he'd be the last one to write about his dealings so as to paint himself the bad guy. I warned him some day South American guerrillas, militant Moslems, or leftist lawyers would give him A, B, X and Y right back, rendered useless.

At the moment Kennedy was shot, a CIA agent gave a Cuban operative a syringe filled with *black leaf* to assassinate Castro. The re-link up with the old Havana mafia never came about.

Neither did Cuba-Spectrum. Willa didn't care about Cuba-Spectrum. She didn't want to know about the project, automaticallly becoming preoccupied with papers, a radio, her stocking, whenever smuggling was discussed. Carex Industries began bidding against Bechtel and United Technologies for government contracts. Willa thought it was just about computer parts. Then computer parts turned into military technology, the kind applied in animated weaponry used in Vietnam; next he would sell to Caribbean (with the exception of Cuba) and South American countries. She thought of the time Luc came to look at a painting she wished to sell and didn't leave until the next morning, but that was eight years ago. She turned to the parcel of papers Monsieur Xavier had left her.

The nineteenth-century letters were carefully placed in alphabetical order in an album. They would be interesting to libraries and possibly to a few individual collectors. Monsieur X. would get some money for them but not a sum which was likely to mean much to the wealthy Odilon. Underneath the album was a leather-bound book which looked over a hundred years old. The initials 'L.C.' were engraved into the brown leather, a few streaks of gold clung to the grooves. Another note from Odilon said briefly that the book had been written by a friend of his great-grandmother. He didn't know if it was worth anything but the woman who wrote it seemed to know a few painters. There was a mention of Baudelaire: perhaps she had had an affair with him, thought Odilon Xavier. If Mademoiselle Rehnfield would take a look at the diary, he hoped she could give him an idea of its value. Dr Rehnfield might include it in the papers she was to turn over to Ferrier if it were worth anything. The diary was in French but she was to be the interpreter. Perhaps no one had opened this book since Fabienne's death.

Finishing the last swallow of coffee, she picked up the

diary, leaving the letters to be put away safely by the maid, went to her room to fetch a blank spiral notebook, then left to take a walk. She turned the corner on the Boulevard Beaumarchais and walked down Rue Saint Gilles; from there she walked to the Rambuteau Metro stop and spent the rest of the day at the Bibliothèque Nationale.

Willa went to the library nearly every day without fear of offending Xavier by her absence. He was never in. A week and a half after her arrival, he was called to Aix to attend to his wife. She liked being alone in the house. It, too, had a glass elevator and several balconies. Laval (or had it been Petain?), she was told, had lived next door. The empty house seemed to envelop her during the hour she lay in bed before she fell asleep. It didn't seem possible the structure could be truly, completely empty. She wasn't afraid of thieves or ghosts, just not convinced of her solitude. Willa tried to picture Monsieur Xavier, small, thin, bald, gold-rimmed glasses. He was so old as to be on the brink of losing the adjective masculine. He would still have the biological habits of a man but he would be an elegant, neuterized shell. He could still refer to his wife in the present tense.

When Monsieur Xavier returned a week later they were to meet at his bank vault where the paintings he planned to smuggle out of France were stored. He was about to have them moved back to his house and from there out of the country. Willa sat in a red velvet chair for an hour, waiting, reading Le Monde, staring down the arcade of the hall, striking up a conversation with a guard. Then a bank officer and a messenger brought her a note full of complicated apologies: events at the Bourse prevented him from attending her and seeing the paintings. He regretted not being able to discuss the papers with her. Unfortunately, these dead artists gave her more company during her visit in Paris than he did, and he hoped some day he could make up for what he owed her. The manager would open the vault for her. Willa thought it was just as well. After reading the diary of his great-grandmother's friend she was curious to meet Odilon Xavier, but actually preferred to be alone with the paintings rather than have to chat it up with the owner at the same time.

There was a Vuillard of two women in a room of ochre, rose and blue-grey. One sat at a table writing, the other sat in a rocking chair, hands clasped; one sitter actively engaged, the other apparently not. A Bonnard still life, violet, ochre, dark brown and ivory. Her descriptions, among the pages I found, had the brevity of frightened writing, as if she were afraid these passages could become evidence of her culpability in the scheme of colleagues F. and X. About one picture there was only a single line: '*Portrait of a Woman in Moroccan Costume*, by Eugène Delacroix.' She didn't describe the picture, sure of either her memory or her future ownership of the woman in Moroccan dress. That I'd found no writing by her on the drawing up until that point was in itself an odd omission, and I wonder about the writing she lost, writing I won't have read even as I finish this last file.

Two days later Willa left Paris with the diary and the letters. She refused headphones because the movie seemed like the kind of comedy you could understand without language. Luc Ferrier met her at the airport. He appeared pleased to see her. They got into his car, his driver and private guard in the front seat. Willa gave him the letters but asked if she could hold on to the diary for a few more days. Her weeks in France had been completely occupied with studying and translating it. In her appraisal of the letters and paintings she revealed to Luc the extent of Odilon's misjudgement of the diary. That was a mistake, because he insisted on taking the journal back to California with him and she might have been able to keep it had she said nothing. Fighting jet lag, helped by pills, Willa stayed awake nearly the whole of those two days. Still she didn't finish the translation. According to a note I found in the LUC-ME file drawer she carefully removed a last section of the diary and it was filed somewhere in the ring of cabinets surrounding me. Monsieur Xavier had given her access to his great-grandmother's letters while she was his guest, but he didn't wish to sell

182

these. Willa may have stolen the 1872 letter to his grand-father, Christophe, or copied it over before she left Paris.

All this occurred in November 1968, a month which goes by quickly, a funnel steeply sloping towards Christmas and the New Year. Willa had barely been back in New York a month when the invisible Monsieur X. died of a heart attack. He realized Ferrier was never going to pay him for the paintings or letters and since they'd been smuggled out of France illegally there was nothing he could do about it. Madame Xavier's strata of existence hovered around the comatose and there were no close relations. Their estate was to be auctioned off. In fact Luc planned to buy some of it but he never returned to France. On 1 December, a bomb went off in Luc Ferrier's house in La Jolla, California, killing him and destroying everything in the house. Presumably the unpaid-for diary, letters, paintings and drawings in his possession were also destroyed. They were never seen again. Two groups took responsibility for the bombing. The first was an anti-war group which had targeted Ferrier as the director of Carex, then building anti-personnel weapons used in Vietnam. He had also been on boards of corporations whose subsidiaries, chemical companies, produced napalm and Agent Orange. Perhaps in the night somebody poked through smouldering sticks, cold ashes and melted tele-phones for the remainders of his deals. The first group which claimed responsibility for the explosion made its research public. No one had heard of the second caller; she hadn't been after Luc Ferrier, but a Mr Masterson. Either Ferrier had been mistaken for Guy Masterson, or, under the name Guy Masterson he was guilty of rape and murder – but this caller surely had the wrong number. Willa looked for residual clues of Guy Masterson in what she considered a vague memory of Luc's less guarded moments. During empty sunny days or alone at night Luc might have trans-formed himself into a corporate werewolf driving up and down the California coast. She only partially considered a mistake had been made in the victim's identity and seemed to have little inclination to doubt the accuracy of both bombers. She wrote that there were rarely any fissures in his persona of power, outside of the statutory feelings of help-lessness he had when he was ill. No manic moments in search of victims. No impulse to squelch an ant. From bug-mashing to rape, these actions were unnecessary expressions of power on the part of the founder of Carex, but she continued to look for characteristics of the man she remembered less well: expressions of derision, cruel parodies, extreme impatience. There had been a human organism who got up in the morning, brushed his teeth, had breakfast and went to work like everybody else. Willa liked to think this was the Luc Ferrier she knew. That he could contain all the contradictions listed on the front pages of news-papers the morning after the bombing was another subject. Knowledge of his other activities was like knowing what someone did in the bathroom in the morning. You didn't need to know, and Willa didn't know until Luc Ferrier was blown to bits.

By the time I came to work for her, twelve years later, she never mentioned him and I knew nothing of their relationship until I had to dispose of her files. Following his death, she translated the remaining fragments of Lucienne's diary and that is what I'm now trying to find.

An old letter stuck to a note she wrote herself in 1979, clipped to an article on the Chinese people fleeing Vietnam in boats:

> What would interest him about this newspaper article is the subject of the black markets that have sprung up in response to the needs of the refugees in the Malaysian camps. Within the camps factions have split apart and formed gangs with some claim to an imitation European ideological analysis. Ferrier would think the politics have little connection to the emergence of a black market. Markets, black or otherwise, form in response to needs not being met. Needs begin with food, shelter and clothing but soon become more complex. There are always deals to be made somewhere, and this interested

him whether black marketeers in Kuala Lumpur or a meeting of agro-corporation heads in the Imperial Valley. Deals, according to Mr Ferrier, could be very simple exchanges of goods and services, but exchanges, however simple, are rarely equal. Somewhere along the line someone might notice the imbalance, the inequity. There had to be someplace to expand to and Luc believed the imbalance to be necessary. It becomes a question of face, of appearances, of what each party, in reality, actually wants.

His opinion, his point of view, remained stationary while most people experience a definite continuum of change as they age. Luc had aged imperceptibly, like a model in a series of shirt ads. He was a little to the left or right of the force of gravity. His brain was not the sort to tally up personal flaws, assets, even likes or dislikes. Self-definition was for the uncomfortable.

Willa's response to Ferrier's death must have been like a film run in reverse. She took quick steps up the street to her door, opened by the doorman, backwards up the elevator, into her apartment, the door locked behind her. For several months she didn't leave her building. She knew more than most people about the covert actions of the foreign service and wars that were really about oil, not communist aggression, but her knowledge wasn't put to any sort of use, save for her own consumption. When I worked for her she hardly read newspapers, wrote a letter in protest once in a while and considered generous tipping a way of making up for certain social injustices. She found it impossible to take sides in arguments, there was so much information to sort out, and she was suspicious of those cock-sure debaters who could. The ideal double agent, she could agree with both pro and con. Books didn't argue with her.

It never occurred to either Luc Ferrier or Willa that what was valuable about the Lucienne Crozier diary was the woman who wrote it, not the fact that it documented her affair with a man whose paintings were worth enough to contribute to a corporate business venture 120 years later.

Closer to the end now, at the VX file, I found a letter from Amnesty International asking if Dr Rehnfield would write a letter to the Argentine government demanding the release of José Maria Morales, sixty years old, missing since 1977. José Maria Morales was born in San Miguel de Tucuman, a small industrial town in north-west Argentina. At seventeen he went to art school and at twenty-one won a scholarship to L'Académie des Beaux-Arts in Paris. In Paris, the letter went on, he had a successful career as a painter, meeting Picasso, Jean Cocteau, even Gertrude Stein. In 1954 he gave all this up and returned to Argentina. He began to teach in the few schools that existed for the children of the Buenos Aires slums and became friends with union organizers before unions were outlawed in 1970. In the middle of the 1970s he travelled into parts of the Gran Chaco, living among the native Indians, studying and documenting their crafts. He disappeared on the way home from teaching on 11 April 1977, one of the *desaparecidos*. The Argentine government will not issue any statements declaring or confirming his death. His family fled to Bolivia, then to Mexico City. There was a picture of José Maria Morales at the bottom of the page. He holds a long tribal pipe in one hand; he and the other Indians smile at the camera. The shutter snaps. They turn and speak to each other in Quechua. A few weeks later Morales returns to Buenos Aires, to the tightly controlled school system. The Paris bistro life is far behind him and his Argentinian days are numbered. I don't believe she ever wrote the letter. The folder only contained one of her notes:

No, not Walter Burns, he took Rosalind Russell with him, locked her in the press room. She got the exclusive with Earl Morgan. She cracked the case. As women have been telling men for decades, you too, Luc, are no Cary Grant. You have Walter Burns's grabbiness, but this isn't *His Girl Friday*. You wouldn't let a girl reporter

186

anywhere near your answering machine. Brenda Starr's heel would get caught in the grate of an employee's washroom, your Pinkertons would knock her notebook out of her hands, scatter its pages to the winds, burn her audio cassettes. Even collaborators of the male persuasion are allowed minor access. Hildy Johnson (Rosalind Russell) interviews the accused murderer, Earl Morgan, in his jail cell. Does he want a cigarette? No, he doesn't smoke; bald, nervous Earl. She gives it to him anyway. Then she hits on the magic aphorism: production for use. That's it, production for use. As in a dream, in which a single figure might represent many different people, Luc has the capacity to perform as a super Earl Morgan as well. He was a true believer in production for use on a global scale and advocated limiting the number of beneficiaries.

Next I opened the YZ file and flipped through her Flaubert notes, plans to translate some of his erotic kinds of records: trips to brothels, prostitutes and the baths. In the back I found a small old portfolio covered with faded, marbled paper, the kind with strings which tie on three sides. Inside were very old sheets of paper, yellowed, their left edges serrated, scarred from the time they were torn from the threads of their original binding, now ashes somewhere in La Jolla, California. The pages were covered by writing in French, in a hand which made much of the tails of letters. Between every other page, written on lined notebook paper, was the English translation. These pages, too, were a bit faded. The last of them had a date written on the lower right-hand corner: December 1968. The formality of her Introduction would lead the reader to believe publication was expected to follow shortly, but expectations can be deceptive. Was this really Willa's plan? Apparently not, since the manuscript lay in the file drawer for twelve years; or perhaps no one had wanted to publish it. With Ferrier and Xavier dead and most of the original destroyed, no one would have challenged her truths as elastic, her lies iron-clad. It's possible that Willa thought the diary too personal, too private for publication. Publication she might have seen as a violation of Lucienne's intention, her trust that the diary should only have an audience of one, maybe two (Fabienne). Willa extended the privilege of readership to herself, and in a moment of curious fidelity to the writer's original intentions, may have decided readership should be extended no farther.

The bibliographic avalanche came to an end.

An hour after the last Marseilles spire disappeared from the horizon, I could no longer pretend we would never be going to Africa. We are following the ancient Phoenicians, Romans, Greeks and perhaps Odysseus, too, who followed this route to Carthage. The ship is called *Le Nerée*, after the old man of the sea who always tells the truth. To avoid a repetition of my father's fate I looked in the waves for slivers of shell or trident, evidence of Triton the trumpeter or Proteus who, like the sinister Dr Koreff, can change his shape at will and cast the future. The hot, dry wind is of the nineteenth century; there are not really any references to antiquity on deck or over the edge. *Le Nerée* is a cargo ship. In the hold is machinery for printing presses, and in return Captain Lautrec will bring back figs, dates, lemons and oranges. I would feel happier if we weren't carrying such a heavy freight. Wooden furniture, or logs, for example, are less likely to sink. I don't mention this fear to Captain Lautrec. There is only one other passenger on the *Nereus*, a silent fellow, about seventeen. I think his name is Jules or Guillaume Kleiner from Alsace.

Few of the sailors are French. They are Spanish, Italian, Corsican, Sicilian, and one is Portuguese. The captain seems reluctant to hear news from Paris and since the description of events on the barricades (even to a sympathetic listener) only revives my dissatisfaction and unhappiness, I don't speak of them. Captain Lautrec never speaks of transporting exiles or fugitives from Paris. No amount of conversational manoeuvring can pry this information from him. Save for the movement of machinery in one direction, fruit and Algerian wine in the other, the people on his ship are sailors or recipients of personal favours. I don't think he knows exactly who we are or the nature of the papers hidden in our trunk. I've learned a great deal about Algeria from him, but we avoid speaking about the February or June Days. 'The fighting in Paris is a terrible spectacle. We run the risk of having overthrown Louis-Philippe only to have replaced him by a true despot.' That's the extent of our dialogue. The captain speaks like a deliberate innocent who is proud of the fact that his steamship carries no emergency sails. Paris is as remote as the Cape of Good Hope. The Mediterranean is his territory. I can no longer identify people according to what they say their allegiances are.

I'm trying to replace instant suspicion with a trust that is just as automatic. Inducing artificial naiveté and idealism is turning out to be a misfired transplant, however. A grain of suspicion is the precipitate of certain memories. If I could enforce naiveté on my spirit, recurrent thoughts of mortality might be truncated to a degree, as if mortality were a horizon seen but never touched. In time, perhaps I can enforce this transformation on myself. Right now I put all my trust in Captain Lautrec, as if to relinquish responsibility and attendant doubts; at least I try to.

Dreams engender everyday circumstances with fear until I wake and the ordinary is rendered powerless again. As I watch the ocean, perhaps see an island in the distance and imagine life on that island, my thoughts have none of the sensory rewards of true experience. I can't sit under its trees, listen to incomprehensible native speech, but only imagine the sounds and the coolness. A dream occupying the same mental space is, for the duration of time spent sleeping, taken for real experience. I am often still shaken by dreams during the first moments of waking. Last night I dreamed my father was on this ship. I was so glad to have found him after all these years but he was elusive and slipped away. The boat was full of strangers.

12 JULY 1848

We stopped for a day in Majorca and walked through Palma, the last European city I may ever see. The inhabitants speak a language unknown to us but it is possible to get a general understanding from sentence patterns and Latinate words. Outside Palma we took a tour of the stalagmite caves with a guide who spoke French. Cones of yellow stone rose from the floor of the cave, sometimes they were so close to one another they seemed a curtain of dripstone. Nature out of control, unrestrained and able to follow dangerous whims. Governments are overthrown and overthrown again, but the steady accretion of minerals goes unabated and unchecked.

Jean found a bit of quartz which, when held a certain way, looked like a man's profile. I suggested we stay in Majorca of the beautiful rolling hills, pomegranates, oranges and olive trees, windmills and Cyclopean relics, last stop before Africa. The benefit is in its remoteness, one might easily hide here; but no, the list, we must continue on. George Sand and Chopin stayed here for a winter at Valledemosa, but no, says Jean, we have responsibilities in Algiers, the list, the boat is waiting. We sailed away from the legendary hide-out of Moorish pirates, the tower of the Almudaina Palace and the blocky cathedral lacking even a rudimentary spire; all have, as I write, disappeared from view.

Jean managed to get Guillaume Kleiner's story out of him. He's seeking his fortune, that's all. In his confession he said he was the youngest son of a blacksmith, a neighbour's girl got pregnant; it would not have been an advantageous marriage and he might not have been the father. Girls made up stories in order to get married. It was an old trick, the blacksmith said, and Guillaume felt foolish not to have sensed the girl's deceit first. Jean thinks he is a lonely but silly boy who believes what he's told and does nothing but look at the sea and dream of becoming a rich man. They talk about boats; the best thing about the sea is it has no boundaries. Guillaume already feels the restraint of society's conventions but he wants to conquer these restraints by leading such a conventional life that he can hide behind its ordinariness. He would like to own a steamship and carry freight across the Mediterranean, outside the laws and perimeters of any state. He thinks, Jean said, he would only have to watch the weather and say his

191

prayers. I asked Jean not to use the simple Guillaume as a source of entertainment. My brother Etienne was just as serious about his own simple ideas.

A cough which began just before we left Paris has grown progressively worse. At night there are moments when I feel I'll vomit up my lungs and my throat can convulse no more. One of the Sardinian sailors heard me coughing each night and told the others that the French woman surely has consumption. Captain Lautrec got angry at their complaint, and told me they are superstitious but there was nothing he could do about it. He once sailed in the Caribbean and the crew's bewitchment by the supernatural or what they believed to be the supernatural was uncontainable. Captain L., anti-clerical, doesn't believe in God. He believes in modern methods. His ship has no sails. There are times when he feels his men are close cousins to the Arabs on the other side of the Mediterranean who believe in such things as *baraka*,* yet I believe he will let them burn my bedding after we disembark – to calm them and perhaps to calm himself, as well.

The silent printing-press parts stored in the ship's hold twitch with unwritten sentences, language waiting to be born.

We took on a new passenger at Majorca, an Andorran monk, Father Pablo Nableau. He is to go from Algiers to a monastery in Constantine. He seeks converts among the Berbers and Arabs. He will not eat until we see Africa, which should be no great hardship since we should arrive tomorrow and turning down the ship's food is not a hardship. He is stern and surely mad at the same time; a severe inquisitor, a man of the *auto-da-fé*. He faces south and clicks his rosaries. The sailors avoid him, Guillaume Kleiner too, as if Father Pablo Nableau would pry confessions from them like oysters. One Spanish sailor, either concealing a

---

* Algerians often believed in the presence of invisible powers or spirits which wrought good or evil and had, therefore, to be treated with respect, honour, or shunned, accordingly. *Avoir la baraka* means to be lucky (*avoir de la chance*). The expression was used by French settlers as well as by Arabs. W. Rehnfield

192

set of Iberian superstitions to top all those of his fellow sailors, or entertaining a cloud of guilt which has followed him from Barcelona, is very attentive to the monk. I think Father Pablo Nableau is above the need for companionship and does not sense ridicule when the agnostic majority express slight interest in him or his faith.

We European passengers have great designs and aspirations on this new continent. Captain Lautrec says of Algiers, *Jazirat al maghrib*, which means island of the west. The city is like an island between the Mediterranean Sea and the sea of sand, the Sahara.

13 JULY 1848

I was standing alone on the deck. Algiers began from the moment we could see the black Atlas Mountains of Kabylia, still leagues out to sea. The city rises very steeply from the harbour. It's built directly up the slope and I thought again of the Majorcan stalagmites, except the rising roofs and minarets of *Al Jazair* appear of unveined white marble, no yellow incisors of the caves. Captain Lautrec pointed out the lighthouse, the Dey's hospital, the Maison Carré and the Cape Sidi Ferrugi which draws the coastline southward. The harbour did not resemble the ports of Marseilles or Palma. This is Africa, and indeed of all the people crowding the piers, hardly any of them were European. I wanted to remain on board until evening, thinking the temperature must certainly grow cooler by then and all these people will have gone home to dinner. This was not to be so, however. The captain instructed me to wear a hat with veils, if I had one; the customs regarding women here are different, and, in ignorance, I begin to prepare for them. I dug from our trunk an object of black net and pink velvet ribbons that had been part of Jean's costumes, one of his disguises after César's murder. I pinned it on my head and we descended, myself between two men.

Waiting for us in his carriage was a friend of Captain Lautrec's, Yves Polignac. If the captain's ideological inclination was ambiguous, his friend, who looked like any prosperous merchant from the continent, was even more ill defined. He wore a long black and white scarf around his neck, the only visual indication that he lived in an Arabic country, and he looked like a happy man. We were introduced as Victorine and Hilaire. Jean would not let go of our trunk even to rest his arms. Captain Lautrec and Polignac discussed what arrangements were to be made regarding the press parts, gave directions to the crew, then we drove away, up to the centre of the city, La Place du Gouvernement. Monsieur Polignac wanted to show us how French Algiers is, how we should feel quite at home, as if Paris had never really been left behind. The square was pretty, planted with orange trees; the buildings had the long windows, balconies, facades of French buildings and would have looked very European except for the appearance of guns everywhere. He pointed out the Hôtel de la Régence and asked us many questions about ourselves. Most of these questions, though personal, were asked eagerly and in connection to the February Days. He and his family weren't allies of Louis-Philippe, he made sure we realized that, but given the power and the opportunity, Monsieur Polignac would duplicate the July Monarchy in every detail. He may tell strangers how wonderful his wife is and how much he loves his family, he might wear long Arabian scarves, but in other respects he's not very different from Charles or Fabienne's father.

We passed through a dusty market, bits of cloth and a few metal objects glinted in recesses reached by a strong afternoon sun. The market was full of men. They were all loud and confused, or at least it seemed so to me. Perhaps it's a kind of order for these people, one I don't understand and am not inclined to sort out. Although Monsieur Polignac tried to draw our attention elsewhere, near the outskirts of the market I saw an Arab neighbourhood nearly burned to the ground. A few sides of buildings remained and families squatted in structures which combined household objects, relics of walls and the principle of the tent but

194

not really a tent at all. A burnt sundial marked the eroded centre of the street. A boy peed on it and ran away. We came out on Bab Azoun Street. It is here, two rows of houses which could have been carried brick by brick from the Quai Voltaire, that the Polignacs live. They are *grands colons*. Monsieur Yves is a self-made man. ('Their origins were not gracious,' Captain Lautrec had said. It has been through his intervention that we are able to rent rooms from them.) The Polignacs do not associate with the *pieds noirs*, recent working-class arrivals who were labourers in France. Six of their eight children have returned to the continent. Only a son and daughter remain and the daughter is soon to be married out of the house to another *grand colon* family.

18 JULY 1848

Jean wishes to find rooms apart from the Polignacs. It isn't just their intrusiveness: I think they are well meaning and don't even care particularly who we are. He simply doesn't like them.

Monsieur Polignac is speculating on land bought cheaply in an Arab or *pieds noir* neighbourhood near the port. He would raze sections and build an oil refinery or factories which would construct the kinds of machinery previously imported. I no longer care to behave like moral police and I dread reproducing the cramped, frightened nature of our last days in France, just copying them over, surrounded this time by a different culture.

Jean met an Algerian Jew, a socialist, in a café. He calls himself Spinoza and I don't understand why he refuses to believe the name must be made up.

19 JULY 1848

The Polignacs have an Arabian servant who makes very strong coffee; the smell fills the house in the morning when she grinds the beans, fading as the day grows hotter.

Madame Polignac thought it would be good for my cough because it is strong, thick and bitter. I haven't told her I've begun to spit up blood. The coffee reminded me of my lost afternoons with Fabienne. I would have liked to take a walk by the sea, but this is not done. A copy of *Le Monde* left on a chair, the sound of a *cornet à piston* – all these accidental things jar my memory and increase my desire to return to France. If the Polignacs, like the sailors, think I have consumption, we may, indeed, have to quit this place. Boats are reluctant to take on consumptives and, once discovered, the crew might set me adrift in a lifeboat or put me overboard. Disease is my body's response to memory, the desire to return. I have often thought that I don't want to be here: the knowledge found its way into my lungs, my bloodstream. My corporeal self has provided a perverse way out. The marks of blood take on the meaning of an accretion, an addition to my identity as Lucienne Crozier. The events which have shaped my perception of that identity: receiving prizes at school, being told one is pretty, or ignored because one is not, moving to Paris, getting married, acts of infidelity, joining the *14 Juillet*. The appearance of the red spots, first sign of disease, this is another one of those sticks marking the road, but one I thought would come later, along with the alterations of age, disability and worry; unpleasant experiences would have by then taken over. We may be told the location, time and manner of our births, but it isn't always given to us to know the manner of our deaths. Physicality occupies one sphere, intellect another, until the former, through illness, overpowers everything. I try to keep the secret to myself, stare at the over-ripe tomatoes in the garden, and thank Madame Polignac for the coffee. A window on the other side of the house has a view of the street and there are only men in it. They are all wearing fezes and each is red in colour; it's like a street full of cherries or pills. The romantic clothes from this continent, not the veils of constriction, were packed in Eugène's trunk. In spite of his perceptions of human suffering, everything he brought back from Morocco

196

was about pleasure. My trunk, were I to pack it now, would have very different contents.

22 JULY 1848

Of necessity I'm attached to Jean in a manner which would have been insupportable in Paris. Since we've arrived and recognized these rules, he sees me as a glued-on appendage, forced on him by circumstances. I don't want him as a constant companion any more than he needs me as a second pair of legs. We both know this but he behaves as if the imposition were desired rather than detested. Once when we did walk out together there was little to do. Women aren't allowed in the cafés. When Moslem women go out they are covered by veils and no men except their husbands are allowed to see their faces. Europeans live under some of the same strictures because the colonialist drive has not yet wiped the slate clean. The frugal economy of movement and limited discourse between men and women of different cultures, or of the same origins, means a woman alone is an occasion for danger. One is with a man or one travels in a group. We are as remote from the wealthy French as from the Arabs they've displaced, and I have no idea where or in what capacity I might ever actually live here. There was no reason to leave France if all I'm left with is the life of a partly quiet, obedient malcontent. I could have joined Charles in Haiti for far less trouble.

Nobody told the woman who ran the café off the Boulevard du Gand what to do. Her physical liberty, her ability to come and go as she pleased, was ensured by economic freedom; she was dependent on no single man or group of men for her income. She controlled her own cash. It all comes down to money. Might I be accused of a memory which mimicked Rémy's drawings of working-class women? I don't think so.

I can find nothing but disappointment here. Europeans may have indulged in romanticism about Arabs and the

Orient, and there is some reciprocation, a love of things French among some Algerians, but I wouldn't call it that kind of enchantment. The rubbing off, the influences and counter-influences which go on here, are sometimes desired, often enforced, and occasionally accidental.

Jean spends his days and evenings with Spinoza and tells me nothing about their meetings except that the list is involved. Is he personally knifing each name, conducted to the right address by S.? Or are they blackmailing these people? Sometimes he waits so anxiously for the mail, and I don't know where his money comes from. I am so much shut in but he moves with relative ease. He was more restricted in France. I'm the fugitive in Algiers. February is a secret here, and all women are the mad woman locked in the attic,* real or theoretical. The truth is I don't really care anymore, but I don't know what it is I do care about in the place of an unattainable revolution, social changes whose architecture I can no longer implement, criticize or even desire.

Madame Polignac has told me the Arab, Moorish, Kabyle and Berber women lead much more restricted lives than we; men consider them inferior in every way, only slightly better than animals. In a situation of forced retirement in which even the youngest male has authority over them, women organize a hierarchical system of power among themselves. Men can have four wives and many mistresses but all are at the mercy of the mother-in-law, an arrangement Madame Crozier would have enjoyed. The Arab family which serves and lives with the Polignacs is representative of a small group of Arabs who, for whatever

* According to Foucault's *Histoire de la Folie* (Librairie Plon, 1961), laws were passed after the French Revolution which required mad men and women who had been confined in prisons to be released. Since there were no asylums in the modern sense, families were responsible for their mad relations. Lucienne probably had not read *Jane Eyre* but she may have been familiar with the middle-class practice of moving mentally deficient or emotionally disturbed family members to attics. This expression might also have had a source in popular mythology. Witches were often relegated to remote towers, castle turrets, etc. W. Rehnfield

reasons, find French culture attractive and have adopted the language and religion.

Michel Polignac is the brother who is destined to remain on the African continent and carry on the family's business. He offered to take his mother, sister and me to the Arab market at La Place de la Chartre, and so began my second outing beyond Bab Azoun Street since arriving in Algiers. Michel is eighteen and spends most of his days with his father, selling machinery they import from Europe to farmers, printers, ironmongers or whoever is in need of imported mechanical parts. He has enormous ears, a large nose and resembles neither of his parents. Wives and daughters of customers who come from outer farms like him because he is amusing. They feel comfortable with a homely man who talks about crankshafts and treadles with a slightly lewd edge as if crankshafts and treadles represented something else.

La Place de la Chartre market occupies a square with a fountain in the middle surrounded by orange trees. The image is a cool one but it was hot, dusty, noisy and full of vendors, none of whom spoke the same language. At the point we entered, cakes, sticky with honey, were sold along with figs and dates. In cases of great poverty, dates are a substitute for bread. Roses, lilacs and freesias gilded up to their blossoms were waved at us, and bunches attached to turbans upset a delicate balance, the gilt weight almost tipping them off the heads of those who sold them. An old woman with three gold rings in her nose offered us oranges from a pile at her feet. She was very old and a freed slave. Animals were set in cages in another section – live hens, eagles, storks, red partridges, black swans, greyhounds – along with the skins of rare lynx, panther and lion. There were Negresses wearing bits of striped cloth and necklaces of red, brown and black seeds bound by bands of copper or silver, a contrast to the Moslem women of whom nothing can be seen but their eyes. Some black women sold milk in boarskin bags, flowers, or the roots of the dwarf palm. One had a tame hyena on a frayed leather leash. The slave trade flourishes in Algeria. Arabs bring blacks out of the African

199

interior and sell them here in the north. A slave can buy his or her liberty as perhaps these did, or, upon the death of their owners, they may be freed. In France where there is no slavery, all a black has to do is step on French soil to consider himself free, but in Algiers, a French colony, slaves are a major trade commodity. Madame Polignac wished to look at djellabas embroidered with braid, bolts of silk shot with gold and transparent muslin chemisettes. Michel and Mademoiselle Claire bargained over a yellow saddle covered with interlocking designs. Money changes hands, animals are slaughtered, slaves sold, fortunes cast. The veiled Chaouia women from the east, near Tunis, are allowed out more than Berbers or Kabyles, Claire says. These are magicians. The practice is passed on from mother to daughter and their market stands are lined with philtres in blue, green and brown bottles, trios or quartets of women beckoning from behind flaps in their tents. Michel translated. 'What would Madame like to remedy? Unlucky in love? Unlucky in matters of money? Childless? No sons?'

As we were leaving we wandered in the direction of drum sounds unlike anything I'd ever heard before. Madame Polignac wanted us to come away but her children insisted on showing me the source of the music. The sound led to black musicians, two playing drums made of skin stretched over a hollowed tree trunk, one playing hollow gourds, and another a pipe made of reeds. A fifth with fishbones and teeth around his neck played a sort of xylophone. Madame Polignac finds the music barbaric, symbolic of how remote some tribes are from civilization. Even the village musicians of her native Franche-Compté were more harmonic.

Another distant drum made her nervous and we quickly left La Place de la Chartre. Claire told me executions are performed in the market. Men with all their hair shaved off except for a tuft on the top of their heads are doomed. I remember seeing five or six of them. The tuft is left so the men can be pulled into the afterlife. Under the

Deys,[*] Algerian barbers often became ministers and ambassadors.

As we were leaving we heard a high-pitched screeching. Although my ear is still unaccustomed to Arabic, there was something erratic in the sound. Michel told me the screams came from the mad woman who lives on the fringes of the marketplace. She lives on what she can scavenge after the merchants have folded their tents, gathering the old bits of food or cloth left behind. She can survive as an object of pity and curiosity but people throw rocks, as well as coins, at her. She walked slowly around the edge of a tent, approaching us. Half French, half Algerian, she had been raised in a brothel, but when she grew up she couldn't learn to work properly in the house, wouldn't perform at all, Michel said when his mother was in the carriage, door locked behind her. The woman's hair was a brown mat and she'd stuck dying gilded flowers in it, the ones that had been discarded. The sun made a halo out of the tangled strands rising above her head. She wore many layers of rags, black and white striped on top; red cloth, another garment, appeared through the holes; no veils covered her head and the opening for her neck was so torn, both her shoulders slipped out. In spite of her near nakedness, men seemed to leave her alone; at least they did that day. She walked towards us, turned an imaginary corner very sharply as if a voice had beckoned her away from us, and so we left the market without incident.

Ordinary windows, walls, courtyards become symbols of confinement and desperation. Each tile, each crack is painfully familiar, the kind of familiarity you recognize when you return home after a long journey, but here the familiarity isn't a happy one.

The Polignacs have a few books. A biography of Lafayette, aphorisms by La Rochefoucauld and a dictionary. The life of Lafayette is a formidable adversary, daring me to confront an endless cycle of revolution, repression and impotent compromise.

[*] Former title of the Governor of Algiers. W. Rehnfield

25 JULY 1848

Muezzin call from minarets, salutations bounce from tower to tower five times a day, almost like church bells marking the hours. The Moslems say no rosaries. They have chaplets which are very similar, beads on a string.

28 JULY 1848

Our rooms are separate from the Polignacs', almost another wing of their house altogether. It was in these rooms that the older children lived before they left home. The separateness is an illusion. Our lives are conducted within their house and our comings and goings are nearly transparent to them.

'Where is your husband? What does he do all day? You say he is a writer but we never see him writing and we never see what he has written. How do you pay rent?'

They don't ask these things. I say them to myself as if the Polignacs were doing the asking.

At dinner Monsieur Polignac discussed his interest in a railway scheme, a shoreline rail which will connect Algiers to Blidah in the west and Constantine to the east. He has already ridden out to the Fort Vingt-quatre Heures to inspect a section of the projected line. Nothing has been built yet and in order to begin many tribal lands will be seized by the *grands colons*.

29 JULY 1848

Because it's not just specks of blood anymore, I'm frightened and can barely remember how it would be to lie in an upstairs bedroom in Boissey Saint-Leger, taken care of by my mother. The heat never stops. I wish I could sleep during the day. Madame Polignac frowns at the sound of my cough. There are moments when I'm nearly doubled over and the sight I present isn't one of a victim of vague, benign complaints. She pretends to be polite but really wishes us gone. She likes the extra money but doesn't like strangers, especially a sick one, in her house. She is less sure of the captain and probably complains to her husband that Lautrec has dumped God knows what on them this time. The trust Yves gives so easily makes him appear slightly foolish to her. Her politeness begins to crackle with a cool distance. Her maternal instinct in the foreground, she doesn't want Claire and Michel exposed to infection.

My thoughts on the boat were the premonition of a queasy optimist, a mental safety net, not worth much really, as if confidence could be instilled by outlawing remorse: the assurance of negation, by behaving like Captain Lautrec and refusing emergency sails.

7 AUGUST 1848

This evening on the terrace overlooking the Polignacs' tangled garden I overheard a visitor from the south, a man who started a large vineyard and brought his friends bottles of Algerian wine, describing the desert. He probably felt he could speak freely with only two men present; he didn't see me. The guest told stories of the practice of torture carried out by the Kabyle tribe in the desert. If they capture any French man, or woman, farmer or Zouave, they bury them up to their necks in sand and leave the captives to die. Sometimes various parts of their bodies are cut off first. He did not describe what the French did to the Kabyles in turn, but the Kabyles, he added, will torture any Arab or Moor as well. They are brutish, animals: any human life is a toy, a source of amusement and experimentation, he said. Another desert torture is the *simoon*, sandstorms more terrifying, more dense than fog, often obscuring the sun, erasing roads as if there had never been any. The storms of the Sudan are even worse, especially near Khartoum. No one can survive them. Walls of moving sand, sometimes thousands of feet high, the description of them encouraged the dark wine grower to pull his lapels close and blow air out through his mouth in pantomime. He looked so saurian, didn't notice that Claire, too, was listening. She is to marry into a *grand colon* family whose lands are encroached upon by both Kabyles and *simoons*.

14 AUGUST 1848

Two nights ago Jean rubbed my back with oil that smelled of ginger, to help the lungs. He repacked a few days ago as if he intended to leave at a moment's notice. His kindness is at odds with the evidence that he is about to leave without me, abandoning me to Madame Polignac who might turn me out as a consumptive.

I agreed to meet Spinoza. I'd never been in a Jewish house in France and didn't really expect or want to enter one in Algiers.

A low wooden door in a back alley behind Bab-el-Oued Street. Although he is our age, S. lives at home with his parents. All his brothers and sisters have married and moved away. His family came from Spain in the fourteenth century, but they have had so little contact with the world of Africa that the house has retained more of the medieval Spain of its origins than the influence of their host continent. S. told us the story of their exodus, beginning with an imprisoned community of Spanish Jews who waited for the *auto-da-fé* without the slightest hope of rescue. They believed that in less than a week there would be no one left to say prayers for the dead. Their leader, Rabbi Simon ben Sinia of Seville, dreamed of a boat and, following his memory, he drew the boat on the prison walls. The boat took on the proportions of reality, the prisoners boarded, and later when their jailers unlocked the door, all the Jews had vanished. The boat landed in Algiers where they were welcomed by the Marabout Sidi ben Yusef. Successive generations of marabouts didn't accept them as readily and they have kept to their own section of the city. In their quarter all classes of Jew are mixed together. They all dress alike, in brown or black. Many resemble Algerians. (Spinoza's mother looks more Oriental, like a Turk.) I don't believe in a graphic boat turned miraculously tangible. They were probably Maranos.

His mother doesn't speak French. She opened the door for us and silently led us down a narrow passageway to what abruptly appeared as a central courtyard paved with marble tiles. She hurried off without even calling his name and we were left sitting on the edge of a square fountain between a couple of thin cypress trees. The courtyard was disorderly, some of its hexagonal tiles were pried loose, corners raised or worn down; one could easily trip. Baskets of washing and clay pitchers were scattered about. Several families besides Spinoza's shared the courtyard and occupied rooms which opened on to it. I am told this design is Moorish and that a single wealthy family might in some cases occupy a whole such building by itself. S. descended from a wooden gallery. He looked like a Moor, the same olive skin, his nose less aquiline, eyes round as some Spaniards' are, and he had straight black hair. His eyebrows met at a point above his nose and in his dress he went further than Monsieur Polignac; three cultures were represented – Arabic, Judaic and European. I don't think he was as glad to see me as Jean said he would be. He led us to a room whose dormer windows opened within reach of the olive trees. The inside was spread with carpets and pillows, no chairs.

It probably began with an interest in Europe, the continent left behind. He can read in French, German and Spanish, as well as Arabic and Hebrew, and his room was lined with books written in all of these. If you were sitting on the floor, a stack might be an armrest. At my elbow were Dumas, Sand, Hugo, Baudelaire, de Musset, Saint Beuve – the beginning of an addiction – but these hidden books were the ones Spinoza had finished with. Perhaps Jean's armrest contained German novels or Spanish poetry. The other stack was made up of Blanqui, Babeuf, Bakunin, Marx, Lamennais and, on the bottom, *The Union of Labour* by Flora Tristan.

Spinoza's father, like Monsieur Polignac, used his European connections to join in a shipping business. Not as prosperous as the Polignacs, the family is only part of a large network which includes other families of their religion all over Europe. Bolts of light Algerian wool, cotton and silk end up in Barcelona, Marseilles, Paris, Frankfurt and Amsterdam. All kinds of European things return, from lanterns to these books and outdated copies of *Neue Rheinische Zeitung*.

S. says to be a socialist in Algiers one must be completely anti-French, and this is easy for him because he's not. *Quarante-Huitards* are safe here, he also says, because the military is more concerned with Arabs, especially after the revolt last year led by Abd-al-Kadir. Even the most conservative colonialists are fundamentally republican in spirit or they wouldn't have left France to begin with. The list of names Jean acquired in Marseilles led them to suspect arrests might begin at any time. That was all they would tell me. The confidence the two men exchanged didn't admit a third. I picked up a book and wandered out into the courtyard. If I sat near the fountain, the sound of water mixed with the sound of conversation. Although no words were clear, I didn't want to hear any of their dialogue, even in an abstract form. I walked to the far side and sat on an overturned basket. A woman ran along the wooden gallery overlooking the courtyard, another appeared at a dormer window, then disappeared. I didn't want any knowledge of their plottings and I'm sure they didn't want me to know either. Who was on the list? Imagined names and lives sprang from what I'd seen only once, a creased white paper folded in half. Is inability to assess risk misidentified as heroism? I don't see where French such as ourselves fit in and want only to return to the dwarfed lemons and dried geranium stalks of the Polignac garden. Better still would be to meet Fabienne at the Tuileries but it's August so her father has probably taken her to Dieppe or Deauville, where she'll flirt with American travellers whose limitations with the language are so amusing to her.

The Polignacs' cook made tabbouleh and *soubressade*, a spicy red sausage, but I could eat none of it. Jean apologized for my health, never been very strong, he said. This isn't ·true. I've never been sick in a serious way until now. I go to our room so the family won't be witness to my coughing spells. They don't know that Jean sleeps on the floor to avoid contagion. If I were not sick he might sleep on the floor anyway. If we weren't bound together by this escapade we might have long ago been sleeping in separate rooms, separate houses. Had 1848 in Paris been an ordinary, unmemorable year, Jean de la Tour might have just been someone I met at a party, wrote a little about here, and saw from time to time at the Café Rocher de Cancale in the Rue de l'Ancienne Comédie.

As I lay on the bed I tried to separate the illness from my disillusionment. Sickly, waited on, passivity both enforced and desired, hidden away – none of this was the fate I would have chosen when I left my mother's house. Immobility is the worst of it. How did I get into this room? We had big ideas and slapped titles on them but I haven't done much of anything. My life looks like an inversion of what I set out to do on a large scale. I might as well be living the life of a lunatic at Charenton*, hidden away from the society I thought I was going to change. The February Days have brought me nothing but isolation. Jean de la Tour specifically is the recipient of the blame here, not the failed revolution. (I suppose I should take some credit but as I write I'm being passive on all counts.) Madame Lucienne Crozier was doomed from the day she married. Even if she'd been true to her marriage, the bourgeois woman she'd have become would have been devastated by the destruction of 4 Rue

---

* Maison Royale de Charenton was a lunatic asylum north of Paris on the Marne River. It is the oldest asylum in the world and was also used as a prison during the revolution of 1789. W.R.

Saint Gilles. She would have been forced to consider the revolution, to look it in the face, if only through the vehicle of property loss. Even she couldn't have stayed completely out of it. I lie on the bed, stare at the ceiling when not coughing, left with a physical and mental skeleton of the woman I might have been. There's no way to remedy my situation short of gender change or death. I began the books I brought back from Spinoza's. *Promenades à Londres* by Flora Tristan. I'm glad we didn't plan to hide out in London slums where poverty shaped a fierce criminal class and the air is filled with smoke and noxious fumes as dense as a *simoon*. I turned to Germaine Necker de Staël, the second book I'd borrowed. She was the first of many women exiled by Bonaparte but gives me no reassurance on the subject, warning of the danger of becoming a stranger to one's own land. During the Napoleonic period it seems to me there were clear sides. Even when courtiers switched allegiances as often as they changed clothes one knew exactly where right and wrong lay. A luxury: maintaining the advantage of reviewing history rather than facing it, and, the pleasure of reading a reliable witness.

> Since women, on the one hand, could in no way further his political schemes, and since, on the other hand, they were less susceptible than men to the fears and hopes that power dispersed, they irritated him like so many rebels, and he took pleasure in saying offensive and vulgar things to them.

1 SEPTEMBER 1848

Jean spun the empty ginger oil bottle on the floor. He has grown dark, wears white half-Arabian, half-European clothes and is always busy with plans. His activity is undeniably furtive. He and his friends are like ants invisibly trotting through their underground tunnels as if thousands of lives depended on them alone. Never limited because of that furtiveness, Jean is full of arrangements. He makes coded notes in the middle of the night. Sometimes I desire him more because the object of his passion is elsewhere. Devotion to a larger cause has always endowed him with heroic stature but he has grown to act more from obsession than from belief. I would like to help him but he says, 'Your health will not permit . . .' Permission and health are not the reasons.

Jean sometimes sits with Yves Polignac and pretends to agree with him. Often it presents no contradictions for him to do so.

'The Zouaves are the aimless scamps of our large cities. Society can't absorb them into any other profession but the uniform. They believe the way to handle the Arab is with a gun and then we have to pay for the results of their brutality in our dealings with our neighbours.' Jean agrees, and his obliging character allows us to stay on here in spite of Madame Polignac's obvious preference.

Before 1830, the Algerians were dominated by the feudal reign of the Ottomans who imposed a system of government riddled with corruption and based on slavery. Yves sees the French as desired liberators. It is, he believes, a particular kind of Frenchman (outside of the soldiers) who comes here. They are a 'breed who question the infallibility of French law'. Independent men, like American pioneers. They were opposed to Charles X's invasion, and when Louis-Philippe annexed Algeria they disapproved of the *régime du sabre*. The army here imposes legal rights in an arbitrary manner yet refuses to withdraw and allow a civilian government to take its place. The military claim their withdrawal would plunge the hapless colonialists into a *razzia* (total war) with the Arabs, so deadly not one would survive it. *Bureaux des arabs* were set up to handle colonialists' problems but the *grands colons*, the military and the Algerians form an unstable triad. Monsieur Polignac insists that his point of view can be defined by his position in relation to Charles X, of whom he disapproved, and the late July Monarchy, whose termination he applauded. The Arabs are to his affairs as the weavers and spinners were to the Croziers, and the irony totally escapes him. He will talk about annexing *habus*, land sacred to the Moslems which ensures the maintenance of mosques, and in the same breath endorse plots to overthrow the military establishment. By last year over 11,000 Europeans held the best land here, so he himself says.

2 SEPTEMBER 1848

On a rare trip Claire, Michel and I took a citadine to the man-made jetty near one of the city gates, eating Barbary figs we bought from a Turkish street vendor. The jetty is made of blocks of lime and gravel. It is a lonely place. We walked as far as we could, almost to the sea. The only person we saw was a coral fisherman. Even more startling for its combination of the man-made and the natural were the gardens Michel wanted to show me before we returned to Bab Azoun Street. We smelled the groves of lemons and orange trees before we passed through the iron gate. The garden looked like an image out of a dream of the African desert, the setting of some of Scheherazade's tales. There was no evidence of the hot, dusty city here; we might have been leagues away, although I knew we weren't. Michel identified myrtle, acanthus, hawthorn, wild olive and karob as we passed them. The arrangement and upkeep of the garden was a combination of the meticulous and the lax, the way I imagine an English garden to be. A breeze, perhaps coming from the sea but bearing the scents of the garden, did much to alleviate the heat. It is hard to describe the heat and roughness of Algiers and it is in counterpoint to the city's oppressiveness that the garden seemed so dreamlike. We stopped by a fountain surrounded by a series of marble ogee arches. I tipped my head back, expecting to see silver paper constellations and a moon glued to an artificially blue sky, but the non-paper sun and sky were quite real and the arching of my back only brought on a coughing spell. Claire gave me some jujube leaves to chew. She said they might temporarily relieve my sickness. I noticed she used a more serious word than cough. I think both Claire and Michel knew what was waiting when we returned to Bab Azoun Street.

The Polignacs wish us to find other rooms in Algiers. They are sorry but the risk of contagion demands it. When I'm well we can come back. Jean said, in a monotone voice, 'No, Madame, I don't think we will.'

4 SEPTEMBER 1848

All the weeks Jean had packed, prepared to leave but he didn't; now there is no choice. Spinoza met us on the corner of Bab-el-Oued Street after our departure from the Polignacs. He was smiling and animated, how happy he was to see us. Spinoza is not his real name. It's Marco. I think he's much younger than he says he is, and I don't entirely trust him. I don't think he's maliciously untrustworthy, he just doesn't see the gravity of things and therefore often appears stupid. Through narrow lanes, almost roofed over by jutting upper storeys and balconies, we finally arrived at our new address. Marco found us cheap rooms near Casbah Street where people aren't likely to ask questions. Casbah Street is primarily about the commerce of women.

The rooms are laid out around a courtyard like the one in Marco's house; bigger, I think, but not as clean or as quiet. Eating, washing, fighting, solicitation – any activity which goes on in the private rooms can spill out into the courtyard. A goat and a couple of chickens which look like they've wandered through a *simoon* make their home near a cistern. The courtyard is divided into a maze by washing hanging above and alongside us, billowing white, yellow, gold and red.

We have two little rooms on the second floor. Windowless on the street side, they overlook the arena of the courtyard. Sitting on a pillow, my back against the wall, I am using my lap as a desk. Jean and Marco have gone out

211

for food. I had thought that since I no longer have Claire and Michel as companions I would have to be included in their activities by virtue of my continual presence. If saturation were all it required for absorption to take place I might be, but the transformation is unlikely. Marco never addresses me, not out of hostility, but out of habit and tradition. It's not that the two of them speak as if I'm not here – my presence is acknowledged – but the possibility of my contributing anything worthwhile to their discussion is denied. I can tell the list has been dropped from their agenda, or at least they don't discuss it in my presence. Now they're working on a plan to blow up the soldiers' quarters at the old Casbah palace of the Dey of Algiers. I raised objections to this plan. The majority of the common soldiers are, at worst, just lacklustre fellows like Guillaume Kleiner, men the class structure has pushed into the army because there is no work in France. The officers of rank should be done away with, not the ones who sleep on the floor in the old Casbah palace.

Marco disagreed with me, saying beds had nothing to do with it. Men are formed, pushed around by society, but they do make some choices and the decision to join the army is one they have to take responsibility for. He told me a story, and this is the only time Marco addressed me directly. When he was a child, one of his friends disappeared. Bits of his clothing were found near the soldiers' quarters, and finally his body was found, half naked, buried near the Marine Gate in the ruins of the baths of the Dey. A witness to the murder turned up, a *shurfa* (descendants of Mohammed and mara-bouts). He had seen three French soldiers with the body near the ruins. It had been spring, around the time of the Jewish holiday of Passover and the Christian Easter. During this season, Marco explained, French Christian leaders, priests, Dominican monks, put the idea into the heads of their followers that Jews were murdering Gentile babies to use their blood for ceremonies. Then the *shurfa* disappeared, probably buried under the fallen columns whose capitals still sprout stone grapes. They'd murdered him, too.

I found the whole story flimsy. Something he made up to convince me, fabricating sentiment to assure me of the merit in large-scale revenge.

They returned with olives, dates and wine, a terrible combination. I could only swallow a little of the wine.

7 SEPTEMBER 1848

Marco found a doctor for me. He spoke a few words of French, brokenly; Marco translated the rest. He prescribed opium for brain fever and quinine for the throat and to calm the effects of the convulsive coughing on the nervous system. I smoke it from a crystal narquilla lent by one of the women who lives facing the courtyard.

28 SEPTEMBER 1848

I've been too ill to write and when I do sit down it seems too late to recover my thoughts. De Staël wrote of the blight of exile, the transformation of one's home into something foreign and alien. Gradually, the hybrid quality of quotidian detail (food, clothing part Algerian, part French) grows to include mongrel thoughts. I assess men who enter the courtyard, predict the price I would ask, imagine their size as if I were an Algerian prostitute. None of them can speak French. I've learned to recognize the women individually by what they look like and the colours they wear. The woman in the rooms next to ours wears transparent muslin garments heavily embroidered in red and gold, threads concealing what cloth will not. Another has strings of coral and jade around her neck. She never removes them. The one who owns the goats and chickens in the courtyard below looks like a Moorish version of Jenny le Guillou. Skin and hair colour are different but their mouths and jaws have the same lines. Since I know no names, I call her the African Guillou. She is older than most of the women here but men still visit her. Sometimes her silks look as if they would disintegrate if one's finger glanced an edge.

Occasionally a man passes through who can speak French. The African Guillou brought such a man to my door. She wished to give me an amulet against illness, he translated. The leather she pressed into my hand was divided into sixteen parts, each containing the marks of these numbers:

40	10	20	8
7	21	9	41
12	42	6	18
19	5	43	11

In each direction these add up to seventy-eight, a number Moslems believe signifies power and fate, rather like seven or thirteen.

Jean and Marco store their arsenal of nitroglycerin, sodium nitrate, sawdust and paper in the other room. They've begun to roll sticks of dynamite, hiding them in a laundry basket during the day.

30 OCTOBER 1848

Dear Fabienne,

Enclosed is the journal you gave me nearly two years ago. I no longer have the strength to write in it and I have so little to write of. No one here speaks French, eliminating any hope of dictating my last thoughts. The untouched book is more than a reproach, it's an innocent-looking box shape which fans out into a blaze of documentation I'd like to forget. It should represent an anchor of security but it doesn't. These past two months I've lived in a world where the only comprehensible language I've heard was the sound of my own consumptive voice and the pattern of my writing.

You may remember Jean de la Tour as the man who took me from your house during the February Days. We travelled here for reasons you can read within. Please forgive my past lack of confidence. I was easily convinced that midnight flights were a matter of life or death. Mystery and urgency don't seem as brilliant as I

214

once thought. The reasons, whether genuinely meritorious of secrecy, or reduced to triviality and inconsequence, aren't important now. You will see this last paragraph as proof of my illness. I'd rather this book were not destroyed or turned over to Jean after my death so I am waiting for a man who can speak French to visit one of the women who lives in the courtyard and have him mail it. My postal system isn't rapid, relies on detours, but I have no other choice.

I also think you should ask Eugène Delacroix for my portrait because I would like you to have it.

I can't think about Jean without feeling bitter. He never used the word exile. I live in a room whose walls remind me of the inside of a skull and I have heard no voice but my own for weeks. I wouldn't choose self-imposed isolation, especially if I still lived in Paris. Some formerly passionate memories are pitched into a silly light from this perspective. A man who waves his apathy and disillusionment around like a flag that certifies exemption for an old cynic only looks foolish. (Eugène's Orphéus was murdered by the Zouaves.) I have enormous regrets but I wouldn't preach them to anyone.

Je t'embrasse,

L.C.

The half-retarded kid from next door came out of his mother's apartment and leaned his head hard against the Wonder Woman sticker on their door. I said hello. He never speaks. I had left my radio on and the two of us could hear it in the hall as I put my key in the lock.

I took my troubles down to Madame Ruth
You know that Gypsy with the gold-capped tooth
She's got a pad down at 34th and Vine

The kid shot a fresh wad of Bazooka into his mouth.

Mixing little bottles of Love Potion #9

I told her that I was a flop with chicks
I've been this way since 1956
She looked at my palm and she made a little sign
She said what you need is: Love Potion #9

She bent down, turned around, and gave me a wink.

I lay the Lucienne Crozier notebook and my mail on the table. The last time I could remember hearing 'Love Potion #9' was in Spartacus, Pennsylvania, and I was leaving home the next morning for Berkeley. My last night in Spartacus I went to the movies at the Orient Theatre but I no longer remember what I saw. I didn't feel too badly about leaving. I came to New York in 1972. *Midnight Cowboy* was playing at the St Marks, around the corner from the place I was staying. There didn't seem to be any Joe Buck in any of the people I saw in the city that first month. They all walked the streets with a sense of purpose. None of them had ever lived in little closed-down industrial towns like Spartacus. I was sure none of them had, and no one in the whole city received mail under a name not his or her own. Living under an assumed calling, made up and attached, I avoided making any acquaintances beyond the slight. I rarely went to the same store twice in succession. Repetition, a conversation struck up unselfconsciously, these posed threats to my fake identity. I thought my loneliness created a solitary low-wattage bulb dangling a

216

few inches above my head, continuously following me around. My scheme for a personal haunting. On the other hand I exaggerated my isolation, as if I were extraordinarily unique, as if a movie director was having his cameraman single me out in a crowd on any given avenue or following me alone on a street. I lived in secrecy but indulged in the idea that my entire life was in the process of being recorded as a dramatic film.

Quite a few people have this bulb hanging over their heads but we possess no special talent for finding each other. It begins with leaving home but might end by giving up memory, creating a fake history and having to stick to it. Everybody has Joe Buck reasons for leaving home. There is a part of people that shelters that kind of reasoning whether or not they actually make it out or not. I left Spartacus because it was appropriate but I would leave California denying I'd ever been east of Chicago.

She said I'm gonna fix it up right here in the sink.
It smelled like turpentine an' looked like India ink.
I held my nose, I closed my eyes,
I took a drink.

It was 1979. I had just seen a movie at the Museum of Modern Art and the English director was talking about trying to make a British road picture and how difficult it was, how impossible: Britain didn't have the tradition of the road picture the way America did. Going places and leaving places. Colonialists and the frontier. Americans have a tradition of going places and leaving places. (The director, head resting on a book in the British Museum – had he dreamed of masses of trailers, vans, covered wagons, ferries, smoke issuing from trains, hitch-hikers, hobos and millions of postcards, in a close-up shot of the machine which keys the mail?) A tradition begun in the manner of colonialist expansionism, pioneers who persisted until the frontier was reduced to a sliver of coastline. But what of those of us forced to leave, those of us assigned the 'fugitive nature', the phrase Proudhon used to describe air and

217

water? (Proudhon hadn't seen *Chinatown*. He didn't know about dam projects, scandals and the preciousness of water in southern California.) We fugitives go places and leave places. What about Robinson Crusoe and the Wife of Bath? Weren't those the seeds of the road picture? Weren't those English fellows the first imperialists to go on the road? In the lobby I ran my fingers over the raised letters, names of major contributors, from Rockefeller to Marx and back again. What I remembered about the movie was the radio, it was always on. The radio spells out a hazy buffer zone between the traveller and everything else in Great Britain. The radio was always on. It's 1982.

I didn't know if it was day or night
I started kissing everything in sight
Until I kissed a cop down on 34th and Vine
He broke my little bottle of
Love Potion #9.

I turned the radio off. My apartment has a view across an airshaft. A little girl in one apartment puts her dolls and animals out on the window ledge. A Chinese family hangs duck and other carcasses out of their window, using the airshaft as an extension of their refrigerator in the winter. The man is very fat, the woman wears a red bathrobe and after 5.00 they speak in loud voices, arguing and cooking into the night. They press towels against the window frames to keep out drafts; layers of pink, white, green, even in August. I never see the girl who leaves her dolls out. Under a bare bulb, the Chinese woman lifts silver threads of noodles and lets them fall back into the pot.

I had taken an art history class at Berkeley and remembered a few paintings projected on the screen in a dark auditorium. Click, click and you wrote as fast as you could until the next pair of slides appeared. The beam of light shot out over a hundred (or more) heads, utterly confused, helter-skelter light particles until intercepted by the silver screen, and then: Gauguin, Gorky, Guston. 'Defend, attack, or modify the following statement as it applies to the following

218

painting.' In the dark, under pressure, memory worked double time, all kinds of facts spilled out faster than you could write, but I didn't remember much about Delacroix and looked him up in an old art history book. It's all too dramatic, that kind of painting; the silent film strips presented more vivid allegories than *The Abduction of Rebecca*. Lucienne is easier to picture. She has long hair, wears long zipperless dresses and calls Mathilde in to do the buttons. What did she use for a toothbrush? What does she do when she has her period? She is in love for the first time but she doesn't hum Beatles songs to herself and she and Fabienne walk down the Rue Bleue hoping to catch a cab and avoid Eugène Delacroix. They would have felt as if they had just gotten out of a horror movie if they could have compared the Princess's story of Herr Dr Koreff to *Dr Caligari*. The movie is over. The credits roll. Princess Belgiojoso closes the door, you hit the street: reality. You walk to the Tuileries pool and throw breadcrumbs to the fish. The *Post*, LAWYER SHOOTS WIFE AND DRIVER, is used to wrap sole on Canal Street. Nobody remembers a tiny Monsieur Peytel.

Lucienne dying alone in Algiers. Occasionally a prostitute hears her teeth chattering and puts a blanket over her, fans her when she's feverish, or tries to make her eat some rice. To Lucienne, the men look like women and the women look like men, phantoms dressed in *kufiyehs* and *haiks*. The women wear gold piastres, clinking as they move. Perhaps there are no men, no French johns trying to translate, but she can't distinguish faces or language clearly. She is dimly aware of Jean's erratic presence by two smells – sometimes ink, sometimes metal and chemicals – and this smell rises above that of rancid cooking oil and coriander. It is even stronger than the smell of the animals by the cistern.

The fat man joins the woman in the kitchen. They stand opposite each other, and under the bare bulb they argue. Was their son working the late shift? Would their daughter come in from Queens tomorrow? For the past week I've

219

been getting up earlier and earlier, completely involuntarily. I fall asleep right away but it doesn't last long and I watch the shaft grow lambent with the first rays of the morning news programme. Most of the film frames are dark. Silent, narcophile neighbours left their shades drawn hours ago.

The last section of Willa's translation contains a glaring error. I know something about explosives. Dynamite wasn't invented by Alfred Nobel until 1866 and yet Spinoza/Marco and Jean de la Tour weigh nitroglycerin and sodium nitrate with eighteen years more to go until dynamite is invented. I laid the last torn pages of Lucienne's diary on my desk next to Willa's pages. The meaning of her English bore little resemblance to the original French. Misreadings grew, took on the proportions of invented fiction on the part of the translator. My pencilled corrections turned into entire passages so I started with my own translation from the beginning of the existing French pages, starting with the first entry after they left Marseilles.

Before my translation begins, I should do a more thorough job of introducing myself. The reader is acquainted with the characters of writer and translator but doesn't really know the biases of *this* reader. I have told you enough about Dr Willa Rehnfield to stretch your credulity, your faith perhaps, in the very existence of a notebook entitled *L.C.*, so now I'll correct the inequity of the scalene triangle.

Some may accuse me of writing an epilogue that is also a memoir. I'm uncomfortable with the idea of a memoir. It implies a preciousness I don't believe I can or want to lay claim to, and memoirs are about looking back. All this is still very immediate to me. My epilogue is a Book II, a running commentary in the margins of the diary. This space, these margins, Dr Rehnfield would probably claim were hers by virtue of the acts of translating and introducing, but I think she's wrong because Lucienne's story and mine run in tandem, then mine keeps going where hers leaves off. Imagine stories arranged like a bank of elevators, one set stops at the first floor through twentieth, the parallel set makes stops twenty through forty. If the

220

reader believes Lucienne Crozier was more of a witness than a participant (and this is probably what made her attractive to Dr R.), then Book II might belong to someone like Communard Louise Michèle. For Lucienne, the confrontation with revolution caused affairs behind her to appear trivial and childish, but she is paralysed into the life of a fugitive rather than galvanized into becoming a revolutionary, which, in part, happens when one is forced to go underground. So the step which follows occurs when it's not enough to be a witness anymore. To all this Willa Rehnfield would have said, no voyeur is truly inert.

Book II, as she conjectured in her Introduction, is Berkeley 1968. Between the two narratives is a hinge: the translator, Willa, the connective tissue between us. Abstractly, like the lines of women's vision at their windows, zig-zagging from one to the next, the first knows of the invisible third through the second.

My mother worked in the public school system in Spartacus. She did not like the supervisors. The school board was anti-union. She complained bitterly to me and to a few other teachers who were her friends, but neither she nor they ever went on strike. My mother was afraid of losing her job, not being able to find another owing to blacklisting, and we'd lose the house. If she led or participated in a strike nobody would rent to us either, she was certain. Our vulnerability, as she portrayed it, and her complaining were uneasy partners. It was a tug of war waged only domestically. In school I was afraid her dissatisfaction would become vocalized, organized, and then we'd be lost but the tug of war would be finished. When I was a little older I told my mother the teachers might win if they walked out, but no, she said, she wanted to retire soon. I had seen strikes on television, men in sandwich boards singing songs. She looked annoyed. Did I think coffee and cakes were served to strikers on a picket line? No, people got their heads bashed in. Did I want to be an orphan?

Violence, planned or random – we are attracted to it and

curious about its perpetrators. From the arena of federal litigation or the arena of the media, the interrogators repeat the same questions. What made you decide to do it? What happened to make you believe in Marxist-Leninist philosophy and Blanquist or terrorist violence to achieve your aims? Some can recite points of light, guideposts and moments of resolve in otherwise dark childhoods. There is the element of rebellion; to get out of Spartacus, so small that knowledge of neighbours is fluid. Everybody knows everyone else in a common pool in which fates are continuously examined and compared. Born into a small town and tagged with its conventional, tremulous expectations, codes are maintained, continuity is the thing. Bit by bit the pattern is eroded by a daughter who stays out all night, a son who vandalizes the Easter floats. The threat of boredom, the ominous premonitions caused by behaviour grown erratic: hair not cut, beds not slept in, bits of a draft card which refused to be flushed away. The known quantities – plaster saints, cigarettes, neck ties and draft cards – take on hideous, unknown properties. A drunk pisses on an overturned statue in an alley and the stolen saint loses the sheen of beneficence, is corrupted. White bits, the selective service registration card swirling in the john, spells jail. Solids suddenly have the elasticity of Silly Putty.

The malcontent leaves and forms a devoted allegiance to what the press sees as an extremist point of view. It is a solution to the rebel's vision of social injustice. There is a moment at which the young perpetrator of future crimes recognizes the use of the middle class in consumer society as a deaf and dumb source of exploitable lives, too devout to veer off course except in moments of insanity. ('LAWYER SHOOTS WIFE AND DRIVER.') When I was at Berkeley the newspapers were full of biographies in search of psychology, illumination, turning points, in search of 'what made you do it'. I'm not clear as to what memories, what moments constitute my constellation, my astrological configuration, the moments which led to my becoming what the journalists called a student radical, and they always

222

asked that question, even if it wasn't directed at anyone except a TV audience. I would now ask the members of the press to turn off their tape recorders. My grandmother met Emma Goldman, and my mother was sent to Workman's Circle or *Arbeiter Ring* classes after school. The Workman's Circle group cancelled classes in observance of Paris Commune Day, May Day and, in October, to commemorate the anniversary of the Russian Revolution, but none of these brief encounters with socialism took hold. My generation, in comparison to theirs, was a privileged and educated one, the first generation of women to go to college in my family's history. Isn't it a contradiction, a tragedy, the interrogators ask when they're trying to be nice, you who had every advantage, why did you blow up buildings, destroy art, cultural symbols, take lives?

Headlines, television specials, radio broadcasts attach themselves to wars, riots, natural disasters and vehicular crack-ups like choking liana around a tree. 'What made you do it?' is only a footnote to the basic core of sensationalism. This symbiotic relationship sells newspapers because even if violence doesn't affect some citizens personally, we are fascinated by it, we watch the police snap on the handcuffs and the ambulance workers load bodies on to stretchers. A crash, an explosion, an earthquake, a volcanic eruption, a fire, a flood, a mudslide, a manic murder, all have their own timing. Occasionally there's time to put on your shoes, brush your teeth, compose your thoughts. The margin of time remaining to contemplate the imminent no doubt makes things much worse. Fascination plays havoc with alienation, opposite poles which must share the same magnet. Corporeally distant from the printed page, the screen and the events represented, their distance is curated by the intellect as well, even when confronted by real live victims. The initial shock and revulsion peel back to 'This isn't me. This is no one I know. I need very much to get home.' The riots I participated in had the opposite effect: rarely random or chance occurrences, these demonstrations were organized. There was no distancing, no sense of disassociation.

There was no pretending it was dangerous for someone else and not for you.

Watching documentary footage of police firing buckshot into a crowd of striking workers in the 1930s or cracking skulls of students in Chicago, watching films of guerrilla fighting or preparations for a larger theatre (missile silos in Arkansas, radar buried in a mountain in Colorado), and all the time you're sitting in a warm room. Terrorism can't penetrate it. The dog might carry something nasty in his mouth and drop it on the rug but unpleasantness, politically motivated violence, no. Soldiers don't haul Spartacus citizens out in the middle of the night, picking people off at random. We played childish battle games which involved more running and hiding around the neighbourhood than actual fighting. Hiding alone behind a garage, looking out at a deserted back yard as twilight came on, mad dogs or kidnappers were more threatening than being captured by the jerky kid who sometimes told dirty stories through our screened-in porch. I never wanted to be on his side. Jizz this and jizz that, one of those kids who seemed sprung into licentiousness from the age of three. Why did I remember him as I ran from the police and again now? A little boy who presented himself as a kind of danger. There were no kidnapped children in Spartacus, no victims of hit-and-run drivers, no childhood cancers, none of my friends ever spoke of being molested. Murder, threat, terror, actual or imminent, took shape only in games. At Berkeley, I know it's frivolous to say it, but as I was being chased by riot police the danger seemed less frightening than the old neighbourhood war games when you didn't know what was around the corner. I was older, more sincere; something genuine was at stake and if I stood still I might get shot or blinded. Governor Reagan had the National Guard brought in, as if the school could be occupied by a military state, like universities in South Korea or the Philippines. As I ran, a perverse memory: hiding behind the garage from an unpleasant boy, as if it were the same thing.

Before I left home it seemed that everyone I knew was

224

protected, far from the line of fire. As a child, the protection may have seemed just, somehow connected to a child's simplified concept of religion: merit versus sin, reward balanced by the punishment. Step on a crack. Break your mother's back. Simple theology, cause and effect. We live in a nice neighbourhood, therefore sins are small, reward great. Senior year in high school there was a small group who had received but earnest ideas about the inequities between classes and yelled at their parents: the condition of the suburbs has nothing to do with justice, of people getting what they deserve. Working with a truncated view of history, they didn't allow for fate. It's just chance where the third generation from the immigrants ends up, the luck of the draw. Coming over on a boat from Vilnius or Palermo, who would have been able to predict that Minneapolis would turn out to be safer than Santiago? You can't anticipate the accident, the natural disaster, but when human cruelty seems more the norm than the exception, you wonder why you've been spared. The idea that rewards are deserved and somehow, somewhere along the line, punishment is meted out, is a persistent idea, however mistaken and naive. Bad conduct isn't always revenged.

One weekend we ran off to New York. My friends and I were recruited by a state university drop-out who was more interested in sleeping with us than organizing. I no longer remember his name or where we met him. He talked about the war in Vietnam and represented a life or a manner of living very different and easily upsetting to the conventions of Spartacus. He represented what might constitute dissent. He deserted us in New York. My friends and I never saw him again. I had been given the address of an apartment on East Sixth Street, a place we might stay. It was summer, perhaps not too far to walk. We walked downtown and east, feeling self-reliant, hot and stupid at the same time. The streets began to look more foreign. A girl with a necklace of tiny plastic grapes followed us from Avenue A to B. We saw junkies, nodding out, eyes closed; a dealer in the Tompkins Square Park, knife unconcealed in his pocket,

225

and a blind man sitting in a plastic chair someone had left for him in the sun.

The apartment door was opened by a man who familiarly put his arm around me. 'You're friends of Tom's' – or whoever he was. 'Fine, great, come on in.' He kept his hand on my shoulder and moved it down my back to my waist, hugging me to him. Suddenly I was part of a network of intensely loyal friends. In less than an hour it became clear that the apartment was not about organizing against the war in Vietnam but dealing. Not out of prudery, what I remember was it just seemed so silly. Here were several men and a woman talking about drug deals as if they were sitting on a Spartacus porch full of capitalists. It wasn't quite the same. The pretence of familiarity and pleasure was different but I couldn't pitch in, my idealism was shot to hell. We were high-school girls from Pennsylvania, that was all. I envied the independence of the long-haired men and single women but I wouldn't be a teenage runaway to join them. They were still bound by guile because they were dealers, but seemed to enjoy the rules of covertness, restrictions which admitted some but not others. They were practitioners of a self-righteousness as stiff as my newly found moral indignation. I knew that much. They saw themselves as social rebels undermining like a squad of termites which only occupy a small space but imagined they were capable of doing great damage. The apartment was dark; walls were painted different colours, one purple, one red, something like that. Using a stack of comic books as an armrest, the man who initially greeted us rolled a joint. Another bearded and sort of fat man told me to loosen up and have a smoke. I did, but the sensuality was lost on me. All my so-well-articulated criticism and contempt of a small town was supposed to be acted upon by this trip to New York. I had planned it that way and it was all coming to zero in this stupid apartment. Even on East Sixth Street between Avenues C and D in 1968 it was all about style. I stood up to leave and the bearded man said he would walk me downstairs. On a landing he grabbed the back of my

T-shirt, putting his hands up it, wet scratchy kisses; Puerto Rican children on the stairs watched. It was supposed to be all right. You were supposed to go along with that kind of thing, you were supposed to swallow your revulsion and I did for a few minutes then pushed him away and ran, children laughing behind me. I left my friends who were intrigued by the long-haired boys and the knowledge that no one in Spartacus would suspect what they were up to. I walked towards Tompkins Square Park, protected because the moment was about running away, nothing more could happen. Two junkies walking quietly a few yards ahead of me began yelling. One accused the other of pulling a knife. He hadn't, he said, but since his partner thought he had, he did. I was between them. Incorporated into the fight, I tried to cross the street but I was in the orbit of expansive anger. Within the mottled perceptions of the other I was an object aggressively in the way and I was going to pay for it. Junkies don't believe in neutrality. A knife came close. I didn't think about children's games at home. There was no connection, this time, between real and made-up danger.

So I left the suburbs in 1968, flying from Pittsburgh to San Francisco International Airport.

The stewardess was apologetic. We would not be seeing *Dr Zhivago*. The distributor had sent a defective print or the wrong one altogether. The deflated Russian aristocracy, the White Army or the Red were not going to shoehorn me into U.C. Berkeley. It was to be *A Touch of Evil*, instead. Charlton Heston and Janet Leigh drove to the California-Mexico border in their convertible and discovered local corruption. We were over Illinois and already in California. The movie reinforced my picture of the state put together from 3,000 miles away: lots of driving to the border in convertibles, making connections, buying drugs – even back in 1958 and surely now, as well. And then there were all the detective stories which revealed intricate webs of corruption in Los Angeles County. One sleepless man (a private detective, a journalist) connected all the links in the chain to pin the murder of the Santa Cruz girl squarely on the shoulders of the oil/cattle/waterworks/construction/ real estate king, the man whose hands always appeared clean, who always got away with it. Suddenly he is discovered for the scum he really is, uncovered for thousands of readers of the *L.A. Times*. The war in Vietnam was escalating, backed by corporations (Orson Welles's character multiplied many times over); evidence suggested the possibility of *film noir* on a global scale. A convertible just like Charlton Heston's blew up with another man and another blonde inside. There was another California that didn't make the movies. I had read about Mario Savio and the Free Speech Movement in Berkeley, seen the demonstrations on television, thought Berkeley would be like the Sorbonne with redwood and eucalyptus trees.

'Nobody gets blown up like that and nobody really wants to meet any Mexicans. The Mexicans don't like us. They don't have any reason to. I saw this picture years ago. I wish they'd been able to show *Dr Zhivago*,' said the tanned woman next to me. On her fingers she wore large opals that looked like swimming pools visible from the plane's windows.

Marlene Dietrich said something about Orson Welles being just a man. The lights would always be on in her wagon. The movie pulled the plane faster and faster towards the west coast.

Noon Rally! Sproul Hall!

The fog begins to burn off around eleven o'clock in the morning, retreating off San Francisco Bay, and then the day will be cloudless, sunny. Summer weather has a pattern in Berkeley; twenty miles away it's completely different – but I didn't learn that until later. As the fog lifted, there were days when students would assemble at Sproul Plaza for rallies, and then there would be the police, clubs, rocks, tear gas, confrontation.

I met Mary by Ludwig's Fountain towards the end of the fall. There were always dogs in the fountain and she called to one, a golden retriever, Polly Peachum. Mary held out strings of French fries trying to get her out of the pool but the dog was sniffing a terrier and couldn't be coaxed away. I recognized Mary from a large class we shared, 'Art between the Wars.' She often sat in front of me and would slide down in her seat when the lights went out and two slides, side by side, appeared on the screen. She was able to see and take notes at an angle. I tossed a French fry to Polly Peachum. Mary was reading *Art in the Age of Mechanical Reproduction* for her paper, didn't like a student with very long hair who sat in the back and called women 'ladies', didn't like the way the teacher pronounced Marcel Duchamp, Dough-sham. One of the students often asked to copy Mary's notes after class because, for various reasons, he couldn't concentrate: drugs, loud music late at night, burnt out, couldn't sleep. He wanted Mary to take care of him. His nervous laugh and self-pitying tone were not very encouraging. She put him off with excuses but he wouldn't leave her alone. She theorized that he ought to feel more self-reliant just by examining the reading list. No Hannah Arendt preceded Benjamin and Brecht, no Frieda Kahlo between Eisenstein and Fritz Lang. No Gertrude Stein. Elimination meant marginalization but she wouldn't address the professor about women missing from his list nor did she ever raise her hand. We took Polly Peachum home. Mary, a year ahead of me, lived in a house on Ashby Avenue. She was from New York and had a kind of self-possession that stopped me from telling her that I had once been in the East Village. Mary wouldn't have let them kiss her or grab her T-shirt. Since I was a new student I lived in a dormitory, in a room I'd been assigned. Before the beginning of the next semester I moved into the house on Ashby Avenue.

At first Mary's involvement in Berkeley didn't revolve around any political group. We went to rallies and riots together, we ran from the police together, and we talked for hours in the kitchen. We had little to do with the others who shared the house, an Iranian engineering student and a woman who was studying landscape architecture. I wasn't critical of Mary's sense of separateness and, in fact, mimicked

229

her aloofness, believing she only insisted on getting involved on her own terms. As much as those were my terms as well, that was all right. I didn't want to join anything, didn't want to be lectured on commitment, and saw a diluted but distinct version of the long-haired boys from East Sixth Street here, and somehow, not far away, would be the drawn knives with someone inextricably in the middle.

'For months the only pictures you've taken have been of plants in Strawberry Canyon and the dog. The dog in the water, snarling at a cat, looking out of a window. I thought you were going to take pictures at the riots. What happened to social documentary and *cinéma verité?*' Mary asked.

'It seems predatory. I sold my camera. It has nothing to do with Thoreau.' The impulse to photograph slipped from calculated desire to self-conscious diversion. Mary would think I was trying to rid myself of dispensable luxuries and hindrances. Rejection of materialism had nothing to do with it, although the $100 helped. 'Using a camera during the riots puts you outside the conflict, removes you from the obligation of choosing sides.'

'Someone has to do the recording. It's not like you're sitting on a bench, eating a sandwich, watching the local psychodrama get played out with clubs. Journalists get beaten up for just standing around,' Mary said.

I had seen a picture of a ring of photographers snapping away as a man was clubbed by police in front of Sproul Hall. The position of the observer, in spite of Mary's archival instinct, seemed androgynous. I couldn't be that kind of witness, was afraid of being that kind of witness even if I had no camera and got teargassed to death. Hinges, filters, the compromise of the half-hearted, the ones who watched. At the time it seemed something to avoid.

I still have several of the photographs I took. Symbols with missing parts turn up. One of the earliest was a picture of some people kicking around a soccer ball. The picture is black and white but I remember the ball was yellow and orange. It was supposed to represent Governor Reagan. I wished I had a lens large enough to shoot the students playing with frisbees at one end of the campus while at the south end others fought with police. If there had been no fraternities, no Callaghan Hall, no Hearst Gymnasium, or Safeway supermarket, perhaps it would have been a different fight. Guerrilla war is most dramatic when played against the backdrop of civilian life or its remnants. Of course the Safeway is open seven days a week, and then one afternoon it's levelled. The panhandlers on Telegraph Avenue, the National Guardsmen in their gas masks, these pictures I've tossed aside. Others of open conflict and the ironic scenes which were part of Berkeley, these I've tried to keep. Years later, on a train going back east, I had an image of myself being arrested by the FBI. I would remain silent. After searching me the only information they would find would be these tattered photographs of the People's Park riots in Berkeley or an anti-Vietnam, anti-ROTC rally. That's all they'd need. Here's one of an officer clubbing a girl to the ground. She had covered her face with her hands and didn't fight back. She looks very young, probably came over from her high school during study hall. Someone nearby, face close to the lens, has a look of terror on his face. There's a billboard in the background for Amoco. Here's one of an officer aiming a kind of gun the county police said they didn't use. A picture of the house on Ashby Avenue, another of a house off Hearst – these are the most incriminating but I've saved them anyway. Another dream I had was about being picked up by a murderer/rapist while hitch-hiking. I try to fight back but can't get the car door open. The landscape contains no signs of rescue during my last minutes and no one knows my real name. My naked body is found with bits of these pictures lying scattered over me like leaves in autumn, a maniac's way to bury his dead. Would the FBI catch up with me then? Would they put the pieces together in their forensic laboratories and then, maybe, figure out who I was? At rallies I often saw the man to whom I sold my camera. By noon the sun was high and the light harsh for taking them.

231

Noon Rally! Sproul Hall!

At the entrance to Sproul Plaza, embedded in the concrete, was a six- by eight-inch brass plaque with raised letters which read:

PROPERTY OF THE REGENTS OF
THE UNIVERSITY OF CALIFORNIA.
PERMISSION TO PASS REVOCABLE AT ANY TIME.

Everyone hung out at Sproul Plaza, and because of the Free Speech Movement, the university allowed student groups or groups with student sponsors to set up tables and disseminate information there. The largest and most popular of these groups were the Radical Student Union (RSU), they were Marxist-Leninist, unaffiliated; the Maoist Students for a Democratic Society (SDS), a faction of which became the Progressive Labour Party (PL); the Young Spartacus League (Sparts), which had a small following; the Student Mobilization Committee (SMC), and the Trotskyite Young Socialist Alliance (YSA). There was also a table for the Universal Life Church. If you gave one dollar you got a card making you a minister and this was advertised as a way of avoiding the draft. The only religious zealot was Holy Hubert. Reactionary, fundamentalist Hubert didn't have a table. He stood on a planter and engaged in shouting matches with anyone who challenged him. Later on there were Moonies ('Cookies and fruit juice upstairs!').

We were sitting in the Forum having coffee when Mary suggested going to a meeting of a group, a particular faction which had split off from the SDS. We had attended many political meetings, without actually joining, from the moderate, informal gatherings of the resistance at a Friends' meeting house in North Berkeley to the heated political debates in overcrowded halls, the meetings of the RSU; and the small, calculated meetings of the Progressive Labour Party coming out of a single party line. The latter had recently planned a demonstration which ended in two weeks of rioting. Mary had reasons; this wasn't just another sample bit of agitprop training. The Forum was dark and smoky. Drug deals were being made around us. Someone had a friend who had just returned from Mexico, from Colombia. Nickel bags, dime bags, voices lowered, sometimes not. Connections established, deals proposed and connections severed. These conversations flooded the gaps in ours. Mary had met one of the members of the group. It was focused on drawing attention to and attacking the corporate support for the war in Vietnam: IBM, Honeywell, Carex, Dow Chemical, those were the obvious targets. General Motors, Westinghouse, Monsanto, almost any corporation in the telephone book had Defense contracts. Mary was more curious about the group than committed to its ideas. My curiosity took the reverse turn. I often felt out of place at these meetings. These organizations presented constructs like waves I admired but which swept me aside rather than along. Finally I was persuaded.

The meeting was in a house off Hearst Avenue. There were only six or seven people besides us in a cluttered room in the front of the house. Stacks of newspapers, books, articles cut out and pinned to the wall, an old black typewriter. I write cluttered but I remember the impression of crowding and emptiness at the same time. There were only a few chairs. At each meeting some people had to sit on the floor. There was a poster of Lenin placed in such a way as to be invisible from the street. I think it was Lenin, perhaps Emma Goldman, perhaps I just want to think the room bore the mark of someone's portrait from another generation. A testament to precedence, you see, because what I do remember about the room is that it always seemed to be in a house newly arrived at or about to be abandoned, a room of transit with no use for the evidence of antecedents.

A man named Win usually began the meetings by discussing his research into a chain of connections, the links between institutions and the everyday, between our pedestrian actions – the quotidian behaviour rarely questioned – and the feeding of the war effort. In other decades, past or future, Win might be a dogged journalist, a private

233

investigator who, for a fee, would peel the sedate layers off the worst kind of corruption. Win was more polite and earnest than most detective novel heroes, although cynical enough. He was too unruly in appearance and manner to get very far as a journalist. A true believer in 'production for use', his research was not to be wasted. Win didn't believe in mass riots, pitting students against police minions, although he would go to rallies and pitch teargas canisters back with the best of them. Despite his participation, he believed riots were a distraction, fodder for television crews. Letter writing, petitions, boycotting, these were footnotes, nothing more. Win wanted to aim at the main arteries. Win was short for Winthrop Auersbach, but none of us was suspicious of the aristocratic sound of his name. We weren't given any reason to be. He approached us with no clutter of received ideas or favourable prejudices. Win didn't offer instant affiliation. Many men burned their draft cards and went to jail; many were earnest and obsessed. Win did all these things but had no mental list of his heroics or achievements in subversion. He didn't care what it all meant, he didn't want credit for anything and I found him more compelling than I admitted to Mary.

Nearly as vocal as Win was Peter. If the group could have been called an organization, Peter was its security wing. He was obsessed with secrecy, obscuring identity and keeping information from people to ensure his own safety. Once, for a month, he had everyone call him Philip M. Ray in order to confuse people, since he believed the FBI was tailing him. Nobody could remember to do this. He would be called 'Peter-I-mean-Philip', then everyone gave up and P.M. Ray was dropped. I questioned his resolve but Win assured me that if Peter were an informer he would take care not to appear so cowardly. Mr Ray was simply afraid of losing his job at the bookstore. Eventually he stopped coming to the meetings, looked embarrassed when he saw one of us in the store, and clearly crossed the street when he saw me coming towards him. His girlfriend stayed on. She did a lot of typing for Win. I couldn't see why these notes and research papers were so crucial. They were, to him, part of what might one day be a very important document. Documentation, history: in spite of his lack of preciousness and seeming concern only for the present, there was something of the preservationist in Win, as if he knew this all-important, highly charged moment were only that. Casualties would consist of what was going to go out of fashion; what would remain vital, he believed, were certain facts.

In the spring, although the Regents tried to ban assemblies, there were rallies and frequent clashes with police. The whole campus, even those who thought they were safely tucked away in classrooms, was affected by the CS gas. During the riots a helicopter sprayed the campus and gas drifted into nearby hospitals. CS is stronger than CN, the kind usually used on civilians: in certain circumstances in Vietnam it was fatal. On the other side we threw rocks, bricks, bottles, and eventually I got sufficiently used to the gas and the hot canisters to throw them back at the police. I moved quickly; you had to move fast. Grey university trashcans were sometimes used to smother the bombs, or the contents of the trashcans were burned and the cement bases thrown like heavy flying saucer sleds. Unless the teargas was dealt with in either of those two ways everyone would panic and run away. Medics would yell, 'Walk!' It was the police's favourite way of breaking up crowds, although even CS gas wasn't always effective.

Teargas makes your eyes water and sting horribly. You can't breathe, and, temporarily blinded, you can't see the police coming at you. There were theories about what would help; egg, vinegar. You just got used to it, after a while the body can. They used pepper gas to disperse people and jeeps equipped with teargas rigs and screens attached to the sides provided a broad front to sweep through crowds. They claimed they used birdshot, but shotgun and special .36 calibre shells were found.

The riot police were drawn from various quarters: the regular university security guards, the California Highway

235

Patrol, Berkeley, Alameda and other Bay area forces. Many looked like cartoon police made of Dick Tracy angles, caricatures of human beings drafted with a T square. They were referred to as fascistic as a matter of course. Teutonic and murderous, yet they were drawn from the California surf. In these situations, however, in their special back packs with sprayers and their gas masks, the riot police looked like giant bugs escaped from a Hollywood back lot, all-purpose extras sent from set to set with no sense of any single complete picture. After a number of riots it was impossible to imagine them going home to families in Marin or Santa Clara. The police, for the most part, we considered dehumanized, indoctrinated, like Robot Men with jet packs, unable to criticize or reflect on the discs with which they'd been programmed. I write about them in metaphor as if they were harmless, futuristic models, as if I don't take them seriously.

It's a mistake. Viciousness is a trait associated with an individual, not a mob, but that's what I think about when I remember the riot police. The language of personal traits seems accurate. The character of each individual opponent equals the character of the mob, and by virtue of being an opponent everyone on that side, collectively and singly, is as damned as the cause they support. Win called them Deltas, the hit men or the dumb, unquestioning arm of the corporate institution. Their allegiance was advertised by American flags sewn on their sleeves. I was curious, and still am, about the biographies of the National Guardsmen and the county sheriffs who rushed so quickly to Berkeley. What were the moments, the turning points in their childhoods, as the interviewers are so fond of asking, which made them choose the military? I don't think the local police really thought about what we represented or who they were working for. The Vietnam veterans against the war might be an untenable contradiction to them but it's easy to look at things naively when you're sure there are only two sides.

The police, as well as the radicals, were often accused of

instigating violence or provoking riots, sadistically beating anyone if they even looked like they had breathed fuck off. It didn't matter if the victim had, in fact, been silent. Observers, reporters were guilty by association for just standing around. Those who wanted no part in the demonstrations tried to gauge when the correct moment had arrived to traverse the campus. Often guessing wrong, they paid for the miscalculations with minor injuries. The timid and the unconcerned tried to skirt riots, and, failing, were swept into them, like walking into a helicopter, books scattered, glasses smashed. For the ones who intended to demonstrate and who did fight back, reprisal was fierce. Women were pulled by the hair and beaten around the face until knocked to the ground. There were some who just followed along, but except for those errant neutrals who got swept in physically by accident, this was a fight whose ideology, left or right, was supported passionately by each side. The effects of property damage were minor compared with the results of police brutality, which probably created more radicals than served as a force of subjugation.

The aftermath, as late afternoon became evening, looked like an epilogue to a brief war, a prolonged skirmish. The looting and trashing were nothing like in a real war, but I think the rallies and police reaction helped dispel the notion of a battlefield as an abstract space, an artificial plain used for war games. Land battles happen where people conduct their lives in some aspect. In this case university property, and sometimes lives, were among the casualties. Windows, glass doors were reduced to gaping holes with jagged glass teeth. Smouldering trashcans, broken windows; a dog might play with a flattened teargas canister. As the next day's *Daily Californian* went to press, announcements would be printed requesting witnesses:

Anyone who saw Elizabeth Klein have her arm broken when arrested by police at approximately 1.00 Wednesday, April 14, you are needed as a witness. The incident occurred west of the dining commons, on the path between Strawberry Creek and the Alumni House. Please call 845-5957

Billy Graham, visiting President Nixon, said, 'Prayer will get us out of our dilemma.'

After a while a pattern became discernible. Speeches at Sproul were followed by marches to Callaghan Hall, ROTC headquarters, and the confrontations with police quickly followed. When I went to SDS meetings I could see how these things were planned, how they developed, and ended. There would be a build-up on each side until a clash occurred. The speeches began by attacking the university's covertly racist policies, its complicity with ROTC and the Defense Department. The speeches became boring after a while. Everyone knew what was coming.

You would often hear all kinds of general observations about the riots. Men would say they were a good place to pick up women because of the excitement of the situation: it was viscerally dangerous, the adrenalin soared. I heard one man talk about the riots as a 'peak emotional experience, like a fantastic orgasm'. It made me want to puke. People were seriously injured, lost their lives, and here's some man talking about these battles, these confrontations in terms of crass sexual metaphors. I was too idealistic; there *was* an element of crassness involved. Many participated on those terms. There was a lot of jingoism about dope, rock music, girls and the revolution. It was something to disassociate yourself from and I did, increasingly so. The danger, the caveman brutality of each conflict, duped us into believing sides were simple: X against Y; clean, neat, unambiguous. Physical strength – though the odds weren't good either way if you were unarmed. Win had a better chance of hurting a National Guardsman than Mary. Discrepancies in strength reduced the situation to certain inevitable dependencies and allegiances. I considered learning Kung Fu.

I was often sick of Win, Mr Seer, Lord High Chamberlain

238

of Every Detail. He ran everything as if he were the only one capable of understanding the complexities of social theory. The vocabulary of theory and practice was his precious bailiwick. Language, ideas, action, he was the mediator and the lockup. He was so circuitous about asking women to type, xerox, tidy up, as if they weren't doing it for him personally but for the common good. Win had a way, when one was alone with him, of making each woman feel she was the one with the brains, the only one who could play on the boys' team and might ultimately share a bit of his territory, might not have to type his notes any more.

Sometimes you didn't know what to expect. You could be blinded, have bones shattered, organs ruptured; you had to draw on animal instincts and had no training for doing so. How much was I willing to stake? Cowardice isn't a clear-cut streak when you're at a physical disadvantage. All the elements for a fairy-tale rescue were in place, and as I stood near Win one day maybe that was when Berkeley seemed not so far from Spartacus. Hiding behind the garage in Sproul Plaza. The only way to accept the danger was to frame potential terror in a context of 'when I was a little girl'. Win could snap billy clubs, take guns away: another image from the nursery. I couldn't look to him for rescue, wouldn't accept the instant Hercules anyway. Should the occasion call for Superman, I might laugh myself to death in the wake of Win's transformation.

A helmet reflected the sun, a scream far off in the crowd, the benign egg shape turned malevolent. Now it seems so anachronistic, so choreographed a kind of fight, each side neatly lined up. Almost like a print of a nineteenth-century battle, uniforms tinted red and blue, each side knew where the other was. No chance guerrilla skirmish, no surprises. But for the moment lines wavered, I couldn't see very far over the heads. Thinking: what if this is it? What if this is it? The fighting seemed to be drawing closer. People began to run. A helmet, sunglasses, no mouth, no language. The riot police were quiet, appeared suddenly, rapid fingers striking into the crowd. A club came down on Win's back, he crumpled for a moment but could still walk. We made our way to the edge of the mob. Blood ran down his cheek from splintered glasses, yet he clutched them in his hand like a damaged but crucial identity card, an odd artefact to save for your grandchildren. I can see old man Win pulling them out of a shoe box along with a battered belt buckle from the Red Army, a Chinese cap – all genuine, he would say, all certainly the real thing. He limped and held on to me tightly. Win was afraid and, never having known him to be afraid, his fear was compelling. We were far enough from the fighting so terror was no longer a contagion.

Injury made Win desperate. The bloody cut on his head (combined with the effects of the tear-gas fog) must have interfered with his vision. He saw lamp posts and bicycles where there were none, stepped over curbs without anticipating the drop. Home, FBI bugs be damned, was never so safe. We washed his cut in the kitchen sink. There seemed no need to go to the hospital or call a doctor. Win was able to stand up straight.

I helped him upstairs. Pain was sending signals up his left side in morse code, Win said. What was going to be wrong? His contorted face seemed a cinematic projection of a nervous system gone haywire. He was glad not to be alone. Win filled the bathtub, took off his clothes and got in. I hadn't seen him naked before. He was always careful about shutting doors, the only person in the house who did. No one saw him without clothes on. He was very thin and the way he stepped so gingerly into the water reminded me of an illustration of Titania's fairies, toes just nipping the surface of the water – except Win was more battered. I pulled the toilet seat down: what do you want me to do, Win? He didn't want me to help him, I was just to watch, make sure he didn't lose consciousness from his head injury and slip under the water's surface.

'Why do you think I took my clothes off?'

'To take a bath.'

'That wasn't the only reason.'

240

'You're supposed to be wounded.' I tried to be as obtuse as possible.

'I don't want to talk about it.' That was the pattern. You were just supposed to know those moments when they happened, not talk about your reluctance, and take your clothes off. When I was slow, he leaned out of the bathtub to help, getting water all over my legs. Win wouldn't pretend any passion or overtly express desire. He was so oblique and matter-of-fact you suspected fervour would be expressed in other ways. It wasn't. Because of the riots our emotions were spent in odd channels and so strange alliances were formed, and broken, in turn.

In Paris students and workers had taken to the streets.

Win's frenzy to document was finally ebbing to some kind of point of action. A long book, a huge boycott, a series of bombings. He had become secretive and went into Oakland a lot, or at least that's where he said he was going. He often took a paternalistic line with women but was also the kind of father who would abandon his self-proclaimed children at the drop of a hat.

Marching to Callaghan Hall on a warm May afternoon, Mary and I were joined by Win. Berkeley had a $70 million contract with the Defense Department and Win predicted major confrontation. Callaghan Hall is low, unimposing, across the street from Strawberry Creek and a eucalyptus grove. The police were already in place and somewhere ahead of us we heard screams; waves of teargas began to blur the edges of profiles. There was a surge, I was pushed forward into the fog and separated from Mary, but I kept my head down and pressed a handkerchief over my nose and mouth. A canister landed nearby, I tossed it back, mostly intuiting the location of the surrounding Armada. The crowd had a thrashing momentum that, in moments of frenzy, could accidentally turn in on itself. A woman toppled against me, I lost my balance and my heel came down hard on something soft: a human hand. It was attached to a small man who had been overcome by CS gas. I helped him to the medics and as I reached the edges of the fighting I saw Win and Mary, who was limping, arms around each other, walking in the direction of Hearst Avenue. I didn't run after them. If I turned my back on the crowd, clouds of teargas I knew to be bitter looked like a gentle mist floating through the eucalyptus glade.

'Drugs, art theft, murder in Oakland, murder in Marseilles, an old American oil rig in Libya, a former governor of California's Indonesian correspondence, the woman who brings in his mail, a man with one wall-eye in a Mission district bodega, a woman in a laboratory exposing *in vitro* cancer cells to oxygen, a man on an oil tanker gazing across the Pacific; all fit into a long-armed acquaintance network, a sensational newspaper story, the story of the year, the one that blows the lid off,' Win said. 'You take all your little. stories and put them into one big story. Shave off a little here, add a bit there and it will all connect. A little dove-tailing, that's what stories are all about, right?

'Let me explain it to you this way. I heard a man on the radio and he had a theory about acquaintance networks. If you can believe his system, any single person in the United States could meet any other single person in the United States through an average of five contacts. The kid who runs the car wash could meet the president of Chrysler Corporation. The man on the oil tanker could meet the woman who works for the former Governor of California. He could find out a lot about his correspondence, business and personal, and where the two overlap. You could say he finds out by screwing the secretary, or you could say she screws him, or even that they fall in love, depending on what kind of story you want. So he gets in trouble, the oil man, finding out things about the governor, and he ends up knifed on an oil tanker, stranded in the middle of the Indian Ocean, headed towards the Strait of Hormuz.

'You have to look for the clues, the connections.

'Cut out a bunch of stories and line them up on your

desk, one right after another, put them in piles according to category. There must be some scientist who will jump out of type, run across the desk and prostitute his research to Mr Petro-Dollars.

'The wall-eyed man suddenly appears in Marseilles with a painting that was hot long before he stole it.

'The painting originally belonged to a Cuban doctor, now living in New York.

'Neither of them wants to talk.

'The sister may have been married to an ex-Nazi in the fifties and you think she's still hiding him somewhere on Long Island.

'And the former Nazi is actually the uncle of the woman who works for the former Governor of California. The moral of the whole thing is that few people are ever really out of power. They still exercise their influence in private spheres, so you have to watch out for everybody.'

I folded my newspaper into thirds and told him there wasn't enough room on my desk for a stack of newspaper articles and there wasn't enough room in our house for even little people to run around, meet for drinks, exchange secrets, hide stolen art, or old Nazis, and read other people's mail. Did I seriously think stories could be linked like pop-it beads?

Mary and I had a basic philosophy about the network of the guilty. Guilt by association, by endorsement: you had to know what to boycott. You had to know who the enemy was, which thresholds not to cross, who not to shake hands with. We didn't go to the Safeway supermarket, never bought non-union lettuce, poured our leftover Cokes and Pepsis down the drain and never drank them again. The absence of economic endorsement, however large, is still a passive kind of action that depends on recruitment and numbers for success. (Later on I heard there was a faction of Weather women who boycotted speech with men.)

It wasn't enough for Win, this systematic shunning. He wanted complete agreement. Not satisfied with waiting for them to come to you and be refused, he was interested in the direct hit. The chain of acquaintances, the network of the guilty – it had a purpose. It was useful to know that, under the name of company A, a man owned a series of porn houses, and under the name of corporation B, the same man owned a string of restaurants near the university. It was becoming too academic. Win was nearly finished with sleuthing out degrees of culpability, depths of nasty deals, ironic connections, hypocritical relationships. Everyone knew the connections of corporations like Standard Oil, Honeywell and IBM with the war. Still, he wanted to be sure, before we left the Med café, that there wasn't the slightest doubt in my mind about the Network of the Guilty. He linked his arms around the back of the metal chair so his chest stuck out.

'The President of the Board of Trustees of your favourite museum in San Francisco is also on the board of the Contel Corporation which owns diamond mines in South Africa, feldspar mines in Angola, Kennecot Copper* in Chile, and Western Tin, to name three of his nine corporate affiliations. Each time you pay a dollar to see his art collection, you support apartheid, the war in South East Asia and the museum's anti-union policies towards its own employees. The president of Carex Industries has a large collection of French nineteenth-century paintings. He designed the concept of bombing Vietnam's countryside with chemicals in order to force people into the cities. If his estate is bombed in retaliation, to make him flee to L.A., all those innocent paintings will be destroyed as well.'

I felt, at times, like a beleagured half convert confronted by a medieval priest, and there was no questioning the demands he exacted: each penance matched my transgressions. Over the water fountain at the Café Mediterranean

* In 1972 Dr Salvatore Allende accused Kennecot Copper of 'digging claws into my country . . . of trying to manage our political life'. After Allende was murdered, his government was replaced by a military junta which made reparations to Kennecot to make up for the previous attempts at nationalization of industry. Win, scenting the CIA behind everything as a matter of course, would have felt even more vindicated looking back on this conversation. Jane Amme

was a sign which read: 'No soliciting or dealing.' It's one of my clearest images of the Med.

Win began the meeting by declaring that there were many targets worth hitting, and in the process of narrowing down his list he discovered the deserving Luc Ferrier. Win had been taking trips to southern California and had investigated the headquarters of the major weapons manufacturers. Each of them maintained complicated security arrangements. There were many snares, final numbers in locks' combinations we couldn't begin to predict. It had been planned that one of the women would pose as a night cleaner, plant the bomb, then leave, but even these workers had special identity cards. You couldn't enter the building without one. We considered having one of us apply for a job under an assumed name, get a card, execute our plan, then leave anonymously, but some job applications, Mary learned, were checked with the police department. It was as if they anticipated trouble, in the form of file riflers at the very least. All of us, except the departed Peter, had been arrested. You practically had to be bonded to mop the floor. Also, each person who entered or exited the buildings had his or her movements monitored by closed-circuit television. Some offices were in large buildings in Los Angeles. There was no point in a twenty-four hour day in which innocent workers wouldn't be killed and there was no guarantee that a warning telephone call before the blast would be taken seriously. Offices were the optimum target. Second choice was the suggestion of bombing the estates of those who occupied the pinnacle of Win's network of the guilty. At first Win rejected this idea.

One day he tried tossing firebombs at the Oakland Army Terminal (where weapons were shipped to Vietnam) from the highway, but none of them worked. As he became increasingly frustrated, the meetings became more erratic.

Her body was found partially clothed in a ditch near a parking lot in south Berkeley. She had been raped and strangled, but not robbed. There was $84 in her wallet and a gold chain around her neck. The second murder took place a few days later. The victim's body was found near a diner which didn't open until late in the morning. It was as if she had been waiting for the owners of the Busy Bee Diner to open up, leaning against the side of the building. They'd never seen her before, they said, even though they'd just interviewed a lot of women for a waitressing job. She'd been raped and strangled like the first but she showed more signs of having fought back. Detectives took scrapings from under her fingernails and sent them off to a forensic laboratory. Three, four, five dead women were found as autumn began. Students were warned not to hitch-hike, not to take isolated routes home at night, to walk in pairs, or in groups. The only clue the police had was a silver cigarette lighter the dead woman at the Busy Bee had clutched in her right hand. It was engraved with the initials, G.M., not hers. She was Carla Pollack. Crisis hotlines were set up. The cautious wanted straight facts, they wanted a predictable pattern to emerge. The frightened were interested in rumour, snatching at any spectacular story that a friend of a friend might have heard. The man was Hawaiian, he had an accent, he had a nervous twitch over his right eye. The police described the suspect as being twenty to twenty-five years of age, a short white man, with long brown hair. It could have been any one of thousands.

I had taken on the mute role of an automatic participant. Except as a physical presence who listened to speakers, broke a few windows, threw CS gas canisters, I was the sort Jane Austen's characters would have called 'a most agreeable and obliging young lady'. One disaffected day Win asked me to type a few pages for him. I refused.

'Even Marx and Engels wrote about the enslavement of women by the bourgeoisie. Just because you're who you say you are doesn't get you off the hook, doesn't make you innocent of everything. Cultural hegemony in Vietnam,' I scattered newspaper clippings to the floor, 'cultural hege-

246

mony in Oakland,' I almost mimicked him, 'it's all patriarchal, Dickface.' The two words, one with connotations of
veneration and power, the other from the gutter, just
slipped out together. 'Do your own typing. Do my typing.'

We tossed slogans at each other. He accused me of
cynicism, lack of commitment, of placing too much value
on my privacy, and, 'Don't we all have to work in some
capacity, however unpleasant?'

Mary was in the room looking pained. I wanted to shout
at her, 'Get rid of the melodrama, I can't stand this torn
devotion act.' In private, to me, she might call him a
theoretical slob but in the room with the portrait of Lenin
she was silent. Since the riot Mary had grown ambivalent
and chary. Her confidences to me were not about Win as a
person with whom she had slept. Skirting Win the hero or
bather, sticking to his political contradictions, you would
think she hated him. In spite of her privately voiced
criticism, we continued to go to meetings. Sometimes as we
walked to the house she would grow nervous, teeth almost
chattering. A malingering symptom, she blamed it on
coffee and a drug I had never heard of. During that month,
the meetings were the only time we saw Win.

My interest dwindled and I began to talk about leaving
the group. Mary, to my surprise, agreed with me. In her
speech Win was prefixed by 'that guy'. She spoke with the
derision of someone who might have been jilted but also
wanted a way out. With the talk of bombings she was afraid
things were going to get out of control and her life would be
taken over by Win and his schemes. She believed he had
good ideas, and, after the smoke cleared, he might be
all benevolence, but in the meantime, his plans had a
malevolent edge. Win was beyond agitprop. When he
detailed how explosives could be stolen from a sporadically
guarded construction site, Mary began to resent, even more
strongly, being asked to do menial tasks. Suspicion and
fear buttressed resentment and we began to talk seriously of
parting from Win. Even if she thought Win's targets deserved
being blown to bits – and Mary didn't have strong pacifist

sympathies – she saw danger in following a man who had become a zealous believer in his own rhetoric. Fear, secrecy, Win as Keeper of the Directives, all these previously minor elements would surface, would take control. We weren't so much afraid of a mistake which would leave us charred skeletons in an accidental factory explosion as of being swept into the kind of commitment that binds colleagues of violence. We just didn't want to be his minions.

The things people do when they're alone: singing along with the radio at the top of their lungs; dancing; addressing mirrors, the captive audience. When he spoke to us, Win acted as if he were by himself in a house of mirrors and radios.

Mary and I talked about starting an archive for the kinds of books and documents that lay on the invisible reading list. We started making lists. It was a vague idea, a resource made up of the omissions, a folderful of lists haphazardly arranged. Win said the women of Vietnam didn't have the luxury of leaving the struggle, that the Lost Women Library (sic) sounded like something from Peter Pan, and what made us think chronicalization ensured survival?

'You're the one who's always talking about rectifying history's erasures. Do you think you have a monopoly on that idea, on those words?' I asked him.

'If you think your history's been snitched from you and polluted, action is what engenders change. Don't talk to me about women as a marginalized sex class. Blow up the massage parlours on Shattuck Avenue,' Win said.

'Go bury your head in the Frankfurt school,' Mary answered.

RAPIST WORKS IN POST OFFICE
MADMAN STALKS BAY AREA
KAMPUS KILLER

It was still light out but barely. I was neither particularly frightened nor cautious so I left the art building the way I came. It was Sunday. I was carrying spray paints left over from making anti-war signs. I stared at the Campanile as if the tower were a beacon although I knew my way. A funny omen, sticking up like that. I had always taken it for granted in the past, like a street sign or a traffic light. The school had paved two asphalt paths from the music building to the creek but I took the dirt path worn down through the middle of the grassy slope. Near the creek it was dark. It was always dark there, even in the middle of the sunniest day. I could see him examine each tree in turn. He was tall, dressed in expensive light brown and blue clothes. At first I thought he might be a professor. When I reached the bridge he approached me and asked if I had the time. His watch, he pointed to his wrist, had stopped.

'I'm supposed to meet my nephew at the Faculty Club. That's one of those buildings up there, isn't it? I'm from Newport. I haven't been here in years.' He introduced himself, familiarly, as Guy Masterson. He was more clinging than a stranger ought to be and told me nervously that his nephew was an associate professor of thermodynamics.

'You must be a student. An art student?' I had a bag of spray paints in one hand. He said something about no longer contributing to the university because of hoodlums and the tragedy of a decent research grant rescinded, but I wasn't interested in having a chat with him. I just wanted to get home. I turned around to point out the Faculty Club where his nephew was supposedly waiting when he grabbed me violently by the collar. In the second my shirt tore I realized the rapist didn't have long hair, could be a town alderman, an FBI agent, could be anyone, but was the greying man behind me. He turned me around, had his mouth over mine so I couldn't scream. His taste was disgusting, violently alien. I gagged so fiercely, the retching noise must have contributed to his perverse desire somehow. Ways of fighting back – hands, feet, teeth – all rendered useless. I recoiled in spasms like seizures. He said something about dirty pants as he held my wrists together with one hand and tried to unzipper my blue jeans with the other. Frustrated, he smacked me across the face and tripped me so I fell to the ground. It's strange how time is suspended for the duration of criminal assault, as if you're in a capsule and life spins on its merry way without noticing you, as if you're operating at such a high speed, you and your assailant are invisible to other human beings. The glade was deserted. It was completely dark now. Masterson was on top of me. He held one of my arms pinned down. My left flailed and pushed uselessly. He shoved it away with such force my hand hit something cool and cylindrical on the ground. He pulled a cord from his breast pocket. My fingers closed around the top of the object. One of the spray-paint cans which had tumbled from my hands just a few minutes ago nestled in my palm, cap popped off. Cord around neck, his eyes bulged out in mimicry of the way mine were about to. I threw the paint into his face. Day-glo pink, Mr Masterson looked like a racoon escaped from someone else's LSD trip. Blinded, he must have been. He made horrible noises but refused to scream. He rolled off me as weightlessly as a marshmallow. I ran.

Nobody picked up the hotline number.

The police didn't believe me, made no connection between a man who was stupid enough to tell me his name and a cigarette lighter clutched in a dead woman's left hand at the Busy Bee Diner. What did I think this was: *Strangers on a Train*?

'How many people in the state of California walk around with the initials G.M.? Could have been Carla Pollack's boyfriend, for all we know.' No one had been admitted to a Bay Area hospital emergency room with pink spray paint in his eyes. 'That's the kind of thing the nurses would remember, don't you think?' Perhaps he had been only temporarily blinded, perhaps he'd washed in the back seat of his limousine, attended by his chauffeur. Because I'd been arrested and released immediately after a riot months ago, the police were not inclined to believe me; they found my sarcasm in bad taste and I accused too quickly. 'Did you think about what you just said? Did he really look like that?' Their idea of a criminal identity was the social misfit drop-out. Mine was a well-dressed man who talked about art. They kept me in the police station overnight, wouldn't let me take a bath, questioned me as if I'd raped myself, beat myself up.

In the smokey little Top Dog the television was always on with the sound turned down and the radio turned up. Hot dogs were lined up on the grill, a replica of a log-jam made of meat. The same old Libertarian propaganda was tacked up, but the man who made the dogs didn't seem to notice. That was all they served. Mary and I sat on a concrete wall outside. It was warm for October and we tossed potato chips to Peachum. Mary's place in her book was marked by a clipping from Win's anti-war research files. We rarely ran into him anymore but his ghost turned up in books, at the bottom of a pillow case full of laundry, a cast-iron frying pan never returned. I pulled the article out of her book. It was several months old, the image smudged. It was about Carex, Inc. Luc Ferrier wasn't smiling as he had been when he told me he, too, was something of a student of art, although there was little of it to look at in Newport.

You didn't need the obsessiveness of a Win Auersbach to learn about Luc Ferrier. Catalogues of marriages, children, acquisitions, these weren't what I was looking for. I checked through Standard and Poor's, back issues of *Business Week*, the *Banker's Almanac and Yearbook*. He had been a member of the Bilderberg group, an organization whose membership was composed of largely European corporate and state leaders. It was a predecessor of the Trilateral Commission and, had he lived to 1970 when that organization was founded, Luc Ferrier would surely have been an active member. You string all the little stories together to get the big one but which scheme had been a footnote to the other? Homogeneity: Ferrier wanted his products to have the same universality as Coca Cola; broadcasts he sponsored should be heard from Lapland to the Cape of Good Hope. His rationale: a certain class of people have genetic destinies mapped out for tedious employment in unpleasant environments at thirty-five American cents an hour, and if they can't speak English that's a marketing problem.

To some people covert greed isn't confused with piggishness. They're entirely separate. One is an abstract, philosophical sin, the other is associated with plebeian excess. Virtues instilled in compulsory chapel were, for Ferrier, sentiments of elasticity. (Where he went to school was listed and certainly chapel there was mandatory.) I've read that fat people dream of consuming the whole world and I think Luc Ferrier was a fat person in an average-size body.

Win would say, well, there you are, he's a global rapist, too. Win's politics and morality were sometimes like a Sunday school lesson memorized too well and naively. He saw too clearly devils dancing around a red-hot fire waving pokers and pitch forks. I didn't care about any of that so much. Losing faith in moral indignation, I just wanted to even the score. Victims often become obsessed with the limitations imposed on fighting back, but I didn't think the terms of murdering this man were based entirely on personal motives.

'Born in 1930, he resides in La Jolla, California.'

From there we went to the telephone book.

The blast went off at night. He was alone in the house, according to the news, and we were glad of that. The part of the house occupied by his servants was only a little shaken and chipped. The Los Angeles Times reported the details of his art collection, how it was reduced to burnt fragments of canvas and bits of marble body parts. Even on television, the ruins of his house were spectacular. The television fire was weak and nearly out; you could faintly hear the surf in the background. As the reporter droned on about the victim's wealth, ambulance attendants carried out a stretcher almost as flat as when they brought it in. Another report said they found an armless, legless torso. Former wives would not speak to journalists. The local television reporter described the perpetrators as 'fringe activists fascinated by arson, bombing and violence'. I don't think he used the word 'terrorists'. It had not yet come into common news language. He never alluded to the fact that this man was singled out for a reason. Back in the newsroom he was controlled, no longer foregrounded by the burning estate. His voice had the network tone of ironic surprise – one of the groups claiming responsibility was an anti-war group, a faction split off from the SDS. The other group, his voice went up slightly, said they were feminists. Several groups had called the *Berkeley Tribe*, declaring they had been the ones who set the charge.

Governor Reagan, a personal friend of the deceased, vowed revenge on the terrorists. There was a close-up of charred shards of pre-Colombian artefacts from what had been the Ferrier terrace: slivers of marble from a bathtub, a corner of canvas, a Renaissance woman's face blew towards the beach.

The FBI was fairly easy to spot in Berkeley. Each agent had very short hair, thin tie, hat, sometimes dark glasses, and they all seemed to wear Robert Hall suits. Nobody else looked anything like them. Once in a while the *Daily Californian* would print pictures of them with captions: 'Reported undercover agents observing Thursday's demonstration.' We didn't take them seriously until one came to the door of the house we shared. He was looking for me but I wasn't home. The knock on the door was alarming although the FBI knocked on a lot of doors as a routine matter. We had a choice. Mr Robert Hall might only be looking for me because of the people I knew; perhaps his ominous call had nothing to do with certain exploded property in La Jolla, California. The latter assumption was injudiciously naive, an assumption as rooted in myth and wishful thinking as the memory of a perfectly innocent childhood. Forget sweet dreams: we began to make plans to go underground. Now I wonder why we delayed so long, intrigued by our own crime and its aftermath. Voyeurism: the hallmark of a pair of novices who hang around to watch the news. Bombing is easily an anonymous crime, we were told, and another charge, unknown to us (Win?) had gone off that same night.

Around this time we were sharing the house on Ashby Avenue with a third woman. Neither Mary nor I knew her very well. Ordinarily she hadn't been in much, and then, at the time of the bombing, she was in all the time. She wore outlandish clothes, as if dress might signify a kind of larger unconventionality. In spite of the long black cape, lots of scarves and hats, she was, in most conversations, like a boy-crazy fifteen-year-old. Sleeping out most nights was like some sort of social obligation, although she didn't always enjoy sleeping with men we never saw. It was just what she did. She didn't boycott the Safeway supermarket, read the *L.A. Times*, thought general obedience would solve most problems, was a devoted shopper of everything and always had the money to do that kind of passionate shopping. When we asked her not to buy milk from the Safeway but to work at the co-op like the rest of us, she would apologize profusely, declaring her mind 'was on a different level right now'. 'A different level, all right,' Mary said, 'the Federal Bureau of Investigation.' Mary didn't trust her. She may have guessed about the bombing. The same network which provided us with explosives was also to help us with some of the papers and background for going underground. I had found her in our room a few times. She claimed she needed to borrow soap or aspirin but if she had snooped she might have guessed about our trip to La Jolla. But then I think she was genuinely, adamantly apolitical, not an informer at all. I knew a lot of radicals, some of whom had already gone underground. The agent could have had any number of reasons for wanting 'just to ask her a few questions', as they say would with deliberate ambiguity.

Finally we split up, promising it was only temporary.

254

Mary moved to Oakland, hair was cut short or grown long. I hennaed mine red and stayed in Berkeley a few days after she left, but I couldn't get away from the shopper in the black cape. I ran into her all over campus although she wasn't in any of my classes. Once she cornered me near the Campanile, the tower used for storage by the palaeontology department. The chimes had just gone off a few minutes before. She knew I didn't have a class. I had no excuses. I couldn't tell her I was going to look at the bones. She wanted to know why everyone had moved out of the house suddenly and why she had always been left out of everything. I felt sorry for her. Perhaps she was nothing more harmful than a shoplifter in those voluminous clothes but I was evasive with her out of habit. I still hold her responsible, indirectly. A few days later I noticed a car with two Robert Hall agents parked across the street and down a few yards from my door. The four-door Ford was there when I got home in the evening and the next morning, too. Mary called from Oakland. Her private nature grew obsessive under pressure of suspected investigation and arrest. Polly Peachum was run over by a Ford. Mary didn't take down the licence number. It would have been them. She was certain. She had found FBI cars at her doors and had declined to answer any bells or knocks. It had taken the investigators several months, but by 14 July we guessed arrests for the Masterson bombing couldn't be far off. We had been so careful and credit for the action was obscured by others who had targeted Ferrier because of his contribution to the arsenals of the American government and other sympathetic powers. That night we took different names and left California.

I tried to take buses to small towns like Tonapah, Greeley or Nebraska City where the only books I could find were Gothic stories and romances, the kind that twirl on silver stands near cash registers. I began to read them, the A&P romances. Here were solutions to problems. Here were modes of behaviour the shoplifter back on Ashby Avenue could identify as worthwhile: victimized, abused

255

women rescued by marriage to rich and handsome husbands, or aggressive career women battling to get to the top of management or administration who end up just wanting to get fucked. Being stuck with these books was part of the price of thinking I'd be less likely to be recognized in a small town. In one book a woman who lived in a village made it a habit to examine the Most Wanted posters in the post office. She later recognized the new doctor on the block as a handsome but dangerous felon from the post office gallery. Fugitives might be expected to follow a route of small bus-stop towns and I was easily convinced, so I switched to the anonymity of big cities. Beginning in Chicago, I even took a train.

Somewhere in Ohio I was in a drugstore buying a pen, another romance, toothpaste and the smallest bottle of shampoo, when the cashier said she'd seen my face before. She was certain she knew me from somewhere. Had I gone to school in Cincinnati? I assured her with false calmness that I had a very familiar face to all kinds of people but I'd gone to school in Detroit. She didn't look as though she believed me. Perhaps she was homesick for Cincinnati and was looking for a reunion, however vague. I stuttered as I said no, absolutely. Maybe I should have lied. A few weeks earlier a woman seated next to me at a bus-stop restaurant between Omaha and Des Moines had kept staring at me in the mirror above the counter. Here was the lonely woman from the romances who studied the posters when she bought stamps and tried to make matches. Although I'd only lately been thinking of myself as living underground, the events of each day, ordinary though they must have been, were part of the mental construct of the chase. No matter how secure I actually was in that bus-stop diner or in the drugstore, my reaction was intuitive, suspicious, posed, ready to bolt. In each store, in every building, before I glanced at a menu, I looked for the exit signs. Useless, but I did it anyway.

Part of the nature of being a fugitive curtails document-ation. I wrote on little bits of paper, kept them for a week, then threw them away. Living underground, being in exile from your past, you begin to look for cures for deracination. A memoir, like turning the projector to rewind, seeing and hearing the film all over again, that's one remedy. I altered names, dates, places, so if the book were found, no one, including myself, would be incriminated. The journal could in no way be confused with a confession. I spent a lot of time in the movies; the FBI would never invade the Orient Theatre downtown or the Cinerama in the shopping mall.

In Albany, New York, I was getting desperate, waitressing in a restaurant on Lark Street where a lot of teenagers stopped on their way to or from Planned Parenthood. It was raining heavily, few people were in the place and I was busy turning my quarters into dollar bills. The United States had begun invading Cambodia; Irving Kristol advised President Nixon to begin electronic surveillance of the left as a control measure. Governor Reagan had compared 'the feat of the Apollo 13 astronauts with the little group of so-called anarchists who have absolutely no excuse . . . The only feeling one can have about them is contempt.' He accused the militant students of throwing CS gas and this accusation reminded me of the police who insisted that a student who had a police bullet lodged in him had shot himself. I followed the press like a true exile or ex-patriot to learn what was going on in Berkeley. The Governor continued to call in the National Guard, saying, 'If it takes a bloodbath to end the violence, let's get it over with.' The words seemed like a toxic spot in my notebook but I wanted to keep a record of them. Stuck in the world of fried eggs, side orders of fries and men who treated waitresses badly, blatant brutality fascinated me. When true drama is a day ruined by burnt toast, I wrote down words like those. There were small demonstrations at the capitol building in Albany but they left me feeling isolated, a participant who'd lost her momentum. The futility of being Jane Amme complemented the peripheral, washed-out temper of life on Lark Street. I would invent what I thought might be short life histories of Patricia in *Breathless*, Florence Keefer in *The Marrying Kind*,

257

tried to feel as they might have felt when walking down the street, opening their doors, taking off clothes, eating a sandwich. How would Jane Amme feel if she were asked to play Jean Seberg? What would Judy Holliday think if she were asked to play Jane Amme? If some jerk started telling her about his nephew, dirty agitators and suitable punishment, would she have reached for her gun and been up at the foot of the Campanile before Guy Ferrier could have pulled the trigger? I tossed roles around as if caught in a giant changing room, bits of clothing flying, expressions tried, rehearsed in reflections. There was no getting out of this dressing room and I found no comfort in Albany's resemblance to Spartacus. My relationship to Spartacus was one of estrangement and memory. Albany was about neither of these.

It had been a year since I'd left Berkeley. I was counting out my change when Mary walked into the restaurant, half by chance. She knew I was somewhere in Albany but not exactly sure where and stepped into the Lark Street Grill to get out of the rain. The restaurant was nearly empty and I only had ten minutes to go on my shift so we sat in a booth and whispered, tracing over the ice cube and boomerang pattern on the formica table top like high school girls from Rensselaerville after they'd just got the pill a few doors down.

Mary had returned to Berkeley in April, right after the verdict on the Chicago Seven had been handed down. That day a riot began so fast there was nothing the police could do about it. The degree of anger was so great and so spontaneous, the riot police had no time to strap on their gas masks. You would think there was a city job designed for a sociologist/demographer who might have predicted the reaction, but no; and the police were unprepared and angry with the annoyance of the unprepared. Half a mile of Shattuck Avenue was destroyed, including a Toyota dealer, a Bank of California, Security Pacific and Crocker Bank. The riot ended by nearly demolishing the Safeway supermarket. Bricks, windows, fluorescent lights, electric doors were all utterly destroyed. Rolls of aluminium foil, paper towels, rolls of white register tape from overturned cash registers streamed over mounds of cans, bricks, shredded boxes of cereal, frozen food, spaghetti, raisins, ripped cellophane from loaves of sliced bread, pools of broken glass, olives, pickles, maple syrup, orange juice concentrate. The corner of Russell Street and Shattuck looked like an archaeological dig, with stray dogs wandering through playing with flattened rolls of toilet paper, battered relics of teargas canisters, or chunks of the grille from a bank teller's window. Government agents were trying to act cool now, she said. There were several known informers, agents who had let their hair grow and wore tie-dyed T-shirts with too many silly buttons. Mary thought Win was still making bombs in the basement of the house off Hearst Avenue.

For most of the year Mary had stayed in Phoenix, a city she saw only as a place of exile. Aside from the recent riot, Berkeley, Mary said, was winding down. Ads from Con Edison and Tiffany's were creeping back into the *Daily Californian*. The *Berkeley Barb* was almost totally pornography and prostitution ads. Our November bombing was a forgotten history lesson. Blame for the riots was still placed on a few 'outside agitators and communists'. The Berkeley administration issued statements contradicting the students' version of the riots. Mary repeated the well-known irony; the university accused students of irrational acts of violence while UCB profited from contracts with the United States Defense Department. Newsmen are attacked by both sides, as always. Mary met one as she was leaving gutted Shattuck Avenue. He wanted to interview her for part of an article for the *New York Times*. He had done his research and was very persistent. He tried very hard in only a few minutes to make Mary feel she could trust him. He was on her side, he seemed to give that signal, and was only a few years older than Win. He asked her what she thought about the bombing of Chase Manhattan Bank, Standard Oil and General Motors in 1969 – 'about violence as a means towards pacifist ends?' She hesitated, considered the *New*

York Times, then ran away from him. She had seen, we both had, a reporter used by the police as a human shield against flying rocks and bottles. That wasn't why she ran. It was just that this one, try as he would, didn't elicit her sympathy and she didn't want to be quoted in his newspaper.

Mary saw him a week later at the Med talking to two women and writing notes as they spoke. The journalist's face was bruised; the eager, earnest look was gone. He didn't seem to recognize her when she sat down at the next table. He told the two women he had been arrested for assaulting an officer with a deadly weapon although he would have had to be a candidate for Mr America to survive that onslaught and still have enough strength to slug a policeman with a lead pipe, as was claimed. It seemed a recitation which, even if true, had become a customary prologue to his interviews, calculated to urge confidences from his subjects.

She was no longer overly cautious. The habit of seeing the FBI and other kinds of threats in every handshake, every man seen twice in the same telephone booth, is hard to discredit. I imagined the dissilient pod of rumours a creative bureau chief up for promotion might hatch. Stories, once sprung, would snowball out of control, growing more damaging with each repetition. On the other hand, I don't really give a fuck. What can they say about me? Then I remember my mother. She hasn't lost her job but is still always afraid of losing it. Stories of people who lost work, miscarried babies, had nervous breakdowns, committed suicide – Frances Farmer, Judy Holliday, Jean Seberg. Mary's facility, her easiness, she never looked over her shoulder; this had become an alien way of being to me. Like remembering how to climb stairs by putting one foot in front of the other instead of dragging the right up to meet the left, I could remember but not re-enact. I was still using the slow, careful method, although I hadn't always.

I left for New York the next day. Mary was going on to Boston and she called the restaurant to tell them I'd had to go home for a long-term emergency. In New York or Boston we decided it would be easier to remain anonymous and find jobs other than waitressing which would pay off the books. I got an apartment downtown near a park which rang quietly with dealers' liturgy. 'Jamaican, loose joints, cocaine, black beauties, sensemilla, am-phe-ta-meens, loose joints, cocaine, black beauties, hop on the Sugarland Express, hey m'fuck, got some blow.'

It might have reminded me of Berkeley but didn't, and there was never a Gérard de Nerval walking a lobster on a pale blue leash, or anyone who seemed to bear an atavistic relationship to him.

I had a high school friend who went to college in the city and through the university's job board I answered an advertisement for a translator's assistant. I got several jobs this way and it was how I met and began working for Dr Willa Rehnfield. Dr Rehnfield was happy to pay me off the books but it was my apparent anonymity that most appealed to her. As far as she knew, I came from nowhere and would return there. I had no record of union activism, knew no foreign nationals or underground radicals, never went to a demonstration and typed fast.

There's a place I go for coffee sometimes. Every day the man who works the espresso machine grows fainter and fainter. Long ago I thought he would disappear altogether. He forgets to shave, his eyes are red, his clothes acquire new wrinkles, stains upon stains. He owes money . . . somebody takes him out back, roughs him up. Nobody knows. Each day he grows fainter and fainter, less and less able to concentrate on pouring coffee or wrapping sfogiatelle in white tissue paper, as if these actions are just histrionics and his real concerns, his actual life, involves other kinds of deals. The old man in a Beckett play who sits on a park bench and twists a paper bag over and over. The one who appears and reappears – driving a taxi or on a bus. All the Virgils, Eugène dear, steering all the Dantes.

I heard a story in my neighbourhood. A man, a very big

man, was arrested on charges ranging from narcotics dealing and extortion to second-degree murder. The FBI based the case on evidence gleaned from the man's garbage. For five years, the FBI agents posed as sanitation workers. They sifted through fragments of paper, notes and letters, a special agent had to be hired to translate the Sicilian dialect. They've come a long way from the Robert Hall suits. I still look over my shoulder when it's raining and wonder about the wall-eyed man in the Second Avenue bodega. I tend to be careless most of the time.

My relationship to Willa Rehnfield's papers is something like that of the FBI tossing through empty olive oil tins and petrified spaghetti looking for the word cocaine in Sicilian. I'm looking for the name Lucienne Crozier. The entries in the modern notebook are the memoirs of a woman who skirted the barricades, and they are written in English. I'm looking half-heartedly for Luc Ferrier, too. Willa remembered him in cabs which took her through Times Square. Years after his death she placed his face behind a black man at the end of a long red tunnel, entrance to 'Les Girls Revue', behind little boy and girl prostitutes in mascara and satin shorts, leaning on Donkey Kong machines. Behind pimps, behind red, white and blue striped wigs, behind do-rags. She knew that under another name he did other things.

In my translation I've tried to be true to the original.

262

The Republic of France left behind, I have never been on a boat like this before. There was a storm at night and Jean told me the story of Danaë and Perseus who were locked into a chest and dropped into the sea by Acrisius but they were saved and lived to fulfil the Oracle's prophecy. By substituting trust in myths for survival instincts acquired through experience, I'm echoing Eugène of whom I was so critical. The mimickry, in this case, is in support of a good analogy: the stories are the same; they were told hundreds of years apart, the names are different. We are Danaë and Perseus dropped into the sea by French rulers not yet calling themselves kings or emperors but afraid, like Acrisius, of exiles who might return.

In the hold of *Le Nerée* is machinery for printing presses; in return Captain Lautrec will bring back figs and dates, lemons and oranges. I don't think he knows exactly who we are or the nature of the papers hidden in the lining of our trunk. He is quite familiar with the customs of Algiers and the various Algerian desert tribes, but we never discuss the February or June Days, or the Algerian rebellion of last year. In the face of vivid memories of the barricades, his ignorance strikes me as a kind of apathetic perseverance. Jean treats him warily but I think he's an innocent who is proud of the fact that his steam ship carries no emergency sails.

Jean has told me I ought to throw this journal overboard. As a record of the past year it contains incriminating evidence. A shadowy, unknown figure pretending to be a sailor might rummage through my things. The ship is turned around, we're taken back to Marseilles and delivered to the police. My trust in people, or lack of trust, shouldn't really be allied with what they say their political sympathies are. Being against Lamartine is no tag of automatic trust and confidence, but Jean believes survival might make such an index necessary.

The papers in our trunk bear a list of names and addresses

of informants for the police. A man who used to work for the police in Marseilles gave it to him, but how does he know it's genuine? There were opportunistic souls among the *Quarante Huitards*, those who believed they had some kind of ideological edge and wanted acknowledgement. The list could be a trick, based on the perilous foundations of other men's arguments and infighting. If I tell him no one in Algiers has read a word of Karl Marx, Jean says he doesn't care. 'Lamartine and the others,' he says, 'will learn you can't save yourself by creating an exile class.' I look for clues in the commonplace because women have fewer choices than men and suffer more for their mistakes.

12 JULY 1848

We stopped for a day in Majorca and walked around Palma, still a European city. Outside of it we walked among the Cyclopean relics: thick walls, some still high, many now shallow skeletons of rooms; monuments. Careless of ancient evidence, I scraped some of the pebbly clay from between the stones with a twig. Cyclopean blacksmiths gave Zeus the thunderbolt which killed Cronus. They disappeared, were replaced many times over by subsequent inhabitants: Phoenicians, Greeks, Romans, Byzantines, Iberians, Carthaginians and Moorish pirates.

There is another French passenger on *Le Nerée*. His name is Guillaume Kleiner and he claims to have stabbed a soldier during the June Days. There had been witnesses. He had ridden day and night to reach Marseilles and finally discovered Captain Lautrec's steamer. An apprentice locksmith from Alsace, he had gone to Paris originally to look for work. He couldn't find any and joined a group in Montmartre, although he didn't agree with all their ideas. He enrolled in the National Workshops and when they were shut down he took to the streets like many other workers. Guillaume hadn't meant to kill anyone; it happened very quickly, he says. He is doing some lock work for Lautrec in exchange for his passage, and has been tinkering around with the printing press parts stored in the ship's hold.

We took on a new passenger at Majorca, an Andorran monk, Father Pablo Nableau. He is to go from Algiers to a monastery in Constantine. He seeks converts among the Berbers and Arabs. Father Pablo Nableau claims to be an ascetic who has observed long vows of silence. He has brought his own food with him: grains, nuts, dried fruits. He is a great admirer of the Bishop of Algiers, the former Monsieur Dupuch of Paris. A man who left the bar to become a Carthusian monk, he divorced his secular life completely and is now a primate. The priest faces south, clicks his rosaries, is as fastidious as possible, and avoids all contact with the sailors.

13 JULY 1848

Out at sea, from so many miles out one can't tell the French neighbourhoods from the Algerian, the rising roofs and minarets of *Al Jazair* appear of uniform unveiled marble.

One of the sailors told me the Arabs would go berserk if they saw a woman's bare head and face, so I left the ship between Jean and Captain Lautrec. All kinds of people crowded the pier: Kabyles who tend to be short, Moors, Negroes, Jews and Christians. There were no women that I could see. Waiting for us on the pier was Monsieur Polignac. We were introduced to him as Hilaire and Victorine. He made me uneasy. Although I wanted to have confidence in Yves Polignac, there was something ambiguous in his presentation of himself as a happy citizen who was even more ill-defined than the captain. He avoided having an opinion on anything. Monsieur Polignac got us past the authorities. No one asked to look in our things. Here was a man with connections. Towards what end does he use these connections? Does he pretend friendship with the Maréchal Braque in order to betray him for another cause, or are we the only ones being taken in? Is he the *petit bourgeois* Talleyrand of Algiers, constantly altering his allegiances?

He can only be a traitor to one side but it remains obscure which one, if any, he might betray. Perhaps he takes no sides. He may be a congenial trader who uses his government connections for his own personal advantage; no wool is pulled over anyone's eyes, all is mutual and open for scrutiny. All is conjecture.

He drove us past La Place du Gouvernement. It would have looked very European except for the appearance of guns everywhere. Yves pointed out the Hotel de la Régence, a reproduction of a symbol of imperial France. His simple eagerness, his sincerity, elicited pity. He seemed so genuinely proud, however dubious the achievements he gestured to. I felt sorry for him in his earnestness, rather like the way I felt coming upon Hippolyte Phébus's damaged bundle of cards.

He told me to avoid the *petit blancs*. To Yves the small landholders are only a little better than the natives. We will be renting rooms from the Polignacs. They have so many to spare and Madame Polignac has been lonely since all her daughters have married and moved away. I don't know what Captain Lautrec told Monsieur P. to make him think we'll be suitable tenants, but for now we'll be agreeable, as if we want nothing more but to establish ourselves in the *grand colon* manner.

14 JULY 1848

Firecrackers, salute the flag: the celebration of Bastille Day in a colonialist dominion is without irony. The assault today is not one of soldiers but of heat. Edges sparkle, glisten, melt, surfaces are warm to burning. Nature and the *colons* are out of control. There is nothing to be done but sit still and drink mint tea.

One immediately becomes aware of two sets of contradictions in Algiers. French influence battling for supremacy against the Arab, altering the architecture, coating the surface of the culture and changing it, converting customs and traditions until all have metamorphosed to the French

266

end of the spectrum. Arabs drink wine in Algeria but in no other Moslem country. Last year Abd-al-Kadir led a revolt against the French, fighting General Bugeaud. Villages were destroyed, many French had to flee their farms. It had been talked of in *14 Juillet* meetings. Kadir is now in exile. Another contradiction exists between the colonialists and the republicans, a contradiction often exhibited within the same household, or the same person, and it results in a very odd hybrid. I don't see how they do it. Our landlords, the Polignacs, for example, are great republicans, quite against the military rule in Algeria, but at the same time they cling to their colonialist posts, proud of the fact they are landowners. Future generations may be a southern version of the Croziers. In France, like the medieval Croziers, the Polignacs were landless. Unlike Captain Lautrec, they're eager to tell us exactly what they thought about the June Days, about French rule in their city, past and present. They were against Charles X's blockade of Algiers, instigated by a swat from a fly switch,* and they were against Louis-Philippe's *régime du sabre*, yet they continue to condone the expropriation of the *habus*, lands sacred to the Moslems, turning them into wheat fields and vineyards, turning mosques into churches. At the same time Algiers is said to be the most radical department of France.

Jean wishes to find other rooms. We were to have been so careful here but, clearly, staying with the Polignacs is a mistake. There was a man he met in a café yesterday who called himself Spinoza. Jean said he was remarkable and pays no attention to me when I tell him that name has to be fake.

22 JULY 1848

In Paris there are men, women, boys and girls, but in

---

* Hussein Day hit the French consul in a dispute over shipments of wheat the French never paid for. Another version of this story puts part of the blame on a third party, a Jewish merchant. Jane Amme, 1982

Algiers there are only men. The Moslems consider women slightly better than animals. According to their religion, women have no souls. It is as if men and women were divided into two spheres. The way the division was described to me, it seemed almost a geographic separation, although I know that's not truly the arrangement.

I was told about Islamic customs by Maria Farouk, a converted Moor who lives with the Polignacs as a servant. Many years ago the members of her family were diminished by war and disease, leaving only a nineteen-year-old nephew, lazy and tyrannical. He had a wife and two children, more on the way, and she knew if she went to live with them she would be like an unpaid servant. Rather than live at the mercy of a man twenty-five years younger than herself, she accepted an invitation, arrived at through circuitous means, to live as a servant with the Polignacs. She was fond of Madame P. and the children and subsequently converted to their religion. Her conversion seemed to matter to Madame at the time. The mistress of the house took religion seriously, but Maria's conversion, like a mosque partially gutted then restored as a church, was a combination of many factors, the least of which involved theological preference. She mixes the religion she was born with into the one she inherited to suit her purposes. In her pocket she carries both rosaries and Moslem chaplets. They make the same clicking sound. Maria doesn't envy the Polignacs marriage and tells me it's not a pleasant arrangement. Islamic marriage isn't a sacrament and divorce can be obtained, according to the Quran, if a husband repudiates his wife three times before witnesses. Still, the decision is up to the man, the woman has no choice except to submit.

When she first arrived at the house, Monsieur Polignac wanted Maria to get a young Arab girl for him. She didn't understand why at first; they didn't need anyone else to work for them at that time. Then she did understand what he wanted but pretended she had no way of finding a girl who would do what he asked.

The crime of rape carries very severe penalties but there

268

are few opportunities for a woman to be raped, as far as I can see. Women are so rarely alone on the street. If they are, they are jeered at to such an extent it appears they're the criminal for walking abroad to begin with.

She took me to her room where none of the family has been and showed me little clay pots full of colours: blue for eyebrows, yellow for nails, red for cheeks and patterns traced on to hands and feet. The Polignacs do not allow this paint to be worn in the house but Maria painted a design on my left hand. Her room smells like attar of roses. Jean noticed the smell when I returned to our room.

It remains to be determined how I am to occupy myself while in exile. In France the class system translated itself, in a curtailed version, to the society of women. In Algiers stratification is shrouded by the veil, and so whatever I might do is still conjecture and I'm afraid will end in disappointment. Many of my days and all my nights are spent in the house. Most of Jean's days and evenings are passed with Spinoza and he tells me little of their meetings except that they involve the list which I'm convinced is a fly-by-night silly business. I remembered a bit of advice and in an ill humour passed it on to Jean although he was unresponsive. I had overheard Jenny le Guillou saying to a delivery boy, 'Somebody you don't know is out for somebody else you don't know. You don't want to get mixed up in that business for a million francs. You look the other way. You didn't see anything.'

I don't really believe in looking the other way but this list smells of the witch hunt. Jean says he is writing at the house of the man from the café with the ridiculous name. Whether the money he has comes from his writings or not I haven't asked. I'm much more concerned with what I'm going to do. Our roles of prisoner and free agent have reversed themselves. Jean has adapted to the rules of Algiers very nicely. He feels no restrictions. He was far more restricted in France. I'm the same woman who went to *14 Juillet* meetings and fought on the barricades in February but I'm treated like a chronic invalid. I'm not a fugitive but I'm excluded from life outside the walls of the Polignac house, which, they say, like certain parts of Paris after dark, contains hellish potential twenty-four hours a day.

I did go out one night dressed in a suit Fabienne would envy. Jean, with Spinoza's invisible help, got me a pair of baggy white trousers, fitted at the ankles and waist, and a long white cotton shirt which came to my knees. It was decorated with blue embroidery which would remain invisible because the whole suit was covered by a *haik*. On impulse I cut my hair short to fit under the *kufiyeh*. When I'm in the house I cover my head with a scarf so the Polignacs won't notice. Jean also provided dark spectacles, a fake moustache, and pointed beard. The adhesive was too old. It wouldn't stay on my chin for more than a few minutes and so had to be abandoned.

Evading the Polignacs after dinner, I changed in an alley and Jean led me by way of back streets I'd never seen before and could barely see now through dark glasses. I wanted to take them off, to be sure I could see him. If in the event I lost sight of Jean I would be utterly lost, doubly so since I speak no Arabic and my knowledge of the life going on behind the shadowy white walls would make me hesitate to cross any thresholds. Languages I couldn't understand were whispered and yelled behind walls as we passed by. At this moment a fear articulated itself and I realized how far I was from enacting even the idea of the life of a revolutionary, alone or with Jean de la Tour. Stretching behind and ahead, a life of costume changes guided literally and metaphorically by a man's hand. Remembering what it was like arriving in Paris from Boissey Saint-Leger, I might tell myself first impressions are always very sharp and very wrong, but those first days in a northern city are buried under layers of sentiment and highly subjective explanations. The objective facts here are contradictory and hopeless.

Along the streets my sense of smell became more acute; here coriander, here cumin and olive oil such as I found in southern France and in Maria Farouk's kitchen. Finally we came to a dead-end street and passed through a narrow door opening on to several flights of shallow stairs leading to the café. This arrangement is often the custom in Algiers. Music I might have thought Turkish or Spanish a few months ago was audible while we were still stairs away from the entrance. There were two Arab musicians: one played a mandolin, the other a sort of reed pipe or clarinet. The *cavadji* sat making coffee, a little removed from everyone else. The coffee is served hot, small cups without any handles. The drinkers sit on benches or sheepskins, smoking from glass *narquillas*, playing chess or cards. I don't think there were any other Europeans present and certainly everyone in the room was a man. Abruptly the music changed and a woman ran into the centre of the café, dancing with blue scarves. I looked hard through my glasses, straining my eyes. There was something wrong, something was amiss, out of proportion in the woman's body. She was a boy. I was so startled I wanted to leave right away but Jean insisted we stay until the dance was finished. He didn't want to attract attention and I don't even know exactly why I was angry. I was certainly the only member of the audience who felt affronted, who was mocked.

25 JULY 1848

I've grown used to the time sequences established by the sound of the muezzin. They now seem more logical divisions of time than hours. Maria told me the names and times of the calls:

Sunrise – Emleber Denor
Noon – Dor
4.00 p.m. – El Hasser
Sunset – El Magruh
1 hour after sunset – El Hatmet

5 AUGUST 1848

Until Jean's recent invitation to meet S., I've been no more than extra baggage dumped on him at the Marseilles harbour. He behaves as if his thoughts are on such a rarefied plane only intellect of the male persuasion could approach understanding. His ideas exist and thrive exclusive of female contribution, or it's as if I'm still being punished for walking out on Proudhon. I've found no Pascales here, nor have I any hope to. Maria Farouk isn't interested in anything which might upset the delicate balance of her singular Moslem/Christian world and I can't really blame her for that. If it's taken Jean this long to decide I'm a good risk, I'll decline the invitation and remain in quarantine.

7 AUGUST 1848

A *grand colon*, owner of a vineyard in the south, was a guest at the Polignacs last night. He brought bottles of Algerian wine and told stories of Zouaves' brutality towards each other and towards Moslems. His conversation revealed something about the nature of Algiers, the placement of the city in relation to the rest of the country and continent. The treachery of the desert isn't limited to the sandstorm. Algiers, Constantine and Oran do seem like islands of civilization in relation to the guest's tales of the northern Sahara. He described the practice of torture employed by the Zouaves. If they capture Moslems, they bury them up to their necks in sand and leave them to die; but worse, sometimes after burying the victims, the soldiers will practise by cutting off their heads from horseback. The soldiers go on long marches. They are famous for them, but they leave those who can't make it to die where they fall out of step. Their battles are enormously bloody; the visitor doesn't understand how France can continue to send men here. For twenty to thirty years, he thinks, French women must have had nothing but male babies. Both *colons* have a strong dislike of the military. They fear Algeria will become a military state and see no need for the vast operations that can only result in making all French and all Moslems hostile enemies. A few soldiers, yes; the *colons* couldn't continue to live in Algeria without some protection because I doubt these two would return to the Arab tribes all they've taken. They want to live peacefully but don't expect concessions from their side to be part of the price.

8 AUGUST 1848

There's nothing for me to do. I suggested teaching Algerian girls. Maria said it's illegal, against French law or Moslem, she wasn't sure which. I might assassinate a colonialist general, particularly a Napoleonic one, get into his bedroom, use a knife, but I'm no Charlotte Corday. All I can do here is dress up as a man. I have begun to consider returning to France. The male/female, Frenchification/Arabization dichotomies may be interesting to some academic, but to me they're riddled with contradictions which hold no fascination. It shouldn't be difficult to obtain return passage with Captain Lautrec and I know too little of Jean's plans with S. to be a liability to either.

The 14 August entry describing Lucienne's visit to Spinoza's house has been accurately translated except for the references to the Polignac garden and to Fabienne at its end.
   The 27 August entry begins with Lucienne's reference to *Promenades à Londres* by Flora Tristan and concludes with the quote from Madame de Staël.
   Jane Amme
   1982

3 SEPTEMBER 1848

No, he says, you can't return to France. It's too dangerous. Should I just get used to being bored? He has already made plans for us to leave the Polignacs. If I will only wait two days. I am disappointed and find myself staring out to sea like a somnambulant lunatic robbed of the power of speech. In a balance of personal or even physical power, how can I be forced to stay? I'll wait two more days. Yesterday I wrote to my mother and to Fabienne. Today I wrote an entirely different letter to my brother on the same subjects.

6 SEPTEMBER 1848

Two nights ago I was awakened by a sound outside my door. Jean had been out with Spinoza, now Marco. Yves Polignac might have been in the corridor had he seen Jean leave many nights in succession and guessed his nocturnal hours. The sounds indicated two people were in the hall and soon Jean entered with another man who removed his *haik*, glasses and moustache to reveal: Pascale. We didn't talk but packed our things and left the Polignacs quickly, silently. There would be no going back with Captain Lautrec now. We cheated his friends out of a month's rent. I regretted not saying good-bye to Maria.

It was as if I were being led through tunnels, the narrow lanes almost roofed over by jutting upper storeys and balconies just visible in the dawn. After walking for about thirty minutes we arrived at our new quarters near Casbah Street. I am again immersed in a world of women and a kind of netherworld structure where people aren't likely to ask questions; everyone assiduously minds their own shadowy affairs. Our rooms, adjoining Pascale's, are part of a complex of rooms arranged around a large courtyard. Eating, washing, prostitutes earning a living – any activity which goes on in the private rooms can spill out into the courtyard. Animals piled near the cistern seemed like inert washing; chickens, I think they were.

Shortly after the last time I saw Pascale in Marseilles she decided to go into exile in Algiers. She did not prefer the city to Amsterdam but the trip across the sea was safer than the northerly land route. Since she has been in Algiers she's nearly always dressed as a man and I suppose I, too, will begin to do the same. Pascale has no reservations; you just do it in as matter-of-fact a manner as possible. Men perform as women for men. Women dress as men. We dress in costume, not because we wish to cross gender lines but because society is imperfect. Disguised in men's clothing the imperfections which are liable to impinge on our movements are limited.

She had met Marco but she's not interested in liberating Algeria from the French in order to establish a socialist state founded on the ideas of Proudhon and Marx, the ideas of the *Quarante Huitards*. It's not that Pascale thinks they're wrong or that they will become despotic, but for her, if she has to wear men's clothing to walk to the corner, their idea of revolution is an incomplete one.

Pascale has two little windowless rooms on the second floor overlooking the arena of the courtyard. Jean and I are in one room, Pascale in the other. We cook together but the arrangement isn't an easy one. Sometimes when Jean and Pascale argue as if they were deciding the fate of millions (from this tiny ministry), I can't see anything but theatre in their debate. They could be travelling performers and carry on before paying audiences. I just wrote this but I don't really believe it.

11 SEPTEMBER 1848

Jean spends so little time here during the day and remains out most evenings as well. We no longer discuss his plans, even in a round-about way. He may not be with Marco at all. Since I never voice my curiosity (Is he with a prostitute across the courtyard? A boy/girl dancer? Do I care?), I can't prevent myself from drawing certain conclusions, as un-becoming as they might be. Boredom and idleness play havoc.

As in Paris, Pascale wants to print a journal, *La Voix des Femmes Algériennes*, and we have begun planning its contents, project who the readers might be. Our language of address is, of necessity, French. Jean accuses me of creating an elite voice since we can't speak to Arabic women and most of them, he says almost vindictively, can't read their own language anyway. Jean is no citizen to point fingers when it comes to living with contradictions. Exile, double exile, triple exile, he knows only the trumped-up romance of the expatriot. I have no desk and write sitting on the floor. We can use Spinoza's printing press.

15 SEPTEMBER 1848

We work at night, leaving the courtyard in our men's clothing, and return just before dawn, inky and tired. Finally the first issue was finished.

Our hours coincide with those of our neighbours and I've begun to recognize them and acknowledge their different identities and ethnic backgrounds. Zouaves often visit here, sometimes drunkenly; they call us names as we leave, never guessing that these Arab gentlemen, under their *haiks*, are former Parisiennes. I'm a little concerned about their presence but Pascale is indifferent. The soldiers are here for one reason; for the moment they'll forget about baiting Arabs. Pascale hadn't heard the kind of stories I did at the Polignacs'.

The woman who lives to the left of us is half Spanish, half Arab, and about my age. She is quiet when we meet in the courtyard but within her room she's very loud. She is one of the few women who drinks openly. Inside her room she has passages from the Quran printed on strips of paper pinned to the wall as well as a small cross. She is very curious about the activities of two European women who do not entertain gentlemen, but the difference in language prevents our having a conversation. One late afternoon she knocked on our door. She had a Frenchman with her who would translate so the three of us could talk. Her efforts at befriending us were so sincere but we had to lie in return. She brought olives, dates and wine but we couldn't tell her our real histories through the mediation of the *pied noir*. Instead we were indigent aunt and niece who had relatives in the Zouaves. She didn't ask us about our costumes and seemed to take it as a matter of course that not all of what we would tell her would be true. She left politely, the noise began next door and we dressed to go out.

One of the women, a Moor who lives downstairs, speaks some French. Sometimes her silks look as if they would disintegrate if one's fingers glanced an edge. Her bit of education and the class of her callers cause her to remain a little aloof to the rest of the courtyard, although she's polite to us when we meet, probably due to her love of things French. Yesterday she gave me a very good false moustache, much better than the one I've used previously, and yet we never spoke of the object or the reason I need it. I thanked her but all she would discuss was the lazy goat near the cistern.

16 OCTOBER 1848

Their writings, though precious and much fretted over, are erratically produced. Jean and Marco are protective of the press. Their work has priority and each time we want to print it is an exercise in the art of persuasion. Two more women, friends of Pascale's, have joined us.

30 OCTOBER 1848

The privilege of using the machinery is to be rescinded. The two men are no longer open to any suggestions; dialogue ends in favour of who is simply in possession of the keys. They are Charles Crozier in *kufiyehs*, pistols hidden in their belts; it's the same. Our divisiveness, as they see it, is at odds with the revolution. We should be supportive, perform in such a way as to facilitate their activities which are so dangerous. What are they looking for? Comfort for the moment when home is finally reached. Reassurance for the moments when terror is imminent. Someone to fill the shells, hour afer hour, someone to oil the press and benignly, aliterately set type, hour after hour. Our arguments to the contrary are useless. Jean talks about gender destiny: men and women are not meant to have the same one. Marco talks about social patterns based on biology, not culture, which are sacrosanct and fixed, not vulnerable to critical analysis. We've tried to find another press as an alternative.

Jean usually enters our room behind Pascale's tiny chamber while I sleep and leaves after I've left in the morning. In a large house with many rooms it's possible for a husband and wife to pass days, perhaps weeks, without speaking or even seeing each other. The tension, geographically spread out so, must be more bearable, even if alleviated only slightly. They, the rich man and woman (with tardy servants), leave trails: breakfast dishes left on the table before the maid can pick them up but after the eater has vanished, a glove left on a table, a newspaper dropped on the stair. (I think Charles's parents may have lived this way for years.) The same system of disregard is imposed in this tiny space. We have no vistas of bedrooms, libraries and lawns on which to leave our marks; no personalized, insignificant detritus. Instead of a space in which these objects and what they represent are reduced, in these rooms such personal effects are magnified. They become the person, carry his smell, his ideas, the disappointment and annoyance he summons just by lying here like a stone. We are cramped but treat each other as foreigners. Even when we behave as lovers, we in some part of ourselves despise the other one. I want access to the press. He doesn't reject my wanting it, but rejects what that desire represents. My loathing is like a mandrake he fathered, nurtured by his power to forbid. Jean is so confident, a confidence based primarily on physical superiority, his ability to run the machine and physically keep me away if necessary. At this ragged point, I want only to even the score through whatever means I can lay my hands on. Revenge is a devouring idea, at least I think it may be. It's not revenge so much; I just think I'm entitled to have my own way in this.

I suspect Pascale would like to turn Jean out but she doesn't say anything to me. He must find it so hateful here. I wonder why he doesn't leave, unless there's still an attachment to me he deliberately obscures. As we face the unattainability of the press, Pascale has designs on a very startling gesture, a kind of action more effective than language which she believes is so slow to induce or procure. She has fallen in love with a dangerous scheme: gun running to Abd-al-Kadir's rebels, such as remain since his exile. To be truly socialist in Algiers you must be anti-French, and Pascale, in her frustration, will lash out at whatever is at hand. She isn't indiscriminate. She's thought about gun running but I think it's as if she were acting on a dare, a dare issued from a big source, not any single individual. It's as if, grown so tripped up by failures, everything about general existing social order dares her to try this, making the desperate appear reasonable. And maybe the scheme is reasonable. I haven't yet been convinced otherwise. What she's really afraid of is being thrown to the dogs. Pascale isn't a coward, isn't a César, but she is a survivor who acts a great deal on instinct, instinct alloyed with intellect although the scale is weighted more towards the former lately. Instinct is why she's here instead of Amsterdam.

More hiding. Like the subterranean cafés, there's always another floor beneath of ancient origins, and we'll go to the centre of the earth if we have to, I suppose. If not for the printed page which has the ability to burrow to the surface, I would feel as if we were chasing our tails, screwing ourselves into the sand.

13 NOVEMBER 1848

I'm alone, sitting in the doorway between the two rooms. Sometimes I'm glad there are no windows. I feel protected, but invisible; sometimes I think I'll go crazy for lack of a way to see out. I won't know soldiers are coming until I hear them on the stairs.

Last Thursday morning Pascale and another woman, both dressed as Arab men, were returning from a meeting about the guns when a Zouave shot Pascale, believing her

279

to be an Arab. She was only wounded in the shoulder. When they realized they'd shot a French woman, they were horrified and she was sent to the Hôpital de Salpetrière, attended by the best doctors because it is the best doctors who always serve the French citizens. I visited once. For pain Pascale has been given morphia and her speech had a glowing quality although she was never one for a happy turn of phrase. Words were coherent, but sentences made no sense. An elderly Marseilles woman in a red wig occupied the bed on one side, another lay near death on the right. Nuns glided in and out between patients so we couldn't really speak. The glow didn't matter. As I was leaving I was introduced to the guilty soldier's commanding officer. He assured me the two Zouaves would be court martialled immediately. He came to visit the victim himself, to apologize, but also to inquire why she and her friend were running around in the dawn dressed as Arab tradesmen. At first he was polite but then less so.

When I returned to the hospital yesterday one of the sisters told me Mademoiselle Pascale was no longer a patient. The commanding officer had recognized her as a fugitive from France and had had both her and her companion arrested on the spot. 'The doctors said Mademoiselle was too ill, but the soldier in charge said if the doctors knew the crimes Mademoiselle had committed they wouldn't have her as a patient in this clean hospital,' a dark old nun told me. I left quickly, but for what reason or to what possible sanctuary I don't know. I sit in my room and wait for the knock on the door as I have waited for two days.

I don't think Pascale or the other woman would give my name or anyone else's unless the Maréchal tortured them. Not to crack when tortured, especially when already wounded and still under the influence of morphia, may require a kind of stoicism no one can count on. If the women are searched, papers with my name on them or old copies of the journal may turn up, and if they really follow all the clues any tangent may lead to even the slightly culpable, those guilty by association. The anticipation of arrest when one has bored so deeply into the earth that there is no place left to go, no other disguise in the closet, is like a prelude to sickness. Sickness is ensured, I have been exposed to contagion, in this case fear of arrest and prison. I wish the soldiers had come when I was visiting in Salpetrière. Internment, return to France or exile to New Caledonia would have begun simply. Perhaps Pascale's confession will end in suicide. The woman next door is hammering more bands of the Quran into her wall. I confuse the hammering with knocking.

17 NOVEMBER 1848

Dear Fabienne,

Enclosed is the journal you gave me nearly two years ago. I expect I may be arrested soon and believe it dangerous for this diary to fall into the hands of French legionnaires. I don't want it to be the means of incriminating anyone else. The details of my life since June 1848 you can read for yourself and I hope you won't interpret my exile as a tragic decision, hastily made, because it was neither. Jean de la Tour you may remember as the fellow who took me from your house during the February Days, but on that day and on other occasions you must believe I did make up my own mind. I hope you won't think I'm writing in a patronizing manner. I don't want you, in your disappointment, to feel I was under someone else's influence entirely. So as soon as the ink is dry, I'll leave the courtyard which has held me for several days and send this parcel off to you.

I also think you should ask Eugène Delacroix for my portrait because I would like you to have it.

Je t'embrasse,

L.C.

It's June first and it feels like it's already been summer for a long time. I was early for work so got off the subway at Grand Central and decided to take a bus uptown. Hot in the tunnels, hot in the station as the trains from Rensselaerville, Montreal and Chicago came to a stop, let their engines cool. I looked down a platform as people left a train which had just arrived. Heads, shoulders, profiles seen against the frames of the train windows, a giant strip of film, stationary, the image of the crowd itself really moving. The people on the outer edges of the crowd moved more quickly up the ramp. A little girl pulled on her pink necklace and plastic pop-it beads fell to the cement floor, rolling towards the tracks. Round pink hermaphrodites with a male face and a female face. An Amtrak mechanic humming 'I Heard It Through The Grapevine' stooped over, picked up a couple of beads rolling his way and handed them to the girl. 'My sweet darling won't you be mine?' A nun sat in a dark corner shaking a box of change in one hand and fingering a string of rosaries with the other.

It wasn't until Madison Avenue that I remembered the conversation about stringing stories together to form one big one. Newspapers were all around me, hundreds, thousands of stories. There was evidence everywhere I looked; it was just a question of putting all the pieces together. But that had been Win's technique and he was out of the picture. Bits of his dialogue still intrude. I was thinking about that afternoon in March; we had been in the Med: drugs, art, theft, murder in Newark, murder in Marseilles. Maybe it would stay summer for eight or nine months.

I'm going uptown to turn my keys over to the executor of Willa's estate.

Lack of use is feeble justification for theft. I didn't feel Willa owed me anything, nor did I wish to cheat her lawyer or rook the library in Amherst out of a contribution. My impulse to break rules is not, I think, the kind of impulse entertained by petty larcenists. In my own way, I've made a large contribution to this tradition, Willa's legacy of

282

papers and art objects, acquisitions brought home by legitimate means or illicit. A portrait, a solitary journal of one hundred and thirty-four years ago, might have become solid investments, property of value in a marketplace which original writer and subject scorned. Accretions of worth twist the turbulent route of the stolen object. Perhaps the cremation of the original L.C. papers was a good thing, although they would have been an asset to Mary's library.

Across my narrow airshaft, above the apartment occupied by the warring Chinese couple, lived a young woman whose shades used to be drawn nearly all the time. Sometimes I would hear her telephone ring and ring. I would see her or her silhouette but she didn't pick it up. She started leaving her shades up and she would stand in the window, newspaper or glass in hand, staring at me. We never waved or conversed. My desk, at a window, faced her kitchen table. I could see what she ate and drank, her mail, sometimes a book on the table, although I certainly couldn't see what it was she read or who the mail was from. Once she sat at her kitchen table, shadow of a long elbow jabbing at the brick wall. Somewhere a radio was on as she filled lined pads.

I stopped writing and just watched her.

Then there was a starless black night. The moon was a sliver and it rained as if the airshaft might have been converted into a water tank. All the windows were shut except mine and those belonging to the woman living above the Chinese. Hers were wide open, shades snapped up. I could hear her telephone but she wouldn't answer it. She had just put down her pen and sat with her back to me. I suppose there was a knock on the door because she rose to open it. Through the rain, acting like the imposition of a grainy television image, I could see three men enter. She put on a jacket and left with them.

For the next week I checked the newspapers. There were three arrests in New York. One woman had been taken in for running a drug ring on the lower east side; one for her recent, if superficial liaison with an arms smuggler; and one on an old murder charge, a *Post* headline from last year. I didn't know my neighbour's name and the one picture of the woman murderer was unclear. She wore sunglasses, her head was bent down. The woman across the airshaft could have been any or none of them.

Several days later I saw someone packing up things in the apartment. Dishes, shoes, a few books and the radio were placed in brown cardboard boxes and sealed with tape. After many months of vacancy, a new tenant moved in but I've begun keeping my shades drawn and know nothing about him.